"Kristopher Triana's work is a volatile mixture of visceral noir and twistedly disturbing passion play that invades the reader's psyche and exposes the raw and throbbing nerve hidden within. His prose is unapologetic and totally without restraint or mercy. There's no denying it. Triana is the Master of Extreme Horror!" —Ronald Kelly, author of *Fear, The Saga of Dead-Eye*, and *Southern Fried & Horrified.*

"One of the most exciting and disturbing voices in extreme horror in quite some time. His stuff hurts so good." — Brian Keene, author of *The Rising*

"*Full Brutal* rocked my world! It's one of the most powerful hardcore horror works of modern times." — Edward Lee, author of *Header*

"Kristopher Triana pens the most violent, depraved tales with the craft of a poet describing a sunset, only the sunset has been eviscerated, and dismembered, and it is screaming." —Wrath James White, author of *The Resurrectionist*

"*And the Devil Cried* is one of the bleakest, most black-hearted books I've ever read…possibly the most reprehensible main character I've ever encountered." —Bryan Smith, author of *Merciless*

"I'm blow away with what Triana can do and will read just about anything he puts out." —*Scream Magazine*

"*Full Brutal* is the most evil thing I have ever read. Each book I read by this guy only further convinces me that he's one of the names to watch, an extreme horror superstar in the making." —Christine Morgan, author of *Lakehouse Infernal*

THAT
NIGHT
IN THE
WOODS

THAT
NIGHT
IN THE
WOODS

KRISTOPHER TRIANA

CEMETERY DANCE PUBLICATIONS

Baltimore

2023

Cemetery Dance Publications
132B Industry Lane, Unit #7
Forest Hill, MD 21050
www.cemeterydance.com

Trade Paperback Edition

ISBN:
978-1-58767-903-2

Cover Artwork and Design © 2023 by George Cotronis
Cover and Interior Design © 2023 by Desert Isle Design, LLC

For the friends I grew up with and the girls of my youth

"When we forget old friends, it is a sign
we have forgotten ourselves."
– William Hazlitt

"Conscience is no more than
the dead speaking to us."
—Jim Carroll

PROLOGUE

*T*hey come to me at night. Those voices like distant dreams. They tell me their stories and I write them down, a secretary taking dictation. I am but a utensil, a pen and publisher in one. It's their show, as it should be. They're the ones with the stories to tell.

Sometimes I wonder if I've ever written anything of my own, or if every single word of poetry and fiction I've accumulated over a lifetime were channeled into me by forces I simply could not detect at the time, let alone understand. People always ask us writers where our ideas come from. Perhaps now I have an answer.

The notebooks fill one by one, each voice taking their turn. That's why I bought this house on the edge of the woods. I want to be a better listener. For too long I attributed the voices to something neurological, my imagination running away with itself, or maybe my cognition starting to slip as I became more of an isolationist. We all talk to ourselves sometimes, don't we? But whenever I check for accuracy, the voices are always proven right. Who would know their history better? They tell me no lies or exaggerations, not even to make themselves seem more interesting or important. They already know they matter and that their truths must be revealed.

I speak for those forever muted.

I am the biographer.

OLD FRIENDS

CHAPTER ONE

She had to pull over for this.

Jennifer was a cautious driver and had been since her kids were little. One of those mom habits that never fade, not even when your kids start driving themselves. She wouldn't have seen the alert pop up on her phone if she hadn't mounted it on the dashboard to use her GPS.

You have a new message from Scott Dwyer.

Jennifer's jaw fell. "Oh my God."

She turned onto a side street into the suburbs, parking in front of a softball park. Meredith Peterson could wait. Jennifer had long doubted the woman would buy. She seemed like she just wanted an excuse to hang out with Jennifer, a lonely woman looking for another single friend to gab with over brunches and to take Caribbean cruises together. It was hardly the worst thing a client could do to her, but Jennifer didn't have the time or the means for new friends.

But old ones sparked her interest.

"Scott Dwyer," she said, wondering how long it had been since she'd said the name aloud. At least a decade, if not two. "Scott freakin' Dwyer."

There were plenty of friends from her high school days who'd found her on social media over the years, and even more from college. But this was the first ex-boyfriend who'd ever looked her up (or at least contacted her after doing so), and honestly the only one she held any real nostalgia for. She'd had a lot of disappointing relationships, to put it kindly. And now, even her marriage had proven a failure—over after seventeen years of marital bliss. No, more like five years of bliss, ten years of mediocrity, and two years of emotional ruin leading to a painful, if amicable, separation. The very fact that it was amicable was painful in and of itself. In a way, it would have been better for there to be more passion involved, two broken hearts at war. Instead, there was nothing but numbness, the most damning evidence that their relationship had lacked passion for a very long time.

The divorce papers sat in her glove box. She'd yet to have time to get them notarized. Maybe if looky-loo clients like Meredith Peterson didn't waste so much of her time, if she could just sell a house and get her boss off her back, maybe then Jennifer could muster the strength to sign that paper and really mourn the marriage instead of dodging the issue, even though she'd been in favor of the divorce. So many maybes. Too many.

And now there was the mystery of Scott Dwyer.

She opened the app and read the message.

Her first love had a lot to say.

AFTER DINNER, Jennifer went to her bedroom with her laptop while Alex did the dishes and Devin took out the trash. Even with their father gone, she insisted on her son and daughter sitting down at the table with her for this one meal of the day, at least when they were both home. The smartphones went into a locked cabinet, assuring real conversation. Tonight, Alex had gone on about cheerleading and how well her junior high's football team was doing this season. Devin, still bitter over the separation, seeming to blame his mother more than his father, had been stoic, barely giving Jennifer more than one-word answers when she asked him about school, not knowing what else to ask about. For once, his silence proved useful. Her mind had been wandering, anyway.

She hadn't replied to Scott yet.

It was best to gather her thoughts and really think about what she wanted to say, even though his message to her had been pretty simple. Most of all, she wanted to write out a draft of the reply in a document, check for spelling and grammar, and then cut and paste it into the message window. She didn't want any typos or autocorrect errors to make her sound foolish. Even after two decades of estrangement, she still felt the need to impress him. Maybe now more than ever. She was older, a little heavier, and silvery at the temples.

In his profile picture, Scott looked good, almost improved. Jennifer was confident she was still attractive at forty-three, but Scott looked better, even though they were the same age. His gray—more a salt and pepper— made him appear distinguished, even rugged, like a man who could chop down trees as easily as he could carve a turkey. Her own gray, though slight amongst the natural blonde, made her look like a young grandmother. Scott had grown a short beard, but it did nothing to tarnish a face that had always been strikingly handsome. And there were those eyes—blue with a touch of green and clear as Bahamas seawater. They'd always been her favorite of his features, impervious to the ravages of age.

No doubt about it. Scott Dwyer was *hot*.

Not that Jennifer was seeking a man. She hadn't leapt into online dating as her friends encouraged her to, telling her it would boost her confidence, if nothing else. Roger had only moved out five weeks ago. She wasn't ready to dive back into the whirlpool of dating, especially after being married so long. She was out of practice, and the thought of dating in her forties was simply mortifying. There was a sense of sadness to it, she felt, a scarlet letter of failure. It made her feel hopeless. Most of all she was scared.

But she definitely wanted to get laid. Long before they'd decided to separate, she and Roger had stopped having sex. It was a strange, unspoken agreement. After the past year of loving-making that was few, far-between, and unsatisfying, they'd simply quit. She found it amazing that neither of them had had an affair. In a way, it was sweet. Even as they drifted apart, they hadn't wanted to hurt one another. But Roger was gone now. He was free to do as he wished—and so was she. There were bachelors in her life, but they were all associates or clients, and she refused to mix business with pleasure. And a one-night stand with a stranger wasn't the sort of thing Jennifer would go for. But someone she knew...

Scott's profile said he was single.

He still lived in Connecticut—in Redford, at that. It seemed he'd never left their old hometown. Staying where you were born and raised was something she couldn't imagine enduring. It wasn't enough for Jennifer to just see different parts of the world, she needed to experience living in some of them, and that meant leaving home. She'd left for NYU at eighteen and never moved back. And once her parents retired and moved to Port St. Lucie, she no longer had reason to visit Redford. But while never leaving your hometown was almost as sad to her as dating in your forties, Jennifer refrained from judging Scott for it. She had no idea what his life had been like after their breakup. Maybe he had moved away and eventually circled back. Even if he hadn't, that didn't make him some kind of loser—different strokes and all of that.

Still, Redford didn't hold the best memories for either of them. The memory of that one night alone…

You're just stalling.

Her fingers hovered over the keyboard. She bit at her bottom lip and reached for her glass of wine. This was more than a mere hello, no matter how Scott might have intended it. This was a knock at a door, one she wasn't sure how to open, but needed to nonetheless. It wasn't just a gateway to Scott and all the possibilities that came with him. This was a door to herself—to the girl she once was and the woman she was becoming, the transition to a much-needed transformation.

She started typing.

SCOTT'S REPLY came less than an hour later.

Hey, Jenny. Thanks for writing me back. It's great to hear from you too and even better to hear you're doing well. A mom? Wow! Sorry to hear about your divorce but it sounds like a peaceful one, so that's good, and like you said, it's for the best. It's so cool you're a realtor and still living in New York even though you left the city. But I would imagine Long Island is a better place to raise a family than Brooklyn or wherever, ha ha.

I'm doing well, thanks. Yeah, I'm still in Redford. Never did move on. Guess I just belong here. Anyway, I've just been thinking about the past lately and how there are a select few people in our lives who are really special. Maybe it's because my parents both died within the past year, but I've come to really appreciate the people who made a positive impact on my life. For me, you're one of those people. I know our breakup was hard for both of us, but I don't hold any resentment. When I think of you, I think of all the good times we had.

Maybe we can talk sometime? It'd be great to hear your voice and catch up.

He left his number.

Jennifer decided on another glass of wine.

She headed downstairs and into the kitchen. Only the oven light was on, the rest of the house in shadow. When she was young, the television had always been on, someone always in the living room. But these days, with phones and computers, it seemed families hibernated in their separate rooms with their own entertainment, their own online worlds.

Well, you've got one hell of an online world now.

She sipped the chardonnay and ran her hand through her hair, thinking about getting it done. She'd have to make an appointment with Maurice. This sudden urge to doll herself up made Jennifer giggle. *Two messages and you're acting like a schoolgirl with a crush.* Was she really allowing herself to get goose bumps over her first boyfriend?

She would call him. Not tonight, but soon. She would schedule it with him for a time when she'd have the house to herself. The messages alone had put her in a better mood than she'd been in for weeks, so she could only imagine what an actual conversation might do for her spirits. That Scott would come back into her life at this particular moment was too perfectly timed, a dose of confidence when she needed it most. It was like some kind of omen for good things to come. Nostalgia was a funny thing, especially when you're a divorcee hovering on the threshold of middle age. And there was something about old friends that just created a sense of instant trust.

CHAPTER TWO

"It's not just a Batman doll," Corey said. "It's a limited edition, resin statue of the Michael Keaton Batman from the 1989 film."

His wife continued chopping vegetables, every clack of the blade like a curse thrown at him.

"Only a thousand were made," Corey said, knowing it wouldn't make things any better.

"Oh, well, then," Gretchen huffed, "I guess it must be worth the money after all."

Her sarcasm, while all too familiar, cut through him better than the knife she wielded ever could. Her back was turned to him, but he could picture her pinched, bitter face, the upper lip curled—her *angry Elvis* look. Her cheeks flushed, eyes flooding with poison.

"I'm sorry," he said, knowing it was only a matter of time before he'd have to apologize anyway. He hated conflict. Always had. "I guess I should've discussed it with you first."

Now she spun around. "Oh, *you guess*? Two hundred dollars on a *toy* and you *guess* you should've talked to me about it first?"

Corey looked at the kitchen floor, leaning on the counter with both hands. One nice thing he buys for himself and she goes bananas, even though Gretchen never hesitated to blow money on everything from expensive jewelry and nail salon trips to paying for everyone's drinks when she went out with her girlfriends, always the showoff. Not to mention the tummy tuck she might have been able to pass on if she would lay off the Ben and Jerry's and exercised now and then. But that was the kind of thing he could only think and never say. Even thinking them made him nervous, as if his wife might spy into his skull and decipher his thoughts, turning them into yet another weapon she could chuck at him whenever he was feeling content. He'd found the statue he'd been hunting for years. It was going to look so good on the mantel behind the counter of the shop. Leave it to Gretchen to spoil it. Maybe he should have told her it was a gift for his partner, Don. They were both comic book fanatics; that's why they'd opened the shop in the first place. But even that wouldn't have eased Gretchen off of him.

"You're sending it back for a refund," she said, going back to the cutting board.

"Honey, I can't."

"The hell you can't!"

"It was an online auction. All sales are final."

She tossed the knife on the counter, gritting her teeth at the ceiling. "Why, Corey? Why do you have to make me the only adult in this house?"

It was an old line that hadn't lost its punch. If anything, it stung more with every year. Being called a man-child was cutting when you're in your twenties, but it was a far worse insult when you're forty-four, and having it come from your own wife added a coating of emasculation to that already sour cake. It wasn't like Corey just loafed around playing video games and reading graphic novels all day. He was a good father to their only child. He co-managed a business, one that was actually successful even during the retail apocalypse brought on by the popularity of online shopping. He brought in good money from an investment Gretchen had been vehemently against. Most months he made more than his wife, something he'd never achieved before. He'd thought she'd be happy about it, but instead, she was resentful of his success and that he enjoyed what he did, whereas she despised her job at the bank. This had put more weight on the structure of a marriage already too burdened. Corey felt that any day the foundation would fall to rubble.

"Next time I'll check with you." He went to her and put his hand on her shoulder. She shook it off. "I said I was sorry." But he wasn't. He just wanted this to end. The sound of the postal truck came to his rescue. "I'm gonna go fetch the mail, honey."

"Fine. There better not be a box with some five-hundred-dollar damned Spider-Man in it, Corey Pickett!"

He took his time outside, thumbing through the letters. An insurance bill, a credit card offer he hadn't asked for, a town newsletter no one ever read. A crisp breeze sent golden leaves blowing across the driveway, clicking like kindling upon the pavement. Even in his flannel, Corey was chilly. Autumn had come in full, and seemingly from out of nowhere. He always mourned the loss of summer. As a child, summers had gone on forever. Now, they raced by in a blink of fireworks, barbeque grills, and garden hoses, and before he could savor a full day of sunshine and fireflies, the season was over, the nights after Labor Day cool enough to see your breath. As he walked back to the house, he saw a pumpkin on the Johnson's front porch that hadn't been there that morning. It wasn't carved, but would be soon enough.

There'd been a time when he'd loved Halloween. Now he did everything he could to ignore it, to act like it wasn't happening.

Corey shook his head to escape his revere. He had enough stress without digging up those bones.

A GREEN Lou Ferrigno roared from the screen of the laptop propped on the counter. Corey never tired of reruns of *The Incredible Hulk*. Sunday mornings were always slow like this, but Corey preferred to work them because Gretchen had Sundays off. He'd rather be in the comic shop alone than stuck in the house with her. More than that, he'd learned over the years how important it was for his wife to have her space. Even when they were newlyweds, she'd scoot away when he tried to snuggle up to her, including in bed. Corey respected solitary activity and knew very well the joys and benefits of isolation, but the constant coldness from his wife was something else entirely. It had taken years for him to accept it, to just give up. The woman he loved showed him no affection. He sometimes wondered if she ever had.

"You'll marry the first one that comes along."

That's what Dad had always said.

Corey had hated that growing up. Now he hated it even more, because the old man had been right. A virgin all through high school, Corey was hopelessly enamored when Gretchen came into his life. She wasn't beauty pageant material, but she spoke to him, which was more than most members of the opposite sex deigned to do. Corey was scrawny, pale, and pimply even at twenty-two. Though he'd hoped to start anew after moving out of Redford when his parents relocated them to Portland, Maine, he'd failed to generate a fresh attitude or even a semblance of a desirable image. He was still the geek with the stack of comics in one hand and a mint-in-box action figure in the other, intransigent with those who told him to "grow up." Back in the '90s, superheroes weren't the darlings of pop culture they were now. Things might have been different if Marvel dominated the box office when he was a teenager. Maybe he wouldn't have been so eager to be with a girl who treated him as an inferior from the very beginning, a presence in his life more judgmental than even his old man had been.

Corey popped open another can of soda and put his feet up on the counter. It was almost eleven. Soon church would be out and the young people would be free. The shop would fill up nicely. He smiled up at his new Batman statue standing proud upon the shelving behind him, watching over the shop as if it were Gotham City.

Things weren't all bad.

As the Hulk slowly morphed back into Bill Bixby, a message appeared on the laptop. Corey pulled the screen closer, seeing the name of the sender.

"Scott?" he whispered.

They'd reconnected on social media years ago, but after some basic catching up the messages faded until they didn't write anymore. They were still "friends" online and hit the *like* button on each other's posts now and then, but there was no direct communication. While not that interested in his personal social media, Corey had to maintain those accounts in order to have additional ones for the comic shop, and these slow Sunday mornings were when he did the most posting and advertising on them. Today, he'd left the browser open.

He clicked on the message and learned Steven Winters was dead.

CHAPTER THREE

"I t's not like I have to go."

Traci wasn't sure whom she was trying to convince, Kordell or herself. Her boyfriend leaned across the table, taking her hand. His dark eyes seemed not so much sympathetic but dulled. Was she boring him, or was he just hungry? The restaurant was busy, and they hadn't been served yet.

"What do you think?" she asked.

Kordell seemed to awaken from a long slumber. She knew then he'd barely been listening.

"I don't know," he said, leaning back into the booth. "I mean, how long do you say it's been?"

"Over twenty-years."

Kordell shook his head. "That's a lot of time to not see a friend."

"Well, once I left Redford, I never came back. Not even to visit. I was too damned happy to get out of there."

"Yeah, I know."

But he didn't know. Not really. Not because he was a bad listener (though, he was), but because she hadn't told him. They'd only been dating for seven months. He hadn't earned that level of truth from her. She'd yet to find a man who did.

The server appeared at the tableside, carrying Kordell's beer and Traci's straight vodka. She made a bubbly promise the food would be right out and then shuffled off toward a pair of impatient-looking patrons waiting to be seated. They were older white women, and one of them was staring at

Traci and Kordell, judging the interracial couple. When Traci stared back, the old witch turned away.

That's right, Karen, Traci thought, *my man is black. Be jealous.*

She sipped her drink even though she wanted to down the whole glass. It'd been a bitch of a day even before the surprise email from Scott Dwyer. Maybe that was one of the reasons the news hit her so hard.

Steven Winters. Dead at forty-three.

It always disturbed her when someone in her age group died. It underlined her own mortality, reminding her of her own fleeting youth and how temporary life was. Her birthdays depressed her, but what was worse was hearing one of the rock stars or movie stars she'd grown up with were now senior citizens. Somehow, their birthdays made her feel older than her own did. But a death was even more intense; especially when it was someone she'd grown up with. Though they'd long ago lost contact, learning Steven was gone seemed to take something away from Traci, a part of her life lost forever.

It made her wonder how people she'd known would feel when she died. She didn't expect it to happen soon, but there were bound to be some friends and lovers who outlived her. When it came to friends from her hometown of Redford, they would be remembering a version of her that didn't even exist anymore.

Traci had never been the nostalgic type. She'd heard from a few old friends over the years, as anyone did, particularly once you started crawling toward middle age, but she'd never felt the urge to pursue yesterday's ghosts. To Traci, people who longed for the past had probably not made much of the present and had a void where their future ought to be. She knew what it was like to be directionless, and to feel the best days of your life were behind you. You could only listen to people tell you you're a mess so often before you started to grant the notion legitimacy. She'd been in that abyss before, but even then, she'd been too busy juggling the present to seek the comforts of the past, few though they'd been. Traci considered yesteryear not only gone, but also rather meaningless.

But she had been curious—only about a mere handful of old friends, but still curious. And when she'd searched online for the old gang, she'd found most of them and read what information was available. But she never reached out. That was an extra step she deemed unnecessary. Traci had seen what Scott Dwyer looked like now and that Jenny Parks had married and become a real estate agent. She'd been unsurprised by Mark Goranson's mug shot. She'd even found that nerdy kid, Corey Pickett, and chuckled at how he looked the same as he had in 1994, complete with Captain America t-shirt.

The only one who'd left no online footprint was Steven Winters. There was nothing to be found about him until now—his obituary.

"So you gonna go?" Kordell asked.

She ran her finger over the lip of her glass, gazing into her drink. Half of it was already gone.

"I don't think so," she said.

But she called Scott anyway.

"WOW. I can't believe I'm talking to Traci Rillo."

"The one and only." She sipped her vodka and placed it on the coffee table, leaning back into the couch. "How are you, Scott?"

"Good, good. Thanks for the call."

"Thanks for giving me your number. I must admit, I was kind of shocked to hear from you."

"Oh?" He sounded disappointed. "Really?"

"I mean shocked in a good way," she assured. "More like surprised, I guess."

"Yeah. I can't blame you for that. I was kind of surprised to hear back from you, honestly. But man, it's so good to hear your voice. Really, really good."

Traci brought her legs up, sitting on them. She was twirling her hair in one hand. As a teen, she'd talked on the phone with friends for hours, spinning the strands around her fingers the entire time, but it'd been many years now since she'd done it.

"So, what are you up to these days?" Scott asked.

She shifted in her seat again and pursed her lips. "Well... I'm a lawyer."

A pause on the line. "Wow. Traci Rillo, attorney at law."

"Crazy, right?"

"Yeah. Or, um, you know… I mean, not totally crazy."

But it was. Though Scott was too polite to say it, he knew what everyone had expected her to become. He was probably amazed she was still alive, let alone supporting herself.

"And what about you, Scott? What do you do?"

"Oh, this and that. Right now, I work in books."

"You mean, like, writing?"

"No," he chuckled. "I run a website that buys and sells used books."

Traci furrowed her brow. "There's still a market for that?"

She regretted it the moment she said it. As always, she turned to her vodka for support.

"You'd be surprised," Scott said, no offense in his tone. "First editions, signed copies, out-of-print titles. Not to mention brick and mortar bookstores rapidly going under, which gives me more business. I make a modest living."

She'd been looking to segue and saw her chance.

"Steven was the writer of our group," she said, but it had sounded better in her mind. The words were too blunt when spoken. "I was just thinking, you know…"

"Sure. I've been thinking about that too. It wasn't until recently I found out he'd been successful."

This was news to her. She wondered why he'd never popped up in her searches if he'd been published.

"Really?" she asked. "I had no idea."

"Well, you'd never know it. He never wrote under his own name. He used pseudonyms, you know? A pen name, like when Stephen King wrote as Richard Bachman."

She wasn't aware of King's pen name, or those of any other writers, for that matter. Traci had never been into reading fiction, particularly anything scary. She tried to keep all forms of horror from her life.

"He wrote as Jack Polar," Scott continued. "Did some biographies and a lot of non-fiction about New England history. He also wrote under the name Susanne Polar when he did movie novelizations."

"I'm impressed."

"Me too. But like you said, he was always the writer of the group—all those poems he used to come up with and stuff."

Traci smiled, remembering some of the notes Steven had passed her in science class, song lyrics made up for a band that never existed. Now she wished she would have held on to them.

"He never put out anything under his own name," Scott said. "Not anything he published, anyway. But I managed to track down some of his works."

"I'd love to see them."

He perked up. "Does that mean you're coming?"

She closed her eyes. She'd walked herself right into this.

"I don't know, Scott. I mean, I'd like to, but it's a bit of a drive. And I'm just very busy, you know?"

Another moment of silence on the line.

"Sure," Scott said. "I get it. You're a lawyer, and you're probably juggling a family on top of that and—"

"No," she said, surprised by her urge to make this clear. "I'm not married. No kids."

"Oh." There was curiosity in his voice, perhaps even excitement. "Nothing wrong with that. I never married either." He gave a sad little laugh. "I always thought there'd be time for kids, but..."

"There still is."

"I guess so. I don't know. Anyway, I just thought you should know about Steven. I figured since I was the only one who still lived here, you might never have known he'd died. It sure shocked me to find out he was still in Redford."

"He was?"

"Yeah. All these years and I never even happened by him in the supermarket or at a gas station or anything. Turns out he was sort of a recluse."

"That is so not the Steven Winters I knew. He was so popular back in the day. Very social. I guess people change."

"It certainly seems that way."

Traci sensed Scott wasn't just talking about Steven. Was he implying she had changed too, that by turning down his invite she was showing a new side of her Scott wouldn't have expected? Did he feel she'd changed for the worse in this regard? Traci always considered her personal transformations as serious accomplishments. She was proud to have altered her perspective as well as her life, especially given her complete lack of resources or parental support. It was absurd for Scott Dwyer or anyone else to expect her to be the same person she had been as a teenager—a little insulting even. No longer was she the girl who just went along with what everyone else said or did. She was a grown woman, in control of herself—a total remodeling that had taken years of therapy, meds, and determination. She liked herself now, didn't she?

"Listen," she said. "Let me think about it. I might be able to come up if it's just for the weekend."

CHAPTER FOUR

Mark Goranson leaned into the steering wheel and took the tube into his mouth. He blew, hoping to hell he'd pass the breathalyzer so the goddamned truck would start. It'd been about twelve hours since his last drink, right? Ten at least. The breathalyzer couldn't detect the weed he'd smoked either. If he failed to pick up Jamie at soccer practice this time, his daughter might give him the silent treatment even longer than she had last week. He got enough of that from his son. What was it now…five years? Dalton held a grudge almost as well as his mother. Jamie's mother, on the other hand, was still tolerant of Mark. He hoped he could keep it that way.

The device beeped and the truck revved.

"Fuck yeah," he said.

It wasn't like he screwed up *everything*, though that was the portrait most people in his life tried to paint. Putting on his worn Red Sox hat, Mark pressed the lighter into the dashboard to warm it up, an unlit cigarette bobbing in his lips as the pickup shuddered along, crying for him to replace the ball joints he'd been putting off. Even if he had the eight hundred dollars to dump into this old Ford, he had other things he'd rather spend it on, maybe something to brighten things up, like a baggie of cocaine or a good night at a titty bar. But his unemployment checks didn't leave enough of a budget for such entertainment, and he was way behind on child support payments.

The lighter popped out and he lit his last cigarette. Damned things were so expensive these days. He'd tried to quit, but those nicotine patches were worthless and vaping was for fairies. Who the fuck wanted to blow smoke that smelled like a Cinnabon? He was running only a few minutes behind, so he pulled into a convenience store and asked for a pack of whatever smokes were cheapest and two scratch-off tickets, then snagged an Icehouse tall boy from the cooler. He turned back, deciding to get Jamie a Dr. Pepper. It was her favorite. He knew that much about his daughter.

Back in the truck, the October air felt good as it surged through the cab. He'd lowered both windows and turned up the radio, shaking his head when songs from his youth played on the *classic rock* station. When had it changed from The Doors and Zeppelin to Stone Temple Pilots and Pearl Jam (who always sounded like clones to Mark, anyway)? It made him feel older than Moses. He pulled into the parking lot a little late, but there were still some other kids on the soccer field. But Jamie just *had* to sulk. So instead of hanging out with them, she was sitting on the bleachers alone. With her hoodie up, he almost didn't recognize her. Mark honked the horn. She looked up from her phone and took her sweet time coming down the bleachers, and he reached over and opened the passenger door for her because it refused to open from the outside.

"Hey, baby girl."

She gave him a weak smile. "Hi."

Just a lousy *Hi*. Not even a *Hi, Dad*.

The gravel crackled beneath the tires as he pulled out, making him think of the cement mixer he'd had to sell to pay back rent.

"How was practice?" he asked.

She gazed out the window. "It wasn't practice. It was a game."

He looked to her, then the road, and then back again. "Oh. I thought it was games in, like, the spring."

"We have them then too."

Mark sighed. If he'd known it was an actual game, he might have been there to watch her play. Had Carol told him it was a game? He was almost certain she'd said it was just a stupid practice. Sometimes it seemed like both of his ex-girlfriends tried to set him up to fail as a father.

They passed by a shopping plaza where a Halloween pop-up store had settled into an empty building left behind by a failed clothing outlet.

A giant grim reaper flashed his rictus grin from an orange banner as it fluttered on the breeze.

Don't fear the reaper…

"So," he said, hitting the lighter again. "You know what you're dressing up as this year?"

Her eyebrows pinched together. "I'm eleven years old. I don't go trick-or-treating anymore. That's kid stuff."

"Oh. Right."

The lighter popped out and he put a fresh cigarette in his mouth.

"Could you please not do that?" Jamie asked. "Second hand smoke is almost just as bad for you as first hand."

He put the cigarette behind his ear. "Sorry, baby."

They didn't speak much after that. When he pulled into the driveway, Jamie practically leapt out of the truck. He kept it running so he could pop open the Icehouse for the ride home without having to start the truck again with beer on his lips. The Dr. Pepper was still in the cup holder. *Shit.* He'd forgotten all about it. He watched Jamie head up the front steps and the door came open, Carol welcoming their daughter home. Mark hadn't seen her in a while. She'd cut her hair short, and he thought it made her look too butch. She also looked fat. Carol waved to him, and he motioned her over to the truck. Jamie went inside without a goodbye. As Carol approached, Mark noticed her new tattoos. Soon her left arm would be sleeved in them just like her right arm, one of the benefits of dating a tattoo artist, the very one Mark had introduced her to when they'd still been together. Nothing like having a good buddy take your woman away. It killed two relationships.

"Didn't expect you to be here," he said. "Thought you was working."

"Got off early. My manager's cutting back on hours 'cause sales have been so shitty."

Mark nodded, wishing he hadn't brought up work because he knew exactly what she would say next.

"You find anything yet?"

"Nah," Mark said. "Still looking. But I've got some good leads."

"Yeah. I hear ya. Things are tough all over."

"Welcome to New Hampshire."

"Yeah, I guess." She scratched at her puffy belly. "Hey, by the way, I was gonna call you, but since you're here—"

"Look, babe, I know I owe you a little money but, like I said, I'm still trying to find me some work."

Carol squinted, looking just like their daughter. "It's more than a little, *babe*, but that wasn't what I was gonna say." She reached into the pocket of her too-tight jeans and pulled out a folded piece of notebook paper. "This guy called for you. I told him you don't live here no more, but said I'd give you his number."

"You gotta be the last woman on earth with a land line, I swear."

"Yeah, well, don't worry. Wasn't no bill collector. Said he was an old friend."

Mark chuckled. "Old friend? Shit."

"You want the fuckin' thing or not?"

He pulled the cigarette from his ear and popped it in his mouth. Then he opened his hand to her. The piece of paper was pink with purple pen scratches—probably Jamie's stationary but definitely Carol's nearly illegible handwriting. At least the numbers were clear.

"Schmidt?" he asked. "That what that says?"

"*Scott*. Said his name was Scott Downer or Dryer or something like that."

The cigarette fell from Mark's lips. His mouth went instantly dry, but it wasn't the only reason he needed another beer.

CHAPTER FIVE

The glow of the waning moon glazed the ripples of the Housatonic. Walls of black mountain rock beset the river, cradling maples that rustled in the darkness in ghostly veils, expelling dead leaves into the night sky. Jennifer had almost forgotten how beautiful this part of Connecticut was, especially this time of year. It would be far more beautiful come daylight, when the luster of a New England fall could be taken in. She strongly preferred the woods by day rather than by night—especially here.

It was early still, but she'd not seen another car in a while. The empty, black roads twisted through the hills, her headlights catching glowing eyes in the surrounding wilderness, nocturnal creatures scampering at the sound of her engine. Now and then she passed a makeshift grave where flowers and wooden crosses had been placed, landmarks of those who'd died in accidents.

Jennifer found she was gripping the wheel with both hands. She exhaled. *You're not scared. It's just nerves.*

She still couldn't believe she was doing this, but she needed a little adventure. Her life had been so uneventful lately, so mind-numbing and drab. These days it seemed the only surprises she got were bad ones: buyers backing out, Devin getting suspended from school, her soon to be ex-husband expecting to take more of their possessions than they'd initially discussed. Lately, she'd been feeling like God's personal hacky sack. Money was too tight for her to take a vacation on her own, but she could certainly afford taking the car across the Long Island Sound by way of the ferry. Her old hometown of Redford was hardly Paris, but she wasn't headed there for the location. She was in it for the company.

Roger took the kids on the weekends. No one had to know what she was doing. Jennifer preferred it that way. Her own little secret. There was a hint of dirtiness there, and a touch of danger, but a fun and innocent danger, like a carnival ride. It reminded her of sneaking out at night when she was young. Funny enough, most of the time it'd been to see the very person she was going to see now.

Her conversation with Scott had been nothing short of riveting. It was not so much what they said, but rather the simple fact they were speaking to one another. Warmth seemed to radiate through the phone as if transferring a natural energy she'd long been unable to tap into on her own. She felt instantly at ease with him, and though they went over the histories of their adult lives, somehow it felt as if no time had passed since high school. It hadn't taken long for them to laugh; not polite laughter, but true laughter—the kind she'd feared was behind her. She smiled so much her face ached. And even when he filled her in on the death of Steven Winters, Jennifer remained in a good mood. She regretted to hear Steven had died so young, but while he had been a friend and she would mourn him in her own way, Steven was not the man she was nostalgic for. That man had been on the other end of the line, inviting her to his house, inviting her back home.

And she would stay the night. They'd agreed on that. Scott had a guest bedroom, so there was no implication in her agreeing to stay. She wasn't planning to sleep with Scott…at least, not exactly. But it had crossed her mind. More than crossed, actually. After all, she had dolled herself up, paying extra for Maurice to not only style her hair but put a coat of dye on it to enhance her fading blondeness to its former glory. And when was the last time she'd worn a dress? It was always pantsuits at work, and once she got home, it was long t-shirts and stretch pants. This powder blue cocktail dress was tasteful; it made her feel sexy, and the Spanx beneath gave her shape that added boost. If only she'd had more time between his call and the actual invitation date. He would have been just the motivation she'd needed to get back on the treadmill.

But despite her body having changed since she was seventeen (whose hadn't?), Jennifer was pleased with what she saw in the mirror tonight. She wasn't always, but her old boyfriend reaching out gave her a spark of much needed confidence. She expected Scott might like what he saw too. So maybe something *would* happen. If the conditions were right and she felt safe, as she expected she would with him, there was certainly the possibility. Ultimately, where the night went would be up to her. It felt good to be in control of her happiness again.

Turning down Crestline Avenue, Jennifer was amazed at her memory for navigating the neighborhood. She didn't even need the GPS now. She passed by Traci Rillo's old house and wondered if she still lived in town or if she'd been one of the ones lucky enough to escape. The girl had never shown much ambition for anything other than chasing boys and smoking weed. Wherever she was, hopefully she'd done a good deal of maturing. Jennifer wished her well.

She rounded the corner onto Union Drive and there was the house Mark had grown up in. From the cleanliness of the yard, it was clear the Goransons no longer lived there.

Steven had lived on the other side of town.

So had…

But Jennifer didn't want to think about that. She was here to celebrate the good times. But with the woods surrounding the old block, it was hard not to think about that night.

On Belmont Street, the streetlights were few and far between, just as they had been twenty-five years ago. A gathering of leaves bustled before her headlights, rolling on the autumn wind. It wasn't until the Dwyer house came into view that her smile returned. The nervousness was of a more pleasant form, more like anticipation than the discomfort the wilderness had brought on. That had always been one of her favorite things about living in New York City—*no woods*.

While Jennifer thought never leaving your hometown was sad, she found there was something bittersweet about Scott living in the house he'd grown up in. He explained how his parents left it to him in their will, and with the mortgage paid in full he'd decided to move in rather than sell it, admitting it was an upgrade from his old place. Perhaps sunlight would prove otherwise, but right now the house looked the same as she remembered it. Years in the field of realty made her guess the uninventive, post-and-beamer domicile had been built in the '70s, but the shingles on the roof looked new, the driveway repaved.

Before turning off the engine, she flicked on the overhead light to give herself a quick check, reapplying her lipstick and giving her hair a quick toss for volume. She turned the car off, hoping Scott hadn't seen her gussying up from his window. Exiting the vehicle, the breeze that had been ushering the fallen leaves touched her and Jennifer shivered as she reached into the passenger seat for her long coat and scarf, even though it was a short walk up the pathway. She left the suitcase. It could be dragged in later. Her priority was a flattering first impression. When she glanced up at the front door, she saw it had opened, the tall shadow of a man silhouetted against the welcoming glow.

Every step pushed her further into the past, the clack of her high heels like the electrical claps of some sci-fi movie time machine. Though she did not feel young again, she did feel at home again, and that was enough for now.

Scott opened the screen door as Jennifer reached the porch. He was even better looking in person. Those eyes could melt tungsten. Her shoulders relaxed, and she smiled with her whole heart behind it. He initiated the hug and she could have kissed him for it, almost planting one on his cheek before deciding against it. His back was wider now, his hands bigger. The scruff of his beard was soft against her cheek, smelling of musk and hair oil, a masculine aroma that stirred something within her.

"Let me look at you," he said, stepping back.

She felt both flattered and self-conscious, but the unabashed joy on his face excited her. It felt like a first date.

"You've aged like a fine wine," he said.

"Oh, stop."

"I'm serious. It's so great to see you, Jenny." He held the door open for her. "Oh, sorry. I mean, Jennifer. It's *Jennifer* now, right?"

She shrugged. "To most people. But for you, I can make an exception."

Not even in the door and she was already flirting.

She held back a giggle as she stepped inside. It was going to be a great night.

AMBER LAMPS were suspended from the ceiling. Wood paneling on the walls. Campy colors blended with light earth tones. Though the furniture and appliances were modern, the interior of the house hadn't changed much. Back in the '90s, its '70s design still hadn't been altered. Now it was even more noticeable. For the right customer, the retro appeal could be an excellent selling point, but most people would find it tacky. Jennifer, however, appreciated its time warp charm. Like everything else, it wrapped her in a cozy blanket of sentimentality.

Scott came back from the kitchen with two glasses of wine. She joined him for a toast.

"To old friends," he said.

"To old friends."

They retired to the living room, taking different sides of the connected couch so they could face one another. Flames in the fireplace added a cinematic glow to everything, adding weight to the magic.

"So," he said. "Steven Winters. Poor guy."

She crossed her legs. "Yes. Very sorry to hear about Steven. He was too young."

It disappointed her that they were starting with this particular topic, but perhaps getting it out of the way was better than avoiding it—elephant in the room and all of that.

"What happened?" she asked.

"I'm not exactly sure. Things are a bit...murky."

She blinked. "Murky?"

"Steven left a lot of interesting things behind."

"Really?"

"There are just certain things most people didn't know about him. But he didn't talk to a lot of people, being a hermit and all. Maybe that's one of the reasons he..." Scott looked into her eyes. The seriousness seemed to slip away. "Oh, never mind. We can get into all of that later. I'm just so glad you came up, Jenny. Steven would have really liked it."

She smirked. "You're probably right. Still, with all respects to the dead, I didn't come here just for Steven."

Scott actually blushed. "I know."

"But it's very thoughtful of you to celebrate his memory."

"Well, it's what he wanted."

She took a sip of wine. "Really? How do you know?"

"He said so in his will."

Jennifer's back stiffened. "Wait…he mentioned you in his will?"

Scott nodded.

"I thought you said you hadn't spoken to him in decades."

He nodded again. "That's right."

Before she could ask a follow up question, the doorbell rang.

CHAPTER SIX

"Jenny?" Corey asked. "Jenny Parks?"

She smiled, but the look of confusion remained. "Hello, Corey."

Scott shook Corey's hand and pulled him in for a hug, patting his shoulder a little harder than Corey was used to.

"You look the same!" Scott said.

"Not you, buddy. Look at the gray and that beard."

"Hey, the big five-zero isn't that far away for either of us."

"Jeez. Don't talk like that, will ya? Gives me the heebie-jeebies."

The men came around the edge of the couch, and Corey put down his backpack. He took in his surroundings, marveling at how the house seemed to have been cryogenically frozen. His own parent's former house, which was right beside this one, had been so reworked and remodeled that it was like a whole different building. But the Dwyer place matched every Polaroid in his scrapbook. Corey looked at Jennifer again, now that she wasn't looking at him, allowing himself a little innocent ogling. The years had been kind to her. Corey's wife not only didn't look this good now, but Gretchen had never looked this good to begin with. Even if Corey no longer carried a torch for his buddy's old girlfriend, the remnants of that innocent crush emphasized his attraction to Jennifer. He could only imagine how Scott must be feeling about her now that she was right here, back in his life, if only for a few days.

"Get you a beer or a glass of wine?" Scott asked.

"Oh," Corey said. "No, thank you. Maybe just a soda or something?"

"Don't drink?"

"Not much."

It was an understatement. Corey hadn't touched alcohol in sixteen years. He hadn't kicked an addiction. He hadn't even been a steady drinker. He simply wasn't comfortable not being fully cognizant and in control of himself, no matter how controlled of an environment he was in. The one time he'd done something to fog his memory was the night he'd always wished he could recall with perfect clarity. If he had to remember it at all, he might as well be sure about what he saw.

"Such a shame about ol' Steven," Corey said. "I'm glad you let me know, man. He was a really good dude."

"Yeah. The best." Scott turned toward the kitchen. "I'll be right back with that soda."

Jennifer drank what was left in her wineglass, almost as if in a hurry. She stood and excused herself. As she passed by Corey, he admired her from the back as she followed Scott behind the wall.

CHAPTER SEVEN

"Can I talk to you?"

Scott came out of the fridge, the gray in his hair more apparent in the brighter light.

"What's up?" he asked.

Jennifer wasn't sure how to say it. "Well, it's just...I mean...I didn't expect anyone else to be here. And I definitely didn't expect Corey Pickett, of all people."

Scott put his hand on her shoulder. "I know."

"You know? What do you mean *you know*? I thought this was about us reconnecting. You and me."

"It is, it is. I'm sorry, Jenny. I thought we'd have more time before the others got—"

"*Others?*" Her chest pinched. "You mean there are *more* people coming?"

"Well, yeah. It's a celebration...in Steven's memory."

The pinch left her chest, replaced by a tremor that flushed her veins. This couldn't be what it seemed like. Scott wouldn't have done something like this, would he? Even if he meant well, he should know better than to...

"Scott...who else did you invite?"

He smiled at her, as if nothing was wrong with what he'd done. If anything, he seemed proud.

"The whole gang, Jenny. The whole gang."

The doorbell rang again. Corey announced he'd get it. Jennifer looked to another door behind Scott, which led to the back porch. She took him by the hand, and he followed her out. There were no lights on in the backyard, so hopefully Corey Pickett and the new arrival wouldn't see them.

"Why didn't you tell me?" she asked.

"Jenny, don't be upset. I really did want to see you first and foremost. You know that."

"Do I?" She crossed her arms, the cold already starting to gnaw at her. "I came a long way for this, Scott. I don't think it was selfish of me to expect I'd have all of your attention. Now you're hosting a party? Some kind of high school reunion?"

"No, no. Nothing like that. I didn't invite everyone from our school days, just the ones from our group."

She put her hand to her forehead. "Oh my God."

"What's wrong? They're all old friends. You didn't have some kind of falling out or something, did you?"

She exhaled. "No, but I haven't talked to anybody from back then since before I left for college. I just…didn't want to. Not after everything that happened."

Even in the darkness she could see his face drop. "That was a long time ago."

"The past is the past, but it's here to stay, Scott. There's no changing it."

"True, but that's not the point of this."

"Then what is? What made you think to do this?"

"I didn't." He looked away. "Steven did. His last wish for us all to be together."

They were silent then. Jennifer heard another familiar voice coming from the house, a less pleasant one. The voice was deeper, raspier, worn down not just by age but also by hard luck and bad choices.

"Listen," Scott said, his hand gentle on her arm. "I didn't mean to upset you. I actually thought you might be more comfortable if it wasn't just you and me at first. I didn't want you to think I, you know, *expected something* from you."

"I wouldn't have thought that."

He shrugged. "It's been a lot of years, Jenny. I wasn't sure what to do. It took everything I had to muster up the nerve just to send you that first message."

When he laughed, she couldn't help but do the same. His lure was magnetic. She hadn't been able to resist Scott Dwyer back in the day and felt just as powerless against his charms now.

"We've got all weekend," he said. "We'll get time alone. I promise."

CHAPTER EIGHT

Mark Goranson looked rough.

He was dressed nicer than Corey would have expected, having remembered the guy as always having more holes in his jeans than a pair of fishnet stockings. These jeans looked new, and he had on a button-up shirt, but his freshly shaven face was haggard and busted. The calendar had etched deep lines upon his forehead and made ditches on both sides of his mouth, his lower eyelids weighed down by permanent darkness, giving him a look of perpetual exhaustion. Perhaps if he had bothered to smile when he saw Corey, he might have been a little easier on the eyes, but not much.

"Shit," Mark said. "*You're* here?"

Corey snorted, hoping it was meant as a joke. "Nice to see you too, Mark."

Mark stepped into the anteroom and shuffled out of his army coat. Somehow Corey doubted he had served.

"Where's Scotty?" Mark asked.

"He'll be right back. He just stepped outside for a minute with Jenny."

Mark raised his eyebrows. "Jenny Parks, huh? So she came?"

Corey nodded but wished he didn't have to admit it. Somehow, he wanted to keep her a secret, something just for Scott and himself. They'd had a lot of secrets like that growing up, things they whispered to one another through two cans and a piece of string that ran between their bedroom windows. Having known Scott the longest, Corey figured he knew more about him than even Jennifer did.

"Any beer?" Mark asked.

"Scott mentioned some, yes."

Having gotten a look around the living room, Mark's eyes finally settled back on Corey, and for one embarrassing moment he was almost afraid of the man again. Mark had never been a true bully to him, but he had picked on Corey, always teasing but claiming he was just joking if anyone took offense. Corey had never stood up for himself, but Scott had sometimes done it for him. Corey always wondered if Mark's low-level hostility toward him stemmed from a jealous possessiveness, that Mark might be envious of how Corey had been friends with Scott longer while Mark considered Scott *his* best friend.

"You're looking good, Corey."

Again, the sarcasm was possible, but not obvious. Corey decided to jab back by not returning the compliment, if it even was one.

"What're you doing with yourself these days?" he asked instead.

Mark soured. He tilted his head back, rising to some unspoken challenge. "I'm in construction. How 'bout you?"

"I own a comic book shop. I know—surprise, surprise." He gave a self-deprecating laugh as a peace offering. "But I love it, and it's mine." He didn't see the need to mention his co-owner. "Still just a kid at heart, I suppose."

Mark was slow to reply. "That's real good, man. I'm happy for you."

His words seemed genuine this time. Corey was a little taken aback. Maybe the irritable, rowdy boy had grown into a reasonable man.

"Speaking of kids," Corey said, "I had one."

"No shit?"

"None whatsoever. Name's Luke. He's a junior at the University of Southern Maine."

Mark smirked. "Luke, huh? Like Skywalker?"

"Yeah. I guess you remember my thing with *Star Wars*. Luckily the wife didn't catch on to why I wanted that name until long after it was on the birth certificate."

"Wife? *You* have a fucking *wife*?"

Corey's smiled faded a little. "Yes, I do. Is that so hard to believe?"

"Nah, man. I didn't mean it that way. Actually, I offer my condolences. I never did marry, myself. I lived with women, and that was bad enough. Know what I'm saying?"

"Sure." Corey didn't want to admit he could relate, even jokingly. "So, no kids either, then?"

"You kidding? I got two. The boy's probably just a few years older than yours. The girl's almost twelve."

"Oh, congrats. Bit of an age gap there, huh?"

"Yeah, well, they came from two different baby mamas, two very different parts of my life. Funny to think though—our sons are older now than we were when we last saw each other. Crazy how time just moves right on like a bulldozer, not letting anything slow it down."

He pulled a pack of cigarettes from his pocket and put one in his mouth, not even enquiring whether or not it was okay to smoke in the house. Before he could light it, Scott came into the living room, Jennifer tagging behind, looking less pale than when she'd exited. Corey wondered what had been so private they needed to go outside. He sensed it had to do with him. Maybe now that Mark was here, it would take some of the third-wheel awkwardness away. Hopefully that was the only source of tension, which Corey sensed was mounting since the moment he'd arrived.

CHAPTER NINE

Seeing Jennifer reminded Mark why he'd agreed to this bullshit in the first place. It was as if Scott Dwyer wasn't standing right in front of him. All Mark saw was a girl from his past who still looked tasty and hadn't brought a husband or boyfriend along. There was no ring on her finger, but there was a faint tan line where one had been. He liked the implications of that.

He had a funny feeling about this reunion. It was like a friend's wedding or something, the kind of event that invited casual sex. Mark felt he had a better chance of scoring with old classmates in Connecticut than he did up in New Hampshire. Here he wasn't the burned out, unemployed, double DUI undesirable he was there. He was the bad boy who'd rocked the pleats right off girls' skirts. That reputation was bound to count for something. Even if a lot of time had passed, chicks remembered who'd been cool, like him, and who'd been dweebs, like Corey Pickett. And while Jennifer had always been Scott's girl, she certainly wasn't now. She was back on the open market.

Scott said, "Hello, Mark."

He turned, looking at him for the first time. "Hey, man."

"Been a long time."

"That's what they say."

"Too long."

"They say that too."

The men shook hands. Mark squeezed a little harder than necessary. Scott offered a beer and he followed him to the kitchen, slowing as he went past Jennifer. She was wearing perfume, an obvious sign she was hot to trot, but looked away when he winked at her, shy. He put out his hand and though she tried to shake it, he brought hers to his lips and kissed the back of it.

"Oh," she muttered.

He wasn't sure if she'd been pleasantly surprised or just made uncomfortable. Either way, he'd gotten a rise out of her, and he'd take it.

"Hello, Jenny." She couldn't hold his gaze when he looked right at her. "Man, you're just as pretty as a peach. Great to see you."

She cleared her throat. "Nice to see you too, Mark."

"Glad you could make it."

"Likewise."

But she didn't seem to mean it. Not yet.

Mark walked away, letting the babe marinate. It would take time to work on Jennifer. He could tell she wasn't the sort of woman you could rush. Besides, before he could really get comfortable enough to work his man magic, he had to get things square with Scott Dwyer.

In the kitchen, Scott handed Mark a cold beer, then refilled his glass.

"You drinkin' wine these days, huh?"

Scott shrugged. "Nothing fancy."

"Was always beer back in the day. We'd rip right through a twelve pack under the bridge, remember?"

"Those were the days."

Mark twisted the cap and drank, smacking his lips. He wasn't sure where to begin and was a little relieved when Scott did it for him.

"Listen, man. As I said on the phone, I know we have a history. Things didn't end on the best of terms. Honestly, I was surprised you even called me back. But I'm glad you did, and I'm very glad you're here."

Another sip of beer. "Shit, yeah. I wouldn't miss this. You kidding? Steven was like a brother to me."

"He was like one to me too." Scott paused, bracing himself for something. "And so were you, dude."

Mark went tense in his shoulders. It was the nicest thing Scott could have said and yet it made him feel cheated somehow. All the drive down, he'd thought of so many things he wanted to say to the guy, and with one term of endearment, Scott had smacked them right out of Mark's mouth. His grip on the grudge loosened, but he wasn't about to let it go.

"Yeah," Mark said. "That's true too, I guess."

"I'm sorry for what happened between us."

Mark took another drink. "That was then. This is now."

"Things change, you mean?"

"They've got no choice to."

"Maybe we can change this for the better. Not just for the sake of Steven's memory, but for our own sake too. What do you say?"

Scott held out his hand again. Mark shook it and even allowed Scott to lean in for a bro-hug, and though he didn't hug back, he patted Scott's arm.

They started talking, learning about each other all over again, Mark taking the rough edges off his life when he spoke about himself. He didn't lie, exactly, just omitted inconvenient truths. No sense in embarrassing himself. If they were putting past mistakes behind them, why not apply that to them all? His brief nights in jail were for minor offenses, anyway. It wasn't like he was hiding that he'd raped or murdered somebody. He wasn't an ex-con. Sometimes he just got drunk, made stupid mistakes, and then had to pay for it.

When he talked about his children, he didn't have to mention how they really felt about him. He could just say how proud he was, that he loved them. It's not like it wasn't true. Being a dad was one of the few things he seemed to have over Scott, who was still a bachelor. Mark envied him for it, but Scott didn't have to know that. Maybe the guy regretted never having kids and would be envious. Mark was certainly envious that Scott was self-employed, something he had failed miserably at. Scott also owned his own house, even if his parents had left it to him. Mark had never owned property and doubted his folks would leave him any when they kicked the bucket. The old man had never been very successful.

Like father, like son.

Minor envy aside, Mark found himself enjoying Scott's company. Whenever Scott had come to mind over the years, it wasn't always a negative. There were plenty of good memories too. It was almost embarrassing they'd managed to let such a simple, meaningless thing damage their friendship. If Mark knew then what he knew now, he never would have reacted the way he had, and the same likely went for Scott. Looking back, it was hard to believe something could've come between them.

Until she walked in the door.

CHAPTER TEN

"This is so weird."

Traci looked to the two men, Scott showing happiness, Mark shock.

"I don't mean that in a bad way," she said. "I just never thought we'd all be together like this again."

She spotted others in the living room. Traci wasn't surprised to see Scott had invited Jennifer Parks, but she hadn't expected Corey What's-his-name. She'd never considered the guy part of their clique. He was just Scott's friend from way back, an occasional tagalong, but little else. Whatever. It didn't put a damper on things. If anything, it added to the surrealism. Being with these four ghosts of an abandoned life was like an acid trip, only with more vivid hallucinations. Her two old boyfriends weren't an illusion, though.

"Traci," Scott said. "So, you made it after all."

"I said I'd try. Guess I succeeded."

They shared a little laugh, and she looked to Mark. His jaw was still slack and his stare hadn't left her. Traci liked that. Even after all these years, she made an impact.

Scott took her bag and went to the closet with it, inadvertently giving her a moment alone with her high school sweetheart.

"How are you, Mark?"

"I didn't know you'd be here," he said.

Her smile faded. "Is that a problem?"

He seemed to snap out of a dream. "What? No, no. I didn't mean it like that. It's just that Scott didn't tell me."

"He didn't?"

This struck Traci as odd. But wasn't *everything* about this odd? Still, why hadn't Scott told Mark she'd been invited too? She'd been hoping her presence was the main reason Mark would have come. Now she wasn't sure why it had been important to her at all. It's not like she wanted to rekindle anything. Far from it. She had Kordell now. What they had wasn't particularly special, but he was definitely more put together than the man who stood before her. Mark looked worn out. He looked *old*. Sure, they all did (except maybe Corey), but Mark seemed to have aged twice as much as the rest of them, even if he still had his hair and it hadn't gone gray like Scott's had. The age was not just in his face; it was in his soul. The good-looking boy who'd driven her parent's insane was no more. If Mark had faded any further, he'd be as gone as Steven Winters.

Traci glanced about the room as she walked deeper inside, almost expecting a funeral dirge to be playing from an organ. She was thinking Steven might be here, lain out in his coffin like the in-home wakes that were common long ago. But why would Steven's body be in Scott's house? She dismissed the silly idea.

Mark followed behind her as she greeted Jennifer and Corey.

He would shadow her most of the evening.

CHAPTER ELEVEN

"You guys remember the basement?"

Scott watched his guests' faces, waiting for them to brighten at the mention of the furnished room below the house. The gang had spent more time there together than anywhere else.

"Oh, man," Corey said.

Scott knew he could rely on him for that excitement. Jennifer, too, gave him a bright face at the mention of their old love nest. Scott looked to Mark, but he'd been in a daze since Traci Rillo arrived.

And who could blame him? Jennifer looked good, but Traci…she looked *amazing*.

Scott had expected her to look beaten down, the female equivalent to Mark. Given the type of girl she'd been, he hadn't maintained the kindest expectation of the woman she would have become. But he'd been dead wrong. Traci's face was as flawless as it had been when she was a teenager. They'd all had some pimples back then, but she'd never suffered a single blemish. Now they all showed wrinkles, but there were none on Traci's face. Age only made her appear more sophisticated, more worthy of respect and admiration. She wore a sharp, navy business skirt and an impeccable blouse, her stockings and high heels extenuating those long legs. Her once brown curls had been straightened and dyed blonder than even Jennifer's hair, and her body looked fit and firm, everything higher than it would be on another woman her age.

The only thing souring her image was the look on her face when Scott mentioned the basement room. He chose to ignore it and looked to the others for enthusiasm. Having them down there was a key part of this. Getting all four of them to the house was no easy feat. That he'd succeeded in doing so impressed even him, but it didn't end there. He had to keep guiding them in the gentlest baby steps.

He flashed his most charming grin, the one that was always reciprocated. "It wouldn't be just like old times without the old lounge, right?" He went toward the staircase, carrying a six-pack and a fresh bottle of claret. "C'mon, guys. You're gonna love this. If you think the house hasn't changed a bit, wait until you see my old room."

Jennifer stepped through the others, cradling the glass of wine that had been loosening her up. It was obvious she was still disappointed they weren't alone, but she grew more forgiving with every glass. There was a desperation to her that was almost palpable. If she'd tried to conceal her attraction to Scott, she'd done a half-assed job. It was flattering, but more importantly it gave him an edge.

She cocked an eyebrow. "Tell me the room still has all those monster movie posters."

Corey, always taking things further back, mentioned the *Teenage Mutant Ninja Turtles* posters that had long preceded them. Scott joined them in a laugh and patted Mark on the arm to bring him back into the moment. It was as if Traci had put a spell on the guy.

"Come on, buddy," Scott said. "It's been too long since we smoked a bowl down here."

Jennifer snickered at the mention of weed. Scott wondered if she still partook, one of those soccer moms who popped an edible at the end of the night and binge-watched Netflix with a pint of ice cream.

"Shit," Mark said. "A little grass. A little Motley Crüe and Soundgarden. Then this really will be fuckin' yesterday."

He joined Scott at the stairwell but didn't head down. None of them had. They were clearly hesitant, wanting Scott to lead them.

Scott held out his hand to Traci. "Wouldn't be a party without Traci Rillo."

She looked at the floor. "I don't know, Scott. Can't we just stay up here?"

His mouth went dry. He'd worried about this but had not come up with a real plan to get around it.

"C'mon," he said, "don't be that way. The basement was always our favorite place."

She crossed her arms, clinking her glass of wine with one fingernail. It was her only reply.

Jennifer looked back at her. "What's the matter?"

Scott winced but tried to hide it. There was enough unpleasantness to go over tonight without Traci coming up with a reason to stay above ground, particularly if it was a good reason.

"I just don't see why we have to go down there," she said.

"It's just for old times' sake," Corey said. Scott was delighted to see him start down the stairway, waving Traci on. "C'mon, it'll be fun."

"It'll be cold."

"Basement's heated," Scott told her.

They were all looking at her now. Despite Traci's newfound maturity, Scott detected remnants of that scared little girl in her eyes. He knew then she would fold, that when pressed by the others all intransigence would disappear and she'd revert to the suggestible, agreeable Traci he remembered. The slick exterior was already showing hairline cracks.

He took her hand even though she had not offered it. "Let's go. He's waiting for us down there."

The others turned back to him.

"Who?" Jennifer asked. "Who's waiting for us down there?"

Scott winked. "Who else? Steven."

CHAPTER TWELVE

Jennifer kicked off her heels and sank into the beanbag chair. All the furniture had remained, including the twin bed she'd lost her virginity on. The old boombox sat atop the dresser, both still covered in stickers for rock bands and radio stations. There was also the tube television with bunny ears, a hand-me-down Scott's uncle had given him. A VCR was below it, the shelves beneath lined with tapes and a rewinding machine.

"This is crazy," Mark said.

And it was. Jennifer wouldn't have felt more at home even if visiting the house she'd grown up in. The first Thanksgiving she'd come back from college, her folks had already redecorated her room. It became an office where Dad proudly displayed his first computer. Scott's parents, however, had done everything but seal the room in Mylar to keep it preserved. Even the old wizard bong was on the nightstand. Scott picked it up and sat down on the edge of his old bed, taking a small bag from his pocket.

"They really kept everything like this?" Jennifer asked. "You didn't just recreate it by dragging all this stuff out of storage or something?"

Scott shook his head as he packed the bong with marijuana. "They didn't change a thing. I know. It's kind of weird."

"Very weird," Traci said. She still hadn't sat down.

Jennifer was glad it was Corey who'd interrupted them first. If Traci had been the first to arrive, Jennifer might have stormed out, no matter how embarrassed she'd be by it later. She and Scott had had a much more serious relationship than he ever had with Traci. Scott only dated Traci for a month, and that was before Jennifer knew either of them. She'd met Scott through her friendship with Steven, and they went steady for over two years, an eternity for a teenage couple. If she hadn't had to move away for school, they might never had broken up at all. Scott's previous relationship with Traci was insignificant, but Jennifer had always harbored a sliver of jealousy, even though the two girls had gone on to become friends. It was even more ridiculous to feel any jealousy now, but her confidence was bruised by not being the only person Scott invited. The fact that Traci looked hotter than a ghost pepper didn't help matters.

Jennifer told herself she was the special one. Scott and Traci had just had their little fling and remained friends afterward. In contrast, the echo of the love Scott had shared with Jennifer was present every time they caught each other's eye. Traci wasn't competition—never had been. She was just an old friend, same as the others. Jennifer patted the side of the huge beanbag.

"Get over here," she said.

Traci came, but her face remained pale, lips drawn tight. She'd seemed so happy when she'd first arrived. What had changed?

Mark was alternating between watching the weed get pushed into the bowl and gazing upon Traci's form. He'd been following her like a puppy and looked just as eager to hump her leg. Where between Jennifer and her old boyfriend was a resurfaced affection, between Mark and Traci she sensed only one-way lust.

"His spirit," Corey said suddenly.

Mark looked at him. "What?"

"Steven. Scott said he was down here, waiting for us. You mean he's down here in spirit, right, Scott? I mean, if any place on earth could bring out the spirit of those days, it'd be this basement."

"I can think of another place," Traci said, her eyes like glaciers.

No one spoke. They all knew what she was alluding to. There'd been a time when they'd vowed not to speak of that place again. Had that vow expired after all this time? Jennifer hoped not. *That* wasn't what she'd come here for. Actually, it was the one reason she'd debated not coming at all.

"You're right, Corey," Scott eventually said, as if Traci hadn't said anything at all. "Steven loved it here. My Dad always said he should charge him rent. That's how often he stayed over."

Mark laughed. "Your old man threatened me with rent too. He was always just bustin' balls, though. He'd say that, but then he'd bring home enough pizzas for everybody. What a great guy he was."

"Thanks, Mark. That means a lot."

Jennifer remembered Mr. Dwyer a little differently. Scott's father had always been cold to her and his mother had been downright mean. She'd never understood why. Even Scott said it was a mystery to him.

Still, she warmed at seeing Scott and Mark reunited. The hostility between them she remembered was continuing to ebb, the memories of better times like a healing salve. Scott had a special touch when it came to all of them. He was the only one of the group who could have gathered them together again. Jennifer was sure of it.

"Steven was a good dude, too," Scott said.

He took a hit from the bong and passed it, his eyes going wet. Mark took an even bigger hit and didn't cough like death was upon him the way Scott had. It seemed only one of them was rusty with pot.

"I thought we could share some memories," Scott said. "Memories of Steven."

Jennifer had plenty of good memories of Steven Winters. Unfortunately, those weren't the ones that often came to mind.

"WE'VE GOT to do something," Steven said.

They were loitering under Fred Lee Bridge, a short connection over a creek that exited the suburbs. It was a frequent hangout on their way home from school. Vast farmland stretched toward the surrounding mountains, and from where they gathered, the group of teens could see the Klinger family's farm with its endless rows of swollen pumpkins.

Traci was passing a cigarette back and forth with Mark, his denim jacket slung over her shoulders. He wore a Slayer t-shirt with the sleeves torn off but showed no discomfort despite the chill of the afternoon. Scott sat with Jenny in front of him, his arms wrapped around her, her head nestled back into his chest. She always felt so good here, so safe.

"Do what?" Mark asked Steven. "You wanna go trick-or-treating?"

Everyone else chuckled.

"Yeah," Traci teased. "Maybe I'll dress up as Wonder Woman!"

Mark snorted a laugh, smoke sneaking through his clenched teeth.

Steven shook his head at the ground. "You guys are assholes."

Jenny said, "Well then, what? I mean, what're we supposed to do? It's not like there's any cool parties going on or anything."

Steven scooched off the rock he'd been sitting on. "I don't know, but there must be *something*. It's Halloween tomorrow. Shouldn't we do something other than sit around Scott's basement playing Super Nintendo?"

"Mortal Kombat not good enough for you anymore?" Scott joked.

"Not for Halloween night. It only comes once a year."

Jennifer couldn't resist. "Don't want to miss it by sitting in a pumpkin patch with a blockhead."

They had another chuckle at Steven's expense, but he shrugged it off.

Traci said, "We're not kids anymore, dude. We're not gonna put on masks or bob for apples. That's lame."

"Of course it is." He tucked his shaggy hair behind his ears. "I wasn't saying we do any of that corny shit. I think it would be cooler to do something...scary."

The group glanced at each other, gauging reactions.

"We can go see one of the new horror movies," Scott said.

"Nah. Too typical. And not *really* scary."

"Speak for yourself," Jennifer said. "I hate those slasher movies Scott drags me to. They make me want to pee my pants."

Mark snickered. Jennifer figured there was a dirty joke on his lips, but he swallowed it back when Scott glanced at him.

Traci said, "Speaking of piss—"

"This ought to be good," Mark said.

"I've got an idea. Let's get some toilet paper. Redecorate all of Redford."

"Hey, I like this idea. We can paper it up and smash all the pumpkins. And I've got a backyard just full of dog shit we can bag and set on fire."

"Come on, guys," Scott said, but trailed off.

"Yeah," Jenny said. "I don't want to do that either."

Traci exhaled. "Jen, you never want to do anything Scott doesn't want to do."

"Nuh-uh. I just don't want to vandalize the whole town. It's childish."

"Fine. Any better ideas?"

Steven walked through a circle of yellowed leaves gathered at the edge of the creek. His flannel fluttered on the wind trapped beneath the bridge, his hair escaping from the backs of his ears. His eyes were like flint, and though he was the shortest of the boys, there was an intensity to him that made everyone forget that.

"Yeah," he said, smirking. "I've got an idea."

JENNIFER SHIFTED in the beanbag chair as Mark and Scott went over all the old stories: Steven hood-surfing on Danny Napier's station wagon until they hit a pothole and he flew off, just missing going under the tires; how he'd taken two chickens from his aunt's coop and let them loose on the football field during the big game; the time he'd brought crickets to school and hid them in classrooms to drive the teachers insane. Jennifer enjoyed hearing them, for some of these memories had been lost to time, fading into the back of her mind until they were no more. It was that way for all of them. Traci told stories Mark had forgotten. Corey told one about Scott and Steven trying to catch his escaped dog, which Scott barely remembered. As the weed took effect and the next round of drinks came, they all loosened up, even Traci, who had all but frozen when she'd first entered the basement. The only one who wasn't buzzing was Corey. But while he'd not drank or smoked, he was just as jovial as the others.

The surrealism of them all being together again transformed into something more pleasant and warm, and when Mark got up to use the bathroom Jennifer saw her chance to sit with Scott on the bed. The wine was going to her head and she knew it, but she simply didn't care. She'd needed this good time and went with her impulses. Save whatever shame clouds for tomorrow. Tonight, she was reverting to a time when there were no houses to sell, kids to raise, mortgages to pay, or heartbreaking divorce papers to sign. Here she wasn't Jennifer anymore; she was Jenny. Young and carefree, the way she'd been before so much had gone wrong.

They would have to talk about it at some point. She knew that. The memory of that Halloween must have popped into each of their minds, even if they'd all been too polite to spoil the mood by mentioning it, other than Traci's subtle nod. Scott was the host of this thing. Maybe that responsibility fell on him. Jennifer just hoped they would wait until tomorrow. Tonight was for better reflections.

"How're you feeling?" Scott asked, smiling as she cozied up to him.

She leaned on his shoulder. "Oh, I am *great*."

COREY SMILED at the former couple falling back into old habits. Seeing Jennifer snuggling into Scott was like some kind of spell. It felt as if they'd all fallen under a protective dome that blocked out the bad things that had happened, sealing them in so they could take this time to heal, the way they should have back then but had ultimately failed to. It was deeply therapeutic. Not just for Corey, but for all of them.

He was glad he'd talked himself into going. His main motivation had been to see Scott Dwyer again, and it surprised Corey that he was enjoying the company of the others this much. He'd never been an integral part of the gang. After they'd turned thirteen, Scott had found new hobbies like skateboarding and heavy metal, leaving behind the comic books and role-playing games with which Corey remained obsessed. Scott found new friends who were cooler than Corey could ever hope to be but, to his credit, Scott never turned a cold shoulder to him. They were still buddies, still neighbors, despite their ever-growing differences. Sometimes Corey got to tag along with the group, but more often was just a third wheel to Scott and Jennifer. Mark and Traci simply tolerated him. And Steven, despite being the wildest of the group, bonded with Corey over Isaac Asimov and Phil K. Dick novels. Steven even liked some comics, dark ones like *Preacher*, *Hellraiser*, and *Sandman*. It was that love for horror that had bonded Steven and Scott from the beginning. Steven was married to all things scary, even more so than Scott with his love of horror movies.

Corey didn't go in for those sorts of movies these days. He didn't even like carrying horror comics in the shop, but there was a small market for them, so he folded to his partner's insistence they bring them in, along with action figures of Freddy Krueger and Jason Voorhees and other big screen boogeymen. It wasn't that Corey was snobby. He didn't frown upon horror like some Sunday school teacher might. He just couldn't enjoy the genre. It too easily triggered him. Once you've experienced real terror, the desire to be scared for fun not only disappears, it stops making sense.

Mark returned from the bathroom with a bottle of vodka. When Traci spotted it, she came out of her seat.

"Hey, buster," she said. "Keep your grubby hands off my stuff."

He smirked. "It was just sitting there."

"No, it was in my bag."

"It was *poking out* of the bag. It's not like I rooted through it. I just thought we could all enjoy some of the good stuff. You did bring it for everyone, right? You're not gonna bogart this whole bottle, are ya?"

Scott raised his hand. "Guys, if you want vodka, I have some Tito's."

He nodded toward a small cabinet in the corner, one of the few things in the room Corey didn't remember being there in the old days.

A look of resignation came across Traci's face. "No. It's fine. We can drink this one. Help yourselves."

Mark pulled two glasses out of the cabinet and poured drinks for Traci and himself. Corey watched Mark move in on the beautiful woman, not leaving her side once he'd handed her the glass. They toasted, but Corey couldn't hear what was said.

Jennifer stretched. "How 'bout some music?"

"Hell yeah." Mark bobbed his head. "Give us a beat, DJ."

"Okay," Scott said. "All I've got is some old CDs and cassette tapes for the boombox here."

"Perfect," Corey said. "Just the right stuff for tonight."

As Scott dug them out, Corey shared a glance with Jennifer and realized if she wasn't drunk, she was teetering on its threshold. Her eyes had gone even softer, and she swayed in her seat, her hand running back and forth over the mattress as if she were petting a cat. She looked so content, so peaceful. It almost made him want a drink. Maybe he could find that serenity if he gave it a shot. The group got to talking again, Mark telling a Steven story, but when the boombox came on, everyone closed their mouths at once. Corey's jaw snapped shut like a bear trap when he heard the music, his spine tightening like a hangman's rope. He crushed the soda can in his hand without realizing it.

No, he thought. *Anything but this.*

Jennifer's smile vanished. Traci went pale and the scowl on Mark's face could make a marine shiver right out of his boots.

Corey went to Scott and whispered. "What the hell are you doing?"

Scott gave him an innocent look. "What?"

Mark stepped forward. "You know damned well what. Turn that shit off right now."

Again, Scott gave a dumb expression.

Corey shook his head. Could Scott really have forgotten? From the looks of the others, he would be alone in having lost the memory attached to this song.

Without a word, Traci stepped through the men, nearly shoving Corey out of the way, and pressed the stop button, putting the basement in silence. Standing over the boombox, she finished her drink in one long shot, and then returned to the cabinet for a refill, still saying nothing.

"Why the fuck would you do that?" Mark asked Scott.

Corey took a deep breath. He lamented seeing the peace treaty Scott and Mark formed going up in flames so quickly, but he couldn't fault Mark for his anger.

"What's wrong with you guys?" Scott said. "What did I do?"

Traci glared at him. "Don't play dumb, Scott."

Corey said, "Maybe he just forgot."

"Impossible."

"Forgot what?" Scott asked. "All I did was put on some music."

Mark pointed at him. "No, you played 'Don't Fear the Reaper.' That's not just any music."

Scott shrugged, arms out at his sides in question.

Jennifer stood, rubbing a tear from her cheek. "Scott, is this really how you want to bring it up?"

SCOTT CLUTCHED the butcher knife. "I don't know about this."

They were sitting on his back porch after school. It was even colder today, bleaker. Jenny had been feeling a chill all afternoon, but it was not entirely due to the weather.

"We can't back out now," she said.

Scott looked suddenly younger to her, almost boyish. His cheeks were flushed from the cold, lips bright red from chewing on them. His hair was a mess, as if he'd been headbanging, and he hadn't changed clothes since yesterday.

"We can do whatever we want," Scott said. "We don't have to just go along with Steven all the time."

She turned away, guilty. "I know that."

"We don't, like, owe him anything, even if he did set us up together."

"I don't think we do."

"Well, it just seems that way sometimes. It's not just you, Jenny. It's all of us. I know he's the smart one, that he jumped ahead a grade and all, but that doesn't mean he's always right, does it?"

"No. Of course not."

Scott put the knife down on the table, resting it on the array of newspaper. She wondered if there were any articles in it about the woods. It seemed likely, but they hadn't checked. Having mercy on themselves, they'd put down the funny pages on the top of the stack, *Calvin and Hobbes* a more pleasant site than the local headlines. Seeing his heart wasn't in it, Jenny took the knife from Scott and studied the best spot to stab. She raised the blade, lunged, and the pumpkin spurted.

"It's Halloween," she said. "You're the one who loves horror movies. I thought you'd enjoy a good scare."

"It's not that, Jenny. I'm not *scared* to go."

"Then what is it?"

He looked into the distance. "It just seems…disrespectful."

She couldn't argue that. Instead, she focused on popping the lid off the pumpkin. Scott held it down so it wouldn't tear.

"It's kind of like when people take pictures in a cemetery," he said. "You know. They dress all goth and think they're so dark or whatever, that they're so cool. I mean, it's a *cemetery*, not a prop. People are really buried there. It's supposed to be sacred, right?"

She gave him a little smile. Just when she thought she couldn't love her boyfriend any more than she already did he'd show another side of himself that opened her heart even wider.

"You're a good person, Scott. And I know what you're saying. But this isn't the same as going to a cemetery. It's not like the…"

She was unable to say what she'd been thinking. Even trying to find the words proved too callous. But Scott found a way.

"It's not like the bodies were left out there," he said.

Jenny stopped digging through the pumpkin guts. She suddenly didn't feel like carving a jack-o'-lantern anymore. She looked into the woods behind Scott's house, almost daring herself to do so, and then quickly looked away.

"I was never crazy about this idea," she said. "But everybody else is all stoked to go tonight. Steven has everybody pumped."

"Yeah, well, sometimes he comes up with some way out-there shit. I think this is one of those times."

"So what do we do? Ditch?"

He shook his head. "I don't know."

Scott picked up the knife and started fiddling with the innards again, stirring them as if they held some kind of answer. Jenny hated when he was wishy-washy. It meant she had to make her own decisions, which she always felt were the wrong ones. She didn't want to disappoint Scott, but she also didn't want to disappoint her friends.

"I guess we could always ditch later," Scott said. "We could go just for a little while, right? That way they can't say we wussed out."

But she knew it wouldn't be that easy, especially with Mark there to instigate things. He'd start clucking like a chicken the moment they tried to leave. Jennifer decided not to mention it. She touched the inside of Scott's leg with one sneaker, initiating footsy.

"I dunno," she said, "I kind of like the idea of sharing a sleeping bag with you."

Scott gave her a knowing look. "It'd be a lot more fun than summer camp."

They giggled. Jenny relaxed again. Scott's hesitation over tonight's plans had been giving her new reservations just when she thought she'd gotten past her initial ones.

When Steven had first suggested it, she hadn't tried to hide her displeasure because she thought he'd been making a joke—a sick, demented joke, but a joke. When nobody laughed, not even tough guy Mark, the gravity of the invitation rushed upon her.

"Wait," Jenny had asked him. "You're serious?"

Steven shrugged. "Yeah. Why not?"

She tensed further when she saw Traci's eyes going wide, Mark's mouth forming a Joker's grin. Behind Jenny, Scott's grip loosened, and she felt suddenly weightless.

"Suicide Woods," Steven said again. "We meet at Scott's house at sundown."

"For what?" Scott asked.

"To go camping."

"In *Suicide Woods?*"

"I don't know about you, man, but the woods is where I always do my camping."

"You know what I mean."

Traci came to Steven and raised her hand for a high five.

"Fantastic, man," she said. "Way cooler idea than the one I had. That is *so* creepy."

Mark joined his girlfriend, puffing his cigarette like a steam engine. Seeing this growing enthusiasm brought the first tingle of dread to the back of Jenny's neck. Mark put his arm around Steven's shoulders and drew him in.

"Dude," he said. "You're fucking *nuts*, Stevey. Totally out of your skull."

Traci snickered. "What else is new?"

"So, we're gonna do it?" Steven asked.

"Hell, yeah, we're gonna do it!"

They looked to Scott and Jenny for confirmation. She gripped Scott by the wrist in a silent correspondence and they sat up together as if to address their friends, but neither of them spoke. Steven's eyes never left them.

"They only just cleared up the last crime scene a day or so ago," he said.

But Jenny knew that. Everyone in Redford was morbidly curious enough to follow the news regarding Summer Haney, and it was particularly at the forefront of the minds of the dead girl's classmates. Jenny had never really known Summer, and neither had her friends. She was a junior, and they were seniors. Scott said he hadn't even realized the girl lived in his neighborhood until she'd been pulled out of the surrounding forest.

Suicide Woods.

Behind the houses on the west end of Belmont Street, the untouched thicket stretched on for miles, fading into the rocky terrain of the mountainside. Scott's backyard led into those woods, and trails ran through them leading to Crestline Avenue and Union Drive, giving Traci and Mark easy access from their sides of the block. The proximity of Suicide Woods only added to the eeriness of them, even though the bodies were always discovered deep within, far from any roads.

Summer Haney wasn't the only one who'd gone there to kill themselves; she was just the most recent. Over the past year and a half, twelve bodies had been discovered, all at different locations in the forest, all between the ages of sixteen and nineteen. The victims were both male and female, and they varied in race. The methods of death varied too, with some being far more gruesome than others, but none of the crime scenes showed any signs of struggle or sexual assault. There was never any evidence of foul play. Every one of these lost children had taken their own lives, but that didn't stop urban legends from circulating, tale tales of a serial killer, a murderous biker gang, and even a story about a cult of devil worshippers. More than anything else, people in Redford claimed the woods were haunted.

"I guess it is kind of spooky," Scott said now, plopping two handfuls of pumpkin innards on the newspaper. "I mean, to go there on Halloween night."

Jenny nodded. "Oh, it is *definitely* spooky. No doubt."

"But you don't like scary stuff. When we watch a movie, you only see half of it 'cause you hide behind your hands." He put his hands over his eyes and cringed. "Are you going to walk through the woods all night like this?"

She batted his arm. "Shut up. Jerk."

When his hands dropped, pumpkin slime remained on his face. She laughed and Scott reached out with slathered hands, coming at her slowly like some orange mummy.

"You're a butthead," she said.

"You love it." He leaned over the table.

"I know," she said, kissing him.

"I DIDN'T mean to," Scott said.

Traci remained at the liquor cabinet, refreshing her drink. She didn't try to hide it the way she did at most social gatherings. Mark had already exposed that she'd brought the bottle of vodka along. They were all bound to think she was a drunk anyway, and hell, they might be right. They wouldn't be the first people to come to that conclusion. Alcohol had chased away more than one man in her life.

"I knew we'd get around to it," Jennifer said. "I just hoped it could wait until tomorrow. We were having such a nice time."

Mark huffed. "Yeah, a regular high school reunion. Only, we're short two people."

Traci tensed. "Mark…"

"What? Scott wants to talk about it, then we'll talk about it."

"Don't."

"It's his fuckin' house, his fuckin' party."

"Hey, Mark, come on, man," Scott said. "I really didn't mean to bring this up. I just put in a mix tape from back in the day and—"

"That's *the* mix tape, dude. The same one from Halloween 1995. The one Steven made."

Corey intervened. "C'mon. It was just one song. It doesn't mean it's the whole mix tape. How would Scott have even gotten hold of it?"

"Wanna bet? Scott, put on the next track and let's find out."

Jennifer sighed. "Mark, you're being ridiculous. The tape was left behind, remember?"

"Maybe or maybe not. Play it."

"No," Traci said, coming back to the group. "I don't wanna hear anymore. One song was enough."

"She's right," Jennifer said. "Every time I hear 'Don't Fear the Reaper' my stomach twists in knots."

"You okay?" Scott asked, going to her.

She stepped back a little. "I'm fine."

Traci put the empty glass on the table. "This was a mistake. I shouldn't have come. None of us should have."

Scott's face fell. "Traci, please, I…"

"Goodbye, everyone." She moved to the stairwell.

Mark blocked her path. "Traci, hold up. You can't drive. You've been chugging booze and smoking weed for hours."

Traci huffed. She knew damn well this wasn't why Mark wanted her to stay. But the others joined him in protest, so she backed off and returned to the liquor cabinet.

Scott approached, looking slack and gray. "I'm really sorry, Traci." He turned to the others. "I apologize to all of you. Really, I didn't mean to put that on. I just grabbed a random, unmarked tape. It's been a long time and I'm a little buzzed. It was a mistake, that's all."

Mark sighed, his anger visibly fading. "You really didn't want to bring that night up?"

"No. I didn't. At least, not tonight. But let's face it; we can't get together without it being on our minds. So maybe we should just get it out there. I mean, shit, it's already out there now, right? Maybe if we talk about it, we can get it out of the way. Get it out of our system."

"Christ," Traci said. "I've spent the past twenty-five years trying to get that night out of my system. Out of my head."

"I understand."

"Do you?"

"Of course I do. I was there too you know. We all were. But I wanted to celebrate Steven's memory tonight. That's what he wanted. I think he knew that if we did, we could face this thing together."

"We already faced it a quarter of a century ago."

"No, we just tried to ignore it and hoped it would all go away. Even now, we haven't so much as mentioned her name."

Traci grimaced. Her veins felt as if they were flushed with ice. "We don't talk about her. You promised, Scott. We all did."

Scott opened his mouth but had no words.

"Wait," Mark said. "How do you know what Steven's wishes were?"

"He said so…in his will."

"How'd you get a look at his will?"

Scott breathed deep and headed to the dresser. He opened the top drawer and lifted out a wooden box, roughly nine inches by eleven. Opening the lid, he removed a manila envelope, holding it to his chest with both hands.

"He made me his executor," he said. "And he left something for each of you."

CHAPTER THIRTEEN

The girl was younger.

She was short and slender, strawberry-blonde hair and a spattering of freckles across the bridge of her nose. Braces. A pink sweater and jeans with holes in the knees. Probably a freshman; a junior at most. A backpack covered in pinback buttons was slung over her shoulder, a rolled-up blanket under her arm.

"Guys," Steven said. "This is Robin Reeves."

The group introduced themselves. When Robin wasn't looking, Jenny gave Steven a curious look. He only smiled.

"She wanted to come too," he said. "That's cool with you guys, right?"

If there were any objections, none were vocalized. The same went for questions.

There were six of them now, but only four sleeping bags. Steven was carrying one on his back like a professional hiker. Traci, Scott, and Jenny had brought theirs along too. Mark, always the show off, said he didn't need one, that he'd slept on the ground plenty of times without needing such amenities. No one doubted it. They had backpacks full of snacks, flashlights, and coats for once the sun went down. Mark brought tabs of acid secured in tinfoil and had somehow gotten his hands on a twelve pack of Budweiser. It swung by his side like a suitcase. Scott had a cigarette box containing four joints, and Steven had even brought a radio with a tape deck. It was gearing up to be a hell of a Halloween.

They gathered in Scott's backyard. The woods awaited. There were still a couple of hours of daylight left, and the clouds had dissipated, giving way to abundant sunshine which, at least for the time being, lessened the creepiness of where they were headed.

Traci said, "You guys didn't tell anyone, right?"

"Of course not," Scott said. "Our parents would never let us sleep out there."

"So your folks aren't home right now, right?"

"No, they're still at work."

Mark put a cigarette in his mouth. "I don't need to tell my folks jack shit. I come and go as I please."

Jenny pitied him for this. She couldn't imagine having parents like Mark's, ones who didn't even notice when their children were gone. A lot of other teenagers were envious of his freedom, but Jenny didn't think it was worth the emotional toll.

"What about you, girlie?" Mark asked Robin.

He was only asking what they all must have been thinking. She was a stranger who looked like she hadn't even hit sixteen yet. It was hard to imagine her parents would let her come and go the way Mark's did.

"It's cool," she said. "My mom thinks I'm at a sleepover."

"You are," Steven said, smirking.

"I mean, with girlfriends. She thinks I'm at my friend Carrie's."

"Will this Carrie cover for you?" Traci asked.

The girl shrugged. "Sure."

Traci looked to the others, seeming unconvinced.

"Don't worry about it," Steven said. "C'mon, guys. Are we ready? There's only so much daylight left. I want to get as far out there as we can."

Jenny tensed. "Why? What's the difference?"

"It's a big difference. It won't be nearly as scary if we can still see Scott's house from where we set up camp. I don't want us to see the lights of the neighborhood at all."

"Right," Mark said. "Besides, deep in the woods is where they always find the bodies."

Jenny took Scott's hand.

"Does anyone have a compass?" Scott asked.

Mark snorted. "What're we, Girl Scouts?"

"We don't want to get totally lost, dude."

"Why not?" Steven asked, wiggling his eyebrows. "That's part of the fun!"

Jenny glared at him. "Steven…"

"Oh, just relax, will ya? Jeez, we haven't set foot in there and already you guys are all freaked out."

"Yeah," said Traci. "It's Halloween. Let's freakin' party."

Robin surprised them by saying, "Maybe we should smoke a bowl. To mellow everybody out."

"Bad ass," Mark said. "I like this chick already."

Steven drew a pipe from one pocket and a small bag of weed from the other. He was packing the bowl when another voice startled them.

"Hey, Scott!"

They turned to the house next door. Corey Pickett was halfway out his bedroom window, watching the group below. Jenny waved to him.

"What's up, Corey?" Scott asked.

"You guys look all packed up. What's going on?"

Mark turned away, sighing and rolling his eyes. Traci groaned.

Steven lit the pipe. "Trick 'r treat, Corey. Come on down."

Corey came outside, flashing his crooked smile, his gangly body like a scarecrow's. Jenny noticed his Yoda t-shirt and had to stifle a giggle. She liked Corey, even if he sometimes spoiled her and Scott's alone time by dropping in announced. He had a way of inviting himself to things, as she expected he would do now. When Steven told him the evening's plans, Corey's eyes went wide.

"You can't be serious," he said.

"Totally serious."

"You guys can't go out there! Don't you know about the trespassing law?"

Traci put her hands on her hips. "It's not private property, man. Nobody owns these friggin' woods."

"That's not what I'm talking about. They made a new law about these woods, banning teenagers from hanging out in there."

"What? No way."

"No, for real. They did it because of all the…you know. They're trying to keep people our age out of there. They think teenage suicide is becoming a trend in Redford, that we all think it's cool to off ourselves in the woods."

Mark blew smoke. "That's fuckin' bullshit. Nobody thinks that."

"They made the law. If they find you out there, they don't just give you a slap on the wrist. They take you to *jail*."

Tingles slithered up Jenny's spine.

Scott gripped her hand a little tighter and looked to Steven. "Maybe this is a mistake, dude."

"C'mon, Scott," Steven said. "You don't really think the cops are gonna walk all the way into Suicide Woods looking for teenagers, do you? They might drive by and scan them from the street with a spotlight, but that's it. If we go deep, like I was saying, they won't see us."

"Exactly," Mark said. "I don't let pigs tell me what to do, anyway."

Jenny hoped Scott would continue to protest, but he resigned any argument and she was too timid to make one of her own. She was growing more worried. Getting lost? Hiding from the cops? These weren't the fun kind of scares; these were actually dangerous.

"You should come with us," Steven told Corey. "You got a sleeping bag or anything like that?"

"Yeah, but…"

"But nothing. Don't be a wuss."

"I'm not. I just don't wanna get busted."

"You won't. Just tell your parents you'll be watching a horror movie marathon at Scott's."

Robin said, "The same sort of story worked for me."

"See? If Robin can do it, why can't you?"

When Corey gave Robin more than a fleeting glance, Jenny saw a glow come into his eyes. His smile was as bashful as a toddler hiding behind his mother's leg. That's when she knew Steven had him.

MARK EXCUSED himself from the basement. They'd agreed to take a break before getting into Steven's will, despite the eagerness to know what it contained. Scott wanted everyone to calm down before they got into it. He was okay with smoking weed in the house, but not cigarettes. That was fine, though, because Traci had come outside too.

"Can I bum one?" she asked.

Mark opened his pack, and she slid one out. He lit it for her.

Goddamn she was beautiful. Even foxier than she'd been back in high school. It pained him to look upon her now, knowing he'd once had that. His past few girlfriends weren't bad looking, but compared to Traci Rillo, they might as well be gargoyles. He was relieved he'd been able to stop her from leaving. She was a little stiff (and who could blame her?), but if he put in some work with her, he might be able to reignite yesterday's fire, if only for a night. It would be worth the extra effort. Hell, he'd give up a finger to bed her one more time.

"What do you think?" she asked.

Mark blinked out of his reverie. What did he think about what? Her hot body?

"What?" he asked.

"About what Scott said. The will?"

"Oh, right, right. Yeah, that's pretty crazy."

"Well, Steven was pretty crazy."

"True enough."

"Scott told me he became a recluse, one of those solitary writer types. That's a whole different kind of weird than he was when we were growing up, but somehow it suits him."

Mark nodded. "Yeah. I can see that."

She took a sip of vodka. Mark was impressed. He was a heavy drinker but mostly stuck to beer. If he'd drank as much hard liquor as Traci had tonight, he'd black out and wake up in the morning feeling like he'd gone twelve rounds with a young Mike Tyson. But he wasn't one to judge anybody, having been busted drinking and driving. Once he'd even been arrested for possession of a small amount of cocaine. And while Traci only seemed mildly buzzed, if she kept knocking them back, that only increased his chances of having sex with her, didn't it?

"What do you think he left us?" she asked.

"No idea. Jeez, after all these years. I mean, why?"

"Scott said Steven didn't have any family. Maybe he thought of us as family in a way, like siblings or something, because we grew up together."

"Maybe so."

She flicked ash. "Mark?"

"Yeah?"

When she looked at him, something about the moonlight gave her a ghostly air. Like some movie magic, she appeared to be seventeen again. He knew it was an illusion, a mild hallucination brought on by getting stoned, but still the effect left him mesmerized.

"There's something I don't like about all of this," she said.

"YOU ALL need to brace yourselves," Scott said. He didn't say it for dramatic effect. What he was about to tell them was a lot to handle. "When I first read this will, it really floored me. Steven had some really...*interesting*... things to say."

He stood before them as if he were giving a Shakespearean monologue, which was befitting in a way. The night had grown heavy with drama and he hadn't even begun to tell them the details. Jennifer sat front and center, leaning in with her elbows in her lap. It was almost as if she were praying to him, for what he did not know. Mark and Traci were against the wall near the stairwell. They seemed to have formed some sort of alliance and Scott wondered what they'd talked about on the back porch. Corey was in the beanbag chair now, looking small and swallowed. Scott would watch him the closest. He was sober and would have the most logical reactions.

"Now," Scott began, "I'm not sure why Steven made me his executor, but given that his final wishes involve all of us, I guess he wanted someone from this group to have the job. He probably only picked me because I still live here in Redford, whereas the rest of you moved away. My close proximity to his house makes it a lot easier for me to collect his things and handle his affairs."

"How did he know we all moved away?" Jennifer asked.

"Actually, I don't know if he did or not. If he did, I guess he was keeping tabs on us. These days it's pretty easy to find people."

"I looked for him," Traci said. "Tried to find him online but there was nothing. No articles or records, and no social media profiles—nothing. If he wanted to find us, why not just create accounts? That's how everybody finds everybody."

"Look, guys; I don't know why Steven did the things he did. All I can tell you is what I read in this." He held up the manila envelope containing the will. "And what I read in this."

He reached into the wooden manuscript box.

It was time to show them.

THE TRAIL was hidden under fallen leaves and twigs. If Steven hadn't been leading the way, Corey never would have been able to follow it. The leaves on the ground had browned, but the ones streaming the trees were various shades of gold. When they caught the late afternoon sunlight, they seemed almost neon. The teens trenched like soldiers alongside walls of black rock, down slopping hills that made bowls of the basin. The air split with the caws of birds that had yet to travel south for the season.

Corey was behind Traci, admiring her from the back. Not ogling, just admiring. How often had he told himself that one day he, too, would have a girlfriend? Maybe not as hot as Traci or as sweet as Jenny, but a girl nonetheless, one he could call his own. He wished he knew how to talk to them. He doubted he would ever be as smooth as Scott and wondered how two guys who'd grown up in the same environment could have developed such a different set of social skills.

Corey was actually the oldest of everyone here, and yet he was the little tagalong. And now, somehow, he'd been roped into coming along for something he had no real desire to do. If anything, he'd been inordinately against it. Not just because they could get in serious trouble, but also because it was just plain morbid. Summer Haney had slit her wrists out here just two weeks ago, and here they were acting like it was a haunted house at the state fair. And what about all the other suicides these woods had seen? This place had earned its nickname.

Halloween used to be about dressing up in costumes and getting fistfuls of candy. He'd trick-or-treated until he was thirteen, at which point he was so ridiculed when he went to school in his Wolverine costume that he'd retired from the holiday. He missed being able to escape into fantasy by dressing up and gallivanting through the streets on Halloween night. The magic of it was something people lost as they grew older and their imaginations were chiseled away by the dominating presence of the real world. Corey was happy to be heading out again on this holiday, but it came with an unpleasant catch, like he'd made a wish on a cursed monkey's paw. If there were going to be any good, old-fashioned Halloween fun tonight, he'd have to create it for himself. That's why when he saw the jack-o'-lantern Jenny and Scott had carved, he'd asked if they could bring it along, and when they agreed, he volunteered to carry it.

"How long do we keep going?" Scott asked.

He and Jenny were bringing up the rear. Corey had heard them talking in whispers, sounding more concerned the longer the march went on.

Steven called back without turning around. "We'll go until we get there."

"We *are* here," Scott said. "I can't see houses anymore. Can you? We're in the woods now. What's the point of going any deeper?"

Mark laughed. "Chicks like it when you go deeper, Scotty. Don't you know that?"

"I'm serious."

"We need the right spot," Steven said. "I'm looking for a deadening."

Jenny stirred. "A what?"

"A deadening. It's what you call a large clearing in the woods."

"Just say clearing then. I don't like that other word. Not out here."

"Starting to get the willies?"

Traci smirked. "It's not even dark yet."

"Hey, Steven," Scott said. "Check it out."

The group stopped.

Scott was pointing to an area where the trees thinned. Two walls of stacked rocks curved around the glade, closing in the open space like a gate. To Corey, it all looked defoliated on purpose, like a cemetery without the tombstones. Red leaves stretched throughout like a lake of blood.

"Prefect-o," Steven said.

They set up camp. Not that it was anything special—just some sleeping bags, blankets, and backpacks. Corey had debated bringing a tent with him but didn't want to be the only person with one. He was certain he would have been made fun of for it, especially by Mark.

Steven and Mark wandered off to piss. Scott and Jenny were talking about the best way to arrange their things, and Traci had popped open a beer. Robin stood away from the others, twirling that fiery hair in her hands. She'd seemed so at ease this entire time, but without Steven by her side, she looked suddenly lost and nervous. Corey went to her.

Though younger, Robin was an exceptionally pretty girl, but he had always had a fondness for redheads, ever since Nicole Sherman in the fifth grade had sat in front of him in class, her long, curly locks a constant distraction. Of course, he'd never told Nicole about his crush. Like all the ones who came after her, she had gotten away. Corey wasn't much better at talking to the opposite sex than he had been back then, but he had courage enough to approach Steven's new friend.

"How's it going?"

Robin gazed upon him with soft, emerald eyes. Her smile was small but honest. They exchanged the basic pleasantries before he got to his real question.

"So, how do you know Steven?"

She furrowed her brow. "What do you mean?"

"How'd you two meet each other?"

"He lives on my street."

"Oh. Well, that's cool. I don't think I've seen you at school before. What grade are you in?"

He instantly regretted asking. Clearly, she was younger. He didn't want to make her feel any more awkward to be with them. But Robin didn't seem to mind.

"I'm homeschooled," she said.

"Oh." He was genuinely surprised. He'd never met anyone who was homeschooled before. "So, you and Steven…"

But he didn't know what to say. He felt as if he'd been interrogating her. That's just how he was with the girls he met. He didn't know what else to do but bombard them with questions, a nervous tick he was aware of but powerless to prevent.

"We just hang out," she said. "I like to do stuff with him."

"Like what?"

"Just whatever."

He gestured to the surrounding woodland. "Stuff like this?"

She was about to answer when they were interrupted by the sound of footsteps crunching leaves. Steven and Mark came out from behind the covering of brush, and Steven took Robin by the hand. It was hard for Corey to tell if the gesture was romantic or not. He might have been holding her hand like a boyfriend, or perhaps like a big brother, like he was guiding her through this strange new world he'd invited her into.

"So now what?" Scott asked.

Steven reached for his radio. "Now we just chill out. Wait for the night. That's when the real fun begins."

"You're strange, Steven," Jenny said.

"And then some." He put a tape into the deck and pressed play. "Check this out. I made us a Halloween mix."

Corey recognized Blue Oyster Cult's "Don't Fear the Reaper" as it began.

"Dude," Mark said, "that is twisted."

Steven blinked. "What?"

"Playing this song out here. I mean, it's totally about suicide."

Jenny leaned forward. "It is? I didn't know that."

"Sure," Mark said. "Listen to the lyrics, how they talk about the seasons and the rain not fearing death and how people should do the same. The guy is telling his girl they could be together forever if they would just be like Romeo and Juliette, and those two killed themselves. I know 'cause they forced us to go to that play the drama geeks did. Hell, the title is 'Don't Fear the Reaper.' Pretty clear, ain't it?"

The others were silent.

Mark blew smoke. "What a perfect anthem for Suicide Woods."

CHAPTER FOURTEEN

"You all know Steven was a writer?" Scott said.

The journal was a black, hardback notebook. The cover was blank, no words or other markings. Jennifer was feeling more lost as the night went on.

"We know," Corey said.

Scott cleared his throat, a hesitation. Jennifer could see the stress burrowed into his eyes. Whatever he had to say, it wasn't coming easily.

"This book is different," he said. "According to Steven, no one has ever even read it. It's written out in long hand."

He paused again.

"What's in it, Scott?" Jennifer asked.

"Yeah," Mark said. "Spit it out already."

Scott closed his eyes and took a long breath. When he opened them, he was finally looking at the group again instead of the floor. "It's a journal."

They waited for more, but nothing came.

"That's it?" Mark said. "Just a journal? Well, shit, man, who cares about that? He was a shut-in, right? What could his journal be about—a record of the weather?"

"That's the thing, you guys. Though this is written like a journal, it isn't written from Steven's point of view."

He opened the cover, revealing the first page. They all leaned in. Jennifer blinked, hoping her eyes were deceiving her.

"Oh my God," she whispered.

The journal had a title page.

The Diary of Robin Reeves.

"IT'S ALL written in the first person, as Robin," Scott said. "But I think it's Steven's handwriting."

"It is," Jennifer said.

"You really remember what it looked like all that time ago?"

"I have some things he wrote back then. I've kept them in my yearbook."

Traci gave her an odd look. "What did he write you?"

"Poems," she said, then saw Scott's face fall. He looked hurt somehow, and Jennifer was surprised by her quick effort to reassure him the poetry meant less to her than it actually had. "I don't think he wrote them *to me*, necessarily. They were just stuff that was in his head that he needed to get out."

"But you kept them," Traci said.

Was there a hint of jealously to her tone?

"I kept a lot of things people gave me," she said. "Keepsakes, you know?"

Corey nodded. "I keep little things like that too—movie ticket stubs, arm bands from concerts. I think I have every drawing my kid ever made."

"You're sure it's Steven's handwriting?" Scott asked Jennifer.

"I'm positive. Before I came here, I browsed through the yearbook and there they were."

"Okay. So that's confirmation. Steven wrote this book, but from the perspective of Robin Reeves. It takes place in October '95."

Traci leaned into the wall. "Oh, God."

"*This* is what Steven wanted us to have?" Corey asked.

"It is," Scott said. "He wanted us all to get together—everyone who was there that night. And he wanted me to read this to you."

Mark huffed. "Oh, for Christ's sake. Even in death he's gotta try and freak us out?"

"I don't think that was his intention. I really think he wanted us to settle this thing once and for all. He thought it would be cathartic."

"Maybe to talk about it," Jennifer said. "That, I can understand. But why would he write a book like this? It's not only creepy; it's in poor taste."

"Like I said, I don't know why Steven did the things he did. I can only speculate to his motivations."

"Well then speculate for us," Traci said, "please."

"Maybe it's just a writer thing. Maybe it was the only way he knew how to get it all out. Writing this must've been a form of therapy for him. Maybe it helped him somehow and that's why he wanted to share it with us, to put our minds at ease after carrying this terrible memory half our lives."

The group fell quiet, absorbing it all.

Jennifer's limbs felt heavy, as if she was being dragged down into the earth. Finally, she asked him. "Have you read it?"

"Some of it," Scott said. "It's hard to explain."

"How so?"

"The only way any of you can really understand is to read it yourselves. So I thought I could read it to you. That way everyone knows the details at the same time. Only then can we really talk about."

Traci's lip trembled. "I keep trying to remind you guys we swore we'd never mention her. We *swore* we'd never talk about this again."

"I think that's because we couldn't find the right words. Maybe Steven did what the rest of us couldn't."

"It's been twenty-five years," Corey said. "Scott's right. It's time to break the silence."

Jennifer watched Scott but wasn't sure what she was looking for. If he'd read even a portion of the journal, he would have some insight into what the book was like. It could be nonsense, the ravings of a man who'd first lost touch with the outside world and then with reality. But it could also be heartbreaking, even terrifying. She didn't fault Traci for resisting. Jennifer had sobered up just hearing about the book. Her sleepiness had disappeared, even though she was on a bed. The basement room seemed smaller now, tighter, and the golden light of the shaded lamps made it cave-like, reminding her they were buried underground.

"Go ahead, Scott," she said. "Let's talk about it."

PART TWO

THAT NIGHT

CHAPTER FIFTEEN

Robin had brought candles. Steven lit them with his Zippo, and when he passed each back to her, she arranged them in a circular pattern before the group, as if they were huddling around a bonfire. Having been an Eagle Scout, Corey volunteered to build them one, but Steven was in favor of the darkness. At the center of this ring of candles sat the jack-o'-lantern, its eyes jagged triangles of fire, the gaps between the teeth flickering. The teens' faces were those of tangerine ghosts in the glow, an illusion of warmth in the arctic embrace of shadow. The blackness was swallowing Suicide Woods. The last light of early evening corroded a blue sliver behind skeletal trees.

Scott put his arm around Jenny to warm her. Even with a hoodie and jacket, she had her legs drawn up, her arms wrapped around them. When he kissed her ear, it was like an ice cube. Earlier, if not for getting stoned, he would have been bored, but now that darkness was falling in full, the first flutters of fear bloomed within him. It was irrational, childish fear, he told himself, but it persisted unabated. He pulled Jenny a little closer.

The mix tape continued. Steven had filled it with tracks about monster mashes, werewolves from London, thrillers in the night, and feeding Frankenstein. A little corny, but maybe that kept things from being too macabre.

"Okay," Mark said, unfolding a piece of tinfoil. The tabs of LSD had the face of Felix the Cat smiling up at them. "Who's ready to trip out, man?"

The group looked to one another, faces contorting in the shuddering shadows.

"I'll pass," Scott said.

Jenny, Corey, and even Traci turned him down. Mark glowered at his girlfriend as if she'd betrayed him, and Traci rolled her eyes, having made her choice for the evening.

"I'll take one," Robin said.

Scott blinked at her. *Who is this kid?*

"You sure you can handle it?" Mark asked.

"Yeah, Robin," Jenny said. "Have you ever taken acid before?"

She shrugged. "No, but whatever. I wanna try it."

"In the woods at night?"

Steven looked up from the joint he'd been rolling. "Robin can make her own decisions."

Scott could have slapped him. What was wrong with Steven, bringing this girl out here with them, encouraging her to blast her mind to bits on hallucinogens? Scott had tried acid once in the safety of his own basement room and even that had freaked him out enough to turn him off it for good. Dropping a tab in Suicide Woods was hardly an ideal way to have your first psychedelic experience.

Of course, Mark was no help. He just held out the tab and told the girl to open her mouth. But she hesitated, the pressure of the group having gotten to her. Mark was disappointed.

"I'll take one of those," Steven said.

Scott shook his head. Now there would be two of them tripping balls, which basically meant he'd be babysitting them, making sure they didn't wander off and get lost, that they didn't spiral into delusions and have waking nightmares. Hallucinogens didn't just distort your vision; they distorted reality, contorting every fiber of the mind until it operated at an unsteady level. During his acid trip, Scott hadn't been disturbed by objects around him seeming to throb and shimmer. What had terrified him was the irrational certainty that he would never be normal again, that the LSD had detonated his sanity beyond recuperation. This proved to be untrue, but at the time the thought brought him hours of stress and horror.

But wasn't that what Steven wanted tonight? For them to feel pure, guttural fear? Wasn't that why scary movies weren't good enough this

Halloween, why they had to camp out in this forest, a place famous for self-annihilation? Scott couldn't believe he and Jenny had talked themselves into this. Night had just fallen, so it was too soon to take off, even though they planned on leaving early. Having played in these woods as a child, he was sure he could find the way back. Pretty sure, anyway.

Instead of putting the tab of acid in his mouth, Steven kept his wrapped in tin foil and put it in his pocket. "You guys know what happened to Johnny Clayton?"

Scott felt Jenny's shoulders tense.

"Killed himself out here," Mark said.

"Right. But does anybody know how?"

"Thought he slit his wrists too," Corey said.

Steven shook his head. "That's what they told everybody. They didn't release the truth 'cause, at first, they were looking into it as a homicide."

"Bullshit," Mark said, chuckling. "Here he goes with the ghost stories."

"Nah, dude. This is legit. See, when the cops give details to the press about a possible murder, they alter certain things. That way when loonies try to confess, the detectives can weed them out, 'cause they'll have the details wrong. They also do it because suspects will screw up sometimes and say things that were never made public, stuff only the real killer could've known."

Robin was staring at Steven, enthralled, entranced. Something about that level of hero worship made Scott envious.

"So what happened to Johnny?" Robin asked.

Steven leaned into the light of the candles, giving himself a haunted visage.

"He did kill himself," he said, "but it wasn't like the others. He didn't slit his wrists. Didn't shoot himself with daddy's shotgun or eat a whole bottle of mom's Valium. Johnny Clayton slit his own throat."

Jenny gasped. Corey's eyes went wide.

"Jesus," Traci said. "That's messed up, Steven."

"Yeah," Jenny agreed. "Don't say things like that."

Steven opened his hands. "I'm not making this up. My dad is friends with the guy who found the body. He said Johnny had torn his throat up with a hunting knife so badly he was halfway decapitated."

"Bullshit!" Mark said, still chuckling. "Nobody could cut their own damned head off."

"It wasn't all the way off, but the cut was real deep. Tore through the Adam's apple, severed the arteries. He said the kid was so covered in blood there was probably none left in the body."

Mark turned to Scott. "You buying this shit?"

"I don't know, man."

Robin asked, "Why did Johnny do it like that?"

Steven cocked an eyebrow, affixing a devilish grin. His eyes were black and reptilian. "It wasn't Johnny's choice. He didn't want to do it, but *they* got to him. They got into his head."

"Who?"

He gestured to their surroundings. "The woods."

"The woods?" Jenny asked. "What do you mean, 'the woods'?"

"It was them. The demons."

Robin whispered, "These woods have demons?"

"No." Steven turned his eyes to the sky. "These woods don't have demons. They *are* demons."

TRACI DIDN'T like this. Though not much of a follower these days, she'd been raised Catholic, and religious indoctrination came with long-term effects. So while she hadn't been to church since she was twelve, and sometimes even doubted the existence of God, there were times she still feared him, and in those times she also feared the Devil. Movies about vampires and werewolves and crazy guys in hockey masks could give her the willies, but what really rattled her were films like *The Exorcist, Night of the Demons, Warlock,* and *The Omen,* because to her, these sorts of primordial evil could very well be real.

She'd never heard anything about Suicide Woods inhabiting ghouls from Hades, but the trees suddenly seemed darker now. Looking at the candles, Traci wondered if Robin had arranged them in a particular pattern from some hippie book of witchcraft. Lots of girls were into that Wiccan crap, but Traci wasn't even comfortable playing with a Ouija board.

"There's no demons out here," Scott said.

Steven smirked. "How can you be so sure?"

"Just because you say something doesn't make it true."

"Yeah," Jenny said, but sounded less convincing. "You're just trying to spook us."

"I'm not trying to scare you," Steven said. "I'm trying to *warn* you. We have to be careful in these woods, especially on Halloween night, when the boundaries between the land of the living and the land of the dead are severed. The gates of Hell are open—one night only."

Mark started singing the theme to *The Twilight Zone*. "Do-do-do-do."

Traci batted his arm. She wondered if the acid he'd dropped was already taking effect, or if this was just his regular assholishness.

"What are they?" Robin asked. "The demons, I mean."

Steven put his hand on her knee. "I believe they're those who died in service to Satan."

"Shut up, Steven," Traci said. "Just shut up."

"You all have a right to know. I couldn't live with myself if I didn't give you fair warning."

"So," Robin said, "they're like ghosts?"

"Not exactly. They're not dead. They're the undead. They died in honor of Satan, so on Halloween night, he lets them roam the earth once again. The people who committed suicide out here were—"

Traci stood. "*I said, shut up, Steven!*"

The others looked at her, but she didn't care. Telling ghost stories was one thing but talking about the prince of darkness was something else entirely. She might not be the good Catholic she'd been when she was eleven, but that didn't mean she'd be part of some sort of devil worship, no matter how mild.

Mark frowned. "Hey, what's with you tonight, anyway? You won't take acid and now you're getting mad 'cause Steven's telling scary stories? What did you think we were gonna do tonight, play *Chutes and Ladders*?"

"Up yours, Mark."

She picked up her flashlight and started toward the trail.

"Traci," Jenny said, "where are you going? Don't go off in the woods alone."

"Yeah," Mark chuckled. "You wouldn't want the *demons* to get you!"

Jenny followed after Traci. Steven came running over and took Traci's hand. She tried to snatch it away, but he gripped her harder.

"Hey," he said, "take it easy. I didn't mean to upset you."

"Yeah, well, you did. I don't like that devil stuff."

"Okay, okay. Just come back to the camp."

"Only if you and that idiot boyfriend of mine cut the crap."

"Sure thing." His smile was all warmth. "We'll talk about something else."

Traci gazed into his blue eyes. As weird as he could sometimes be, there was a sweet sensitivity to him that was rare in other boys. He truly had the heart of a poet. He never seemed feminine or weakened by his capacity for empathy. If anything, it made him seem more mature and better able to understand the opposite sex. It also made him hard to stay mad at.

"So, you're not going to talk about demons anymore?" she asked.

Steven put his hand on her shoulder. "No way. You know I wouldn't do anything to hurt you, right?"

COREY DECIDED to keep the mask in his backpack. He'd thought it would be fun to break it out, maybe wear it to tell scary stories around a campfire, but it was a demon mask, a latex one that covered the entire head, with little horns and plastic fangs. After Traci's volatile reaction to the mere mention of demons, the last thing he wanted was to upset her further. It would probably get him slapped. Mark might even kick his ass, even though Mark had been teasing her. So Corey kept the mask at the bottom of his backpack, behind his emergency change of clothes and thermos full of soup.

Oh well. At least they had the jack-o'-lantern.

The joint was passed around. Corey had always been fearful of drugs. Those after-school specials were corny, but there had to be some element of truth to them. But he never lectured his friends on the dangers of using them the way his parents did him. That'd be just what he needed, to come off as some goody-two-shoes who would bring down the party with statistics inconvenient to the fun. Worse than that, he might be taken for a *narc* that would rat pot smokers out to parents or teachers or anyone else who would listen. And so, he left it alone, but had never partaken.

Still, it seemed everyone was smoking pot nowadays. When he'd first seen Scott smoke a joint, Corey had been shocked. But not long after that, Corey caught his older brother, Ryan, puffing from a bong with his girlfriend. Their parents were out for the night, and no matter how loud Corey had turned up the TV, he could still hear the girl's sensual moaning upstairs. He'd worried his parents would smell the tangy miasma of marijuana once they got back, so he turned on all the fans and opened the windows, even though it was a crisp winter evening, not wanting Ryan to get caught.

Eventually, Corey learned that even some of his classmates' parents smoked pot, solidifying how common stoners really were. It was something he never would have expected. His life was so armored against such things. The nerd life didn't offer many forays into the dope scene. But here it was, Halloween night, and he was with a group much cooler than himself. Even the young, new girl was smoking weed. So when Traci passed the joint to him, Corey put it to his lips, closed his eyes, and inhaled.

At first, there was nothing. Then his chest began to hurt. He coughed as if ten flies had just flown down his throat. The others laughed, Scott patting him on the back until he could breathe again.

"Well, look at this," Steven said. "It's a Halloween miracle."

SCOTT ALWAYS got horny when he drank. That was all right with Jenny—a few beers had the same effect on her. Carrying the blankets, they journeyed out of the deadening alone, using Scott's heavy-duty flashlight to guide their way. Steven and Traci had smiled at them knowingly as they'd left the group, and Mark had snickered like a troll, but Jenny was too buzzed to be bashful. She wanted time alone with the boy she loved. It was a romantic way of looking at teenage lust.

Following the path, they came upon a small clearing where white birch trees made a ring around them like a picket fence. Jenny draped one blanket over a bedding of fallen leaves and they got down on the ground there, Scott on top of her, her arms ensnaring him, claiming Scott as hers and hers alone. He pulled the other blanket over them, cocooning the two lovers as they kissed and petted. Jenny shivered to touch him. His back was wide with muscle, but his flesh was soft with youth. Even his cheeks were smooth, Scott having developed very little facial hair yet. He went up her shirt, fingertips electric against her bare belly. When he cupped her breast, she exhaled, going warm on the inside, face pinkening. When Scott sucked on her neck, goose pimples danced across her body, and she drew her legs tighter around him. She was collapsing under his power, a willing chattel to the magic of a tender sorcerer. As he unzipped her jeans, Jenny breathed in the scent of him and closed her eyes.

But it wasn't her who cried out.

The lovers froze. A voice had risen from the dark drift of the forest. It was low cry, almost a whimper, but it echoed off the dead trees as if they were in a rocky canyon. Scott lifted his head. Jenny scooted back and raised herself up on her elbows. They scanned the darkness with naked eyes, but the shadows yielded nothing. Blackness. Silence. Scott reached for the flashlight.

"Don't," Jenny said, taking his wrist.

She wasn't sure why she'd stopped him. Her body lost warmth. Even with Scott still on top of her, she felt unbearably exposed.

"You're trembling," Scott said.

She shushed him. They listened, but there was only the rustle of foliage against the gentle breeze.

"Probably just a chipmunk or something," Scott said, his fingers venturing back to the band of her panties.

"That was no chipmunk."

He nuzzled her cheek. "Chill out, okay? It's fine."

She wanted to believe that, especially as his hands explored her again. But the moment she closed her eyes, the moan returned, louder this time, more anguished. All the saliva left Jennifer's mouth.

Scott jolted, tossing the blanket off. Before Jenny could object, he'd snatched up the flashlight and turned it to the woods.

"Who's out there?" he called.

Jenny tensed, unsure if her boyfriend was being brave or just stupid. She followed the beam of light, seeing only bark and branches and the beginning of a seemingly endless hillside beyond.

"Mark?" Scott said. "If that's you, you'd better cut it out and get out of here!"

The forest regressed to stillness. The moaner was mute again, whispers hushed.

Jenny got to her feet and buttoned her jeans.

Scott sighed in annoyance. "Don't get up."

"I don't feel safe here. Let's go back."

"Baby, come on—"

"We can't do it here, Scott. Somebody's out there."

"They're just messing with us. More of Steven's Halloween bullshit." He cupped his hand to his mouth to amplify. "Steven! If that's you and Mark, I swear I'm gonna kick your asses!"

A voice rose from the shadows. Though distant, Jenny recognized it as Steven's, calling out from the direction they'd come, but she couldn't understand what he was saying. He sounded jovial, not anguished.

And then there was Mark, a little louder than Steven. "Keep the noise down, you kids!"

Jenny shuddered. "It wasn't them. They're still at the camp. That groaning was much closer."

"Well...maybe it..."

But Scott had nothing.

Jenny grabbed the top blanket. Normally she would have folded it, but right now, she just crumpled it into a wad. "Come on, Scott. Let's go back."

"Damn it..."

"I'll make it up to you later, baby. Please...let's just hurry, okay?"

Scott huffed. There was a rustle in the thicket. Jenny jumped back, clutching her blanket to her neck. Scott spun the flashlight in every direction, and when the beam caught the bushes, they were shaking, the branches clacking like firecrackers. Something had been in them. Jenny shrieked and grabbed onto her boyfriend, tugging at his sleeve, trying to drag him back to the trail.

He started to follow, and the guttural cry became a terrible wail, piercing the blackness. The bushes were rustling on their left, but the wail came from their right.

There's more than one.

Jenny dropped the blanket and ran, pulling her boyfriend with her.

CHAPTER SIXTEEN

Jenny exploded out of the woods, Scott tumbling after her. Corey stood. The looks on his friends' faces made him go cold. Scott was ghostly pale, and Jenny's cheeks were streaked with tears. Once in the clearing, Scott pulled her into him, and she buried her face in his chest.

The others got to their feet.

"What is it?" Corey asked.

But Scott and Jenny were still catching their breath.

"You see a bear or something?" Traci asked.

Scott shook his head. "There's someone out there."

The group fell silent. A single bead of sweat formed at Corey's spine.

"You saw someone?" Robin asked.

Jenny turned to face the others. "We heard them. At first, we thought it was one of you guys just trying to spook us, but…"

Steven asked, "What did they say?"

"Nothing…it was more like a cry. Like an *angry* cry."

"And whispers," Scott added.

Corey put his hands in his pockets, making sure the Swiss army knife was still in his jeans. He gripped it for comfort. At least he had something to protect himself. He'd heard marijuana could make you paranoid. Was that why he was so alarmed? He didn't believe in demons, but maybe there was someone else in the woods with them.

"Think it's a hobo?" Mark asked.

"I don't think so," Scott said. "They sounded kind of…crazy."

"Dude, haven't you ever met a hobo? They *are* crazy."

"Yeah," Traci said. "Homeless people set up camps in the woods all the time."

She came up beside Mark, taking his arm in both hands. Corey couldn't believe how quickly she forgave him for everything. Maybe it was true what they said about women liking jerks. Corey was a nice guy, and therefore always alone.

"They probably just wanted a little peek," Mark said with a smirk. "Like a peeping Tom, right?"

"There was more than one," Scott said, ignoring Mark's teasing.

He told them how there'd been groaning to one side of them and a rustle in the bushes to the other. Then he started gathering his things into his pack. When Jenny went to help him, Steven put up his palms.

"Whoa, whoa. Everybody just calm down. I'm sure there's a logical explanation. It was probably just animals."

"Bullshit," Scott said. "Someone's out there, and they are *messed up*. We need to get out of these woods before they come looking for us."

"Dude, we just got here. It's not even close to midnight."

Scott and Jenny just kept on packing.

Corey went to Steven and spoke in hushed tones even though everyone was close enough to hear. "Maybe it's best we leave. I mean, it seems like nobody's having fun."

Mark let out a beer burp. "Speak for yourself, dweeb."

"I'm having fun," Steven said. "Robin, how about you?"

The new girl was a blue wraith in the moonlight, so lithe and innocent looking, almost childlike in the heart of the shadows.

"I'm fine," she said, noncommittally.

Traci puffed from a cigarette as if to excuse herself from speaking. Steven watched her until she nodded in agreement. Though Corey didn't know her well, he'd seen how agreeable she could be, especially with boys. Traci was very suggestible despite her tough exterior and always seemed to go along with the crowd, not wanting to be ostracized. Acceptance seemed most important of all. Corey wondered where such insecurity came from, her being so good-looking and cool. If anything, he should be the one to do anything to fit in.

"Let's check it out," Steven said, pointing to the trail.

Jenny shot him a glare. "Steven…"

"C'mon, we'll investigate. I'm sure we'll find it's nothing. This'll put everyone's minds at ease. Let's not let whatever this is chase us out and spoil our Halloween."

"I'm not going back there."

"Jenny, that's the direction we came in from. If you want to leave, you'll have to go that way anyway."

"I know that! We can go around."

"Off the trail? In the dark?"

She seemed about to snap back but had no retort. When her eyes misted again, Corey wanted to hold her and wished Scott would.

"I'm with Stevey," Mark said, laid back. "I say we check it out. If it's nothing, we can stay here and party. If some bum is just fuckin' with us, we beat his ass."

Mark raised his flashlight under his chin and gave them a sinister smile while wiggling his eyebrows. If he thought it made him look like a bad ass, he was wrong. Corey thought he looked like an ape. Mark's eyes were entirely dilated now, the eyes of a great white shark.

"We're not going back to that spot," Jenny said.

"Okay then," Steven said. "You and Scott stay here, and the rest of us will—"

"No! We gotta stick together. Who knows how many of them there are?"

"Jenny, please. You're being silly. I mean, 'them'? Who's 'them'? You said you didn't see anyone. All you heard was a noise. Whether we're gonna go or stay, we have to check it out to see if we're safe, right? Look, there's five of us if you and Scott want to stay here at camp. Or you can come with us, making it seven. If there really were two people out there, we'll have them outnumbered. It's our safest bet."

Jenny didn't speak. Her eyes told Corey everything he needed to know. Though he'd never been able to read a female before, he was sure Jenny was thinking the same thing he was right now.

What if all those teens didn't really kill themselves?

THE MOON went behind a freight of clouds, only a sliver of powder-blue light knifing through the trees. The forest seemed to contort, the tree limbs bending and rising, throbbing as if each branch breathed. Mark's body ached from the LSD, but the visuals were spellbinding. Clear waves rippled before his eyes like heat rays on a desert highway, and when the breeze freed leaves from branches, they flapped along like a legion of vampire bats. He watched them soar, feeling nearly weightless, as if he could join them in flight if he just got a good running start.

He followed Steven and Robin—directly behind the girl so he could admire that little peach of an ass. He wondered if Steven had done her yet. She was young, but ripe for the plucking. As her hips swayed, they became hypnotic, leaving trails of light in the shadows. When something touched his hand, Mark flinched, having forgotten Traci was walking beside him.

"Getting scared?" she teased.

"Nah. Just trippin'."

"I'm starting to wonder if this is a setup."

"Huh?"

"What if Scott and Jenny are just trying to scare us? Maybe they're taking a shortcut right now so they can cut us off and jump out of the bushes."

Jenny and Scott had remained at the camp, and that little wiener Corey stayed behind with them. What a wuss. Why on earth had he come along? Shit, why was he *allowed* to tag along for *anything* they did? The pathetic nerd lowered the coolness of the entire gang. Mark despised even being seen with Corey Pickett because it made him a dweeb by association. Well, maybe it was Corey who would be getting a good scare tonight. Mark would love to make the little virgin soil his shorts. He pictured them as Spider-Man Underoos and snickered, and then realized he'd forgotten what Traci said.

"What?"

Traci rolled her eyes. "Never mind."

Clouds engulfed the pregnant moon, spreading darkness like a curse and drowning out what little light the night sky offered. They had only the light of two flashlights, one carried by Steven, the other by Traci. It was *her* flashlight, and she refused to let Mark hold it.

"Have we gone far enough?" she asked Steven.

Mark couldn't see him, only the weak beam of his flashlight.

"Almost," Steven said. "At least, I think so."

"One of them should've come with us so we'd know the spot when we got to it."

Mark grimaced. This was stupid. There was nothing out here. Scott and Jenny were just scaredy cats who couldn't handle being in the woods alone. They'd probably scream just from seeing a turtle.

"This must be it," Steven said.

They stopped in a small clearing surrounded by a grove of birch.

"Look," Robin said. "There's their blanket."

Traci aimed her flashlight. Wadded up, Mark thought the blanket looked like a giant, used tissue. The ends seemed to unfold, reaching for him with a hundred cloth tongues. He stared, mesmerized, wacked out of his skull.

"What's that?" someone said.

Mark wasn't sure who'd spoken. Even the gender seemed obscured, the voice androgynous. The beams of the flashlights swirled. There was a crashing sound, like a tree limb falling, and Mark stumbled into the path's shoulder of rocks. Thorny bushes tore at him as he fell backward, needle points slicing his arms and face, cutting his lip and forehead. He stupidly reached for something to grab on to, and his hands sunk into a briar of thorns. They pierced his palms as he landed in a pile of moldy leaves.

"Son of a…"

He looked into a sky with no stars. The tree limbs were like skeletal fingers closing in on the universe, closing in on him. Mark struggled to his feet, the LSD dizzying him, and stumbled through the briar back to the trail. It suddenly occurred to him that no one had stopped to help when he'd fallen, and he'd hollered and cursed the entire time. Surely they must have heard. Were they pissed at him for something?

When he was sure he was back on the trail he looked in both directions. There were no silhouettes of the others, and he couldn't spot even the faintest trace of a flashlight.

"Hey, guys?"

The only response he got was a chorus of crickets.

Mark's jaw went tight. He wasn't enjoying his acid trip now. The drug was only adding to his confusion. The woods were pitch black, and because of the acid in his system, his vision was obscured and wouldn't adjust to the darkness. He yelled for his friends again, louder this time, but to no avail. And he couldn't remember which way they'd been going, and therefore wasn't sure which way led back to camp.

"Mother fu—"

Something scurried past.

Mark heard it more than saw it, a rustle in a cluster of brush. He licked his lips but his tongue was like sand.

The thing scurried again.

This time he could make out the small shape as it darted across the path from one bush to another. Mark gasped. It was a short creature, but not scampering on all fours like a dog. It was anthropomorphic. It stood upright, then ducked into shadow again. Mark's air caught in his throat. He stepped back, away from the spot where the dwarfish shape had been. He wanted to scream for his friends now but didn't want to alert the thing to his presence. Perhaps it had not seen him yet.

It was so dark, so very dark.

Mark decided there was only one path to take, and that was away from this little bastard, whatever it was. Either he'd catch up with the others or he'd make it back to camp. Right now, the pressing matter was getting the hell out of this grove.

Taking a few steps backward, Mark turned around to run, but something tripped him again. He fell to the ground, skinning his knees and palms. A sliver of moonlight appeared on the dirt like light from an opening door. When Mark brought his head up, he saw a pair of gnarled, wet feet. They were human but had no toenails. The ray of moonlight widened, revealing pale, stout legs dabbed with river slime.

Mark trembled, having fallen mute, and when the creature stepped toward him, he saw it was female, the crotch hairless, the chest flat. She had a bald head, but her face remained cloaked by shadows. Her plump hands were at her side, also without fingernails. When she turned her palms toward him, there was a terrible moan.

STEVEN SPUN the flashlight. "Mark!"

Traci was gripping the back of Steven's jacket, afraid of losing him too. Her flashlight shook in her hand. Beside them, Robin had her head titled back, watching the treetops as if Mark would suddenly appear up there.

"It's like he vanished into thin air," the girl said.

Traci hated to hear it because it was true. She'd been hoping she was the only one who hadn't noticed anything when Mark went missing. If Steven or Robin had seen or heard something, they'd at least have something to go on. But as they backtracked, there was no sign of her boyfriend. And though it would be just like Mark to pull a stunt to scare them, she doubted that was the case this time. As they'd gone deeper into Suicide Woods, she'd been rattled by a creeping dread, the kind of irrational, superstitious fear she rarely felt since she'd exited adolescence. It was the same sort of dread she'd felt when her imagination ran away with her, like when she washed dishes after dinner while facing the window, picturing a pale face appearing in all that darkness. It was the kind of fear that slithered up her spine when she was home alone and the house creaked. Only this time the fright was extended further.

"Where the hell is he?" Steven said. He seemed to be talking to the woods, as if they held all the answers. "Could he have gotten lost? I mean… he was tripping on acid."

Traci called out for her boyfriend again, peering through the dense ink of the thicket. It suddenly occurred to her that she'd sobered up completely. She'd had enough of this Halloween shit and wanted to go home. Well, not to her house, of course, but to one of the others'. They could be in Scott's basement room right now. They could be warm and stoned, watching TV with a pizza.

They could be safe.

THERE WAS a scream.

Jenny nearly leapt into Corey's arms, just because he was standing closer to her at that moment than Scott was. Corey held her. He was shaking too. Somehow that made Jenny even more afraid.

The scream seemed to come from all directions, even though it was but a single voice. It was high pitched but sounded male. Scott had nearly dropped the backpack when the sound ripped out of the forest. The three of them drew closer together.

"What is this?" Scott muttered.

He sounded angry. For a second, Jenny thought he was jealous at her being in Corey's embrace. As she slinked out of it, she realized Scott hadn't even noticed. He was staring into the woodland with fists clenched.

"Let's just go," Corey said.

"What about the others?" Jenny said.

Corey gulped so hard she could hear it. She turned her flashlight toward him. It was fifty degrees out, but sweat had formed at his temples.

"We'll probably see them along the way," he said.

"That scream…" Scott said. "I couldn't tell which direction it came from. Could you?"

They both shook their heads.

"What if it's Steven or Mark?" Jenny said. "What if they're hurt?"

"That didn't sound like pain. It sounded like…" Scott watched every shadow, every flutter of leaves.

"Like terror," Corey finished for him. "It sounded like terror."

He gathered his things. Having not unrolled his sleeping bag yet, it didn't take long. Corey said he was leaving the pumpkin behind. The thought of the face flickering its orange clown grin alone in the woods made Jenny quiver.

With Corey packed up, she looked to her boyfriend.

"What do you think we should do?" she asked.

Before Scott could answer, there was another scream. This one was deeper, more of a roar, like a person imitating a lion. And they sounded *huge*.

Jenny shook. "Oh God…"

Scott slung his backpack over his shoulder and handed Jenny hers. There were no more debates.

All they could do was run.

"JUST STAY here."

Traci stared at Steven, flabbergasted. "What?"

"I'll be real fast," he said. "I just want to check."

The three of them stood at the edge of a steep incline that veered off the trail and down to a stream. The bank was a row of large, black rocks that looked like the bottom jaw of a great crocodile. One slip and they'd fall into its mouth.

Traci shook her head. "How would Mark have ended up—"

"He could be anywhere," Robin said.

Traci flinched, surprised the girl would cut her off.

"Robin's right," Steven said. "I'm thinking he might've fallen and rolled down the slope, you know?"

Traci took him by the arm. "Steven, we never came anywhere near here."

"But Mark might've. He's obviously lost, right?"

She wished she knew the answer to that. They'd seen nothing, heard nothing. There were only the obsidian woods, the sea of tree limbs and chattering leaves.

"I'll be real fast," Steven said. "There's no sense in all of us going down there. It's too steep. We could break our necks."

"That's my whole point!"

Traci was concerned Steven could get hurt, but even more concerned he'd disappear on them as well. Then it would be just her and Robin, which was better than being alone, but not much.

"I'm going down to check along the creek," he said. "I won't get hurt, and I'll be back in a flash."

Before Traci could make another objection, Robin went to Steven and kissed him on the cheek.

"We'll be right here," she said.

Steven put his flashlight under his chin so they could see his face. There was a small smile there and Traci marveled at how calm he seemed, as if he were certain everything would work out fine. Once again, the thought of sabotage entered her mind. Maybe the boys were leaving the girls alone in the forest on purpose, to make it all the more terrifying when they reappeared wearing zombie masks and wielding fake machetes, making the girls flood their panties in fear. She was so freaked out right now that she found herself hoping this were true. At least then it would all be just a game.

Crunching through tall, brown grass, Steven made his way down the slope. Traci kept her flashlight beam on him until he was too low to make out, and then she watched his flashlight, following the pale star of it as he journeyed toward the rocks below.

Robin stepped closer to Traci. "Are you scared?"

In the darkness, Traci couldn't make out the girl's face. She remembered it being soft and cute, but now that it was hidden Traci had a sudden, baseless fear Robin's face had transformed, that the skin had turned puke green and her braces had bust from sprouting fangs. She felt at any minute two red slits would appear where the girl's eyes should be. The thought made her shake her head. Was she really afraid of this little pompom? No. She was afraid of *everything* right now. Tonight, even the most innocent creature became a ghoul.

"Don't be scared," Robin said.

Traci felt cold fingers wrap around her own. She flinched and Robin shushed her gently, a mother cooing a baby to sleep. Traci could feel the girl's breath against her neck. It smelled of cherry hard candy.

"What're you doing?" Traci asked.

Robin's voice fell to a whisper. "You don't need to be afraid."

Traci wanted to push the girl away but something kept her knees locked and her shoulders held high. She was shaking, and it embarrassed her.

"I'm right here," Robin said.

The girl cozied into Traci, pushing against her like a kitten. Feelings of warm comfort and inexplicable dread battled for possession of Traci's heart. She couldn't decide or define what she felt. Her lips trembled, the little hairs on her body rising. Her eyes closed only for a moment, but when they snapped open again, she couldn't see the glow of Steven's flashlight anymore. She wanted to call for him, to scream his name until her throat was raw, but when she opened her mouth, only a whimper came out.

Robin hushed her, nuzzling closer, closer than any girl had ever cuddled up to Traci before, but still the girl's face was nothing but a sphere of darkness.

"Don't be afraid," she kept saying. "Just don't be afraid."

CHAPTER SEVENTEEN

Was he running in circles?

Mark scanned his surroundings. It all seemed the same in the dark, just woods and more woods, an endless labyrinth of dying leaves. Either the trail had thinned to nothing or he'd wandered off it while running from the dwarf. At least he'd lost her, or so it seemed. She could be anywhere behind the trees, frolicking like some bloodthirsty leprechaun, waiting for the right moment to strike her prey.

What the fuck was that thing?

He'd been unable to see her face. Mark was grateful for that. Her horrible body had been disturbing enough. He tried to shake the images of fingers without nails from his mind but could not.

Few things had ever frightened him. Mark's most prominent fear was of his father, a bitter man corrupted by his own failures and the envy he felt for anyone who had succeeded at anything. He blamed nepotism and other forms of favoritism when anyone was promoted before him, and it led him to constant job-hopping, one low-paying vocation after another.

More often than not, dear old Dad brought his work stress home with him and unleashed it upon his family. Though he'd never hit Mark or his sister or mother, he was always screaming and cursing, calling Mark a worthless piece of shit and his mother and sister the C-word. They were always so ungrateful, always disobedient. Dad would get right in their faces when he hollered and lectured, forcing them to back into walls as his finger wagged in their faces, spittle flying as his face turned red. He was so loud all the neighbors could hear. The other kids on the block teased Mark and his sister for it, doing cruel imitations of his old man, even quoting him word for word. So many times, Mark's mom threatened divorce, but she never went through with it. As a child, the thought of his parents divorcing scared him. Now he wanted it more than anything in the world—a home without the old man, one where he didn't have to walk on eggshells, afraid to so much as say hello to his own father.

That was fear—the purest form of it. Fear of one's own parent could be paralyzing, for it was they whom your instincts told you to run to when faced with a threat. Even now, at seventeen, this terror in the woods made Mark want his mother, despite how neglectful she could be, more focused on her soap operas and getting stoned than raising her children.

Growling in frustration, he trekked through the forest. He could be dropped off on any street corner in Connecticut and find his way home, but even the woods near his own neighborhood were an impossible puzzle. He thought of a mouse stuck on a glue trap, struggling but going nowhere. If not for his fear of the dwarf finding him, he would have just picked a spot to sit and wait for morning light, making it easier to see his way out. But that wasn't an option tonight.

Mark called the names of every one of his friends, even Corey and the new girl. The thought that they might have left him behind made his stomach sour. Had that same creature chased them away?

He froze as a terrible thought hit him.

What if they've been caught? What if they're dead, crumpled in pools of blood with bite marks all over them?

It seemed entirely possible, and that was the worst part of all.

WHEN THEY were convinced they'd put enough distance between them and whatever thing had been roaring in the night, Jenny, Scott, and Corey stopped to catch their breath and find their bearings. They were still on a trail, but Corey couldn't tell if it was the same one they'd come in on that afternoon. Was the marijuana confusing him? He'd only taken three hits as the joint had gone around. He felt different afterward—strange even—but hadn't felt confused until now. He took his glow-in-the-dark Boy Scouts compass from his pocket. It only whirled, never landing on a final choice.

"What the heck is going on?"

"Must be broken," Scott said. "I mean, you've had it forever, right?"

"It was working when we came out here."

"Well, it isn't now, so you might as well stop playing with it."

Corey frowned at Scott's tone. He sounded more than just frustrated. It worried Corey that he might be blamed if they got lost, even though there would be no good reason to put that on him. He looked to Jenny for support, but she was bent over with her hands on her knees, still catching her breath. He wanted to go to her, to hold her again, as if he could be some kind of hero. That brief moment she'd been in his arms had felt righter than anything he'd ever known.

"Which way then?" Corey asked. Let Scott play leader if he knew so much. "We followed the trail right behind your house. You probably know the way best."

"Dude, you live right next store. You know these woods exactly as much as I do. We used to play out here all the time. Not this deep in, but still."

"True enough. But ever since that first suicide, I stopped coming in here."

"So did I. So where does that leave us?"

Corey sighed. "Right here."

"Guys," Jenny said, standing up straight. "Let's just keep moving. I'm pretty sure we're going in the right direction."

Corey almost asked what made her think so but decided to let it be. The way they'd been going was at least away from that horrible roaring. It was a relief to not hear it any longer. Either the person had stopped doing it or they were far enough out of earshot. Corey hoped for the latter.

They continued down the path into a low basin. The dip in the land sparked a feeling of déjà vu. Corey hoped that meant they were getting closer to home. The thought of his warm room with shelves stacked with DC comics and Philip K. Dick books seemed more welcoming than ever. He had his small TV with built-in VCR and a stack of sci-fi movies he'd taped off HBO. His room was a bubble that sealed him off from the stressors and rejections of the outside world, a fortress of solitude where he wasn't picked on or laughed at. He could draw without someone peeking over his shoulder to mock his work. He could dance without fearing he'd be seen singing along to Paula Abdul and Duran Duran. There were no exams to worry about, no gym classes to fail. In his room, he was in a perfect state. It made him wonder why he'd left it tonight. He could be watching Disney's *The Legend of Sleepy Hollow*. Instead, he was living it. Why had he come along for this?

But he knew the answer to that. First, there was the opportunity to be with pretty girls. Even if he would never make a move on them, just being in their presence made him feel more grown up, more masculine. There was also just spending time with Scott, whom Corey considered his best friend. He'd been worried they were drifting further apart. But the strongest lure had been the chance to do something that proved he wasn't a chicken shit loser who bowed out of anything he could get in trouble for. Now he wished he'd obeyed his cowardly instinct. Corey's first thought had been not to go, but he'd taunted himself into it.

Now his Halloween was scarier than he ever would have imagined.

He followed Scott, just as he always had, just as he always would. Here the basin was so carpeted with leaves that they rose up around Corey's ankles. The moon was a tease tonight, intermittently giving them light just to take it away again. But they had two flashlights—one to show the way and one to scan the bushes for any sign of company.

Corey realized he hadn't thought of Steven and the others since leaving the camp. It shamed him to know he was just focused on saving himself. He wanted the others to get out of the woods too, but what could he possibly do to help when they couldn't find them?

Scott stopped. "Do you hear that?"

They fell silent, not even breathing. When Corey heard the noise, all the moisture left his mouth. The music was faint at first. Then it grew louder. Either its source was being turned up in volume, or it was coming closer.

"Oh my God," Jenny whispered.

Fear made the three of them shake, even though they couldn't explain why.

Corey reached for his Swiss Army Knife as "Don't Fear the Reaper" echoed through Suicide Woods.

TRACI WANTED to go home. Moments ago, she'd wanted to go back to Scott's house, and that was still the better option, but now she was willing to settle. Home wasn't her favorite place to be, but it was better than these goddamned woods. She'd had just about enough of this Halloween. With the boys gone, her worry intensified. It irked her feminist sensibilities, but it was a bitter truth. Boys made her feel safe. That was one of the reasons she always had to have a boyfriend. The thought of being without one was somehow threatening. Even Mark, who could be a real insensitive asshole, gave her a sense of comfort and worth. Best of all, she didn't feel alone the way she did at home. Her father had a whole new life with his do-over family and rarely bothered to visit now that Traci was 'all grown up.' And her mother was either at work or hopping from one bar to the next, only making brief appearances late at night with some stumbling man who looked at Traci as if she were dinner.

Mark wasn't perfect—no guy was—but he was a bad boy and, as hypocritical as it was, that drove her mother nuts. She hated that Traci was dating Mark now instead of Scott. At least that drew Traci some attention. But while Traci liked Mark's appeal as a rebel, he was also good-looking and a great lover. He'd been the only boyfriend to bring her to orgasm, and she'd had many boyfriends and had been having sex since she was thirteen.

Traci and Scott had dated for a while, but while he was an adequate lover, he was too gentle for her tastes. She'd only started dating Mark to make Scott jealous after he'd broken up with her. But it hadn't worked. Now that she and Mark had been together a while, she sometimes felt she might even love the jerk in a way, if she even knew what love really was. Movies had taught her that love was more than just getting stoned together and screwing in the abandoned house down the street when their parents were home.

She wondered if she'd ever be worthy of love, and figured she'd have to get out of Redford before it could happen. In this town, she was just Traci

Rillo, daughter of Barbara Blankenship—just a pair of no good, dirty, town whores. She'd have to escape her own reputation and the lies and rumors about her that had spread through school.

But first she had to escape these woods.

"Should we go after him?" she asked Robin.

Both girls stared below. There was still no sign of Steven.

"He said to wait here," Robin said.

"So what? We don't have to do everything he says."

"But—"

"But nothing. Just because your boyfriend—"

Robin giggled. It seemed so inappropriate right now. How could she laugh when they were alone in the forest?

"What's so funny?"

"Boyfriend," Robin giggled. "Steven? My boyfriend? Did he say that? Wow."

The girl gave off a strange vibe when she asked this. Traci couldn't tell if Robin was excited by the possibility or eager to mock Steven if he made such an assumption.

Instead of replying, Traci called out for Steven again.

"You don't have to be so freaked out," Robin said.

When Robin took her hand this time, Traci pulled away.

"I'm not afraid!"

"It's okay if you are, Traci, but you don't have to be."

"Stop saying that."

A beam of moonlight shone behind Robin, silhouetting her.

"I was afraid once," she said. "I was eleven and lost sight of my big brother, Donnie, when we were at the mall. I looked all over, you know? And the more I looked, the more scared I got, because I just couldn't find him. I had a little money, so I wanted to get to a payphone and call my parents, but they were both at work and I didn't know the numbers by heart. They were on a note on the fridge at home."

She turned to Traci, inching closer.

"Have you ever gotten lost as a kid?" Robin asked. "It's the scariest feeling in the whole world. I didn't know what to do. I wanted to hide.

Isn't that weird? I guess I just wanted to feel safe, like an animal in a hollow log. So I went to the movie theater they had there and bought a ticket. The ticketholder was a teenager who didn't even raise an eyebrow at a little girl coming in alone. I even remember the movie. I had already seen the kids' movie I'd bought a ticket to, so I snuck into an adult one. It was called *The People Under the Stairs*. Have you seen it?"

Traci shook her head, still watching the stream below.

"I didn't know it was a scary movie," Robin said. "I'd never seen something like that. I got so frightened sitting there in the dark that I was too scared to get up and leave. I just sort of sunk into myself, waiting for the movie to be over so the lights would come on. That's when the man came and sat beside me."

Traci looked to Robin then, but her face was only a round shadow. Moonbeams illuminated the free strands of her hair.

"A man?" Traci asked.

"He sat right in the chair next to me. He had a full tub of popcorn and a soda and a box of candy. When he passed them to me, he said 'don't be afraid.' I knew I shouldn't talk to strangers and take candy from them, but I was so relieved to be with an adult. He could protect me from the crazy things in the movie. He could help me find my brother. So I ate my popcorn and drank my Coke, and when he put his hand between my legs, I didn't say anything. I didn't even put my knees together when he went higher up my skirt and put a finger into my panties."

"Jesus." Traci was suddenly breathless. "Robin, were you okay?"

"He touched me down there while he masturbated, but that was all he did. I thought when the lights turned on, he would help me find my brother, but instead he left before the movie was even over. I thought maybe the movie had scared him too much."

"That sick bastard! How could he do that to you?"

Traci went hot in the chest, anger flushing her. It wasn't until later that she would think it odd for Robin to have told her this story while they were alone in the darkness, as lost as Robin had been as a child. At the moment, she was only sorry for the girl and furious at both the man who molested her and the brother who'd failed to keep her safe. Why was it always men who hurt you and let you down? Husbands who cheated on their wives and abandoned their families. Fathers who either forgot or never cared that their daughters needed them. Guys you wouldn't put out for, so they told everyone in school you'd had sex with them all in the woods, letting the boys line up for their turn.

"It's okay now," Robin said, sounding so much younger than Traci.

"Did you tell someone?"

"No. I thought maybe it was my fault."

Traci's face pinched. "Robin, that's terrible. Of course it's not your fault."

"When the lights came on, I took my candy and went to see the kids' movie I'd already seen. Funny how I remember the name of the scary movie but not the G-rated one. While I was watching it, an usher came in the theater with a flashlight. My brother was with him. I guess he knew me better than I thought, 'cause he figured out where I would go. But before I even saw that it was him, I knew I was rescued when I saw the ray of the flashlight. That's when I realized it was the darkness that really frightened me, more than the movie or the stranger or even being lost. So now, when someone's scared in the dark, I just want them to know they don't have to be afraid."

Traci allowed the girl to wrap her arms around her now, no longer sure who was comforting who.

"And what about what's *in* the dark?" Traci asked.

MARK LOOKED up when he heard the music. It had to be Steven's tape deck. That meant he was close to the camp! He called out for his friends and again got no reply. But as he stepped into the brush the music grew louder. And he recognized the song. He'd never been so happy to hear Blue Oyster Cult.

Sprinting through the forest, he wondered how he would explain the creature he'd seen. His friends would probably just laugh and tell him he should lay off the LSD, but he knew the difference between drug-induced visuals and actually seeing something real. Even acid didn't create vivid gnomes from nothing. But the others would never believe he'd been knocked over by some woodland ghoulie. Maybe they had to. Mark didn't have to tell them the truth. All he had to do was corroborate Scott and Jenny's story that there was someone else in the woods. That should be enough to motivate everyone to get out of this place.

The song grew louder, literally and figuratively music to his ears. The ghostly vocals soothed him despite the death coercion of the lyrics. He bounced over a fallen log and hustled across the thicket, kicking through leaves and swatting away brush. He was cut up and out of breath, but the worst of this night was behind him now and relief flooded him.

He spotted a faint orange glow behind the circle of trees, and as he pressed on it grew stronger. His eyes focused. It was not one glow, but three little ones with a longer one running horizontally beneath the others. The collective glow flickered like a light bulb during a thunderstorm.

And it was moving.

Mark slowed his pace. He'd thought what he was seeing was the circle of candles at the campsite. But these lights were hovering a good five feet off the ground. He might have thought the others were carrying candles through the dark, but the glowing dots were too close together, and the slit beneath could still not be explained.

"Hello?" he called out.

He instantly regretted it. What if this wasn't his friends but the dwarf? But how could it be? The lights were too high off the ground.

He dared again. "Hello? Is someone there?"

The woods began to crackle. Someone—something—was moving fast now, and the little, orange lights were coming with them. The dots grew into triangles, the slit into a smile of jagged teeth.

The jack-o'-lantern, Mark realized. He was being chased by a jack-o'-lantern.

Its mouth opened and closed, hungry for Mark's flesh, thirsty for the blood pounding through his heart. And though he could make out the shape of the pumpkin, he could not see who was carrying it. It seemed to be soaring through the night on its own. "Don't Fear the Reaper" grew louder and louder until it was all Mark could hear, a relentless refrain drowning out his own screams.

CHAPTER EIGHTEEN

"It has to be Steven," Scott said. "It's his boombox and his mix tape. He's messing with us. I know it."

He wanted to believe it, even as the sick, hollowing doubt riddled him. The tingle returned to the back of his neck. Jenny had both hands on his arm. Corey stood immobilized by the serenade coming through the shadows.

Then they heard the screaming.

Jenny gasped, squeezing his arm tighter.

"That sounds like Mark," Scott said.

Mark Goranson was shrieking, adding another level of dread to the song.

"They're fucking with us!" Scott said.

"I don't think Mark's that good of an actor," Corey said. "He sounds like he's running for his life or something."

Jenny shivered. "Scott…"

She fell quiet, her tone having said everything.

Scott's anger rose, deeper and meaner. The guys were torturing his girlfriend with this crap and he was downright pissed about it. Though he'd be relieved to know it had all been a joke, he'd still want to plant his shoe in Steven and Mark's asses.

"Enough!" Scott shouted into the gloom. "Joke's over, you guys!"

Jenny called out too. "You scared us, okay? Congratulations. Now c'mon already! Stop it!"

But the screaming continued, raw and bloodcurdling. And it was getting louder, the screamer drawing closer. The song crawled down to its end, and now the only sound was those terrible cries.

"Something's chasing him," Corey said.

Scott shook his head. "You know how Mark is, dude. He'll do anything to mess with someone. And Steven just loves this Halloween shit."

"Listen to him!" Corey insisted. "He's freaking out."

Jenny tugged on Scott. "Let's get out of here. Whatever's chasing him will come for us too."

"There's nothing chasing him!" Scott said.

He felt certain of it now. Jenny tugged but Scott refused to budge. Though he could not see Mark, he knew he was coming right at them. Once he reached them, his screams would turn to mocking laughter, but the asshole wouldn't laugh long with Scott's fist in his mouth.

Jenny cried, "Scott!"

"You wanna hide? Hide. I'm not running anymore. When Mark gets here, this little game will be over."

But Corey disagreed. Of course he did. He always jumped at the chance to side with Jenny. Anything to get on her good side. It was the only way he knew how to get the fairer sex to smile at him—complete compliance.

"C'mon," Corey said, taking Jenny's hand. "We can hide behind those rocks."

He nodded toward a series of boulders at the edge of the slope. Jenny took one more pleading glance at her boyfriend, but he stayed firm, telling her it was fine. Seeing her hand in Corey's added to Scott's brewing umbrage, but he told them to go ahead. They tucked behind the assortment of rock and turned off the flashlight.

When Mark exploded out of the bushes, he jumped back at the sight of Scott and fell on his butt with a thud. But once he recognized his friend, Mark hurried to him, surprising Scott when he wrapped his arms around him. His big, tough buddy was shaking like a newborn foal. If he was faking, it was totally convincing. At least he'd stopped screaming.

"Oh, man," Mark panted. "Jesus, dude, am I glad to see you."

"I'll bet," Scott said, still doubtful. "You done with this now?"

Mark stepped back. His eyes were wet. Maybe he'd joined drama class just to pick up pointers for this, Scott thought, Mark and Steven having planned this prank far in advance. Mark wasn't one for hard work, but it was possible.

"Scott, something's out here, dude. You and Jenny were right." He looked back and forth. "Hey, where is she?"

Scott turned toward the boulders. "C'mon out you two. It's totally safe." They rose up.

"Thank God," Mark said. "Guys, we need to get the fuck outta here—*fast*. Someone was chasing me, but I think I lost 'em. Now might be our best chance."

"Cut it out," Scott said. "This isn't funny anymore. You've got everybody way too freaked out."

Mark's brow dropped. "Me? What the fuck are you talking about?"

"You and Steven. Playing that creepy song and screaming in the dark, making sounds like a werewolf. You were probably the one peeking on me and Jenny, weren't you?"

Mark's mouth fell. "Dude, I would never—"

Scott shoved him, hard. It felt good.

"Dude," Mark said, "knock it off! I didn't do nothin'."

He told them how he'd stumbled and lost track of the others. How someone had been stalking him.

"You serious?" Corey asked.

"As a heart attack."

Jenny touched Scott. "I think he's telling the truth."

Corey nodded, agreeing with her once again.

"Yeah," Scott said, "well, I still think this is bullshit, but I want to get out of here."

"I'm not lying," Mark said. "You've gotta believe me, dude."

"I don't have to believe jack. Even if you weren't helping to do all this, Steven must be behind it."

Mark shrugged. "Maybe. He's the one who likes talking about demons. I only came out here tonight to party. I don't want to play any trick-or-treat shit. Halloween pranks are for kids."

"I'M GOING down," Traci said.

Robin shook her head. "But Steven said to—"

"Steven also said he'd be right back. What if something happened and he's down there hurt?"

Robin's mouth hung open. Apparently she'd yet to think of that. "You really think so?"

"I don't know. That's why we have to look for him."

"I just want him to come back."

"Me too, but how long have we been waiting? At least half an hour, I'd say."

Robin exhaled. "It feels like forever without Steven."

"Well then, c'mon."

Traci moved to the slope and when she took her first steps down, she reached out for Robin and the girl took her hand for balance. They descended side by side, hand in hand like children skipping. The incline was not as treacherous as it had appeared from the top, and they made it safely to the pebbled bank of the stream.

It was darker down here, colder. Trees smothered the moonlight, making it harder for the flashlight to cut through the forest. Traci shined the light on the stream, following the water as it flowed down the bramble of black rocks. She stopped when the ray fell upon an assortment of flowers. They caught Traci's eye because they were fresh, the roses and tulips bright as spring, some of the buds not even all the way open. It was the last day of October. Wild flowers would be dead.

"What is that?" Robin asked.

Traci stepped forward and the light revealed a small, worn teddy bear. An A-frame stand held a wreath and a ribbon was draped across it like a beauty pageant stash.

"It's a memorial," Traci said.

The sash read: *We love you, Holly Reese.*

Robin came closer to the shrine and when she squatted beside it, the beam of light fell upon her. Traci could see her face again. No fangs or green flesh, just the heart-shaped, freckled face of a girl.

"I knew her," Traci said.

"Really?"

"We were in junior high together. We weren't best friends or anything, but we were friendly, you know? She was a nice person."

"So what happened?"

Traci sighed. "What do you think? This is Suicide Woods. There's a reason everyone calls it that."

"Oh...yeah."

"It was so weird when it happened. I mean, Holly was popular and got good grades. Her parents were really nice, made good money. Nobody could understand why she would've done it."

The memorial was placed at the edge of the stream, propped upon the rocks. Judging by the conditions, it must have been recently revisited.

"So, this where they found her?" Robin asked.

"Yeah, guess so. A guy and his sons came out here to fish and there she was. She'd filled her coat and jeans with rocks and drowned herself where the water connects to the river. The stream must've carried her back to the bank."

They were silent then. Traci had forgotten everything else—the missing boys, Scott and Jenny's story of something in the woods. There was only the face of Holly Reese in her mind, smiling and laughing, hair bright as sunshine. It was bizarre how these warm recollections now felt so macabre. The smiles seemed painted on, the laughter smothering what should have been a cry for help. When she'd first heard about Holly, she'd wept softly in her room so no one would hear. Holly was the first person Traci knew who had committed suicide, and the first person her age who'd died. It seemed important to grieve her without interruptions.

"Well," Traci said, "I guess we should keep looking for—"

Looking up, Traci's breath left her.

Robin was gone.

CHAPTER NINETEEN

The face was blood red. The eye sockets were so deep Corey could not see the eyes. The head had no ears or hair. Several small horns lined the forehead, and the lower jaw sported saber-toothed tiger fangs. The face hovered between two pale trees like a red balloon tied to a child's wrist. And it was watching him.

My mask, he realized. *That's* my *Halloween mask.*

He'd brought it with him tonight in the hope of wearing it just for kicks, but Traci's vehement objection to anything devilish had forced him to push it down into the bottom of his backpack, the same backpack he was carrying right now. How could someone have gotten to it? Corey's stomach went hollow.

"Holy shit…you guys…"

He turned to the others to point out the demon's horrible head. He'd been following behind Scott and Jenny. Mark had been walking beside him, not wanting to be at the rear alone. In the split-second Corey paused to make sure he was seeing what he thought he was, the others must have moved on, not realizing he'd stopped walking. He scanned the trail with the flashlight and the beam revealed only forest.

"Guys?"

How could he have lost them so quickly?

Corey spun the light in all directions, calling them by name. His chest pounded.

He turned back to the demon face. It had not moved. It was locked on Corey like a cougar on the hunt. He almost wanted to act like he hadn't seen it, so it might just leave him alone, but he'd already jumped at the sight of it. The demon knew it'd been spotted. It knew Corey was scared.

Swallowing hard, he turned the flashlight upon the demonic face. It looked like his mask, but was it? It seemed more vivid and alive now. In the darkness, the head appeared to hover on its own, but now its body was revealed to Corey in all its grotesquery. The demon had scabbed-over skin, its entire body one russet, crusty rash. If not for the chest swelling with every breath, Corey would have thought it was some sort of prop, a mannequin decorated for the holiday. But the detail was all too convincing—warty limbs; a skeletal chest showing the ribcage; three crooked legs with feet gnarled and black as if they'd been burned, one of which was actually a hand.

I'm hallucinating.

Marijuana was a hallucinogen. People never talked about as if it were, but that's what the drug was classified as. Could three puffs of a joint really cause this intense of an illusion? Maybe someone had spiked it with something. He thought of Mark and his tabs of acid, how he'd been annoyed at everyone's refusal to join him in a psychedelic trip. Had he done something with the remaining tabs? Had he spiked their drinks, making them see and hear things?

Slowly the demon raised its hands. The palms split open, scabs cracking and weeping, revealing tiny, human mouths. The gums bled as yellow baby teeth sprouted through them.

These infant mouths screamed like newborns.

So did Corey.

JENNY WHIMPERED, the heaviness of it all threatening to snap her sanity in two. As soon as they found one person, they lost another. She, Scott, and Mark had been calling for Corey for several minutes now. None had even seen him wander off or lag behind. It was as if the woods had opened up and swallowed him, a thought that made her cold.

"I can't take this…"

Scott held her, and she buried her wet face into his flannel. There was no way this was some mean prank. Mark might do something like that, and maybe even Steven for the sake of Halloween tradition, but there was no way Corey Pickett would ever try to frighten her like this. He was too sweet. They could no longer entertain Scott's theory that this was all some elaborate ruse to scare them. She believed Mark. And whatever had arrived when she and Scott began to make love, it was not a joke. The malevolence behind it all was palpable, a black energy she could actually feel. She knew, without question, the things that had chased them wanted to hurt her. She couldn't explain it, so she hadn't tried. But the feeling had been just as pure and raw as the terror she felt right now.

"What if something grabbed him?" Mark said. "Whatever was chasing me could've snuck up on us."

Scott glared at him. "Don't say things like that."

"C'mon, dude! You still think we're all trying to pull some gag?"

"Maybe not you, but somebody. It could be anybody in those woods. Maybe its Jack Clark or Randy Farris. I don't know."

Jenny winced at the mention of the school's worst bullies. Two bulky meatheads who would rather dunk people's heads in toilets than achieve. It didn't matter if you were boy or girl, or black or white. Those two tortured their classmates at random—equal opportunity sadists. The only friends those jack-offs had were each other, and their only joy in life seemed to stem from torturing people.

"You think they followed us out here?" Jenny asked.

"They could've. Maybe they found out what we were doing tonight and decided it would be fun to scare us."

Mark snorted. "No way. How would they even know where we were going? We all agreed not tell nobody. And none of us would ever talk to those assholes if we could avoid it."

"Maybe they had the same idea to come out here tonight and happened to see us."

"C'mon, man, you're talkin' shit and you know it! Why can't you just accept there's something out here that's after us?"

Scott cocked his head. "What do you mean *something*?"

Jenny said, "We've been thinking it's a person. Do you think it's some kind of animal?"

"No…" Mark said. "I mean…I dunno what I think it is. But I don't think it's Clark and Farris, and I don't think its Steven either. Something's out to get us *bad*."

Scott started to say something but Jenny grabbed his arm. There was no sense debating it anymore. No matter what this thing was, they needed to find the others, starting with Corey. She called his name again, louder and louder until she was crying.

DARKNESS.

His arm had hit branches while he was running and he'd dropped the flashlight. Corey did not break stride. Darkness was better than death, better than letting the demon gain ground.

This can't be real…

But it was. The horrible, newborn cries of the demon's palm-mouths trailed behind him. Corey heard the thicket crackle as the creature ran after him, the trio of legs thudding to the earth when it leapt, and the hot snorts of its breathing. He wanted to look back to see how close it was on his tail, but he did not dare. To do so was to die. He was sure of it.

Corey tried to keep his life from flashing before his eyes, but his mind betrayed him. He thought of his mother's love and his father's guidance, of how lucky he'd been compared to some, how being popular and getting girls weren't as important as a good family. There would be time to date someone and change his image; or at least, there would have been time. With this strange beast barreling down on him, his time on earth might just be up.

It made him feel cheated. He couldn't die like this, lost in the woods alone. There was college to look forward to next year. He was going to be a comic book artist. But now there was only the rich threat of Hell. Wasn't that where the demon would drag him? Or would death be but a sleep he would never wake from? He wasn't sure which option frightened him more.

His mind was reeling with these frantic thoughts when he went over the edge. He hadn't seen it coming, and when he reached the bluff, he tumbled into the air. It was a short drop, but he didn't land on his feet. There was no time to even groan. He bounced back up and charged on, crossing the stream, his sneakers flooding with frigid water. It wasn't until he'd crossed to the other side that he noticed the silence. With the splashing finished, he was able to listen again for his predator, but the baby shrieks had gone silent and there were no running sounds or hog snorts.

Corey slowed. He turned to look.

The demon was gone.

He scanned the blackness, expecting to find the beast waiting on the other side of the stream, possibly scared of the water. Corey couldn't imagine why it would be, but it wasn't any more bizarre than everything else that had happened tonight. He stared at the bank as the moon snuck out from behind the clouds, watching, waiting.

Nothing.

"Oh, man…" He bent over, gaining breath. "What is happening?"

When he looked up again, it dawned on him that he was completely lost. Scott was right. They had spent their childhoods in these woods, playing manhunt and war. Corey and his big brother, Ryan, had done the same until Ryan went off to college, him being eight years older than Corey. Before all the suicides, Corey used to come out here to read comics like *Man-Thing* and *Swamp Thing* because they had to do with the wilderness. But despite all those visits to these woods, Corey's memories offered no discernable directions, and his shuddering fear wasn't helping his cognition. Adrenaline scrambled his mind. But one thing was for sure—he did not want to cross over the stream again. The woods on the other side were where the demon lived. Whatever portal to Hell had opened, it was somewhere on that end, so Corey Pickett was going to stick to this side.

Corey checked his compass, but it was just as useless as it had been earlier. He almost threw it into the bushes out of frustration but decided better of it. It might start working again. He took the Swiss Army Knife from his pocket and clicked the blade out, gripping the handle so hard his knuckles ran white. Corey followed the stream. It had to lead to a bigger body of water. If the stream led all the way down to the Housatonic River, he'd be able to find a road.

It bothered him that he could not remember where exactly the stream ended. It seemed like something a Boy Scout should have learned about his own backyard. He had the feeling he'd followed it before, but again his memory was hazy. The woods were impossible to make any sense of tonight.

"Corey."

He gasped at the sound of his name. The speaker sounded soft, feminine—not the demon. Or so he hoped. It took all he had to look.

Robin stood just a few feet away. She was alone on top of a small cliff over the trickling waters. The girl was ghostly pale and shone blue in the moonlight. She stared at him, expressionless.

Corey sighed with relief, but the feeling didn't last long. There was something off about the girl's posture. Robin seemed lifeless, an erect corpse. She did not take steps toward him. She didn't move at all. Robin had said his name and nothing more, but her mouth was open and her eyes were half closed and unblinking.

"Robin? Are you okay?"

A breeze tossed the girl's hair about her shoulders like bonfire flames. She remained stoic, reminding him of a movie zombie, and he called her name again. And though Robin's lips did not move, he heard her whispering, sounding as if she were right in his ear.

"Don't be afraid," she said.

But he couldn't help it. He was trembling again, and while Robin's behavior disturbed him, he found himself walking toward her, drawn to her. She was beautiful and innocent, but this wasn't the lure. Corey ached for her as a form of comfort, the girl seeming suddenly maternal even though she was younger than him. Maybe if they faced these terrible woods together, they just might make it out unharmed. In his mind's eye he saw them emerging from the forest at the first gray light of dawn. They were smiling and holding hands. And when Corey snapped out of this daydream, he saw they really were holding hands, but it didn't make him smile. Right beside him now, Robin's touch was of ice. When she whispered again, her mouth still didn't move, but he felt her freezing breath against his cheek.

"Can I see your mask?" she asked.

Corey blinked. "My…my mask?"

"Yeah. The one of the Devil."

Had he told her he'd brought it along? He didn't remember showing it to anyone or even mentioning it. He slung off the backpack and unzipped it, bypassing his snacks and thermos. There was the mask, the one mirroring the demon that had been chasing him, certifying that whatever it was, it hadn't been wearing his mask. Corey had had it all along.

He handed it to Robin, confused but compliant. He'd never been able to say no to a girl. She held the mask face-up and stared at the creepy visage. He wanted to tell her what he'd seen, what had chased him, but felt he'd only make himself look like a fool.

"You know why we wear these on Halloween?" she asked, sounding as if she already knew.

"For fun," he said with a shrug. "Dressing up is part of the holiday."

"But haven't you ever wondered why we dress like *monsters*?"

He shrugged again. She obviously had something to say, so he decided to just let her proceed.

"Why?" he asked.

"Halloween is a special day. It's like Steven said. Tonight's when the land of the living and the land of the dead are severed. We dress up like monsters to trick the real monsters, so they won't recognize us and drag us to Hell with them."

Corey opened his mouth, but no words came out.

Robin turned the mask right side up. She told him not to be afraid. Then she told him something else, something he would never forget or repeat to anyone. Then she put the mask over his head.

CHAPTER TWENTY

Traci had never hugged anyone so hard.

Steven chuckled as he put his arms around her. His levity was baffling. He was totally at ease and this behavior seemed almost mocking.

"Hey," he said, patting her back, "it's okay."

"Jesus Christ, Steven, you scared the living shit outta me."

He'd appeared behind her like a wraith, as if he'd been zapped into existence by that transporter beam from *Star Trek*. One second, she was alone, screaming for Robin, and then Steven was there, so inordinately carefree it bordered on the absurd.

"What happened to you?" she asked.

He shrugged. "My flashlight died. I got lost in the woods."

"Steven…" Traci wiped away a tear. "Robin's gone."

"What?" He smirked. "No. She's not gone."

"I'm telling you—one minute we were talking and the next she just vanished."

"Traci, she's *not* gone."

She stepped back, giving him a quizzical look. He seemed so sure of himself. She waited for more, but Steven didn't say anything and soon didn't have to.

Robin walked out of the bushes in a causal tiptoe, careful not to stumble over the unearthed roots. She gave Traci a little smile, braces glimmering when the flashlight beam fell upon her. She even waved.

"Robin!" Traci was relieved, but then came the anger. "Where the hell did you go?"

The girl tucked her hair behind her ear, a display of bashfulness. "I saw Steven."

"You left me alone without saying a word. Why didn't you tell me? We could've gone together to check."

"We didn't have to check. I knew it was him."

"That's not the point!"

Steven intervened. "Traci, what Robin means is—"

"She knows how to talk, Steven."

"All I'm saying is—"

She threw up her hands. "Look, whatever. She's been a weirdo all night, anyway. I'm sick of it. I just wanna get outta here. *Now.*"

"But our stuff is still back at the campsite."

"I don't give a fuck. It's just sleeping bags and snacks."

"My boombox is—"

"I'll buy you another one. Let's just go, please."

"Wait," Robin said meekly, "What about your friends?"

Steven nodded. "We have to find them."

"No!" Traci said. "We can't keep doing this. We're all going in circles trying to find each other and losing each other because of it. I say we just try to get out. Once we get back to the neighborhood, we can call for help, get the police out here to do a search."

"We can't do that," Steven said, taking her by the shoulders. "We call the cops and we're all busted, remember? We're not supposed to be out here. My Dad will shit bricks if I call him from jail."

"Yeah," Robin said. "My parents will hang me."

The girl's choice of words made something go cold in Traci's chest. Tears welled in her eyes, infuriating her. Whenever she got frustrated or felt totally helpless, she cried like this, silent tears that rolled down her cheeks no matter how hard she fought to keep them back.

"I'm getting out of here," she said. "Please don't make me go alone."

Steven's face went slack as he gave her puppy dog eyes. It was not a tease. He seemed genuinely sympathetic. "Oh, Traci. I didn't realize you were this upset."

"I'm not upset, I just want to go home. Now. *Right now.*"

"Okay. It's cool. Maybe you're right. We're not getting anywhere by chasing each other. Let's head back to Scott's house. Who knows, everybody else might be there already, waiting for us, right?"

She wanted to believe that but simply couldn't. There was an energy to the surrounding wilderness that assured they weren't empty. Someone was out here. When Traci closed her eyes to release the tears, she saw Scott's face in her mind, a projection from within. It soothed her to think of him, but pained her to imagine him still lost out there. It took a moment for her to realize she'd thought of him before Mark. It was a problem that would have to wait for later.

A familiar voice came from above, shouting for Corey.

"Mark?" Traci shouted back.

The two groups exchanged calls and Scott, Jenny, and Mark came scrambling down the incline and joined them at the bank. Mark took Traci in his arms, a gesture that surprised her. He never showed affection for her in public and only hugged and kissed on her when he was initiating sex. His unexpected passion was a window into his fear. Something had shaken him to his very soul.

The group expressed their relief to one another. All except for Scott, who shot Steven a murderous look.

"What the fuck, Steven?" he snarled. "What the fuck's the matter with you?"

Steven's face fell. "What do you mean?"

"You know damned well what I mean. You've been trying to scare us all night!"

"What're you talking about, dude? I haven't—"

Scott shoved him, hard. When Steven nearly fell over, Robin gasped and came to his side. Traci turned to Jenny, wondering if Scott's girlfriend could explain his indignation, but all she saw in Jenny was exhaustion and dismay. Traci hoped Mark would intervene. Instead, he just watched the confrontation.

"I don't know what your problem is," Steven said, "but you push me again and I'm gonna push back."

Scott stepped forward and Traci took his arm, a little surprised Jenny hadn't already.

"Why're you so angry?" she asked.

"All night he's been playing Halloween pranks, trying to freak us out." Robin shook her head. "Nu-uh! He's been with me and Traci almost the whole night. We only lost sight of each other for a second."

Traci knew it'd been longer than that, but she didn't want this to turn into a fight, so she backed up Robin's claim.

"We heard your mix tape playing," Scott told Steven. "You were chasing us with it, weren't you? Chasing and screaming like a maniac."

"I don't even have my boombox," he said. "It's back at the camp with the rest of my stuff. I'm telling you, man, I don't know what you're talking about."

They explained to Steven all that had happened, how they'd been stalked by an unseen aggressor. Steven insisted it wasn't him.

"I believe you," Mark said. "Guys, that thing that was after me definitely wasn't Steven."

Scott exhaled. "Then what was it?"

Mark turned his head away, a sign he was hiding something. Traci recognized the look, but if the others did, they made no mention of it. She noted it for later. He might be willing to tell her in private.

"Can we please just get out of here?" she asked.

Jenny nodded emphatically.

All eyes were on Scott now. His shoulders had relaxed, the rage behind his eyes fading. He stepped closer to Steven.

"Sorry, dude," Scott said. "You being behind this was just the only thing that made sense to me. Now I don't think anything makes sense at all."

They shook hands.

"It's cool," Steven said. "No harm done."

Finally, Jenny spoke up. "Guys...where's Corey?"

INITIALLY, COREY thought it was his friends.

He nearly shouted out to the people walking through the grove of trees. But there were too many of them, and some were taller or fatter or shorter than anyone he'd come out here with. He tucked himself behind at tree and crouched low, watching the shadowy figures move into the deadening.

One carried a small, brass burner on a chain. The canister billowed smoke Corey could smell even from this distance, a potpourri of aromatic herbs. His labored breath bounced back at him within the mask. He'd almost forgotten he was wearing it. The trapped air slicked his face with moisture, but he still wouldn't remove it, especially now that he saw these strolling strangers. Something about them made him want to hide in every possible way.

We dress up like monsters to trick the real monsters, so they won't recognize us and drag us to hell with them.

Corey counted thirteen people. They spoke in low tones and though he could not make out what they were saying, their voices were clearly those of adults, not teenagers. But the one up front appeared under five feet tall, a child among the grown-ups. They didn't follow any trail. They just journeyed through the thicket as naturally as bears, and though Corey had been hoping for someone to rescue him, he sensed these people wouldn't be helpful or even friendly. From the looks of them, they did not want to be noticed. He could only hope they wouldn't spot him. He watched as they disappeared into the night like ghost ships and didn't budge until he no longer smelled their incense.

Corey had not been raised with religion. Though they'd never put a label on it, his parents were agnostic. He'd only been in churches for weddings and the funeral of a great aunt he'd never met until she was laid out in her coffin like a mummy. But still he prayed now as he gathered up the nerve to leave his hiding spot behind the tree. He apologized to whatever higher power was listening that he had come into these woods for fun, a place where so many young people had taken their own lives. It was disrespectful and he wanted to make up for it by doing charitable things. But first he would have to get home safely. If God (or whoever) could just give him some help to escape Suicide Woods, Corey would never return. He'd be too busy delivering meals to the elderly and ladling out chicken noodle soup at the homeless shelter.

He dared a single step, the dry leaves crunching, sounding so brutally loud. Corey waited, listening to the unbearable stillness. There were no scurrying animal sounds, not even the night song of crickets. The autumn breeze had left him when he needed it most. If it would just come and rattle the branches, it would create enough noise for him to hide behind. He moved on the balls of his feet, taking slow, long steps at first, picking up speed when he was sure he was alone.

How had it happened? Robin had been *right beside him*. She'd been holding his hand, leading him up the stream as if she knew where she was going. Corey hadn't questioned her. It seemed silly to him now, but he'd followed her like a puppy. They'd walked alongside the stream until they reached a dirt trail and then followed it into the forest, but when low-hanging branches turned the path into a tunnel of leaves Robin's fingers slipped away from his and he was too shy to snatch them back. She ducked under the tightest section, the branches brushing her back as she passed under, and even in the dark Corey could tell those abundant leaves were the same color as her hair. His breath caught in his chest when the girl slipped out of sight, and though he followed quickly behind her, he knew she was gone even before he came through to the other side, finding the path deserted.

But the woods were occupied. The group of strangers had been moving across the grove in a curious parade and he'd hidden instead of searching for Robin. He hadn't even had time to call her name. She must have seen them first and ducked for cover. But if she had, then where was she now? And why had she been acting so strange? Why had she said those things?

Corey scanned the woods for her as he crossed through, sticking to the trail, but without his flashlight, he couldn't see much. It didn't seem safe to call for her or the others. It made him feel like a coward. Robin was probably lost and scared out of her mind. This was his chance to be her hero, but instead, he was making a silent retreat, focused entirely on saving his own yellow-bellied ass. He wasn't Batman, wasn't Spider-Man. He was just Corey Pickett. A nobody. A loser. A shit.

Demons. Corey shook his head. *How could I have been so stupid? It couldn't have been real, it just couldn't.*

It was a costume, a mask like the one he was wearing right now, maybe even identical. It had all looked so real, but it was also dark in these woods and, despite the beam of his flashlight, the shadows gave off black illusions, distorting reality into fantasy.

I'm never smoking weed again.

He also still suspected Mark of lacing his drink. That had to be it. What other explanation was there?

Demons. Real demons.

But Corey couldn't accept that. Not only was he not religious, he wasn't superstitious either. He didn't believe in demons, ghosts, werewolves, or unlucky black cats. He didn't avoid walking under ladders and had never thrown spilled salt over his shoulder. Demons weren't real. Halloween masks were. Hallucinations brought on by drugs were. And these goddamned woods certainly were. They were his true nemesis tonight, not some red devil straight out of a horror movie, and he was determined to defeat them.

But what of the people he'd seen? Were they, too, a hallucination? Corey doubted it. They'd had no horns or wings. He was certain they were human, but that only made them more intimidating. If they were real, they could cause real harm.

He moved faster but kept his steps soft and watched for any fallen branches that might trip him. Even though removing the mask would help him see better and free up his peripherals, Corey left it on. It made him feel safer, just like the Swiss Army Knife in his hand. It didn't make sense, but it didn't have to. On Halloween, you wore a mask. There was comfort in that, however ridiculous. And Robin had been the one to put it on him. He felt removing it would hurt her somehow, like he'd be rejecting a heartfelt gift.

Leaving her behind will hurt her much more than that.

Corey stopped. He looked back to the grove he'd just fled from. She was back there somewhere—alone, afraid.

You're eighteen years old. You're not a kid anymore.

Corey headed back the way he'd come.

You're a man. Act like one.

AFTER SOME discussion and more than a little arguing, Steven convinced them to let him and Robin search for Corey while the others headed back to Scott's, because Corey might have made it home already. Jenny wasn't sure this was the best route to take, but she could think of no better options. Steven lacked the distress that was weighing down the others, and Robin was his docile accomplice, so they'd parted ways and Jenny's group had not been walking long when Scott perked up.

"Hey, look!" he said.

Jenny saw rooftops in the distance. They were silhouetted by a sliver of light, the first sign of dawn. Had they really been out here all night? Traci cried out in relief. Mark cheered like he was at a ballgame. The four of them went into a jog, huge grins spreading across their faces. But while Jenny was flushed with relief, there was still the pang of fear—not for herself, but for the three they'd left behind. She told herself they would be all right, especially now that morning was coming. They'd be able to better see and the woods wouldn't play tricks on them. Steven and Robin would find Corey, and he'd find the way because this was his neighborhood.

Halloween was finally over.

When they reached the end of the trail, Scott's backyard came into view. He put his arm around Jenny.

"Everything's going to be okay," he said.

There was a rustle behind them.

A demon emerged from the bushes.

CHAPTER TWENTY-ONE

He wasn't sure how he'd made it out.

Corey had been retracing the steps he'd taken with Robin, and suddenly he passed through a small hole in the brush and stepped right into Scott's backyard. He hadn't had the slightest inkling he'd come remotely close to the neighborhood. Spotting his friends, Corey removed the mask, comfort filling every inch of him.

"Christ, Corey," Traci said, "you scared me to death!"

Mark snickered with nervous laughter. They were all still jittery, but their universal relief was palpable, on the verge of celebration.

"Why were you wearing that stupid mask?" Scott asked with a touch of suspicion.

Corey could have lied, but a lie wouldn't make any more sense than the truth.

"Robin," he said. "She put it on me. For luck, I guess."

"She with you? Is Steven?"

"No…I lost track of her a while ago."

"They're looking for you," Mark explained.

The words cut Corey like a dull blade. Steven and Robin were still out there. Corey paled. He dropped the mask on the ground and slung off his backpack. The gray in the east was blossoming into a deep purple.

Deep Purple. Is that the band who sings that damned "Don't Fear the Reaper" song?

If he never heard it again, it would still be too soon.

Corey looked back to the trail. They were out there somewhere. *She* was out there somewhere. He made a few trance-like steps toward the opening of Suicide Woods and Scott took him by the arm, the others practically ordering him not to go back in. They came at him with various forms of logic, but it all sounded like mere excuses to Corey. But he wanted to adopt those same excuses, wanted to think of them as legitimate explanations for what they were doing.

"You really think they'll find the way out?" he asked.

There was a brief silence as no one answered. They simply couldn't commit to it. Scott nodded. It was the best any of them could do.

At least the sun was coming up. There were no monsters during the day. No demons or ghosts or weirdoes traveling through the woods. The cold was at its most unforgiving this time of day, but soon the earth would warm and even if November brought its usual rain, it would be a welcome change from the bitter night.

"So, what now?" Corey asked.

Scott put his hands on his hips. "I guess we wait, right?"

There was no school today, so they had nowhere to be. Even if it weren't the weekend, Corey would have chosen to play hooky for the first time. He wanted to crawl into bed and fill his mind with the comforting brain food of *Batman: The Animated Series* and *Family Matters* reruns until, hopefully, he fell asleep.

"Mark?" he said, daring to ask. "Did you put something in my soda?"

Mark curled his lip. "What? No...what the fuck're you talking about? I didn't do nothing to your stupid soda."

"It's just that—"

"Don't try and put this shit on me, dickweed. I wouldn't waste good acid on you."

Traci looked to her boyfriend, and Corey detected a hint of distrust in her eyes. The others were watching Corey now, waiting for more, but he chose not to share what he'd witnessed. They would only think his "child-like imagination" had run away with him, a backhanded compliment he'd heard too many times.

"Must've been the weed then," he said, pretending to shrug it off. "I've never smoked it before. Messed with my head, I guess."

Jenny stepped forward. "Corey...did something happen to you out there?"

He couldn't tell them. He just couldn't.

"It's all okay now," he said. "Right?"

There was a sadness behind her eyes that made Corey avert his gaze. He knew then that he truly loved her, that Jenny's beauty ran even deeper than he'd realized.

When Scott put his arm around him, Corey felt somewhat guilty for his feelings toward his friend's girl, but he hugged him right back. It felt good. It felt safe.

It felt like home.

"I SHOULD get home," Traci said. They looked at her incredulously. Tears of frustration began to rise and she crossed her arms over her chest. "My Mom is gonna kill me if she wakes up and I'm not there."

But it wasn't exactly a danger. Mom tended to be the one who disappeared on weekends, spending the days hungover and the nights gallivanting from one drunk tank to another with the boyfriend of the month. Even if Mom were at home, it was virtually impossible she'd be awake before noon. She was a total night owl. But despite the woman's many flaws, Traci wanted to see her mother now, thinking it would alleviate this bad feeling she could not name.

Mark went to her. "I'll walk you home, babe."

"You guys," Scott said, "you're really gonna leave before we know what's happened to Steven and Robin?"

A tear rolled down Traci's face. "I'm sorry...I just..." Her voice squeaked, both eyes welling now. "I wanna go home, Scott. Please...just let me go home."

She didn't know why, but she wanted permission from him, from all of them. She wanted them to tell her it was acceptable behavior to leave. Traci hoped Steven and Robin were safe, of course, but even though she was out of the forest, there remained a thick vibration of dread. Just being close to Suicide Woods frightened her. Even being with this particular group of people right now gave her a sense of unease. She wanted this whole thing to come to end and knew it wouldn't until she walked away.

Scott sighed. He put his hands on her shoulders. His eyes were so deep and warm it made Traci's heart swell. She thought of how Scott's visage had carried her through those dark moments tonight and wondered, not for the first time, if she were really over him.

"You don't have to do anything you don't want to," he told her. "Never."

These words would stay with her the rest of her life, returning to reassure her when men were too sexually aggressive or when she just couldn't stand going to work another day at a job she hated. This being the first time she heard it, the message was almost shocking in its clarity, the kind of thing you don't realize you need to hear until someone finally tells you.

"You'll call me when they come back, right?" Traci asked. "To let me know?"

Scott nodded.

She put her arms around his neck, tucking her head into his chest. There was muscle to his pectorals that had not been there when they'd dated. If Mark or Jenny had a problem with their embrace, Traci simply didn't care right now. Robin had told Traci to not be afraid, but it was Scott who'd fought to make it so she didn't have to be. She felt his arms go around her waist and couldn't help the warmth that spread below her belly.

A hand fell on her shoulder, pulling her back, out of the dream of Scott and into the cold light of a much harsher reality.

"Okay, okay," Mark said. "That's enough. Remember whose girl she is now, Scott."

Traci tensed.

Scott moved away from her. "C'mon, Mark—"

Mark stopped him. "I'm just sayin'. She don't need you to take care of her. That's what I'm for."

Scott threw up his hands. "Never said otherwise, dude."

"Yeah, but you act like it."

Traci glanced at Jenny, wondering if she'd take offense, if she hadn't already. Jenny was watching her too, but there was no vehemence there, only concern. Traci realized then that no matter how much they got along or even liked one another, there would always be this low-level tension between them, an undercurrent of rivalry. Jenny would never fully trust her around Scott, just as Traci could never really accept he belonged to Jenny now.

"Look," Traci said, pulling Mark back. "It's been a long, bad night. We're all just tired and freaked out. Let's not fight. Mark, please walk me home. 'Kay, babe?" She didn't really care for his company right now, but she also didn't want to go alone.

Mark glowered at Scott, and Scott just shrugged, too exhausted to argue. He went right to Jenny and put his arm around her, but it seemed forced, all for show. Jenny nuzzled into him anyway, and Traci *knew* that was all for her. Suddenly feeling sour inside, Traci wondered if the events of this night had done more damage to her group of friends than they realized. It bothered her as she and Mark headed home, as did her thoughts of Steven, and the weird, weird girl he'd brought with him tonight.

SCOTT WANTED to call out for his friend but feared he'd wake up his parents. There was already a chance his folks knew he'd been out all night. His mother still treated him like a kid when it came to checking on him. Sometimes, when he was lying in bed, he'd notice her in the doorway, peeking in on him sleeping to make sure he was there and breathing. He'd teased her about it, saying he would buy her a baby monitor, but this smothering behavior had begun to irk him. It made sense if she did this sort of thing to the twins. Jaclyn and Tucker were only eight. But Scott was almost ten years older than his siblings. It was time to cut the umbilical cord.

His mother was most protective when it came to whom Scott dated. This was what really bothered him about her treating him like a kid. He could make his own decisions. He loved Jenny whether or not his parents approved of her—and they certainly didn't. Mom never tried to hide it, not even when Jenny was *right there*, so they tried to avoid her when they were hanging out together.

It didn't make sense.

Jenny was polite, did well in school, and came from a respectable, healthy family. She was the type of girl everyone else's parents adored.

Traci, on the other hand, was the exact opposite. She was a tomboyish punk and widely considered a tramp, and her mother was the town's "community cock-wash," as Scott's uncle had so crudely put it. But Scott's parents loved Traci and sometimes even talked about her as if Scott was bound to get back together with the girl. His mother insisted it was meant to be, and Scott couldn't fathom why she'd come to such a conclusion. But parents were strange. His were no exception.

"I'm gonna head up," Corey said, nodding to his house. "I was thinking I could scan the woods with my binoculars. See if I can spot them."

But Scott knew the real reason Corey was leaving. It was the same reason they all wanted to. Just before he turned to go, Corey gave them a grave look. Scott didn't know what to make of it at the time, but as they would drift further apart over the next year, he would think of this moment as a period put at the end of their friendship.

As for right now, he couldn't worry about issues with Corey or Mark or even the girls. He had to focus on Steven. Scott couldn't shake the feeling that he'd left his friend in danger. He'd been so busy being mad at Steven for the frightening occurrences tonight that he'd forgotten how close they'd grown. Lately, Scott had begun to think of the guy as his best friend, replacing Corey and Mark, beating them with a combination of coolness and intellectualness. Steven could keep up with Scott mentally in ways Mark couldn't. He was able to get girls, willing to take chances and experiment with life, all things Corey failed at. Steven was a popular guy but never let it go to his head, shoving off his social prominence, smart enough to know trends fade and high school politics wouldn't mean a damn thing once they went off to universities. Scott admired that about Steven, and also his unique ability to tell stories. He read pulp novels and splatterpunk horror like Scott did, but also more advanced works by Dostoyevsky, Gabriel García Márquez, Tolstoy, and Gore Vidal. He loved and recited poetry, something Scott had never been able to grasp. No one doubted Steven would become a writer. Majoring in communications wasn't the dead end for him that it was for others. He was a great guy, a good friend, and Scott had accused him of childish pranks. He'd even *shoved* him. While Scott still couldn't explain what had really happened out there, he now felt certain Steven had nothing to do with it.

Again, he wondered why Corey had been wearing that mask.

No. Corey couldn't have done anything to scare them. He was the most gentle, mellow, and nonthreatening guy Scott had ever known. He'd never been the type to toss a spider in a girl's hair to get her attention. He was nice to the point of weakness. Corey said Robin had put the devil mask on him, and he was just the type of guy who did whatever a pretty girl told him to.

The sun split the horizon in a red haze, and the shadows receded from Suicide Woods. Scott hated this goddamned forest now. The events of the night had permanently tarnished every fond childhood memory he had of the place. He never wanted to set foot in there again, but now that dawn had broken, the pall of evil the woods possessed dissipated considerably, and he grew anxious as he waited for any sign of his friend.

"I think I should go back in and look for them."

Jenny gasped. "No! Please, Scott, don't go back in there."

"It's no big deal. It's light out now. I won't get lost."

"What about the thing that chased us? It's probably still out there."

"But so are Steven and Robin. Besides, we only heard yelling and—"

"Growling!"

"I can play it safe and stick to the trail. I'll just scan the trees and call for them. You can stay here in case they come back."

His girlfriend huffed. "I'm not gonna just stand here on your stupid lawn by myself."

"So, you want to come with me, then?"

"No way! Are you crazy?"

Scott ran a hand through his hair. "We have to do something."

"Hey, I want Steven back too, but maybe we need to accept we can't do this alone. Maybe we should wake up your Dad."

"Now you're the one who's talking crazy."

"I just think your parents, or maybe Corey's, might know what to do. I'd be willing to go talk to mine about this, even though they'll ground me until I'm forty when they find out I was in the woods all night."

"We'll all be screwed if anyone else finds out where we were."

Jenny shook her head. "I don't care about that anymore. I'd rather us be in trouble than dead."

Coldness crept up Scott's spine. "Dead?"

"It's all I could think about out there. All those other kids who died. What if they got lost out there just like we did? What if whatever was after us tonight…"

She trailed off, but Scott knew what she was trying to say. It was a thought that had been curled up like a rattlesnake in the back of his mind. So far, he'd kept it from striking, but Jenny's confirmation made it rattle its tail once again.

"I don't know what's going on," Scott said, "but I know no one will believe us. We'll just be labeled as a bunch of punk kids who thought it'd be so cool to play around in a place where other kids have died. We'll *never* live it down. And getting arrested for trespassing or something could put all our chances at going to good schools at risk. Steven wanted to avoid that at all costs. So do I."

Jenny's lip trembled. She was so pale and melancholic. Exhausted, purple rings had formed under her bloodshot eyes. He'd never seen her like this. It pained Scott to witness it now. There were some things a boyfriend couldn't just kiss away.

"I'll be right back," Scott said. "I promise."

Reaching for the flashlight in the grass, he noticed Corey had left his devil mask behind. It lay crumpled on the ground, discarded and forgotten, a guest who'd overstayed their welcome.

Scott could understand why Corey didn't want it anymore.

BEFORE JENNY could decide where to go or what to do, the shadow appeared behind the rows of trees. When she recognized Steven coming down the path, she whispered his name, the intensity of her relief bringing tears to her eyes. She sprinted toward the mouth of the woods with Scott right behind her. The initial happiness she felt at the sight of Steven was so strong she didn't register that he was alone and what that implied. But when she saw his face, that hollowing sensation of horror found its way back into Jenny's belly and snatched her heart again.

Steven didn't look at them. His head was down, staring into the dirt. The vacancy of his expression made him appear in a trance, like a boy in a walking coma. It wasn't until Jenny reached him that he snapped out of this gloomy reverie. Looking into his eyes was worse. The irises seemed to vibrate in the sockets, the whites showing too much. When she took his hand, it was shaking.

"Steven? What's going on? What's happened? Where's Robin?"

His lip trembled. "Robin…"

Scott stared at him, mouth agape. Steven seemed a ghost of himself and it gave Jenny the awful, irrational feeling he would stay broken like this forever. She now believed any tragedy was possible in those terrible woods, no matter how awful or senseless or unexplainable, and she was about to learn just how right she was.

"Where's Robin?" Jenny asked again. "Is she okay?"

Tears flooded Steven's vacant eyes. He said only two words, but that was all it took to change their lives forever.

"She's dead."

PART THREE

THE JOURNALS

CHAPTER TWENTY-TWO

He'd been reading for some time now.

Was it half an hour? More?

Traci wanted to stop Scott, but while the narrative made her uncomfortable, it also intrigued her. Steven had always been a good writer, but this was something else entirely. Here, he was writing as Robin, detailing the events of that night from her point of view. Though Traci had only known Robin Reeves for a single night, the memory of her had been burned into her mind, preventing the usual scar tissue the brain forms to protect itself. Traci remembered the girl all too well, and Steven's impersonation was both uncanny and unnerving. The words were so on point they even made Scott sound like Robin in a way, his inflections mixing with a breathiness that was unlike him. Steven had resurrected the girl through the magic of words. It was spooky.

When Scott reached one particular part in the "diary," Traci dropped her glass, and it cracked when it hit the floor.

"I told Traci to not be afraid," Scott read, "but she was so upset by the time we lost Steven, so lost in the dark. As we stood along the stream, I could see beneath the mask she wore. Not a Halloween mask, but an everyday mask, the kind people make to protect themselves. Behind it was a lost little girl, the kind who tries to hide somewhere familiar and safe, only to be taken advantage of by—"

"Stop it," Traci said suddenly.

Scott looked up from the journal. "I'm sorry, I—"

"How does he know?" she asked.

"Know what?"

"What Robin and I talked about by the stream. She told me…something that happened to her, back when she was a kid—a *lost little girl*. How would Steven know what Robin and I talked about when he wasn't even there?"

Mark shrugged, tilting his drink. "Guess she must've told him."

"No. I don't think so."

Scott flipped the page, searching. "Maybe he says in here…"

"This is morbid," Traci said. "This whole thing. Us being back home and Steven writing this and asking you to read it to us after he died. I mean, what the hell are we doing here?"

After twenty years of not crying out of frustration, it seemed the old habit had crept its way back. Traci sniffled. She needed another drink. Make it a double. As she went to the cabinet, she saw how low the bottle of vodka was getting. It made her nervous. The last thing she needed was alcohol withdrawal, those miserable aches that made it impossible for her to sleep.

She opened the cabinet to check on the other bottle of vodka Scott had mentioned earlier that night. Seeing there was a decent amount, she exhaled in relief and sipped her double.

"What now?" Corey asked.

Traci realized how tense he had grown. A single vein stood out in the center of his forehead. He looked fearful but anxious to hear more at the same time. They all did. Even Traci wanted to know more. She needed an explanation as to why Steven had written this curious eulogy.

Scott picked up the broken glass and tossed it into the wastebasket. He went to Traci, and when he put his hand on her shoulder, she was reminded of a simpler time long gone. She wasn't as enamored with him as she'd once been, even if Jennifer was embarrassingly obvious in her unabated desire, but Traci was impressed by him. He was much more soft-spoken and even-keeled than he'd been back in the day. The maturity suited him. They'd both done a great deal of growing up. If things had been different, maybe they could have—

"We can stop if you want," Scott said.

He sounded like a gentleman lover, taking things slow, ready to back off if the lady wasn't ready for things to escalate. She wondered if he was still tender beneath the sheets the way he had been when they were young. Traci had always preferred sex to be harder and faster, like being hit with a sledgehammer of lust, but now, rather abruptly, she thought of how nice it would be to have a sensual encounter, more erotic than ravenous. Would Kordell be able to give her that? Did there have to be love before there could be romantic sex, or could it be faked like an orgasm? It'd been so long since someone had kissed her and really meant it.

"Do you want me to stop?" Scott asked.

You don't have to do anything you don't want to. Never.

She looked to the others. All eyes had fallen on her.

"I think we all want to know," she said. "Even if it hurts."

JENNIFER HADN'T realized she'd pulled the blanket over her.

The journal was like an all-too-convincing ghost story, a true crime show crossed with a horror novel. And it contained details she'd forgotten, things she hadn't wanted to remember. It also divulged new information, even secrets, like the sexual assault story Robin had told Traci. Steven had written it, and Traci had confirmed it. What else would he whisper from beyond the grave?

Scott read on, the dead confessing for the dead.

"I'd never celebrated Halloween before," he said as Robin. "I always had to go to Hallelujah Camp. In my family, celebrating anything other than God was breaking the third commandment. We didn't even get to have fun on Sundays. No way I was going to have fun on Halloween! Mom said it was the Devil's holiday. Dad said it was Pagan and therefore sinful. It was forbidden. I think that's the main reason I went along with Steven that night. I wanted to see for myself.

"I saw so many new things with him. All the stuff my parents kept from me, I got from being with Steven. He was so cool and smart. I just wanted to learn from Steven instead of the Bible for a change. My love for my God will never waiver, but my parents enforced Him in ways that led me away from Him."

Here Scott paused.

Jennifer saw his face pale as he read the next line.

"I don't remember when I first saw the demons."

COREY STOOD up so fast he knocked over the lamp, sending unwanted shadows through an already tense room. The last time his body trembled like this was when he and Gretchen took their honeymoon in Tennessee, staying in a luxury cabin in the Great Smoky Mountains before driving out to Memphis and Nashville to see the sights. His new bride loved old country music and Elvis, so they had to visit the musically significant cities.

One night in Nashville, a terrible thunderstorm raged while they were in a motel room. The wind howled like a steam whistle, vibrating the windows and the roof. The power went out, taking away the TV news that had been tracking the twister as it drew closer. When the tornado finally ran down the highway just east of the motel, Corey and Gretchen went into the bathroom and jumped in the tub, listening to the twister rage. Judging by the wreckage they saw in the morning, the tornado had just barely missed demolishing the motel. In that bathtub, Corey had shaken like a puppy and been embarrassed to be so afraid in front of his new wife. That was the last time he'd trembled the way he was now, like a child being shoved by a bigger bully. He wondered if the others noticed. When he looked at them, they wore similar expressions of unease. Mark, in particular, had gone sour, his eyes wide.

"Demons?" Mark said.

Scott nodded. "That's what it says."

Corey thought of the scab-encrusted ghoul that had chased him on three burned legs. All these years he'd told himself it was a hallucination. It was the only way he could handle it.

"What else does she say?" Jennifer asked.

He noticed how she was referring to the writing as Robin's now. That couldn't be right though. Steven had written this long after Robin was gone. This was just therapeutic fiction.

"Demons are always with us," Scott read, "just like the angels. They walk among us. Sometimes they look like you'd imagine, with red, warty skin and curly horns. Sometimes they're more like trolls or gremlins. I know. I've seen them. But sometimes we don't recognize them for what they are, and that's when they're the most dangerous. That night, Steven told us demons were in those woods—that the woods were *made of* demons. We should've left then and there. But I guess I was the only one who believed him."

Scott looked up at the others, waiting for a reaction.

"I remember that," Jennifer said. "He talked about Halloween night and how it was the time demons could escape Hell."

Corey remembered too. He looked to Traci, reflecting on her outburst. He thought of the latex mask and how Robin had—

"You hated that," Mark said to Traci. "Hated all his Devil talk."

"I still do."

Scott asked, "Should I keep reading?"

"Yes," Corey said. "Please, continue."

Traci downed what was left of her drink in one gulp, and Mark got a cigarette before seeming to remember he had to smoke outside. Seeing his hands when he held the pack, Corey realized he wasn't the only one trembling.

Mark saw something that night too, Corey realized, for the first time. *I wasn't alone in that.*

"Suicide Woods," Scott read. "It is a place possessed. To kill yourself is a terrible sin. God won't let you into Heaven after that. And if you can't become an angel, what else could you turn into but a demon?"

JENNIFER'S SKIN crawled.

She hugged her knees to her chest as Scott read on, Robin/Steven describing all that had happened that night, including things that had happened in private, even reciting everything Scott and Jennifer had said when they'd been about to make love in the woods but were scared off. For the sake of good taste, Scott skipped over the details of their foreplay, but judging by his blush, the writing gave every detail.

Had Steven been spying on them? Had Robin?

It didn't seem possible, for when they'd run back to the camp, the two were sitting there with the others. If they'd gone off to peep, someone would have confessed to it by now. Corey would have tattled to Scott about it. Mark would have made a dirty joke.

But how else could they know?

"This is spot on," Scott said, his face grave. "This is everything we said."

"Exactly," Traci said. "Now you see what I mean."

Mark grumbled. "They must've had video recorders or something hidden in the bushes."

"That's a real stretch," Scott said. "Video cameras weren't cheap in those days. And even if they had them, how would they know the exact spot Jenny and I would pick out?"

Mark sighed, having no answer. At least he was trying. It was a better attempt at an explanation than Jennifer could come up with. Scott read on. The documentation was stunningly detailed. So many small things they'd all forgotten. The flash of remembrance flickered behind their eyes, retreading over things they'd worked hard to forget.

When Steven had emerged from Suicide Woods alone and told Jenny and Scott that Robin was dead, Jenny initially didn't believe him. She kept pleading with him to tell her it wasn't true. It had to be a misunderstanding. Maybe Robin just fell asleep and looked like she was dead. Maybe she was playing a Halloween prank. Judging by Steven's gray face and haunted eyes, she doubted he was behind any ruse. The horror he exhibited was the purest she'd ever seen. But it had to be a mistake. Robin couldn't be dead. She just couldn't.

"What happened?" Scott had asked Steven.

At first, Steven said nothing, and a terrible suspicion crept across Jenny's mind. Had Steven...*done something* to Robin? An accident? Had the girl done something to anger him, maybe resisting when he wanted to have sex? Had he struck her, not intending to kill her, but then she'd fallen and hit her head on a rock? Jenny couldn't imagine Steven being violent with a girl, or anyone weaker than him, for that matter. With other boys, he would finish a fight, but never start one. He detested violence.

"Steven?" Jenny asked, but she had no more words.

Finally, Steven broke his silence. "She killed herself."

Jenny had taken two steps back then, her hands covering her mouth. Even Scott's eyes had grown wet.

"No," Scott said, voice cracking. "No way, man. This can't be true. No fucking way."

"I wish I was wrong," Steven said.

"How? I mean…we were all together less than an hour ago!"

"When she and I went looking for Corey… I don't know what happened, but…she just *disappeared*. One second she was there and then the next…gone." He took a deep breath, trying to steady himself. "I've never felt so lost in all my life. I didn't know where I was anymore. There was only pitch-black woods. I called and called for her and…nothing. Even if I could figure out how to get back, I couldn't leave without her. She's just fifteen…"

"But you did find her," Jenny said in a hush.

He nodded, tears falling. "There's a big sycamore tree along the stream, not far from the trail back here, as it turns out. One big branch is suspended over the water. That's where I found her. You guys…she *hung herself*."

Jenny whimpered. "Hung herself?"

"God…I don't know how she got up there! It's *so high*. Must be fifty, sixty feet up. And I don't know where she was keeping the rope. Her backpack is still at the camp. She wasn't carrying anything when it happened."

Scott grabbed Steven by the lapel of his jacket. "She must not have done it! Jesus, Steven. Someone must have killed her!"

Jenny suddenly felt dizzy and sick.

"Someone was out there," Scott said. "We all heard things and saw things."

"I didn't," Steven said. "Besides…she was alive when I first found her."

Jenny gasped. "Oh my God."

"Robin was standing on top of the branch with the noose around her neck. She was looking right at me. She seemed so…*serene*. She wasn't scared or upset or anything, but she looked very pale. Not just her face, but her hands too. It was like I was looking at a ghost of her rather than the real thing."

His choice of words made Jenny quiver.

"Did she say anything?" Scott asked.

Steven looked up. "Yeah. She said 'Don't be afraid.' That was it. She told me not to be afraid and then she jumped." His lip trembled. "She hung herself *right in front of me!*"

Steven couldn't say any more. He was sobbing.

Jennifer snapped back to the present. She'd forgotten much of that night, but this part of it had no distortion. The memory showed no signs of fading. The basement room returned to her, and she looked to the others. They all had their heads down, listening to Scott in a mild state of dread.

Jennifer interrupted. "Does it say why she did it?"

There was a long beat where no one breathed.

"That's what we really want to know, isn't it?" she asked. "All these years, that's what has troubled us the most. *Why did she do it?*"

Scott bit his lip. He looked not just tired but older, as if the past few hours had been years. His hair seemed grayer, the lines on his forehead deeper.

"I don't know," he said. "I'll have to keep reading."

"C'mon, man," Mark said. "You must've read that part first, right? Right on the day you got it."

"No. That's not what Steven wanted."

"Yeah, well, with all respects to the dead, why're we obeying his rules with this thing? He'd dead, and it's just a book he wrote."

"No," Traci said, staring into space. "I think it's more than that."

Corey stood. "I think so too. I don't think this is the sort of thing we can just skim through."

Mark put up his hands in a gesture of quitting. "All right, then I'm just gonna say it. It's the same thing I said that night when you guys came in Scott's car and got Traci and me before we made it home. Whatever happened to that girl, Steven had something to do with it."

Scott shook his head. "Damn it, Mark. Not this again."

"Yes, *this again*! I mean, he must've, right? He was the last one with her. We all saw that tree; it was way too big for someone her size to climb. She never would've been strong enough to get up there on her own."

It was true. They'd all seen the sycamore.

DESPITE HOW they hadn't wanted to go back into the woods that night, they had to do it, and they had to do it together. So, Scott, Jenny, and Steven had gathered the others again, getting Corey out of his house by tapping rocks against his window. They picked up Traci and Mark down the street. There was just enough sunshine to make the woods less threatening, and Steven told them they wouldn't even have to leave the trail to see Robin. He hadn't been lying. It only took a few minutes for the group to reach the creek, and there was the small body of Robin Reeves, slack and creamy white, spinning gently on the autumn breeze.

Traci screamed. Scott went rigid and Mark threw up. The others wept. When they regained what little composure was possible, they discussed what to do about it.

"We have to call the police," Corey said.

"We'll be screwed!" Mark said. "They'll think *we* did it."

"No, they won't."

But Corey wasn't very convincing. It wasn't a certainty, just a desperate hope.

"We're in so much shit," Scott muttered.

Traci buried her face in her hands and fell to her knees. Mark didn't go to her. Instead, he went to Steven.

"What did you do?" he demanded.

Steven stared at him. "I told you. She did it to herself."

"That's impossible. Look at that fucking tree. Not a lot of knots or branches. How could she have gotten up there on her own?"

"I don't know! What, you think I carried her up there? Talk about impossible. I couldn't make it up there either, let alone while carrying someone else."

Traci moaned. "This can't be happening…"

"We're in so much shit!" Scott said again, pacing. "Everybody will find out we were here, that we were partying and doing drugs, that we brought a fifteen-year-old girl into the woods at night. Even if she committed suicide, everyone will look at us like we're guilty for as long as we live. We'll be pariahs. Our own parents will disown us! Christ, we'll be arrested! There goes college scholarships. There goes our whole futures!"

"He's one hundred percent right," Mark said. "We report it and we'll be treated like we committed some crime. We own up to this, we're fucked forever."

Jenny stared at the two boys. "But…what else can we do? We can't just…just…leave her here."

Mark glowered. "Why not?"

Silence. Shock.

"I'm sorry," he went on, "but she'd dead. Nothing's gonna change that. Us ruining our lives won't help anything."

Jenny watched Scott. He ran his hand through his hair, unable to look at her. So she turned to Corey. He was always ready to agree with her, but she couldn't even tell him what she wanted to do because she wasn't sure herself. She wanted her old life back, the simpler life she hadn't realized was so simple. School, her family, her hobbies, her dreams. The thought of losing it all hollowed her core.

"Look," Mark said, "Robin did what she did. She wanted her life to end. But she doesn't get to decide if our lives have to end too."

Jenny surprised herself by agreeing with him.

"If we were to leave her…she'd be found eventually, right? A girl turns up missing—they're gonna check Suicide Woods at some point, and probably sooner than later. This is where most of Redford's runaways turn up."

She thought of Robin's corpse turning black in the legs from gravity settling her blood. Horrible images scattered her thoughts—the body decomposing and attracting insects, her belly swelling with rot, her slack mouth becoming a breeding ground for flies to nest their maggots.

Traci looked up. "Can we really do this?"

"We gotta," Mark said. "Jenny's with me. Scott, it sounds like you are too."

Scott waited before nodding in resignation. Mark went to his girl-friend, comforting her now that it would get him something, and when Traci agreed, Jenny felt suddenly weightless.

This is really happening.

She looked to Corey again. This time he was staring right at her, his nose pink and wet from crying. She knew what his answer would be, what it always was. It didn't matter how he really felt. He took the opinions of others too seriously to have strong ones of his own.

"Okay," he said, and that was all.

That left only Steven. He hadn't said anything yet and it made the mood all the heavier. His brow was furrowed, struggling with a moral dilemma. She didn't realize it now, but at that moment, something had shifted inside the young man, shifted and snapped. She only came to understand that as time went on and Steven grew more distant—not just from the group, but from the world. The smart, charming young man who wrote her poems had just begun to sink into the cold swamp his soul would become.

"I'm going to the police," Steven said.

Some of them cried. Others groaned in frustration. Jenny closed her eyes, retreating to the darkness inside. Despite what she'd been pushing for, she knew Steven was right.

"We don't have to do this," Mark said.

"Suicide is technically a crime, you guys," Steven told them. "If we leave the body, we'll be accessories after the fact. We could go to prison for that. Not just jail—*prison.*"

Mark put his fists in his hair and pulled, kicking the dirt. "Damn it! Goddamn it!"

There were more whimpers and lamentations.

Jenny had to sit down.

"I wouldn't leave her out here, anyway," Steven said. "I'd never let her just hang there like that. It isn't right. Robin was a sweet girl. She matters."

No one argued that, but they didn't show any agreement either.

"Don't worry," Steven said. "You guys weren't there when it happened. No one needs to know you were out here with Robin and me. I'll go to the police myself and tell them the two of us came out here alone."

"You can't," Scott said. "Don't you see? You'll be ruined."

"You do that," Mark said, "and they'll pin this on you, man. They'll say you killed her."

Steven was stoic. "But I didn't. Robin killed herself. That's the truth and they'll see it's the truth."

Traci came to Steven. She wrapped her arms around him. "Are you sure you want to do this? Your reputation, your life… I mean, you'll be—"

"I know." He patted her back. "But better one of us than all of us. I brought Robin here tonight. I should be the one to see she makes it home."

They talked in circles, weighing the options again and again, but Steven never wavered. He'd made his decision. The group shared embraces and wiped away one another's tears.

"Mark and Traci," Steven said, "did anyone see you walking down the street? Any cars pass you or anything."

"No," Traci replied, Mark nodding. "You know we hadn't gotten very far."

"And all of you are sure you didn't tell anyone else you'd be in Suicide Woods last night?"

The group assured him they'd kept it secret.

"You all get home," Steven said. "And do your best to make sure no one sees you, especially your parents. We need them to think you were all tucked in your beds all night, or that you'd come back early from your sleepovers or whatever. The cops will find out Scott and I are friends, but I'll say I didn't stop by here because I wanted Robin and I to be alone."

"Dude," Scott said, "won't that make it worse for you? It'll sound like you were trying to have sex with her."

"That's fine. I'm seventeen, so it wouldn't be statutory rape. We're both minors. And they have ways to check if she was raped. They'll see she wasn't. And she and I have never had sex together, either. I'm pretty sure she was a virgin."

Jenny had been holding back this question all night. "Steven…what exactly is your relationship with Robin?"

All eyes fell on him. She hadn't been the only one to wonder.

Steven didn't even blink. "She was my friend."

No one pressed the matter.

"Time's wasting. I know folks sleep in on the weekend, but they'll be up soon enough. Get on to your homes. Scott, give Traci and Mark a quick lift, and then come right back home and go to your room. Corey, you too. Jenny, you're parked down the street, right?"

She was, to avoid Scott's parents knowing she was there.

"Okay," Steven said. "Go home. Now."

"What about you?"

"I'll gather the rest of the stuff at the campsite and get rid of it. There's not much left, so maybe I can bury it. Then I'll walk a few blocks down to the Jiffy Mart. Hopefully people will see me walking alone and remember that. I'll use the payphone to call 911."

"Steven, I—"

"Just go, Jenny."

As the group got moving, Scott turned to Steven one last time.

"We owe you, man. We owe you big time and we won't ever forget that."

BACK IN the present, this memory made Jennifer sigh. Now that they'd all gathered back here for the first time since that night, she realized just how right Scott had been. No matter how many other things they may have forgotten, no one here would ever forget Steven's sacrifice. If it were any of the others who had died, they wouldn't have all come together like this. Maybe one or two, if they had the time and the means to make it, but that would be it. A card to the family, perhaps. An old photo shared on social media. But not this full gathering of the survivors of that horrible Halloween. Only Steven could have brought them all together again. They owed him that. They owed him everything.

But here was Mark, all these years later, accusing Steven anyway.

"Mark," Jennifer said, "the police looked into Steven. They interrogated the hell out of him several times. Remember?"

Corey agreed. "Yeah. They found no evidence he had anything to do with it. He had no scratches on him, and Robin had no bruises. No signs of a fight between them, no struggle. They ruled it a suicide. And we all knew Steven. He had no history of violence. He never could've done something like that, a good guy like him."

"He was," Scott said. "He was the best of us."

Jennifer got off the bed and refilled her drink. She walked to Scott and leaned into the wall beside him, looking down at the journal in his hands.

"Steven took the time to write all of this down," she said. "We can take the time to read it."

CHAPTER TWENTY-THREE

"What do you think?" Scott asked Jennifer.

The group had taken a break in order to collect themselves. Corey had gone to the kitchen for a soda, but Scott could tell he really just wanted to be alone. Mark followed Traci outside for a cigarette or two, just as Scott figured he would. He finally had some private time with Jennifer.

"What do you mean?" she asked.

"About the diary."

"I think it's bizarre, but I can understand why he wrote it."

"You think so?"

"Well, don't you? Like we were saying, it was therapeutic. I think we can all relate to that. I know I can." She took another drink. Her eyes were getting bleary again. "We all need to, sort of, *get things out.* Free ourselves from the things that haunt us. We all have basic needs and, more often than not, we have to satisfy them ourselves."

He looked into her soft, dark eyes. So lovely, so desperate for something she'd been lacking for far too long.

Jennifer Parks. Single again at forty-three-years old.

Scott could tell she'd gotten her hair done for this. She'd worn perfume, jewelry, a new-looking dress. Even heels. More than any of the others, this visit was an escape for her. She'd had no idea what she was in for. Scott figured it had to be disappointing for Jennifer, at least so far. Maybe he could change that. Maybe he owed her that much.

He brushed a strand of hair away from her face, looking down at her with a small smile. She smiled back, and when he leaned in to kiss her, she closed her eyes and puckered. Their lips met and she opened her mouth for him, letting him back into her a quarter century after their last touch. Her palms moved up his chest and Scott put his hands on her hips, and in that gentle embrace there was a sense of hope, of there always being a chance to make things right.

The sound of footsteps above made them pull away from each other, but the desire to draw even closer was a frenetic energy, crackling between them like an electric shock, an alluring tension. He'd kissed her for her benefit but had enjoyed it more than he'd expected.

Jennifer was blushing now. Pink was a good color on her.

"I need to show you something," he said. "Just you."

A LETTER in Steven's handwriting.

Again, Jennifer was reminded of his poetry and the notes he would pass to her in class. Did kids write notes to each other anymore, or was it all emails and texts? She hoped some of them embraced the magic of actual, handwritten notes, the poetry of passionate youths that would never be so passionate again. She tried to remember the last time she'd gotten a handwritten letter of any kind, in the mail or otherwise. Even when she and her husband Roger had first fallen in love, he'd never been the creative type, and as time went on, he expressed himself less and less. His sweet words came in the form of Hallmark cards, someone else saying it for him. Flowers were for birthdays, not *just because*. It got so Jennifer was lucky if her husband even said "I love you" on a call before he hung up.

Had Steven ever married? Did he have children? Was he survived by anyone other than this group of friends he'd sacrificed himself to protect? Thinking of it now, as an adult, she was surprised by how grown-up Steven had acted back then. What teenage boy was that levelheaded in a time of crisis, especially one that would break most adults? What teenager deeply understood the nobility of truth and the importance of keeping those you care about safe, no matter what it costs you? Only someone like Steven Winters. Jennifer didn't think of herself as a shallow or selfish person, but as a teen, she'd been far less virtuous. Her own interests had always come first. She supposed most people were focused on their own game at that age. But Steven had been focused on what was right.

She looked at the letter as Scott unfolded it. They were standing very close now.

Had she really just kissed him?

She wanted to blame the wine and the weed, but she couldn't fool herself. She'd wanted to kiss him even before she saw him in person. His crushing handsomeness and gentle demeanor pulled her in like a riptide, spinning her into helpless desire. His eyes were so blue they were dangerous. She was wooed by feelings of credence and the fondness he instilled in her without even trying.

So she'd kissed him. So what? Actually, she'd just allowed herself to be kissed. Scott had initiated it. That made her feel good—to be wanted and appreciated. After Alex was born, her body had changed for the second time, and Roger grew less interested in making love, at least with his wife. How often had she found porn sites on the computer's search history? It wouldn't have bothered her so much if they'd still been having sex, but the fact that her husband preferred to pleasure himself rather than have sex with her had stomped on her confidence. She'd tried lingerie, knee-high socks, high heels, vinyl. She'd tried to be the seducer, but rarely did it have the desired effect on the man who'd vowed to cherish her always. At times, Jennifer just felt so old and spent, yesterday's pretty girl next door having aged out. It made her feel so undesirable, not just to Roger, but to any man. Scott proving her wrong tonight only further endeared her to him.

She was staring up at him, and he grinned boyishly and guided her eyes back to the paper.

"This isn't part of the Robin diary," Scott said. "This is a note straight from Steven, writing as himself. I think you should read it."

She did.

CHAPTER TWENTY-FOUR

They come to me at night. Those voices like distant dreams. They tell me their stories and I write them down, a secretary taking dictation. I am but a utensil, a pen and publisher in one. It's their show, as it should be. They're the ones with the stories to tell.

Sometimes I wonder if I've ever written anything of my own, or if every single word of poetry and fiction I've accumulated over a lifetime was channeled into me by forces I simply could not detect at the time, let alone understand. People always ask us writers where our ideas come from. Perhaps now I have an answer.

The notebooks fill one by one, each voice taking their turn. That's why I bought this house on the edge of the woods. I want to be a better listener. For too long I attributed the voices to something neurological, my imagination running away with itself, or maybe my cognition starting to slip as I became more of an isolationist. We all talk to ourselves sometimes, don't we? But whenever I check for accuracy, the voices are always proven right. Who would know their history better? They tell me no lies or exaggerations, not even to make themselves seem more interesting or important. They already know they matter and that their truths must be revealed.

I speak for those forever muted.

I am the biographer.

CHAPTER TWENTY-FIVE

S omething about the note made Jennifer cold, and she went to the bed and tossed the blanket over her shoulders. "What does he mean?"

Scott shrugged. "I think it means just what he wrote."

"What? That he heard voices?"

Scott folded the paper and slipped it back into the envelope. "I think he believed it."

"Believed what?"

"The diary he wrote as Robin—I think Steven believed he was channeling her. That she wrote the book through him."

Jennifer drew the blanket tighter. "So...he was crazy?"

"Maybe schizophrenic. Something like that. He was different even back in the day, and as an adult, he turned into a hermit who wrote about hearing voices—"

"It could just be poetry, or a piece of an unfinished novel or something."

He came closer. "C'mon, Jenny. You've heard all I've read from that diary. Why would he really write something like that? I think he was imagining voices near the end of his life, and I think one of them was Robin Reeves."

Jennifer took that in. It was a somber thought, but what did it change?

"So, then," she said, "we're honoring the wishes of a mentally ill man. He was still our friend."

"Of course he was. I'm not saying otherwise. If he had gone mad, that doesn't change how we all feel about him. I just wanted to show you this because, well...I guess I just didn't want to be the only one with this information. Look here." He went to a box on the floor and took the lid off. He reached in and held up a black journal and two spiral notebooks. "There's more of them. Diary after diary. And they're not just about Robin."

He held one out to her. On the cover, Steven had written a title: *The Diary of Johnny Clayton.*

Jennifer's breath stopped in her lungs. Scott handed her another.

The Diary of Holly Reese.

There were more, dozens of them.

"Oh my God," she whispered.

"They're all like that, Jenny. Steven wrote one for every kid who killed themselves in Suicide Woods."

"YOU REALLY think Steven had something to do with it?" Traci asked.

Mark took a long drag off his cigarette, hot-boxing it, his nerves pinched and raw. It seemed no amount of intoxicants could get him back to normal. Now, all he wanted was to get some sleep. They could worry about Steven Goddamned Winters and his freaky book in the morning.

"I don't know what I think," he admitted.

Traci sipped her vodka. How many had she had tonight? How was the woman still standing and not on all fours with her head in the toilet?

"You know," she said, "there was a time, after things had settled, that I started to think about who else might've killed that poor girl. I never told anyone about it, but I jotted down different ideas. I started reading true crime books and stuff like that, like I could create a profile of the murderer."

"And?"

"At first, I entertained the idea of some drifter. Homeless people do set up camps in the woods. Maybe there was a serial killer passing through town, something like that. But then I looked at the immediate suspects."

"And who were they?"

She faced Mark. "Us."

"*Us?*"

"All six of us who were with her the night she died."

He puffed again. "That wouldn't make sense. We were all together when Steven and Robin went off alone."

"No, we weren't."

Mark gave her a puzzled look. Then his eyes went wide. "Wait…you mean Corey?"

She nodded. "He was still out there, in those woods."

"Shit…that's right…"

"We just never really considered it, did we? Because Corey was such a…"

"A nerd. A wimp."

"For lack of better words."

"Hold up. Steven said he saw Robin kill herself with his own eyes."

"What if he was wrong?"

Mark blinked. "How could he be? He *saw* it."

"Maybe he just thought that's what he saw. It was dark. We'd been drinking and smoking pot. And remember what Steven did when you were handing out acid? He put it in his pocket. Maybe he took it later that night and just never mentioned it. Or maybe he accidently touched the paper and the acid absorbed into his skin."

"You're saying he hallucinated the whole thing? We saw her up there too."

"She was already dead by then. I'm saying, maybe it looked to Steven like Robin had jumped off the tree and hung herself, but what if she wasn't alone up there? Maybe someone was in the shadows, someone who put that noose around her neck and pushed her."

Mark lit another cigarette with the butt of the last one. "If Steven saw it, and the rest of us were together…"

"That leaves Corey Pickett," Traci said. "He's the only one we can't account for the whereabouts of. And he's the only one who came out of the bushes *wearing a mask*."

There was movement in the house, and they turned and looked through the sliding glass door. Corey was going back to the basement steps. They watched him from the back porch like hounds tailing a rabbit.

"No way," Mark said. But maybe there was a way. "You really think…"

"Like you said, I don't know what I think. Corey came off like even less of a killer than Steven, and he still does. But don't they always say it's the quiet ones you've got to watch? Corey was a nerd, right? He was eighteen and I can just about guarantee you he hadn't so much as kissed a girl. That kind of sexual frustration really eats at a person. Especially a guy. What if the quiet nerd snapped that night and took it out on a girl who couldn't defend herself the way older ones like me and Jennifer could?"

Mark shook his head at the ground. "That is some story. And you never told anybody this?"

"Not until just now."

"Man, oh man. I don't know why I never thought of that. Is this why you became a lawyer?"

She furrowed her brow. "Oh…oh, yes. Yeah, that's right."

Traci seemed flustered. He hoped he hadn't offended her. Mark thought a thousand lawyers at the bottom of the ocean was what you called a good start, but he didn't think that had come through in his tone.

"I think we should go back in," she said. "Who knows what the others might say behind our backs."

AS COREY came into the room, Scott was securing a lid onto a cardboard box. Jennifer stood over him, using a blanket like a cloak. She looked as if she'd just woken up to a loud noise in the middle of the night.

"Sorry," Corey said. "Did I startle you?"

She seemed to come back from a dream. "No, no. Come on in."

Corey put his soda on the end table and drew back, as if to make himself smaller, then wondered why he'd had such an urge. While upstairs, he'd checked his phone. Not for missed messages, but to Google a few things and check the time. Inside Scott's basement was like a Vegas casino—no clocks, no windows. Somehow, Corey had never noticed this before. He didn't like it.

"It's getting late," he said.

Scott got to his feet. "You're not leaving, are you?"

Corey was the only one sober enough to do so. But he had enough trouble driving at night even without being sleepy. His eyes weren't as good as they used to be, especially in the dark, and the thought of making the long haul back to home with no one to keep him awake made him uneasy.

"No," he said, "just commenting."

Scott exhaled with relief. It seemed odd to Corey. Why did all of this stuff with Steven and the diary seem to matter so much more to Scott than the rest of them? Was it because Steven had assigned the task to him directly in his last will and testament? Corey felt like they were all being pulled into a black hole here. Time was being distorted. The past had become the present. Would *that night* in 1995 never end?

When Traci and Mark came down the steps, she wouldn't look at Corey, but Mark glared at him with eyes like skinning tools. Corey almost asked what his problem was, but Scott spoke up, drawing everyone's attention.

"There's just a few more pages to go," he said. "I thought we could finish, if you're all up to it."

"Yes," Jennifer said. "Maybe now we'll know what really happened to her. Or, at least, what Steven thought happened to her."

Traci took a seat and Mark joined her. Corey noticed they seemed closer now. All this talk of the old days must have rekindled something, even if it was just a tiny flame. Good. Let Mark focus on the one who got away instead of on him. The more the guy drank, the less Corey trusted him. He put his butt into the beanbag chair and let it swallow him. It was time to finish this.

Scott returned to the Robin journal and read. "Steven wanted to look for Corey. The others said they should stick together and find help for him once they got out of the woods, but Steven wouldn't hear of it. He is a great friend and cares about everyone so much."

Corey felt all eyes fall on him, reflecting their guilt. They'd voted to leave him out there. No one had ever told him that, but it made perfect sense.

Scott turned pink in the face, obviously embarrassed. He read on. "But we never found Corey. And then, I got lost. The woods just opened up on me again, and they wrapped around me with their roots and branches and tree limbs and carried me into the darkness like I was on a magic carpet of leaves. The roots became like people. I could almost recognize them behind the wooden knots of their faces. And this time, I was *afraid*. I thought I'd taught myself not to be scared. I told other people not to be. The woods had taken me many places that night, but still I'd felt free as I disappeared and reappeared like a time traveler. But this time I knew I was a prisoner. The woods had me."

Scott's brow furrowed at what he was about to read next.

"They had come for me, you see? Was it branches wrapped around my wrists and ankles, or was it the boney claws of demons? I heard their tongues clicking at my ears. I felt their fingertips upon my face and smelled their sour breath. I screamed, but there was no sound. When I looked for Steven, at first I couldn't see him, but then there was a pale dot moving far below me, calling my name. I was so high up. He seemed a thousand miles away, and I'd never wanted to be with him more. But *they* had me now. So I waved, just in case this was goodbye.

"People say the beasts come out at night. But it's not the night; it's the darkness. Whether the darkness of the woods or the darkness of a movie theater—it's all one. In darkness, the evil things know they won't be seen. In the shadows, they can do whatever they want to a little girl. I knew this about them even before the head demon spoke."

Traci made a small whimper. Mark had gone chalk white. Corey wanted to console everyone somehow, but knew it was impossible. How could he calm them when he was just as disturbed?

"Should I keep going?" Scott asked the tense crowd.

Jennifer's voice was almost a whisper. "Just finish."

Scott became Robin once again. "They were gathered around me, and the leader had a rope. One of the others had some kind of bowl with sweet-smelling smoke coming out of it. They were male and female, all different shapes and sizes. One of them was a dwarf. They spoke in tongues; all except the leader. His voice was so loud and clear, like he was talking from inside my brain. And maybe he had gotten in there, because all he told me was the same thing I'd been telling myself over and over again. 'Don't be afraid, Robin. Don't be afraid.' And the crazy part is, I wasn't." Scott's voice waivered. "And then they told me this would save Steven and the others. They said I was worthy and special."

Scott trembled as he read the final words. "That's when they killed me."

CHAPTER TWENTY-SIX

"**G**uys," Corey said, "I have something to tell you."

Scott handed Traci the box of tissues she desperately needed. Tears smudged her makeup. She wasn't the only one sniffing. The last page of the diary was simply devastating. It made her ache inside. She looked to Corey, not knowing what to expect.

"That night," he said. "I saw some things—some really, *really* scary things."

Beside Traci, Mark went rigid. She thought of what he'd told her once they'd left the others the morning after that Halloween, when they'd been walking home as the sun came up. When she'd pressed him, he'd spoken of a creature that had chased him through the forest, but Mark had taken so much acid that she hadn't believed it was anything more than a hallucination. Now, she thought differently.

"What did you see, Corey?" Jennifer asked.

He twiddled his fingers. Mark leaned in, staring at Corey. Though she wasn't sure why, Traci took Mark's hand, and he interlinked their fingers. She noticed how Scott was inching closer to Jennifer. When he looked up at Traci, she looked away.

Corey steadied himself. "The demons Robin was talking about—or, I mean Steven was talking about...I think I saw them too."

"You *what*?" Traci said.

"When I was lost in the woods alone, there was a group of people walking around out there. At least, they looked like people. It was so dark. All I saw were shadows, really. But one of them was much smaller than the others. And another one was carrying this brass burner thing. I could smell the smoke."

"Jesus," Jennifer said, indignant. "You mean we weren't alone out there and you knew it? Why didn't you tell us this before?"

Scott placed his hand on her shoulder. "Easy, Jenny. I'm sure he'll explain."

There was a new glint to his eyes that made Traci curious. Scott seemed nervous after the reading and even more nervous as Corey confessed. Was he starting to believe the same way Traci was?

"Look," Corey began, "I didn't say anything because I didn't think you guys would believe me. I thought you'd make fun of me, that you'd say I was a scaredy cat and a wuss, that I was being an imaginative child. Besides, once I was out of the woods, I didn't know if I really believed it myself. I was stoned for the first time, and I've never been able to see that well in the dark."

"Well," Scott said, "there you go. It must've been nothing, just your eyes playing tricks on you."

"But I could smell the smoke. And I heard them talking."

Traci asked, "What were they saying?"

"I don't know, but they definitely weren't other teenagers. The description in that book—"

"C'mon," Scott said. "You don't mean to say there really were demons out there, do you?"

"Well, maybe not exactly but…I also saw something else that night. It was even more frightening, and I got a much better look at it."

He told them of a demon, red and horned and three-legged, with screaming baby mouths on its palms. Traci's skin went to goose flesh. Corey was so earnest and clearly upset, she found herself believing him and said a quiet prayer under her breath. She rarely prayed these days. God hadn't helped her maintain her relationships or keep a good job. Hadn't helped her bad dreams. He hadn't even helped her with what she prayed for assistance with the most—the bottle. If Traci living a happy life wasn't in His divine plan, what was the point of praying anyway? But she still believed in God, and still believed in the Devil, too. Just hearing Corey's story made her feel the beast's presence.

Scott crouched beside Corey. "You really saw it?"

"I swear to you, man—to all of you. I've lived with this horror in the back of my mind most of my life. For years after it happened, I had the most vivid nightmares. So, I tried to keep myself from falling asleep. I guzzled coffee and ate stay awake pills. But you have to sleep eventually, and when I did, the demon would always be there, as if he'd been waiting for me. Then it would chase me all over again, just like it did that night."

Jennifer leaned in. "Maybe it was only a dream to begin with. Maybe you fell asleep in the woods and—"

"No," Corey said, more firmly than Traci would have imagined him capable of. "I know what I saw. It wasn't a dream or a figment of my imagination. This was real." Corey got out of the beanbag and went to Mark. "You know I'm right. You saw it too, didn't you?"

Traci turned to her old boyfriend. "Mark?"

He looked at her, his face like a corpse's. He said nothing.

"I can tell," Corey said. "I saw it on you earlier tonight, that look of holding something back, that look of barely contained terror. Tell me I'm wrong."

Mark stared into his drink. "Shut up, man."

"Tell us what you saw. Tell us what you know."

All eyes fell upon Mark. He suddenly shot out of his seat, booze spilling from his glass. He pointed at Corey, close to his face. "Shut up, I said!"

Traci grabbed his wrist. "Mark, don't."

She remembered this anger. Apparently, it hadn't faded with time.

Corey didn't budge. "I'm not afraid of you anymore, Mark."

"Yeah, well you should be! I can still use your ass as a footstool."

Scott got between the two men. The three of them started talking over one another, and Scott pulled Mark away from Corey, protecting him, same as always. Corey never would have hung out with the rest of them if it hadn't been for Scott vouching for him, even pushing for him to tag along. It had annoyed Traci back then. Now she found it endearing.

"I don't know what happened," Mark said to the others. "Why don't you all ask Corey, huh? He's the one who saw all these people in the woods but never told anybody! What if they killed Robin, huh? What if he was the only witness and he didn't do shit about it?"

Corey's face soured.

Mark went on. "What were you doing all that time you were alone in those woods, huh? And why the fuck were you wearing a demon mask?"

Now all eyes fell on Corey. His chest deflated, and he went back into a slouch.

"Everyone take it easy," Scott said. "We all saw and did weird things that night. We were just kids. We didn't know how to handle any of it."

"I'd still like to hear his answer," Traci said. "Why were you wearing a devil mask, Corey? You were alone in the woods. What was the reason you had that on? Were you trying to scare someone?"

"No."

Jennifer stepped forward, looking like a spooked child with the blanket drawn over her. "Were you trying to make us believe there really were demons in the woods, like, going along with Steven's story?"

"Exactly," Mark huffed. "If there was a demon out there that night, it was *him*."

"That's not true!" Corey said.

An epiphany came to Traci then. Her eyes went wide. "You're the one Mark saw...it was you all along."

"What?"

"The demon he saw in the woods that night."

Mark spun. "Traci!"

"Mark, please. We have to get it all out there."

"I knew it," Corey said. "You *did* see something."

Mark flushed—from anger or embarrassment, Traci wasn't sure which. Before he could rage at Corey again, Traci did it for him. "You put on that mask 'cause you knew Mark was tripping on acid. You thought you could freak him out with it, maybe get a little payback for all the times he picked on you."

"I did not!"

"And it worked, didn't it? Mark told me he'd seen a demon in the woods. He was just high enough to think you were one, wasn't he?"

Corey's brow furrowed. Had she busted him or was he just confounded by all she'd put together? She felt like a detective interrogating a crook in a movie, a tough prosecutor attacking the witness stand.

"None of this is true," Corey said.

Mark surprised them all with what he said next. "He's right. There's no way it was him I saw. The thing I was saw was far too short to be Corey in disguise. And I couldn't even see the face, only the body—a *female* body."

Scott stepped in. "What *did* you see? What did it look like?"

Mark gave him a quizzical look, and Scott stepped back.

"It was a midget," Mark said. "A naked midget."

"A *midget*? What the—"

"Or a dwarf. Little person. Whatever the best term is."

"Just tell us what they looked like," Corey said.

Mark frowned. "I just did, dude. It was a naked lady midget. Couldn't see the face. And she had no toenails or fingernails. Like some kinda mutant."

Corey ran his hand over his head. "Oh, man. The small one I saw with that group walking in the woods. I'd thought it was a child, but maybe it was that same little person."

Scott shook his head with a smile. "Guys, please. I think we're getting carried away here. I mean, what're we saying? That there were some sort of evil little people in the woods that night? Like this is some backwards horror version of *Snow White and The Seven Dwarves*? Like *Ghoulies* or something? Let's be real."

"I only saw one dwarf," Mark said. "Coulda been real."

"You were—"

"All of you need to stop saying I was just high! I know the difference between real and imagined. This was *real*."

Corey nodded. "And I know the difference too."

Traci watched Scott. It was admirable that he still tried to bring sense to all of this. He'd always been that way, always searching for the logical explanation. But was he trying to calm the others or himself? Or was he just trying to take control of the situation, him being a man and this being his house. He'd started all of this; perhaps now he aimed to finish it. But he would need more than doubt when he had a room filling up with believers.

Traci looked to Corey and Mark. "I like to think I can spot a liar, and you two aren't lying. Something was out there with us that night, and I don't think it was human."

Scott appeared ready to object again. She expected him to say he believed they believed what they'd seen, but belief did not constitute reality. But he was sensible enough not to argue this any further, at least not right now.

She wondered what Jennifer was thinking. It was just as hard to tell as it had ever been. Reading men was like flipping through a pamphlet—simple and easy to understand. But reading a woman was like picking up a copy of *War and Peace* that had half its pages glued together.

"So what now?" Traci asked. "Where does this leave us?"

SCOTT DIDN'T think they could handle any more tonight, so he didn't press them. He was finally getting some answers, but if he pushed the others too hard too fast, they would shatter like fine China. Then they would just turn on each other all the more. Scott couldn't have that. There was still more to do. That's why he'd questioned their beliefs and suspicions. Solid answers weren't the solution. Not yet.

"Maybe we should call it a night," he said.

Traci shook her head. "Now that we've made some headway? No. We're close to figuring out something that has haunted us for decades."

"I know how long it's been. We can wait a little longer. We're all tired and have had too much to drink."

"I'm not tired, and I can't wait any longer to know what really happened to Robin Reeves."

The room fell silent.

Corey broke it. "I have a question. It's for all of you."

They watched him, waiting. Scott tensed, guessing what might come next, and when Corey spoke, he was proven right. A dull pain entered his temples.

"We've been talking all night about what happened to Robin," Corey said, "but does anyone know what happened to Steven?"

WHEN SCOTT first told Jennifer of Steven Winters' passing, she'd immediately thought of cancer. Maybe it was because the disease had taken so many of her friends and relatives. She just assumed if Steven died in his early forties something fatal must have come upon him rather quickly. But when she'd asked Scott, he'd told her he wasn't exactly sure, that things concerning Steven had been "murky." Before she could ask more questions, Corey Pickett had arrived, then the others, and this strange night had begun.

"When I went to the bathroom, I checked on my phone," Corey said. "I was looking for any kind of obituary on Steven, but couldn't find anything."

"I did that yesterday," Traci said. "I didn't find anything, either."

"Scott," Corey said, "how did you find out he was dead?"

Scott shrugged. "His attorney came to the house. Brought all the paperwork."

"Did he bring a death certificate?"

"Yeah. He showed it to me."

"Do you have it?"

"No. The lawyer kept it. I figured it goes to whatever family Steven has left."

"What did the certificate say was the cause of death?"

Scott shifted in his seat. "It said it was undetermined."

A rush of sorrow went through Jennifer. She could see that same rush as it went across Scott's eyes. Thinking of Steven dying alone was bad enough. Now it seemed his death was merely shrugged off by officials, just another weirdo hermit found dead. She wondered how long his body had been alone in the house. Had he decomposed to the point where his cause of death was impossible to decipher?

"Scott," she said, "do you know if there's going to be a funeral?"

"Far as I know, this is the only memorial service he's going to get—the five of us, right here. I think he knew that. I think he wanted it that way. Steven wasn't the same guy after what happened to Robin. You all remember how much he changed. It warped him somehow. I mean, just look at the diary he wrote for her. He'd cracked, you guys. He didn't have anyone in his life anymore, so he became obsessed with the people from his past, particularly Robin. Maybe he didn't want us to just honor his memory. Maybe he thought it was time we honored hers too."

Jennifer reached for his hand. He was more thoughtful than ever. Here they'd all been focused on the darkness of that night, the sense of evil they attributed to it. The trauma it left them with made it easy to feel like victims. But the real victim was the young girl who'd had the life snatched from her heart. When it'd happened, they'd been too focused on their fears to mourn her. As adults, they were all too eager to forget it happened at all. Scott made a valid point. It was time to mourn Robin Reeves, the girl they'd left hanging from a tree.

"There's no way we can know," Traci said. "So now Steven's death is a mystery too."

A chill crept through the room like a gathering shadow. Jennifer saw its darkness cast upon everyone's faces. Everything within her rose into her chest, like the moment of weightlessness just before a fall.

"Maybe Scott's right," she said. "Maybe we need to sleep on it. Things will make more sense in the morning."

THE HOUSE had three bedrooms on the main floor. Scott had long ago explained to Jennifer that when the twins had grown older, they'd needed their own rooms, so he had volunteered to move into the basement. Now he slept in the master bedroom, and his siblings' old rooms served as a guest room and an office easily turned into a bedroom with the addition of an air mattress. Including the basement bed and the couch, there were enough places for everyone to sleep.

"I'll take the couch," Scott offered. "I wouldn't want any of you to be uncomfortable."

"Don't be silly," Corey said. "You're a gracious host, but we're not going to keep you from your own bed. I'll take the couch." He chuckled. "I should be used to it anyway, the way my wife likes to boot me out of the bedroom when she's had enough of my nonsense."

"Then I'll take the air mattress," Scott said.

"No, no," Traci said. "I'll take it. I've slept on plenty of them over the years. It's no big deal."

Mark took the opportunity to show some chivalry, insisting he'd take it so the ladies could sleep in real beds. Traci said it didn't matter to her where she slept as long as she could stay out of the basement, so Jennifer volunteered. It would be sort of nice to sleep in the same old bed she and Scott had snuggled up in whenever his parents were away. Of all the rooms in the house, the basement was where she felt the most comfortable.

"I set up blankets and pillows in all the rooms," Scott said. "You guys know where the bathroom is. Help yourself to whatever's in the kitchen."

The group began to disperse.

"I know it's been a great deal to absorb," he said. "We've dug up a lot of things tonight, and there's still more to talk about. But I think we'll all feel a lot better after we get some rest."

Scott carried Jennifer's bag down to the basement as the others prepared for bed. Now that they were alone again, she wanted to ask him more about the additional journals, the ones Steven wrote for the other suicide victims.

Victims, she thought. *Is that the right word to use?*

But she knew Scott was exhausted. She was too. They were the ones to recommend everyone go to sleep. But now that it was just the two of them, Jennifer wondered if they'd really just wanted the others to go away. They were alone again, and the privacy suggested intimacy. Despite everything that had happened tonight, she hadn't forgotten what brought her back to Redford in the first place.

"Got everything you need?" he asked.

"Um, yeah. I think so."

"Okay."

He paused, and their eyes locked. Jennifer wondered if one of them would bring up the kiss, either by talking about it or doing it again. She certainly had the urge. Though she didn't think there was anything wrong with a woman making the first move, she was used to the man doing it, and preferred it that way. She liked to only cue a man to her interest, using her body language to tell him what she was ready for—a sway of the hips, a step closer, a bat of the eyes, a parting of the lips, or holding a stare the way she was with Scott right now. She always wanted to be the taken, not the taker.

"Well then," Scott said with a smile. "Good night, Jenny."

Not even a peck on the cheek.

"Good night, Scott."

As he went up the stairs, she wondered if she'd done something wrong. Had she been married so long she didn't know how to flirt anymore? Had she turned him off somehow when they'd kissed? Was she too awkward about it?

The door closed behind him. Jennifer unzipped her dress and told herself she was being silly. Scott hadn't made a move on her because he was a gentleman. He didn't want her to think he'd only asked her out here to have a quick fling with an old flame. Besides, there were other people in the house. Things weren't exactly private.

It was a relief to remove the bra and Spankx, and she'd forgotten how comfortable a satin slip could be. It was plain white, nothing special, but it did match her panties, which was more than she could say for her usual rushed paring of undergarments. Still, it was somewhat provocative, the panties being thong so not to show lines beneath the dress. She hadn't planned to seduce Scott with lingerie, but in the event he did get to see her in her undergarments, she wanted to look nice. It was a cool night, but she preferred a cold room to sleep in, so she slept in just this combo and pulled the blanket up to her waistline, tucking out her feet.

As she lay there, thoughts of Scott were replaced by repeats of all the night's conversations. She thought about the readings and the books, curiosity eating at her mind, keeping her awake.

She took the blanket off and clicked on the light.

The box was right there on the floor.

No, she told herself. *It's not yours to pry into.*

But after all she'd been through, didn't she deserve to learn all there was to know? Maybe these journals really were nothing more than the ramblings of an insane man, but what if there was something more to them than that? Jennifer Parks considered herself a woman of science. She'd never studied it beyond college, but she lived by it. She listened to the experts and didn't fall for health industry scams or the ludicrous declarations of anti-vaccination moms. She didn't have to "believe" in evolution, because it was cold, hard fact. She didn't even have a religion. These days it seemed less and less people in this country did. Therefore, could she really entertain the concept of demons, ghosts, and goblins? They were not the stuff of science; they were the stuff of cheap horror movies—the sort of rubber-monster mayhem Scott had dragged her to see once upon a time. Such creatures had no basis in reality.

So then why did all of this scare her so much?

Why did she want to believe the others when they said something supernatural had occurred? Why did she have the absurd feeling Steven really had communicated with Robin somehow, that she could talk from beyond the grave? Jennifer hadn't seen what some of the others had that night, but she'd felt the same creeping dread out there in the woods. She'd felt a *presence*, same as anyone, and had been equally afraid of it. Science couldn't explain everything. Some things remained unknown. Was it so hard to believe something beyond the realm of known science existed in Suicide Woods? Something...*evil?*

Jennifer took a deep breath.

She opened the box.

CHAPTER TWENTY-SEVEN

The twin mattress was comfortable, and the guest bedroom offered plenty of space for her things. Still, Traci was anxious, almost claustrophobic, but it was better than staying in the basement. Maybe it was just a fear of being underground, a mild phobia she'd always had. It would be so easy to get trapped if a storm knocked down the house or something. But Scott's basement, in particular, made her anxious. It wasn't just a mental reaction, either. It made her every nerve pinch and angry butterflies riot in her stomach. She was a heavy drinker, but needed extra to stay down there as long as she had, even with the others there with her.

She couldn't remember if she'd felt that way about the basement room back when she was young. She'd certainly spent a good deal of time down there. Scott had the most welcoming household of the group, so his room became a regular hangout, even though his parents grumbled whenever Jennifer came with them. Though they never objected, they never treated Jennifer as kindly as they did the others, particularly Traci. She recalled that very well. She also recalled making love to Scott in that basement more than once, back before Jennifer was in the picture. So, if anything, that room should give her a sense of warm nostalgia, not a creeping dread she couldn't explain.

The guest bedroom wasn't bad; she was just still amped up from everything that had happened tonight. She hadn't wanted them to quit, but now that she put her head on the pillow, she had to admit she was exhausted. Taking the container from her purse, she popped out two Trazadone. The pills were the only way she'd fall into deep, REM sleep, even if she were in her own bed. She swallowed them with a sip from her refreshed glass of vodka, which she always kept on hand in case she woke up needing it in the middle of the night. She closed her eyes and tried to think about anything other than Robin Reeves by fantasizing about going to the Bahamas with Kordell. She imagined she had money. She imagined she had a good life. Her eyes closed and she drifted off, visions of a better world falling into darkness.

She dreamt of the basement.

Traci was both an adult and a child, her current consciousness implanted into the body and soul of herself at age eleven. Despite the place not being furnished into Scott's bedroom, she still recognized it as the basement of the Dwyer house. It had no light fixtures yet, so candles lighted the way. The walls and floor were gray concrete, cold to the touch, and Traci shivered in her nightgown.

Someone took her hand. At first, she thought it was her mother, which oddly made her feel sick, but the hand was too large and hairy. Little Traci looked up at the shadowy figure of a man. He was in his thirties, stocky with a bit of a belly. He wore his brown hair in a buzz cut, making his head look all the squarer. Even in the dark she could see his eyes, so warm and blue, so trustworthy. He was familiar to her, a friend of her mother's maybe. She wasn't sure. She only knew she was happy to see him. The darkened room wasn't so scary now, but as he patted her shoulder, other shadows appeared behind the flickering candles. She and the man weren't alone.

He whispered something to her. She couldn't decipher it but knew he meant to calm her, but as the figures moved forward, they reached out to her with cold fingers. They caressed her gently, making her skin crawl, their hands in her hair and gliding up and down her arms. They were using words she didn't understand, maybe some other language. They didn't hurt her in any way, but still, their touch was invasive, and she began to tremble.

The man held her tighter, the only hand on Traci that was warm and moist. This time when he whispered, his words were crystal clear.

"Don't be afraid."

Traci awoke sitting up. She gasped for air, cheeks wet from crying in her sleep. Already the details of the dream were fading, but the feeling of helplessness remained, like a bad cough long after the flu was gone. She took a drink, nearly finishing the vodka.

There was a creaking sound outside her door, and she pulled the blanket up— a little girl wanting her mother, wanting to go home. Another creak followed the first. Someone was walking down the hall, straining the hardwood floor. She told herself it was just someone going to the bathroom. *Of course it is.*

It was just a bad dream. Get a grip on yourself, girl.

She did so by gripping the bottle of Trazadone again, shaking another pill out.

Just a bad dream.

THEY WERE just like Robin's—each diary a tale of a Redford teenager's last day on earth. Each had its own unique voice. Some had sophomoric spelling and grammatical errors, strange for Steven. Others seemed painstakingly edited, with lines crossed out and started over again. Jennifer skimmed through the volumes, seeing consistencies in the stories. All of the suicide victims had gone into the same woods. They went in alone. Some wrote of troubles in their lives—poor grades, a bad breakup, an abusive parent, a lack of popularity—but none told of any plans to end their lives. Many of the victims claimed they had good lives and were happy, that they'd only been using the woods as a shortcut or just went out there out of curiosity after all the bodies were discovered. Some had gone to visit the sites where their friends had spent their final moments, placing flowers and cards for Tabby Shyrock or pouring out a beer in honor of Johnny Clayton.

All the journals were dated between 1993 and 1995. Jennifer remembered Robin being the last body found in Suicide Woods, at least before she moved away. She hadn't heard of any others over the years, but also hadn't followed up on it. For her, denial was a key factor in moving on. But she wouldn't ignore things now. The books were filled with foreboding, the dark use of language foreshadowing the inevitable conclusions. Each diary read like a nightmare, not always making sense but maintaining steady dread.

And they all spoke of demons.

Jennifer bit at her cuticles as she skimmed the different journals.

There were four of them. They had arms like roots, and they wrapped around my wrists and dragged me into the water...

...I appeared in random places like I was jumping through time...

...I felt the cold steel of the dagger as it was pulled across my throat, and the blood warmed my chest, feeling good until I snapped out of this dream state and realized I was dying...

...they took me into a clearing and bound me...

...it was coming for me, a red monster with three legs that howled like a wolf and screamed like little babies...

Her throat went dry as she read through these death confessions. The voices seemed so true to her—not like Steven creating characters, but like actual perspectives from various young people facing bizarre killers. Some were fraught with pure, gut-wrenching terror. Others seemed strangely at ease, docile in accepting their fate.

At the bottom of the box was a purple, hardback journal that caught her eye. There was nothing written on the front. When she opened it, she saw the handwriting was different, not Steven's. It had elongated loops and other touches that were clearly feminine. The first line made her go cold.

This diary belongs to Stephanie Winters.

WAS THIS really the best thing to do? Scott shrugged to himself as he walked down the hall. Had *any of this* been the best thing to do?

What a long, strange trip it's been, he thought. And the trip wasn't over. Not by a long shot.

As he moved past the doors to the guest rooms, he paused and listened. Mark was snoring. Traci's room was silent. He thought of her stretched out in there, asleep and beautiful. He simply couldn't help it.

Scott walked on slowly, not wanting the floorboards to creak any louder than they already were. It was an old house and it liked to complain. He tiptoed past the living room. Corey was curled onto his side, facing away from Scott, inflating and deflating with soft breaths. He watched him for a few seconds, just to be sure, then made his way to the basement.

JENNIFER HEARD the footsteps before the door cracked open, giving her just enough time to put the stack of journals back in the box and secure the lid. She scooted back into the bed, lying on her stomach, but didn't have time to turn off the amber lamp before there was a little, one-knuckle tap, and Scott appeared in the doorway.

She opened her eyes as if she'd been sleeping, then realized she hadn't put the blanket over her. She had one leg bent at the knee and the other stretched out behind her, her slip rising over the bent leg's thigh. One of the slip's straps hung over her shoulder, but her breasts remained covered by the satin and her hair.

Scott's eyes wandered over her body for a quick second. "Sorry. I couldn't sleep. Thought you might be up too, but—"

"It's okay." She repositioned, propping up on one elbow. "I wasn't really asleep yet. Just…resting my eyes."

His boyish smile returned. "Can I come in?"

She was certain he knew the answer was yes before she even said it. He closed the door behind him and sat down on the bed, elbows on his thighs, his hands held together between his knees. He was wearing a tank top shirt of thin material that showed off his broad shoulders. His arms weren't massive, but they were athletic, the muscles toned and hard. A single vein stood out on one bicep.

How she ached to touch him.

Though she was drawn into Scott, thoughts of the journals remained. Jennifer wondered if he'd read through them much, if he'd discovered as much as she had. She wanted to ask him but was afraid to admit she'd been snooping. But wouldn't he have known the temptation would be too hard to resist? He'd left her alone with the box after telling her what was inside. Had it been some sort of test? Had he wanted her to take that initiative to read them on her own?

Jennifer could have spoken, but she thought better of it. When he turned to look at her, she knew all questions would have to wait. Right now, in this basement that had once been so special to them, there were no questions—only one, perfect answer.

When he leaned in to kiss her, she leaned back slowly, taking his head in her hands, their lips wet and warm and wanting. This time when she bent her leg, it was to let it glide up his side as he moved upon her like some nostalgic fantasy made flesh. Here in this time capsule of a room, they were insulated from the rest of the world. Every other part of her life melted away beneath Scott Dwyer. And when the time came for him to turn out the light, she moved his hand away from the switch, wanting that soft, amber glow to remain, just enough to see his body, just enough to see those eyes—those deep, blue eyes.

PART FOUR

WHAT LIES WITHIN

CHAPTER TWENTY-EIGHT

Mark needed more coffee. Scott had made an impressive breakfast, with eggs, bacon, bagels, and fresh fruit. He had milk and cereal, OJ and tomato juice. But it was the coffee Mark really needed. It'd been a mistake trying to keep up with Traci Rillo last night. The woman drank like a fish—like a *whale*—and he wasn't used to vodka. He was too old for binge-drinking the heavy stuff. Luckily, it was only his head that was paying for it. So far, the breakfast was staying down.

He'd watched Jennifer as she helped Scott prepare the meal. They'd moved through the small kitchen like a pair of newlyweds, all smiles and giggles and nudges they thought no one else would notice. It was Jennifer who had made the pancakes, and Mark had almost expected her to poof some powdered sugar onto Scott's nose. They'd been that sickeningly cute. The pancakes were good too, not like the always-burnt dough discs Rhonda used to make. That woman could burn a glass of water. At least she had cooked for him. Carol's idea of a good meal came from a drive thru.

He must have banged her, Mark thought, watching them.

Jennifer had the look of a woman who'd had her first orgasm in a long time, that glow of relief that flushes their skin. He imagined her walking outside, singing a merry tune, greeted by little birds that would land on her outstretched arms and sing along with her.

He tried not to let the envy make his headache any worse. Scott had scored while Mark had snored.

He should've snuck into Traci's room last night. Something had made him chicken out. With the way things were going in this country, he no longer knew what was considered seductive as opposed to some form of sexual assault. It made him afraid to make a move on a woman. Mark figured it was best to let them come to him these days, but they rarely did. He should've made more of an effort to stay in shape. He shouldn't have gotten old. Eventually, the whole bad boy bit lost its charm. Most women didn't want a man over forty who still wore a motorcycle jacket and carried a wallet on a chain. Maybe that's why he always maintained a constant buzz. So long as he stayed high, it bothered him less that he didn't have a woman.

But there'd been a spark between him and Traci last night. They'd bonded, hadn't they? She'd held his hand. She'd confided in him. Had he missed a once-in-a-lifetime opportunity? Traci was one fine piece of trim, far better looking than Rhonda or Carol or the random lushes Mark sometimes picked up at the pool hall. Had he failed to cash in his golden ticket? It wouldn't be the first time he'd blown his big chance at something he'd never have a second chance at.

Back when she'd broken up with him, Mark had blamed everyone but himself. He especially blamed Scott Dwyer. Mark had never gotten over the feeling that Traci held onto her ex, as if she were just passing time with Mark until Scott got sick of Jenny and took her back. He saw the way she looked at him. He noticed when Scott consoled her, like he had that Halloween. And so, he'd got it in his head that Traci was dumping him to try and win Scott back, that Scott had led her on, and when he finally confronted his friend, they'd had a bitter fight that ended in fists, ruining the friendship.

Mark carried his coffee to the back porch and lit up a cigarette.

The air was crisp and clean. It seemed a shame to pollute it. Yellow and red leaves fluttered across a clear, autumn sky. Fall had come on so quickly. He rarely got a chance to smell the roses, as they say, so he gazed at the golden maples and burning bush hedges, enjoying the scenery until he remembered where it all led.

Suicide Woods.

He moved across the lawn, looking for the opening. The trail had grown over some, but it was still there. The air felt suddenly more than crisp. It was cold like a walk-in cooler. He thought of the fairy stories he'd once read to Jamie, back when she was still young and happy to spend time with him. The Black Forrest. Trolls who lived under bridges. Big, bad wolves chasing little girls through the woods. Every tall tale contained a nugget of truth, didn't it?

"Sleep okay?"

Mark jumped, having not heard Traci come out of the house. She was dressed down in jeans and a sweater but looked just as sexy as she had last night. She asked for a cigarette and puckered her lip-sticked mouth around it, waiting for a light. He stepped into her to keep the breeze from blowing out the flame, and their closeness excited him. Her sweater was a V-neck and he glimpsed cleavage, pure and white as snow. It was hard to look away.

"Yeah," he said. "I slept fine. That air mattress is surprisingly comfortable. How 'bout you?"

The purple under her eyes said it all. "Not great," she told him. "Bad dreams. Must've been all that talk about demons."

"Maybe so."

They looked toward the woods. The trees flowed on the wind, leaning inward, waving like welcoming hands. Mark felt that chill again and noticed Traci shiver beside him.

"I never thought I'd be standing at the edge of Suicide Woods again," she said.

"You and me both, babe."

He couldn't help it. It had just slipped out; that old, generic nickname he'd always used when they were together. Damn, he hoped he hadn't offended her. He almost apologized, but when he looked at Traci, he saw no tension there, so he let it be.

"What do you think he has in store for us today?" she asked.

Mark's eyebrows drew closer together. "Scott?"

"He's the one who's been steering this whole thing. He brought us back home to dig the skeletons out of the closet."

"Well, that's what Steven wanted."

"That's what Scott *says* Steven wanted."

He stared at her. "What're you thinking?"

"I'm not sure. I just feel like he's been rationing out all these revelations, like he thinks we can't take the whole truth all at once."

"You think he's hiding something?"

"It's not that. Scott's always been a great guy. Maybe he's trying to protect us from something he doesn't think we can handle knowing."

"Shit." Mark shook his head. "If there's more to this than a dead girl saying she was killed by demons, maybe he's right to think we can't handle it. After last night, I've had enough spooky stories to last me the rest of my life."

"That's just it, Mark. I don't think they're just stories."

She looked to the woods, and he followed her gaze. Branches and decaying leaves continued to wave them in, gentle and silent, as if telling them there was nothing to be scared of.

COREY INSISTED on doing the dishes, so Scott and Jennifer went into the living room to finish their coffee. It was hazelnut and Jennifer breathed it in deep, the smell as nutty as she was feeling right now. She had to stifle the urge to giggle like a schoolgirl as she curled up on the couch, resisting the urge to snuggle Scott. It was hard not to nuzzle right into the crook of his arm after last night.

She still couldn't believe it. But why not? Obviously, it was something they'd both wanted. It was more than a *want* for her. It was a *need*. The touch of a man she desired was just as exhilarating as being desired herself. This good-looking guy who she trusted completely was the only one who could ever take her further than she'd thought she was capable of. There'd been no awkwardness to their lovemaking despite years of separation and all the other lovers that fell in-between. It wasn't like they'd picked up where they'd left off; it was better than that. They'd brought new talents to old passions. Jennifer had never experienced anything like it. And from the gleam in Scott's eyes, she was confident she wasn't alone in that.

Jennifer had no illusions about where this would go. They lived too far apart to try for a relationship. There would be no "Scott and Jenny Part II." But that didn't mean she couldn't fantasize about it. She knew she was being silly, but sometimes being silly felt damn good, didn't it? Maybe she could at least make this an extended stay to give them a couple of nights together once the others headed home. She rarely called in sick and didn't have any immediate clients lined up for showings. Roger wouldn't mind hanging out with the kids for an extra day or two, and even if he was too busy, Devin was old enough to be the man of the house while his mother was away.

She was just about to ask Scott if he wanted some company for a long weekend when the sliding door came open. Mark and Traci entered. Jennifer would have to wait for another opportunity. She wasn't ashamed of what she and Scott had done, but she might be a bit embarrassed if the others found out. She was a modest woman and thought such things were meant to be private. Scott, always the gentlemen, would never kiss and tell. This was their little secret.

And so were the journals.

Jennifer wondered when to bring them up to him. If she was going to spend more days with Scott, she couldn't start them off on a dishonest note. A lie by omission was still a lie. She had to tell him she'd skimmed some of the diaries. Not only was it the right thing to do, but then they could also discuss them further. She hoped Scott planned to reveal them to the others today. The information they held was far too pertinent.

Stephanie Winters, she thought.

"So, what now, Scotty?" Mark asked as he plopped down in the armchair.

Traci took a seat at the far end of the couch. Corey came into the living room, drying his hands on a dishrag. The group seemed to orbit around Scott, drawn to the energy of whatever he had in store for them. His face settled with a stark, mysterious determination, an official among expectant citizens.

"Last night," he said, "all of you were beginning to believe in demons. Now that it's morning, have your opinions changed?"

The others shared awkward glances.

"No," Traci said. "I believe. But I always have."

Scott looked to Mark, who Jennifer expected would be the most cynical, but instead he stuck to his story about the impish creature that had attacked him all those years ago.

"I don't know if it was a demon or what," he said, "but it was real, and it was real weird."

Corey nodded. "I'm not religious, but you could say I'm spiritual. Because of all that's happened, I do believe in demons. Call them evil spirits, or ghosts, or whatever—it's really all the same with just a different name. A demon is a demon. And I think Suicide Woods is home to them."

Scott leaned forward. "You think that's why so many kids died out there? Do you think demons killed Robin, like the diary says?"

Corey nodded reluctantly. So did Mark and Traci. Now all eyes fell on Jennifer. She sat on her legs, warming her feet, the mug sending pleasant coffee vapors across her face. Under other circumstances, this would feel like a cabin retreat. If it were only her and Scott here, it would be just as good as one. But this wasn't the weekend getaway she'd been hoping for. Things had gone from dark to darker, and there was no sign of it relenting. If someone asked her if she believed in demons while she'd been reading the secret diaries, she would have said yes, despite all her reservations and a lifetime of disbelief in such things. But now, sober and back to some semblance of reality, she wasn't so sure. She needed more answers. There was only one person who might have them.

"Scott, should we...?" Jennifer almost asked if they should reveal the journals to the others, but then pulled back. "*Should we* believe in demons?"

It was the best way she could spin the question back without giving a definitive answer.

Scott folded his arms like a schoolteacher awaiting his students' feedback. He wore a bulletproof look of confidence in what he was saying.

"The woods behind this house," he began, "they're a bad place where bad things happened. I think the negative energy of tragedy and death can permeate an area where they occur. It becomes, sort of, *haunted*. Not with the spirits of the dead, exactly, but haunted by the emotional impact of their deaths, both that of the victims and those who survive them, like their family and friends. I also think the emotional impact felt by the killers haunts these spots, too. It's like cursing the earth."

Traci asked, "So you do think they were murders and not suicides?"

"In some cases, I think that's possible."

Tell them, Jennifer thought. *Tell them about the other diaries.*

"What about Robin's case?" Traci asked. "Do we believe she randomly hung herself? Or do we acknowledge that all our memories line up perfectly with what is said in that journal?"

Scott clasped his hands. "I think you answered your own question, Traci." The room fell silent.

"So what do we do?" Corey asked.

"Robin Reeves is dead and buried," Scott said. "No one else is going to care about a girl who died a quarter century ago. No one's going to investigate."

"Yeah," Mark said. "Cops ain't gonna dig up a grave based on this."

"They won't now. We waited too long."

The group looked to Scott with expressions of hurt, of guilt.

"Don't you see?" Scott asked. "If we had just told the truth that night and admitted we were all there, all these stories would have come out instead of us keeping them locked in. By pretending none of it happened, we abandoned Robin in those woods not just that night, but forever."

Jennifer was unable to hold anyone's gaze.

Corey's mouth hung open. "Jeez, Scott. Don't talk like that."

"We didn't know," Mark said.

"But we did," Scott said, "even if we didn't realize it. We all saw strange things out there, heard strange things. We felt their presence. But we kept it quiet. We didn't even tell *each other* everything we knew until last night. I really think Steven wanted us to memorialize Robin by coming together like this. I think her spirit remains in the woods behind this house, tormented by the demons that took her. And I think only we can free her from them, so she may finally know peace."

CHAPTER TWENTY-NINE

Corey needed a drink.

The urge surprised him. He never touched the stuff, but the weight of what Scott suggested made him want to reach for an emotional crutch, anything to calm his fried nerves.

"You must be crazy," Mark told Scott. "You can't really expect us to go along with this, can you?"

"I know it's a lot," Scott replied. "But I think it's the only way we can put everything to rest, once and for all. Not just for Robin and Steven, but for ourselves."

Traci had gotten out of her seat and gone to the kitchen window, staring outside where Suicide Woods loomed like a tide rolling in.

"I can't go back there," she said. "None of us can go back there."

"We have to, Traci."

Mark stood. "Bullshit. We don't have to do a damn thing. Jesus, man, was this your plan all along? You get everybody all worked up about this demon garbage and—"

"We all did that," Jennifer said, "not just Scott."

Mark shot her a smirk Corey didn't appreciate. Last night, Corey had woken up as Scott went down to the basement. He could guess what had happened between the old lovers. If Mark knew it too, he'd better keep his mouth shut the same way Corey did. It was none of their business.

"Of course you pick his side," Mark said to Jennifer.

"It's not about sides," Corey said.

"Then what is it about, huh? Haven't we torn open these old wounds enough without going out there and scaring the shit out of ourselves all over again?"

"That's why we go now," Scott said. "While there's plenty of daylight."

"And do what exactly?"

"We honor her memory. Look, I have something else to show you. Something Steven left for us. Us and Robin."

Corey put his hands on his hips. Even he was getting frustrated with their host. "More surprises, man? Can you please just lay everything out to us already? This isn't a game of *Clue*, Scott. This is serious."

"I know it is," Scott said, his face grave. "That's exactly why I've rationed it all out. If I'd thrown everything at you guys the moment you walked in the door, you would've thought I'd gone insane. But I haven't and neither had Steven."

He started toward the stairwell to the basement. Corey sighed. Jennifer rose from the couch, walking with her arms crossed, not looking at anyone. Mark shuffled over begrudgingly. Traci hadn't moved from the window. Something about her stillness spooked Corey.

"You comin', Traci?" Mark asked.

She didn't turn around. "You go ahead. I'll be right down."

"You okay?"

She turned just slightly, showing her profile. "I said, I'll be right down!" She sniffed, collecting herself, and looked away again. "Sorry. I just need a minute. I have to, um, use the ladies' room first."

But she stayed at the window, watching the autumnal display beyond. Corey followed her gaze, seeing more than the trees. He saw what lied within them—black shadows, bad memories, and all the building blocks of horror. Traci was staring it all in the eye as the others journeyed below.

Entering the room, Corey glanced at the battlefield of the bed sheets, all crumpled in disarray with the pillows scattered. The mental image of how they'd gotten that way made him both excited and ashamed, so he looked away, shaking the image of a nude and rapturous Jennifer Parks from his head.

Corey had thought he'd gotten over his old crush. He'd thought wrong. He still cared for her and wanted it to show. Was that why he was still here? Did he just want to be the good guy again, the nice guy? He knew all too well where that had gotten him in the past. Why must he learn the same mistake over and over?

But if there really was a chance to make peace with themselves over the case of Robin Reeves, he was willing to do almost anything to see it through.

In the far corner was a stack of cardboard boxes and plastic totes, this section of the basement used for storage. Scott shifted them around, revealing the labels they bore in black marker: *Christmas Ornaments, Photo Albums, Dad's Tools, Mom's Knickknacks.* Scott selected one of the boxes, and when he picked it up, its label faced outward.

Corey wasn't surprised by what it read.

Halloween.

REALIZING SHE was alone, Traci spun sharply around. She'd wanted a moment alone, but now that she had it, she was suddenly petrified. Gazing across the living room and kitchen, the stillness became instantly unbearable. She felt the presence of Suicide Woods behind her, a concentrated evil pulsing like a great, black heart—a *demon's* heart. She hurried through the kitchen and into the living room. Her pulse was racing. She was chilled, and yet sweating.

When she looked to the stairwell leading to the basement, her throat went tight. Though she wanted to be with the others now, to escape this terrible isolation and the danger it somehow presented, she knew she wouldn't make it down those steps in this state.

She went down the hall to the guest bedroom. Beside the Trazadone was a container of Xanax. It wasn't a panic fix-all, but it was as good as it got. She rushed to the nightstand and chased down the pill with the thin sliver of vodka left in the tumbler. Sitting on the bed, she hugged herself and leaned forward, head between her knees as she took in slow, long breaths. Her throat began to open. She made a mental note to go back on the inhaler. It'd been a long time since she'd had an asthma attack. It frightened her.

When she started to breathe normally, she laid back on the bed and let the anxiety medication do its magic. She closed her eyes and tried to think of that tropical dream vacation with Kordell, but found he wasn't even in the picture. Her boyfriend didn't matter. Traci only wanted the warmth of the sun as she stretched out on the beach with a cocktail. She could almost hear the gentle waves of the Atlantic and the scattered calls of seagulls. There would be no need for pills here. This was where she belonged.

Suddenly a shadow moved across the sun, and at this first hint of darkness, she retreated from the daydream. Opening her eyes, Traci stared at the ceiling, wondering if happiness was even achievable anymore. It seemed to be something reserved for the young, but she hadn't even had it back then. Even as a little girl, she'd searched for it in vain. She'd had no one to tell her where to look for joy. Her mother had lived and died leaving nothing behind but a bad reputation, Traci's only inheritance. Had Mom found happiness, floundering from one barroom bozo to another? If that was a happy life, Traci would keep her miserable one. There had to be more to existence than this. Maybe that's why she believed in a better world that came after this one. Maybe she had to.

When she exited into the hall, she realized she really did have to use the bathroom now. As she moved down the hallway, she saw the door to the master bedroom was ajar. She thought nothing of it and would have kept moving if she hadn't caught a quick glimpse of the framed photos atop the dresser. There was a face grinning back from behind the glass, back through time.

Traci's chest went tight again. She forced her lungs to steady and took a step closer to the door, pushing it open slowly. Daylight knifed through the blinds, making zebra stripes across the frames and the people the snapshots contained, moments captured like prisoners.

The man was in several pictures. He was tall with a bit of a belly, his head like a block beneath a buzz cut. His arms and the backs of his hands were coated in thick hair. His smile was warm, but it struck Traci as menacing somehow, something dark lying just beneath the surface. Her knuckles ran white as she gripped a frame and brought it up for a closer look. In the photo, the man from her nightmare had his arm slung around a young Scott's shoulder.

They had the same eyes.

Blue. Deep, deep blue.

SCOTT WOULD have preferred to wait for Traci to come down, but the others were growing impatient. Even Corey was being a little combative. If Scott didn't move things along, he might very well lose them, despite how much progress they'd made. They believed now. If he frustrated them with any more secrecy, they might leave and never return. Then this would all have been for nothing. Scott couldn't allow that, so he put the box on the end table and opened it.

Despite the label that read "Halloween," the cardboard box did not contain any decorations. There were no Styrofoam tombstones, honeycomb witches, or ghosts made of old sheets. It was not marked "Halloween" because it was a collection of holiday items, but because that was when he intended to open it. It was not quite October 31st yet, but the season was upon them, and that was enough.

He kept what was inside out of the view of the others so he could reveal it by holding it up. He wanted them to receive the full effect of seeing it head on. Brushing away the packing popcorn, he lifted the item carefully, using gentle movements to wiggle it free.

He hoisted it and watched their faces fall.

Traci burst into the room.

JENNIFER HELD the trembling woman against her, stroking her back up and down.

"What's wrong?" Corey asked again.

But Traci was crying too hard to answer. And she hadn't even seen the wreath yet.

"It's okay," Jennifer said. Then, not knowing why, she said, "we're all in this together."

Scott came to the women and gently pried them apart so he could get a look at Traci. He slouched so they were at eye level, but she wouldn't look at him. She turned her wet, pink face away. Jennifer figured she was embarrassed from the outburst, but she detected something else in Traci too, something ominous she couldn't quite identify.

"Traci," Scott said. "C'mon, look at me."

She shook her head.

"What's the matter?"

His face was fraught with sympathy, his sweet eyes like sapphires. Jennifer knew this calming tactic of his very well. It bothered her a little to see him using it on another woman. The hands that had been upon her naked flesh last night now rubbed Traci's shoulders. Jennifer told herself she was being ridiculous, that she was acting like a jealous girlfriend after a single night's fling, but the jealousy remained.

Finally, Traci spoke. "I'm…I'm not sure. I just don't feel safe here."

"C'mon now. I'm right here. We're all here together. There's nothing to worry about." His smile was rich with charm. "Don't be afraid."

Traci went white as chalk.

She trembled intensely. Jennifer feared she was having a seizure. She went to her, and Traci stepped away, toward the staircase, turning as if to run.

"Traci…" Mark said but trailed off.

Scott followed her. "Traci, wait. Please, wait."

But she was already flinging open the door. It wobbled from the force of her pull, and she stumbled as she went for the first step . Her head connected with the doorjamb, and she spun around, blood trickling down her forehead as her eyes rolled in her skull.

Jennifer shrieked. Her reflexes failed her. Scott was the only one who moved fast enough to catch Traci before she could hit the ground.

CHAPTER THIRTY

Scott was on top her.

Traci felt his bare skin against hers, the sweat on his back moistening her hands, the push of him between her legs. She drew them tighter around him, her desire palpable, a sensation that exhilarated and yet concerned her. She felt out of control, a crazed abandon completely untethered from her will. They were in his bed in the basement, an Alice in Chains album playing on his boombox, a pair of Coors Light cans resting on the end table beside them. She remembered how he'd used to sneak them from his father when they were only sixteen years old and—

Father.

The scene shifted, spiraling like black water going down a drain. Scott's young face became even younger as he smiled down at her. He kissed her lips, and when he came up again, his hair was shorter, his cheeks more flushed. He couldn't have been older than twelve. When she ran her hands over his little, bird chest, she saw her hands had grown smaller, the hands of a prepubescent girl, the nail polish gone.

This wasn't right. They hadn't slept together until they were several years older. Traci had lost her virginity at a young age, but not *this* young.

The swirling vortex above them became dotted with orange stars. Their light made Scott glow, his head like a neon pumpkin. There was no longer desire upon his face. Instead, he was warped by fear, the sort of baffled terror only known in childhood. But still he thrust.

The orange stars drew closer. Traci realized they were small flames. And when they moved in, she saw the candles and the hands that held them. They were adult hands.

Naked grown-ups hovered over the children as they reluctantly made love, smiling down upon them with macabre, possum grins. A woman with dyed red hair came closer and blotted Scott's sweaty forehead, and then looked down upon her daughter with eyes brimming with pride.

Another proud parent came into view, his large body hovering over them in a mountain of hairy flesh. He patted his son on the back and winked down at Traci with a dazzling blue eye.

CHAPTER THIRTY-ONE

"We need to take her to the hospital," Corey said.

"Take it easy," Scott told him, blotting at the thin trickle of blood on Traci's forehead. "It's just a bump. She'll be okay."

"She's been knocked out! You know how bad that is for a person?"

"He's right," Jennifer said. "We really should take..."

Traci stirred in the bed, her eyes fluttering open. She started when she saw Scott, inhaling deep. He ran his hand over her head, patting back her hair. She looked around the basement room at the others. Her breathing steadied.

"You hit your head and fell," Scott said. "Got a little bump on the noggin, but you're all right."

"She needs to see a doctor," Corey said.

"She's fine!"

Scott's agitation baffled Jennifer. Why was he being so insistent? Was he afraid of getting sued or something? That didn't seem like him. But snapping at Corey didn't seem like him either.

Traci sat up, Scott ready to brace her with arms outstretched. Whatever fear had sent her scrambling before had faded with her return to consciousness. She seemed at ease now, if a bit confused.

"I'm okay," she said. "I don't like doctors."

Scott grinned over this small victory. "See that? She's fine."

Corey didn't argue it further.

Traci looked to the liquor cabinet and asked for a drink.

"You sure you don't want some water?" Jennifer asked.

"I'm fine," Traci said.

So, Jennifer didn't argue. Mark fetched a glass of straight vodka, filling it nearly to the brim.

Thanks a lot, Mark, Jennifer thought. *How brilliant of you.*

Traci drank with closed eyes. Jennifer watched her briefly, and then returned her attention to the wreath Scott had taken out of the box. At first, she'd thought Christmas decorations had been mistakenly put into the Halloween decorations box, but when she saw the photo in the center, she realized what she was really looking at. It was an old professional photo, probably a school yearbook picture. She recognized the girl immediately. Red hair, freckles, braces. She even had on that same pink sweater. The cloth scroll ran across the top of the wreath, pinned there with little bows. The words were written upon it in delicate cursive.

In loving memory of Robin Reeves.

Jennifer swallowed hard.

Traci gradually got to her feet and poured herself another drink.

Jennifer pitied the woman. It was three in the afternoon, but they'd all slept in after the long night and had been awake for only a couple of hours. Cleary Traci Rillo was more than just a social drinker.

When Traci turned around, she noticed the wreath. She was expressionless as she moved closer to it.

"A memorial?" she said, stating it more than asking. She looked to Scott. "You want us to take this to the tree, don't you? The place where she died."

He nodded. "Yeah. I do."

"I feel like…like I'm going crazy." She sniffed. "Why do I feel like we'll never be able to move on from this? No matter what we do."

"This will help, Traci. I know it will."

She sighed, wiping away a single tear. Silence fell upon them then, heavy and thick. Traci ran her hand over the rim of the wreath and gently touched the photo of Robin, running two fingers across it like a tender blessing.

"We do this," Scott said, "and it's the last thing. Other people surely left mementos and letters at that tree for her over the years, but never us.

Never the ones who were there that night. We have to acknowledge our grief. We have to acknowledge what we did. We do this, and then we're done with all this for good."

In a way, Jennifer wanted to go along with the idea. Maybe it would give them solace. Paying one's respects to the dead was always cathartic. Human beings created such rituals with good reason. Tears were sacred. At the same time, she wasn't comfortable going back into the woods. Not so much because she was scared of them, but because she was scared of how emotional they all might become by being there. So far, they'd only discussed Suicide Woods, and they were all nervous wrecks. Traci seemed to be mentally disintegrating before their very eyes. If they went out there, would the others fall in behind her, deteriorating into nervous breakdowns? Jennifer didn't think literal demons would haunt them, but their own personal demons would, the sadness and self-rage eating at them like starving rats. Returning to Suicide Woods was going down a staircase that might not be easy to go back up again.

Before she could express this, Traci put down her empty glass and straightened her posture. Her eyes were bloodshot, but there was a new hardness to them, a strength summoned from some hidden reserve.

"You're right," she told Scott. "But this is the end of it. When it's done, I'm going home and getting on with my life. And I hope you all understand why I won't see or speak to any of you ever again."

GOD TOLD her to.

Traci felt his presence wrap around her heart, an unstoppable force for good. As she'd dreamed that black dream, her subconscious prayed for His help, and as she'd come out of the nightmare, His guidance continued into the waking world. He told her what needed to be done. Atonement. Confession. Contrition. All led to peace. She believed in the demons of the woods. She believed Scott was right when he said they needed to memorialize Robin to free her spirit from that horrible place. But every instinct told her going back to the woods would be disastrous. It went against her health and safety. The emotional toll would be devastating, with or without interference from any dark, supernatural forces.

But what was the alternative? She'd returned to Redford, hadn't she? Even if she told herself she'd come here under other pretenses, she'd known damn well what awaited her here. The memories hadn't left her no matter how hard she'd tried to erase them, drowning them with booze and blasting them out of her head with pharmaceuticals. She threw men at the bad memories, a line of boyfriends who showed her she was actually worthy of love, only to find her mental demolition unbearable once they got close enough to have to deal with it. This led her through long bouts of isolation and abstinence as a way to protect herself. But the time for self-reflection was even more poisonous.

It was not just the memory of Robin Reeves that had crippled Traci; it was the memories of Redford. This town was a spiritual leech that had proved impossible to peel from her soul. And the longer she stayed here, the clearer that became as flashbacks and nightmares brought something to the surface she would have preferred stay buried, denial being a better medication than all the pills and vodka in the world. She only vaguely retained the images from the dreams she'd been having, but the feeling they left her with was hollowing and arctic. They made her feel destabilized, throwing her off balance as she struggled to move past whatever they contained. They made her feel dirty, even evil. She didn't want to confront them; she wanted to flee them.

Were they punishment?

She often felt she deserved any and all of the bad things that happened to her, whether it was a boyfriend who liked to smack her around or a cancerous growth that had to be cut out of her insides. Was it God's will, or was it the long-lasting effects of contact with demons?

Traci couldn't cry about it anymore. Years of sobbing only dragged her farther down into the pit. Fear was a paralyzing emotion, but guilt was far more brutal.

She had said they couldn't go out there again. Now she doubted there was any other choice.

It was their only chance to escape Hell.

Perhaps they'd been living there all this time.

"CAN I talk to you?"

Mark had gone outside for a cigarette. He needed one—badly. When he'd first heard the porch door open, he'd thought it was Traci, but instead Corey Pickett came up beside him.

"Yeah," Mark grumbled. "Go ahead."

Corey sighed. "Look, I know you've never liked me, but—"

"That's not true."

"Isn't it?"

"No. It's not. I mean…I don't know, man. I was just a troubled kid back then. My home life was shit, and I just had an attitude with some people because of it, okay? Maybe that's not an excuse, but, well, at least it's an explanation."

Corey raised his eyebrows. Mark didn't blame him. He too was surprised by his words, especially because he meant them. Mark had never been the apologetic type. In fact, he hated saying he was sorry. Nearly every relationship he'd ever had—with women, friends, and even his own kids—had suffered as a result of it. Right now, he felt like he needed someone, *anyone*, to not think of him as just an asshole. He was in a tense situation here and wanted an ally.

"Wow," Corey said. "That actually means a lot to me, Mark. Thank you for that."

Mark preferred to avoid anything emotional, so he got back on topic. "So what did you want to talk to me about?"

Corey looked over his shoulder conspiratorially. "This going into the woods business. Besides me, you're the only one who really saw those *things* out there. I was wondering how you felt about going back."

There was a rustle that turned their heads. Only dead leaves fluttering through equally dead grass. Mark released a cloud of smoke and looked down at his boots. If there was one thing he hated more than apologizing, it was admitting he was afraid.

"I don't like it," he said. "I don't want to go in those damn woods."

"Me either. So…why did we agree to do it?"

"I don't know why I do anything, man. I really don't. But you saw how determined the others were. Hell, I thought for sure Traci was gonna scream when Scott suggested it. I don't know what turned her around, but she did a one-eighty, didn't she?"

"I'll say. But she's been acting strange this whole time."

"Not as strange as ol' Scotty."

Corey held his gaze. "You think so?"

"Shit, yeah. Don't he seem different to you? I mean, from the way he was back in the day."

"Well, sure. But we all change as we get older."

"Nah, dude, it ain't just that. He's like...*weird* now. All these secrets. I still don't think he's told us everything, do you?"

Corey looked away. "No. Actually, I don't."

"Righty-o. I worry there's something he's not telling us. Something important. Traci wants to face this thing once and for all, and Jennifer is so nuts about Scott she'd follow him into a burning building. They're going with him to Suicide Woods. I just want to make sure the planting of that memorial is all he really wants them to do."

"You think...you think he's up to something?"

"Not exactly, no." Mark sighed. "I just have this weird feeling, man. Somehow, I think the girls might need us. Scott's had this all planned out from the start. He's sort of manipulated things, right? Even manipulated us. What if they get out there and he springs some other shit on them, stuff that will keep them out there even longer? More requests from Steven or whatever else. The longer they stay in the woods, the more likely the demons—or whatever the damn things are—will have the chance to fuck with everyone again. I just want to keep an eye on Scott so we can move this thing along and get the hell out, and we can't do that if we don't go. We're in this thing now, Corey, like it or not. We have to ride it out to the end, come hell or high water."

SHE FINALLY got a moment alone with him.

The others had left the basement, and Scott was gathering the wreath to bring it upstairs. Jennifer stopped him.

"What's up, Jenny? You doing okay?"

"Not really," she said, rubbing her arms against the chill. "I need to tell you something, and I hope you won't be angry with me."

He put the wreath down, cool and collected. "It's okay. You can tell me anything."

Scott started rubbing her arms for her, moving his strong hands up and down so the friction would give her comfort. She enjoyed having his hands on her again. Perhaps a little too much. The last thing she wanted to do was make it so he'd never want to touch her again, but she had to talk to him about what she'd seen.

"The journals, Scott. I read through some of them last night."

She'd hoped she could read something in his face, but he only looked at her blankly.

"Okay," he said.

Jennifer blinked. "Didn't you read them?"

"Yes. I did."

"Well, then...don't you think we should tell the others about them and what they said?"

He shook his head. "No. Please, let's not do that."

"But why not?"

"It'll only scare them."

"They're already scared. So am I."

He pulled her closer, giving her soft shushing noises. Surely, he meant them to be soothing, but they made her feel patronized. "It's all going to be okay, Jenny. Don't be—"

She gently pulled away. "Don't talk to me like I'm a child. I'm a grown woman. I don't need to be placated."

He bit his upper lip. "I'm sorry. You're right, of course. I didn't mean to be condescending."

"Okay," she said, backing off but still a little guarded. "It's just that, since I've been back, I feel like we're all in some kind of time warp, you know? It makes me feel like I'm seventeen again, and I just sort of lose myself in that. But I'm not a teenager. I'm an adult, crazy as that sometimes seems to me. I'm a mother. I have a house and a job and responsibilities. Being here—being with you—it takes those things away somehow. It's weird. I don't know how to explain it."

He nodded, telling her it was all right without having to say it. He gave her a smile as fleeting as a summer day.

"Look," Jennifer said, "about last night…"

"You don't have to explain anything."

"I know. That's not where I was going with this. I just want to say that last night was…well…it was really wonderful. I needed that. Not just sex with a man, but with you. Last night should show you how much I trust you."

"It does."

"Good. I want you to trust me too. That's why I told you I looked at the diaries."

He put his hand on her shoulder. "I do trust you, Jenny. Always have."

She held back the mist that came to her eyes, the good kind of crying. She was being silly again, going into girlfriend mode when it wasn't appropriate to do so. Why did she get so gushy around him? And why was she so suggestible? She felt they could mourn the dead right here. She didn't want to go back into those horrible woods to swim deeper into a pitch-black memory. Not for Robin Reeves or Steven or anybody. But she'd agreed. Some of it was peer pressure, not wanting to be the only one to say no, but more than anything else, she didn't want to say no to Scott.

"Thank you for trusting me." She rolled her shoulders, tossing her hair over them, bracing herself. "So, the rest of the journals. They all read from the point of view of those who committed suicide, but all written by Steven. Except there's one at the bottom. A purple one."

She waited, leading him on, hoping he'd interject. Instead, he just stood there, waiting on her. He didn't move. Didn't even blink.

"Scott…who is Stephanie Winters?"

He looked at the floor. "I was hoping we wouldn't have to get into this. I should have taken the journals upstairs last night."

Jennifer's heart dropped. "I'm sorry. I just had to know what they…"

He put up one hand. "It's not your fault. I understand. I would've looked through them too if I were you. I just hoped we wouldn't have to delve so far into them. You're the only one I showed the other diaries too. I just felt you'd better understand why I was doing all of this if you knew about them."

She wasn't sure she understood that, but she didn't question it. She waited for more.

"All of the journals in that box were written by Steven," Scott said. "All of them, including Stephanie Winters."

"But the handwriting's totally different."

"I know. Steven was an artist, remember? He created different styles. He had…*issues*. Now, I happen to believe the voices he heard really were the souls of those who died in the woods. I think Robin led them to him because he was a writer and could document their stories. But there is no Stephanie Winters. That's all Steven." Scott paused, looking her in the eye. "Stephanie was his alter ego."

CHAPTER THIRTY-TWO

Jennifer held her breath.

"Steven was…confused," Scott said. "He wasn't transgender, exactly, but he had this other persona that was a young woman—a teenage girl, really. And that girl, in his mind, had also been a victim of the demons. I don't know if he developed this persona as a way to better identify with the victims telling him their stories or what. I mean, he took on all sorts of pseudonyms with his writing projects, including a female one. Maybe this was another one of those and he just got carried away with it until it became a psychosis."

Jennifer sat on the bed. She felt dizzy. The shocks had been coming one after another, solid blows from a more powerful opponent. One minute she believed Steven might have actually communicated with the dead somehow, and the next minute she thought he was simply unhinged. Maybe both were true. If the souls of dead kids were telling her they'd been murdered by demons, she probably would have cracked too.

"What does it say?" she whispered.

"What?"

"Stephanie's diary. What does it say?"

He shrugged. "It's just like the others. It's written from the POV of a teenage girl, who is actually Steven, of course. She goes into the woods one day and is pursued by demons. She gets lost out there. The woods become like a labyrinth, and she's trapped there as night falls. The demons corner her and kill her, and make it look like suicide."

"How did they kill her?"

Scott sat down beside her and took her hand.

"Jenny, it doesn't matter. It was all in Steven's head."

"Just tell me. Please."

"Okay," he said with a sigh. "This one is particularly gruesome. And Steve's writing is so...*visceral*. The girl in the story was dragged up a tree to be hung, like Robin was. I think Steven was working through his feelings about that by writing this. But when the demons threw her off the branch, something happened and the rope snapped. She fell onto a pile of jagged rocks on the bank of the stream and broke nearly every bone in her body and..."

"And what?"

"She cracked open her skull. Everything came out of it."

Jenny put her hand over her mouth. "Jesus."

"This is why I didn't want to tell you. And besides, it never happened, anyway. This was all just in poor Steven's tormented mind."

There were footsteps above them, and Jennifer was grateful for the end of silence. The room had become more constricting as Scott told the story, like a tank being pressurized. She got off the bed and went to her suitcase.

Scott tensed. "What're you doing?"

"Don't worry. I'm not packing up to leave. I'm just getting another sweater." She grabbed one of wool, along with a scarf. "There's only so many hours of daylight left. If we're going to do this, let's do it."

MARK GATHERED the few things he might need. A bottled water. Cigarettes and lighter. A joint to calm his nerves. Most importantly, he brought his pocketknife, the one he always carried in his front pocket, clipped to the denim. He wasn't going back to demon-haunted woods without a weapon. He thought of saying a quick prayer, but decided against it. He wouldn't even know how to do it if he tried. He'd heard before that there were no atheists in foxholes. Mark had learned there weren't any in a jail cell either, nor in a toilet when one had their head over it, puking their guts out. Times like that were when he spoke to God, and even then, he only half believed what he was saying would have any effect. It was more of a what-have-I-got-to-lose sort of thing.

But he didn't want to think about anything spiritual right now. He had this superstitious feeling that doing so would jinx them. That a prayer would irritate the demons, bringing them out of the ground or the trees or wherever it was they lived.

Wondering if he would need his coat, he tried to check the weather forecast on his phone, but the app wasn't working. He really needed to upgrade, but that was just more money he didn't have. The guest bedroom he was in also doubled as an office. He looked to the desktop computer. It would only take a minute to check. When he shook the mouse, the computer awoke from sleep mode. He moved the arrow to tap on the internet browser, but as the monitor lit up, he was struck by the desktop image.

It was a picture of a woman in a sleeveless white blouse, with long brunette curls and a smile that could make a man's heart skip a beat. She looked to be in her late twenties, dark, lovely eyes and a youthful glow to her cheeks. Her hands were placed upon her swollen belly. She was full pregnant, looking ready to deliver that care package any second.

Beside the woman was Scott, looking to be in his early thirties. His arm was around her, and he was nuzzling his head into hers. He wore a silver wedding band on his finger, and the same gushing smile the woman had on her face, the kind of happiness only seen in people who were still in the honeymoon phase of their marriage. Behind them was a postcard-worthy scene of autumn, a covered bridge draped by a canopy of bright crimson leaves. To either side, pumpkins and gourds rested on haystacks, scarecrows with Raggedy Anne faces watching the couple with button eyes.

"What the fuck?"

Mark looked to the folders scattered across the screen, wondering if they held answers to the many questions he had about Scott, about everything. They bore typical file names—*tax records, book sale listings, insurance documents*. There was one that caught his eye.

Katie.

Was that the name of the woman in the picture? Mark looked over his shoulder at the door. It was mostly closed. As far as he knew, Scott was still in the basement with Jennifer.

Mark clicked on the folder.

He'd expected more photos. He found them, but they weren't what he expected. The images were black and white, filled with static blips. The first few were just amorphous shapes, but as he scrolled through the others, the image of a fetus appeared, sonograms of what had to be Scott's child.

There was movement in the hall.

Mark rushed the cursor to the top of the screen and put the computer back into sleep mode. As it faded to black, he felt the first drop of sweat roll down the small of his back. He stood facing the door, listening. When he peeked through the crack, he saw Scott going into the master bedroom. On top of Scott's dresser was a backpack, already packed and ready to go.

"SURE YOU'RE ready for this, Traci?" Jennifer asked.

The women were standing in the kitchen, drinks in hand. Even Jennifer had wanted one.

"I'm as ready as I'll ever be," Traci replied. "I don't know if I'm right or stupid or crazy or what, but I'm going. Last place I ever would've thought I'd return to; I'll tell you that."

"I know," Jennifer said. "Me too."

Corey came out of the living room, rolling his suitcase toward the wall. He'd repacked it. "I need to head out as soon as we're done. My wife's already sent me several texts." His eyes were wrought with worry.

Traci doubted it was because of his wife's nagging, if she'd really been nagging at all. She figured he just wanted to escape as soon as possible. Traci certainly planned to. What little fun this reunion had brought was over now, as dead as the people they were doing all of this for.

Mark exited the hallway. When he saw the bottles on the counter, he went for the bourbon, filled a tumbler, and drank it straight. His eyes were wrought too. Everyone's were. They were exhausted by something that had yet to begin.

"Is this really happening?" Corey asked.

Before anyone could respond, Scott returned from his bedroom, a backpack slung over one shoulder and the box containing the wreath in his hands. He smiled at them as if they were going to Disneyland instead of Suicide Woods. He seemed bizarrely excited.

Traci took another sip. Was Scott just trying to keep their spirits up? Was he just trying to be the strong one? Give them hope. Keep the faith. It was the only way his anticipation made any sense to her.

"What's with the backpack?" she asked. "I thought we were just going to be in and out of there."

"We are," he said. "This stuff is just in case. Some bandages if one of us gets a little cut by a thorn bush or something. A trowel if we need to dig into the soil to secure the wreath. A little water. Stuff like that."

Corey nodded, forever the Boy Scout. "Good call."

Traci looked at all the men, suddenly sizing them up. That there were three of them and only two women in this group was not lost upon her. She trusted them for the most part, but trusting men had gotten a lot of women raped and murdered. And many times the bodies were found in the woods. She told herself to stop being paranoid, that she'd been watching too many true crime shows. These were old friends, not drifters she'd just met in a seedy bar. But still, did she really *know* them? This whole trip had hurled more and more revelations at her, things she wouldn't have believed before she'd come back to Redford. She hoped there wouldn't be any more surprises, from the men or Jennifer or the woods or, worse yet, what lied within them.

"So," Scott said. "Are we ready?"

She told Scott the same thing she'd told Jennifer.

This was as ready as Traci was going to get, which was hardly ready at all.

PART FIVE

THE RETURN

CHAPTER THIRTY-THREE

The group of five stood side by side, colonial soldiers preparing to face their oldest enemy. The trail awaited like a swallowing throat, the tall grass on either side browned by the cold nights of October, the bushes run red, crowns of leaves encircling them with gold. The sun had drifted behind clouds that moved too slowly for Jennifer's liking, crawling across the sky like giant sloths. The air was crisp, smelling clean and empty. Normally this briskness pleased her. Today it seemed ominous, foreboding, as if it were whispering something she couldn't quite make out.

To her left, Traci stood stoic, her blonde hair spinning about her. When strands brushed across her face, she didn't push them away. Beside her was Mark, looking more determined than Jennifer had ever seen him before. But determined for what? Right beside her was Scott, his gray beard doing little to disguise his contentment. He looked more than pleased; he looked proud. Clearly, he wanted this more than anyone. To his right was Corey, coat zipped up to his neck, hands in his pockets. Looking at him in the natural light, Jennifer had to wonder if he'd slept at all.

"This is it," Scott said. "For Robin. For Steven."

"For all of us," Traci added.

"For all of us."

"Do you remember the way?" Mark asked.

"I do," Scott said. "It isn't far at all. You remember, right, Corey?"

Corey turned at the sound of his name, looking like a kid who'd been called on by a teacher when they hadn't been paying attention.

He nodded unconvincingly. "Yeah. I think so."

"In and out," Mark said.

"We'll be as fast as is reasonable," Scott said. "We can't rush this. We have to treat it with the seriousness of a funeral. Otherwise, there's no point to it."

Jennifer noticed Corey checking his watch. Leaves tore across the porch behind them, sounding like a crackling fire— little, martial drums for their battle cry. There was a collective energy to the group Jennifer could feel, pulsing like a single heart, the accumulation of dread and regret marrying a sense of purpose, of moral obligation.

Scott took her hand.

Then he took the first step.

COREY KEPT his hands hidden so he could pick at his thumbs' cuticles when he wasn't clenching his fists.

Back into the belly of the beast, he thought.

In his mind's eye, he saw warty flesh and curling custard horns. The stench of earwax and skunk glands and wet metal. The godless screeching of infant mouths in scabby palms, their tiny teeth like pale candy corn. But mostly he thought of Robin Reeves, and somehow that frightened him even more.

Was she really out there, suffering to this day? Was it possible? Was any of this?

Even as the group journeyed into the woods, they seemed to line up exactly as they had when they'd entered them all those years ago, only now it was Scott who led them in Steven's absence. The feeling of déjà vu made Corey's mouth go dry, and it was more than the chill on the wind that gave him goose bumps. Not for the first time, he felt as if they were moving backward through time, reliving that night on more than just a mental plain. All known physics became invalid and time became fluid, malleable. They were swimming against the current but making progress.

Soon they were under a dense canopy of trees. The dome of foliage dropped silence upon their surroundings, and it occurred to Corey that no one would hear them scream from here. Whatever horrors happened here remained secret, a Genesis garden capable of hiding all its sin. He kept his head down, watching the trail before him, stepping through a minefield of gnarled roots and acorns.

How long had they been walking? Again, time seemed distorted to the point of insignificance. He checked his watch, realized he hadn't registered what it read, and then checked it again. It was four o'clock. But though he was sure he'd checked his watch before they left, he couldn't recall what time it had been then. His stomach went hollow and he picked a cuticle, feeling the burn as his flesh separated. Though he couldn't see it, he knew it would bleed. Would this bloodletting be enough, or was there much more to spill tonight?

"Wasn't there a stream here?" Jennifer asked.

Corey realized she was right. Judging by the dip in the land, they should have reached it by now. He remembered that much about the landscape.

"We're getting closer to it," Scott said.

His hand was linked with Jennifer's. Their arms swayed just slightly, making their bond into a pendulum. It stung Corey to see it. Here were two people who hadn't seen each other in decades, and they were expressing more affection by physical touch than Gretchen had shown him in years. His wife would never attempt to hold his hand. When he took hers, she allowed it, but always found a reason to pull it away within a minute or two. It was the same with a kiss. She would kiss him back, but never initiate one. This lack of tenderness sent a message to him he simply refused to read. There was no need to open that envelope, for he knew what was inside. He was too old to start again. Too old and set in his ways. Corey knew what he liked and no longer had the fortitude to mute it. He was a comic book nerd and a movie geek, and he wasn't going to hide it in order to move on to someone new if his wife finally left him. Corey Pickett preferred loneliness to lies.

His toe bumped an exposed root, derailing his train of thought. How had he sunk into sadness over his marriage at a time like this? Dread had given way to despair so quickly, and all because Jennifer was holding Scott's hand. It was absurd. He thought he'd matured beyond the rejected boy envy of his youth. But he'd thought he was over Jennifer Parks too. Perhaps he'd given himself too much credit.

They reached a grove of white birch and entered a deadening blanketed by leaves, creating a large circle of saffron. Corey didn't recognize it at all. They couldn't be all that far from where he'd used to live. So many times he'd played out here, he and Scott pretending they were Luke and Han Solo fighting storm troopers on Endor. Could the woods have changed this much? This was more than a few missing trees taken out by wind and lightning. This was a complete transfiguration of the landscape.

"This isn't right," he said.

Jennifer looked back at him, but Scott kept on walking, taking her with him.

Traci turned to Corey. She was ghostly pale now, like a beautiful corpse. "What do you mean?"

"The woods," he said. "They're all wrong. They don't make any sense."

Scott called back without turning around. "It's been a long time, man. You're bound to have forgotten details."

Traci looked all around, eyelids pinching. Her lip began to twitch. "Corey, are we lost?"

Scott answered for him. "We're not lost. Just follow me. We're getting close to the stream now."

But Corey didn't hear the trickle of water. He didn't hear anything at all. No hawks cawing. No crickets chirping. No scuffle of chipmunks and squirrels. There was a threatening hush to the woods, the deadening earning its eerie name. He fought against thoughts of his time alone with Robin that night, but the words she'd said floated through his mind like a song stuck in his head. All these years and still he'd never repeated those words to anyone, not even last night when the group had opened all the closets to release the skeletons within. He'd confessed to seeing demons, but the secret of Robin's whispered message he'd kept for himself. It was like an incantation to him, one that would prove true if ever spoken aloud again.

He realized they weren't on a trail anymore. They were moving through the clearing, but the spindly trees on the other side didn't come any closer.

Though the ground moved beneath his feet, the trees remained the same distance away, as if the earth was spinning against him, creating a treadmill effect. When he looked up, the foliage was so thick and lustrous he could not see a single sliver of sky. They were entombed under a blanket of dying leaves stitched together by skeletal branches. But when Corey looked down again, he realized the group wasn't blanketed by the strange array of wilderness after all.

Only he was.

He was alone in the woods.

COREY HAD been dragging behind, staring at the trees overhead. Even when Traci had called to him, he hadn't replied. He'd been focused on the leaves to the point of seeming hypnotized, but he'd continued walking, bringing up the rear. But once they'd crossed the clearing and stepped down from a grassy bluff, she realized Corey had stopped following.

"Hold up," she told the others.

They all stopped as she called out for him. The only answer she got was her own voice bouncing back in a ghostly echo. She scrambled back over the bluff and into the deadening, scanning each direction, her breaths growing short and quick.

Corey was gone.

She called his name. She screamed it. Her hands went to her skull, and she had to stop herself from pulling out hair. There were footsteps behind her, and she spun around hopefully.

It was only Mark.

He scanned the clearing and cupped his hands over the sides of his mouth, calling Corey's name. The yelled it together, Traci pushing her voice until her throat was sore. As fresh tears blinded her, she turned to Mark and buried herself into him. He wrapped his arms around her. She wasn't the only one who was shaking.

"Enough of this shit," he said. "We're going back. Right now."

"What are we going to do?"

"I'll bet he turned back," Mark said. "Corey was always a smart guy. Let's follow his lead and get the hell out of here."

He turned around and called for the others. From where they were standing, they couldn't see down below where they'd left Scott and Jennifer, so they stared toward the bluff.

"Hey guys," Mark said. "Come on, we're heading back to the house! We're done with this shit. Let's get out of here before anything else goes wrong."

But when they reached the bluff, they realized it was too late for that.

"WHAT IS happening?" Jennifer said, unable to keep the tremor out of her voice. "Scott, where did they all go?"

He took her hand again, trying to pull her back from the clearing. She'd heard Mark saying they were going back to the house, but when she'd stepped onto the bluff, none of the others were there. Corey, Traci, Mark—*vanished*. She gripped Scott's hand tighter, afraid to let it go, as if he would vaporize if she didn't maintain constant touch.

"They went back to the house, I guess," Scott said.

He tugged her along again, but she resisted. "Wait a second. They were here a second ago. Now they're nowhere in sight."

She called their names.

Scott turned her to him. "They went back to the house. Coming here must've been too much for them."

"Well, then I want to go back too."

"Jenny, please. We're so close."

"Scott, I—"

"*Please*, Jenny. I can't do this alone. We're so close to finalizing this. It's time to right a wrong. It's long overdue."

He put down the cardboard box, opened it, and removed the wreath. He held it up so she could see Robin's picture. The girl smiled back at her, all butterflies and sunshine, as if she would never die at all, let alone die shortly after the picture was taken. Scott held it out to her.

"Take it," he said.

"I don't want to."

"Hold it in your own two hands and tell me it doesn't feel right."

Jennifer shook her head. "Nothing about being here feels right. I knew I shouldn't have agreed to this. I'm sorry, Scott. I didn't want to disappoint you. But I'm scared, and I want to go back now."

A darkness fell over Scott's face then, like the falling of night. The blue of his eyes became the icy color of glaciers, his brow dropping. His nostrils flared.

"You can't do this *one thing* for me?" he asked.

Something in Jennifer's chest pinched, something tight and cold. Scott's entire demeanor had changed in a snap, as if his personality was on a timer and the alarm had just gone off. She'd seen him frustrated and angry in their youth, but since their reunion, he'd been so calm and collected. So adult. So masculine in his ability to handle these turbulent situations. This sudden shift made him seem alien to her now. She realized just how long they'd been apart, how much she had changed. Scott had changed too, and there had not been nearly enough time to learn just how much. Twenty hours could not cover twenty-five years.

"Scott...I'm sorry... I just—"

He let go of her hand a little too forcefully for her liking.

"God-fucking-damn it!" he said, cursing at the ground.

Jenny took a step back. When he noticed her do this, the darkness that had befallen him rapidly dissipated. His eyes widened, all the blood leaving his face.

"Listen," he said, simmering down. "I need to do this. I'm going down to the creek. I had hoped you'd come with me. I thought the others might chicken out, but I really thought I could at least count on you, especially after last night. But if you really want to go back to the house, I'll understand."

He looked to the trail ahead.

Jennifer's stomach dropped. "Scott, you don't expect me to go back alone do you?"

He shrugged. "It's not that far. And I'm sure you'll catch up with the others."

"I'm not going off alone in these woods. Not for one second."

"And I'm not leaving without putting this memorial where Robin died. This is our benediction, and I aim to see it through. If you want, you can wait here. I'll be back shortly."

"Scott, you can't just leave me here!"

"For God sakes, Jenny, I don't want to. But I made a promise to myself, to Steven, to all of you. I'm going down to the creek. Now are you coming with me or not? It's your choice."

The air felt suddenly colder, more like winter than fall. A shadow had crept across the thicket, the cloudy skies muting the world to a tombstone gray, a false dusk. She stared at Scott and he stared right back.

"Some choice," she said. "That's no choice at all, is it?"

"I can't decide for you."

"But you have." She crossed her arms. "I guess I saw something that wasn't there."

He looked from side to side, scanning the trees.

"Not in the woods," she said. "In you."

Scott dropped his gaze. "Jenny…"

"It's okay." She smiled though her eyes grew wet. "I'm just realizing I'm even more desperate than I thought I was." She let out a self-deprecating laugh. "I let my imagination run away with me. Not your fault."

Jennifer knew she was being passive-aggressive, but she was also speaking the truth. She had lulled herself into the misleading comfort of memories, but as the saying goes, you can't go home again. She and Scott had been in love once upon a time, but that fairytale had ended many chapters ago. So while there was an instant attraction to him, it was built on a flimsy foundation of nostalgia. They were just old friends, not rekindled old flames. She'd been foolish to crush on him so hard so quickly. But while he might not be what she'd wanted him to be, Jennifer doubted she was all he'd hoped for either. Scott wasn't a bad guy, just a disappointment. That was just as much her fault as it was his.

Ever since he'd sent her that first message, she'd built him up in her mind as this oasis in the cruel desert of her middle-age derailment. She'd attached to him the carefree feeling of the twilight of her youth, a feeling from their shared yesterday. But that happiness had come from more than Scott Dwyer; it was the happiness of her youth itself, of being young and free with no work worries, no mom stress, and no failed marriage eating away at her soul. The easy joy of youth was not something Scott could give back. No one could. And judging by the look on his face, he understood this too.

"Jenny," he said. "I'm just a man."

And it was all he needed to say.

She took the wreath from him and started back on the trail, going deeper into the woods.

"Come on," she said softly. "Before we know it, it'll be dark."

CHAPTER THIRTY-FOUR

Corey began to cry. He couldn't help it. He'd always been sensitive and had never grown out of crying the way most men seemed to. How could they control it, whether it embarrassed them or not? In his youth, Corey had been ridiculed for it and became afraid to cry in public, but that hadn't put an end to it. Even as an adult, emotionally manipulative, sappy movies still managed to make him tear up, and he had to pretend to be just rubbing his eye or scratching his cheek instead of wiping away a tear, not wanting Gretchen to notice. He figured she usually did but was too disgusted with him to mention it.

He was mature enough now to know there was nothing wrong with a man crying, but that didn't mean other people thought the same way. For some, either a man could produce testosterone or tears, but not both.

It wasn't the only thing that made him feel like less than a man. Whenever he brought his car to a garage for service, he felt like a ten-year-old around all the greasy, oil-stained mechanics. Other than how to drive, he knew nothing about cars. He'd never even changed his own oil and had no interest in learning how. He didn't like sports, didn't drink beer, and didn't eat red meat. Over time, he'd learned to accept his oddity as a male, and found he was not the only one of his kind. He'd made friends with so many other comic book-reading, sci-fi movie-loving, Milk Dud-popping nerds over the years. Guys who didn't know a socket wrench from sandpaper but could tell you the names of every crewman who'd ever been aboard the Starship Enterprise and the full titles of every *Friday the 13th* movie. Let the jocks and mechanics have their swinging-dick bravado. It wasn't going to bother him anymore.

But that was before his son became a teenager.

As a boy, Luke had loved all the same things his father had. Superheroes and action figures were Corey's son's bread and butter. But, by the time he was thirteen, he'd left them all behind, and Corey could only stand by and watch as Luke became athletic, joining baseball teams first, then football. He'd participated in Olympic-style wrestling after school and lifted weights in the garage. By sixteen, he was bigger and stronger than his father, and bought an old El Camino he'd managed to get running on his own. And he was great with girls. They stopped by to see him all the time, swooning over him like he was the front man for a boy band. And though Luke loved his father and never tried to emasculate him, it still happened naturally. Corey grew to feel like an old lion being usurped by a younger, more virile male. It didn't help matters that Gretchen showed so much pride in Luke and gave him all the affection she held back from her husband. It was like some Freudian nightmare.

He stood in the clearing, his head in his hands as the tears rolled.

My son is better than me, he thought. *Soon he'll realize it and he'll hate me just as much as his mother does, if he hasn't already. He's stronger, more charming, and more skilled than I can ever hope to be, and once he's through with college he'll be smarter than I am too. I'll disgust him. He'll be embarrassed to call me Dad.*

The woods seemed to warp around him, the branches elongated, bending at impossible angles. Just like all those macho bullies, the woods had seen him cry and pounced on him for it. Again, his deepest, private anxieties about his life had bubbled to the front of his mind, even though he knew he should be focused on escaping the forest. It was as if he was out of control of his own thought process.

Corey shook his head vigorously, trying to empty his head of negative thoughts. He had to stay alert. He had to get out of here.

He was still standing in the deadening, and his throat had gone raw from shouting for the others. Light was dimming, as if time were being fast-forwarded to twilight. As the breeze grew colder, Corey hunched up his shoulders and went into a run, going for the tree line. This time the forest allowed him to reach it, but he wondered if that was really a good thing. The trail was not where it should have been. When Corey glanced back, the clearing seemed much farther away than his steps should have achieved. The leaf-covered earth moved up and down like a breathing chest, and Corey kept on through the woods before the deadening could change its mind and draw him back into it like a frog catching a fly.

He leapt into the fray, into the soulless, gathering dark, an intense grayness permeating Suicide Woods like omnipresent vapor. If he could only see the sun, he would at least know which way was west.

He remembered how his old compass hadn't worked that night, but returned to functionality once they'd made it home. Corey took his phone from his pocket, doubting it would be of any use to him, but he had to try. He hoped to pull up its GPS, but when he clicked on the application, the screen only went black.

"To hell with this."

He dialed 911. The screen told him it was connecting and a jolt of relief went through him, enough to make him smile. He put the phone to his ear, waiting. The wait continued. It didn't ring.

He looked at the screen again. *Call failed,* it read.

"You bitch!" He tried again. "Come on, come on."

But he only got the same result.

"No!"

He wanted to smash the goddamned thing against a tree. Instead, he put it in his pocket. Maybe if he kept walking, he'd find a signal. Best not to try the flashlight though. Not with the battery only at half power.

"Great, Corey...just great."

As he moved on, the gray lingered, casting long shadows that played tricks on his eyes. His struggle with low lighting was a high concern right now. He moved faster, wanting to make the most of what little natural light was left, for he knew once darkness fell, he might never see daylight again.

THEY DIDN'T talk as they headed down the path to the creek. Scott knew they were getting close. He felt it more than remembered it. Soon they'd reach the tree where the young girl had been killed. Then he could really get to fixing things, to making all of this better for everyone. That's all he wanted, all that mattered. If he'd disappointed Jennifer, he supposed he could live with that, as long as she was here with him right now, here with him for this.

He cursed himself again for having left the box of journals in the basement room last night. He'd only wanted to give Jennifer a supervised taste of them, to get her to believe. That's why he'd shown them to her. But he'd never intended to leave her alone with them. He'd just had too much to drink. Booze combined with his and Jennifer's sudden kiss had clouded his thinking, and when he'd gone up to bed, he'd forgotten all about the box. Stupid. Careless. A move that could have been detrimental. He'd realized this error before he shut his eyes for the night and had gotten out of bed and gone back to the basement room, hoping Jennifer would be asleep and he could sneak in and grab the box. But she'd stirred, and that smooth, white slip looked so freaking good on her. He'd wanted his former girlfriend again, and more importantly, she wanted him. Reciprocating her passion would further endear her to him, so he risked a sexual advancement that paid off handsomely.

Later, when she confessed to reading the diaries, he had kept his cool, coming up with good reasons not to tell the others. He'd impressed himself. Mom and Dad would have been proud of him. He was determined to do what was right, even if it was incredibly overdue.

They were so close now, so very close.

He smelled the cold water before he even heard it.

MARK'S TEETH were grinding, and he couldn't stop. He wanted to punch something, to scream profanities and kick every one of these damned trees down.

How many years had he stayed out of the woods? Not just Suicide Woods, but *any* woods? After that Halloween, he'd never gone camping or hiking ever again. He didn't go canoeing or even fishing. Whenever he visited a park, he kept to the concrete. Once his children had grown, he avoided parks all together, and that suited him just fine. He got enough fresh air and sunshine working construction all day. Or, at least he had, when he'd still been working. He hated anything outdoorsy because it always gave him the low-level nausea of fear. If he were to try and go camping overnight, he probably would have had a full-blown panic attack. Now that he was facing a creeping dusk in the very woods in which he'd seen that demonic dwarf, he felt one coming on was just about certain.

Traci wouldn't let go of his arm. She clung to him with both hands. That was good. They had to stay close, maintain sight of each other as well as physical contact. It would only take these woods a split second to separate them.

All they had now was each other. The forest had swallowed up the others.

Both their phones had failed. Mark patted the knife in his pocket, glad he had brought it along. He wanted to take it out but worried the sight of it would only amplify Traci's terror. Right now, they didn't need a weapon, anyway. He hoped things would stay that way.

"Okay." He pointed to the edge of the clearing. "We came in from that way, right?"

He looked to Traci. She was staring at the ground, trance-like. He put his hand over hers. It was a block of ice.

"I'm a liar, Mark," she said.

Mark tensed. "What?"

"I said…I'm a *liar*." The corners of her mouth curled down. "I'm not a lawyer, I'm a bartender. I never went to freaking law school. Never even went to college to tell you the truth. The only jobs I've ever held were waitress, bartender, or cashier. Back in my twenties, I'd been a stripper. Most jobs I couldn't hold on to, 'cause of this." She reached into her coat pocket, retrieving a flask Mark hadn't known she'd brought along. "I'm a drunk, Mark. Because of that, I just fail over and over: jobs, relationships, life. I suck at everything."

She started to sob, her chest heaving, shoulders shaking. He tucked her into him and held her tight. He wanted to tell her everything would be all right, but he didn't want to lie to her. It seemed she'd had enough of lies.

But why had she chosen now to tell him these things?

He rubbed her back up and down. God, she smelled so good, all light and flowery and girly, clean in a way the last few women in his life had never managed to be. He thought of Carol and how disgusting she'd become. By contrast, holding Traci, Mark knew all her secret places would be as pure as spring water in the sunshine. It didn't matter how many men she'd had or that she'd been an exotic dancer, that she wore a lot of makeup or obviously had breast implants. Traci wasn't a whore. *Carol* was a goddamned whore. Rhonda, the mother of his first child, was an even bigger whore. Mark had doubted Dalton was even his until the boy grew up to look just like him.

If only he'd stayed with Traci somehow, his life wouldn't be the flaming, ten-car pileup it was today. Having a good woman on his arm, as he literally did right now, would have made all the difference. They'd come from the same rough background and therefore understood each other in ways no one else ever could. It didn't matter to him that she was an alcoholic. She was still a good person. And holy cow, she was so painfully beautiful. To walk around with her on his arm would make other men sick with envy, and that would boost Mark's confidence enough to help him get a job, despite how he was getting older and didn't have the strength and stamina required to do the only kind of work he'd ever been good at.

Traci stepped back, drying her tears and taking long, deliberate breaths. He watched her chest and rise and fall, and it made him ache for her all the more. The woman was gorgeous, inside and out. That's why he could never have her.

He was a fuck up. A loser. Just a deadbeat dad who couldn't remember his children's birthdays. He couldn't even remember to pick them up at soccer practice on time on the few occasions his exes even bothered asking him for help. They barely tried anymore. Mark got stoned and drunk and forgot all the things that should have mattered to him but simply didn't. One arrest for drunk driving hadn't been enough to straighten him up. Neither had the ones that followed. Even a year of riding the bus and taking taxis to work because his license had been taken away hadn't been enough of a wakeup call. He was too stubborn to learn and too lazy to care.

Mark Goranson was forty-three years old, and this was where he was in life.

"I don't really know why I told you this," Traci said. She took a drink from her flask. "I just feel like…like a piece of shit all of a sudden."

"Me too."

"I think it's this place. It's draining us. It wants us to hate ourselves. It wants us to *kill ourselves*."

Now that she'd said it, he thought so too. But this wasn't about him. Nothing ever was.

Traci sniffed. "I'm human garbage."

"C'mon, Traci, you're great. Any guy would be lucky to have you. I'm talking lotto-winner lucky." He smirked. "Your boyfriend must be dancing on the ceiling every day."

She sighed. "He's not really my boyfriend. He's more like a friend with benefits. He…he doesn't even *know* me. How could he? Even I don't know me."

"But I do. We go way back. We never should've broken up in the first place, babe. I know how awesome you are, even if you don't realize it."

Mark felt strong then. Projecting a demeanor of calmness and caring made him feel more mature than he'd felt in a long time. He'd been watching the way Scott did it, and though Mark would never admit it, he idolized the guy for that. Scott was just so well put together, and the women fawned over him because of it. Time had developed him, cultivated him. Time had not been as kind to Mark. It had not enhanced him the way it had Scott Dwyer. It had only worn out his flesh and crippled his initiative, even diminishing his desire, making his life choices more and more myopic. If he couldn't be like Scott, at least he could fake it.

"And I'll tell you one thing," he said. "I'm gonna get you outta here."

AS SCOTT arranged the wreath and mementos, Jennifer took slow steps along the creek, chilled by the shadow of the sycamore tree. Pale sunlight shown through the branches, as if highlighting the spot Robin Reeves had hung from. The feeling of guilt here was palpable, visceral, and if being in the woods was creepy, being at this spot was downright frightening. The atmosphere made her flesh crawl.

What had really happened to that poor girl?

What had really happened to any of the young people who'd died out here?

Jennifer crossed her arms for warmth, covering her hands. How the hell had she committed to this? In theory, it had sounded good, at least back at Scott's place. Now that she was here, the memorial service seemed so futile. It was too little, too late. And it came at the expense of reopening too many psychological scars. How had Scott coaxed her into coming into these woods in the first place?

She walked slowly up the bank, black pebbles crunching beneath her feet. Scott had opened his backpack and was arranging small items around the memorial. Jennifer sighed to herself. She shouldn't have said all of those mean things to him, telling him she'd seen something in him that wasn't actually there. It was a cruel shot to take, and he hadn't really deserved it. But she didn't deserve to be kept out here when she wanted to leave. Still, watching him decorate this thoughtful shrine, it was hard to stay angry with the guy. He obviously felt he was doing something deeply important. He needed this. That much was certain.

But she didn't know what to do with herself. That's why she'd been walking along the creek. She stayed close to Scott, of course. If she lost sight of him too, she'd have a massive heart attack. But the arranging of the memorial seemed specific to him. He was being very particular about it, and she didn't want to intrude. If he wanted to say a few words when he finished, she would bow her head with him. She just hoped he didn't expect her to say anything special. She was never good at that sort of thing. All she would know to say was she was sorry. And she was. She really was.

Jennifer picked up a stone and skipped it down the creek. It bounced thrice over the surface of the shallow water and sunk out of sight. Looking up, she took in the colorful foliage on the other side. It really was beautiful this time of year. Under different circumstances, the scene would be tranquil.

She was just about to turn around when she saw something behind a cluster of jagged rocks. It was brightly colored, not earth tone like the foliage. Whatever it was, it was vivid green and pink, with white puffs tucked in-between. The images reminded her of Easter Sunday, of springtime. She moved up the bank, trying to see around the crags. The colors behind the jagged rocks were so bright and warm.

They looked like fresh flowers.

Jennifer came to a thinning in the creek where a makeshift bridge of rocks and fallen branches—little more than a beaver dam—had been laid across the shallowest part of the stream. It was less than six feet to the other side. She took a few careful steps across, leaning for a better look. The bright colored thing was an arch of shrubbery, decorated with ribbon and a sash.

A wreath, she realized. *A memorial.*

She looked back to Scott. He was still fussing over the one for Robin and hadn't noticed Jennifer standing over the creek. He was digging up earth with his trowel to secure the legs of the wreath. Other small tools lay beside him in the dirt.

Jennifer gazed back across the creek. The memorial on the other side obviously wasn't old. The flowers had not wilted despite the frigid nights, and there were small frames on the ground in front of the wreath that still stood upright. The sash had been twisted by the wind but remained clean. She walked to the bank on the other side and moved slowly toward the memorial.

Scott hadn't mentioned any other recent deaths, had he?

When she came upon the shrine, she squatted before the wreath and picked up one of the photos. It was of a cute brunette girl, maybe fifteen or so. She had her head cocked to one side and was holding a gigantic teddy bear. Something about her eyes seemed familiar.

Jennifer picked up another.

She gasped.

The same girl was in this picture, but instead of hugging a teddy bear, she was hugging a man. Though he'd aged and Jennifer had not seen him in decades, there was no mistaking the face of Steven Winters. Looking at the girl's eyes again, she realized why they were familiar. They were the same as her dad's.

Jennifer put the photos down and looked at the sash that had been tangled by the wind. Its letters were bunched together, making the words illegible. She pulled it back into place so she could read it.

She stopped breathing. Her fingers began to shake along with the rest of her, the wreath vibrating in her hands. She lifted it and spun around. Scott was standing on the other side of the bank, watching her.

"Scott," she called. "Come quick. You need to see this!"

He came, but not quickly. He walked across the little bridge, looking especially pale in the dying light. Even his lips had lost their color. She came towards him with the wreath, holding it before her like an offering. She pulled the sash taught, making sure he could read it. Scott looked it at it, but Jennifer didn't register anything going on behind his eyes. She turned the wreath back to her, making sure she hadn't been mistaken, but the name remained the same.

In loving memory of Stephanie Winters.

Jennifer trembled. She looked into Scott's eyes, hoping to see something more than the powder blue she'd once fallen in love with. He remained a blank slate. Was he just confused? Was he scared?

"Scott," she said. "Don't you see? Stephanie Winters wasn't a figment of Steven's imagination. There're pictures of her back there. She was real. I think she was his daughter."

Scott took a long, slow breath, the first sign of life he'd shown since he'd come across the creek. Jennifer gave him a sad little smile, not knowing what else to do or say.

She didn't notice the knife until it was halfway inside her.

CHAPTER THIRTY-FIVE

Traci had been lulled all along. She realized that now. A dark conductivity had influenced her, guiding her back into these woods despite her better judgment. She'd been tricked. An unknown manipulator had coerced her, and she'd been hypnotized by the force between the trees. Even now it was twisting her emotions. That had to be why she'd broke down in Mark's arms and told him things she never would have confessed to otherwise. The energy of Suicide Woods was subtle but pitch black.

Was this why so many had taken their own lives out here? Did the woods itself convince them they didn't deserve to live by using their own insecurities and anxieties against them? Did it tear up their souls until there was nothing left to say no?

Or were demons the true slayers?

She remembered Steven once saying that the woods didn't hold demons, but that they *were* demons. The sycamores and maples and evergreens, the dirt and the rocks and the streams—all demons in another form. She hadn't known what to make of that at the time. Now it seemed so brutally clear, a truth she wished she didn't know.

Mark got excited when they found a trail. "I think this is it, the one we came in on."

Traci wasn't sure. Everything looked the same now, which had not been the case when they'd arrived. The woods were melding together to muddy her and Mark's vision as well as their thoughts.

She let him guide her anyway. A trail was better than no path at all. It had to lead somewhere. They crunched over a bedding of acorn tops and crisp leaves, each footstep sounding as loud as a shotgun in the unnatural hush of the forest. Would the demons hear them and come dashing across the thicket, claws clicking like sharpening knives, fangs oozing with grease, eyes bright with fire? She couldn't shake the feeling of being hunted and it kept her looking in all directions, glancing over her shoulder repeatedly.

"This is the way," Mark said. "It has to be."

Traci was glad to have him with her. When she'd first arrived at the house last night, she'd thought Mark was a little creepy and Scott was down-home. Now those opinions had flipped. Mark was flawed, but moralistic. Scott was an enigma whose mysteriousness grew more troubling by the minute. His actions had gone from noble to questionable to downright worrisome.

And he was alone with Jennifer.

SCOTT DIPPED the pocketknife into the stream, washing it of Jennifer's blood. When he was satisfied it was clean enough, he wiped it dry on his pant leg, snapped it shut again, and put it in his coat. He rinsed his hands and wrists. There were no visible stains on his clothes. One stab to her stomach had been enough. There was no call for savagery.

He turned away from the stream and looked down at his first love. She was on her side, turned away from him, perfectly still in a pond of red, her hair covering her face. He had the urge to take some memento, a piece of jewelry or a lock of her hair. He wanted to cover her with a blanket or something. But he resisted these impulses. He'd read up on these things and knew covering a body was a clear indication to police that the killer knew the victim. That was if they found her at all, and if her body even remained out here. If he wanted a memento, he didn't need to take it off her corpse. There were plenty of items in her suitcase back at the house.

Scott sighed.

He hadn't wanted it to happen like this. Of course he had to kill her, but he hadn't been ready yet. Yes, Jennifer's death was long overdue, but he still hadn't felt prepared, and the tenderness of their lovemaking last night had made it all the harder to follow through with what had to be done. He'd wanted to tell her why she had to die, but when he looked into her eyes, he found it impossible to do so. Even though he'd shown her the diaries and explained what they meant, she still wouldn't have believed him or understood. Had it not been for his father, Scott wouldn't have believed it either.

The only journal he hadn't been honest about was that of Stephanie Winters. He'd told Jennifer the truth when it came to what happened to Steven's daughter, but lied about her being a work of fiction. The girl was real, or at least she had been. If he'd known someone had created a fresh memorial for Stephanie (it must have been some friend or distant relative he'd overlooked), he would have destroyed it when he was here two days ago, back when he was still forming the plan. He'd thought he'd been so careful. He hoped he hadn't missed anything else. His father had taught him to expect the unexpected, and Scott felt he'd done well on the fly, coming up with last minute explanations to questions Jennifer and the others had thrown at him. And he was damn proud of how he'd managed to coerce them all into returning to Suicide Woods, something he had initially believed would be impossible.

He recalled that night with his father now, how they'd been sitting by the fireplace having drinks, before the chemotherapy made Dad too sick to keep anything down.

"They all have to go back there," the old man had explained. "Otherwise, the effect won't be strong enough. Think of them as fuel for the machine. You may get somewhere on a low tank, but if you really want to complete the journey, you need to fill 'er up."

Scott had nodded. He was gaining so much wisdom. He only wished his father had informed him of the truth earlier. Mom was already gone. She would never see her boy achieve what she'd dreamed for him.

"To appease the demons," Dad had told him, "you have to finish what we started. You're the only one who can do it. The others have been waiting for you. Back in '95, we screwed it up, and that made us all believe you weren't the one, that you couldn't have an effect on the gateway if things hadn't worked out. That disbelief cost us too many years. But I always held out hope, son. In my heart of hearts, I knew we'd all been right to choose you, even when you were just six years old. Maybe if we'd let you know back in '95, you could have helped us that Halloween."

"Why didn't you?" Scott had asked. "Why'd you leave me in the dark about all of this until recently?"

His father had shook his head. "We just didn't think a teenager could handle it. Frankly, I still believe that. It wasn't time to bring you into the fold yet. You were a good-hearted boy—you *still* are, really—and you would have resisted us back then. And once Katie came along, I thought you would be better off having the simple, normal life she provided. But she's gone now and you're an island of a man. You have a better understanding of how the world works, how we all have to make sacrifices."

Standing in the woods now, looking down at Jennifer's body, Scott finally understood what his father had meant. He went across the creek to gather his things, and then trekked back into the woods to find the others.

COREY CROUCHED in the bushes as the shape moved across the glade. He held his breath, watching the humanoid figure. Had whoever it was— *whatever* it was—spotted him too? Though the growing darkness made the person hard to make out, Corey knew it wasn't one of his friends. He could not only see that; he could *feel* it. The figure seemed to drift rather than walk, like it was hovering just an inch above the ground. Corey wanted to duck his head to hide completely out of sight, but he knew he needed to watch what this shape was doing, where it was going.

His mind flashed back to the crimson ghoul with three legs. Had it come back for him after all these years? Could it smell Corey's blood pulsing through his veins, hear his heart pounding like a funeral drum?

The humanoid came to a stop, causing Corey to shiver, thinking he'd given himself away somehow. But it did not turn in his direction. The smell of burning herbs hit Corey's nostrils, a miasma he had not forgotten, and another humanoid shadow came across the glade to join the first one. They held an infuser on a chain, and black fumes rose from it as if announcing a new pope. There was movement behind the birch trees. More figures appeared. The one closest to Corey was definitely a human being.

He was a tall, lean man dressed in camouflage and combat boots. The top of his head was bald, the sides and back a ring of silver hair, and there were deep wrinkles across his brow. Corey guessed him to be in his sixties. The first one Corey had seen came beside the man. It was a female. At first, Corey thought she was wearing some sort of black cloak or cape, and it made his stomach go hollow, but when he looked closer, he realized it was a trench coat. She wore knee-high black boots and a russet scarf that matched the color of her hair.

An elderly, African American couple approached the others. The man had fluffy white hair and a matching beard, and the woman wore Coke bottle-thick glasses and an obvious wig that appeared blue in the fading light. Both had dressed casually. The couple smiled at the other two, and the men shook hands. Corey leaned forward but couldn't make out what they were saying.

He thought of the group he'd seen in the woods twenty-five years ago. Was it possible…?

Corey got a head count. There were seven of them in all, until one more appeared from between two rust-colored bushes and joined the circle. This one was short enough to be a child, but the face revealed otherwise. The little person wore a hooded sweater with the hood covering their head, but as they came closer to the black couple, Corey saw some slight wrinkles that spoke of age, but he couldn't tell how old they were. As the little person came closer, they appeared to be female judging by the shape of her head and her hairless cheeks. The eyes were pink like an albino's, and it seemed she had shaved off her eyebrows. He didn't even see eyelashes.

The dwarf, Corey thought. *The one Mark saw that night.*

She greeted the others—her voice confirming her gender—and they all said hello to her. This time Corey could make out the conversation.

"It's been a long time, folks," the little woman said. "Never thought we'd be doing this again."

The tall man nodded. "It's a miracle we have the chance to."

"The magic may have faded, but it's never gone." The little woman pulled her hood down, revealing a completely bald head. She had a prominent forehead, a flat nose, and plump lips. Her smile showed tiny, malformed teeth. "And I never gave up hope."

The old black woman shook her head. "I was worried for a while there. That man was getting way too close, nosing around like he was. Who knows how much he collected on us."

"Well," the tall man said, "that's why he was taken care of."

"And that's what cinched it for me," the little woman said. "That's when I knew we'd been right about the boy all along."

"I just hope we were right about the girl too. There's still time for them to be productive, but not much."

Corey squinted.

What the heck were these people talking about? And what were they doing out here? He felt certain they were the same people from that Halloween long ago. It couldn't be a coincidence they were in Suicide Woods both times he and his friends were. From what they were saying, they hadn't been here in a good, long while, too. Had they been waiting for them to return?

"The girl remains potent," the little woman said. "Every time I cast the stones, they tell me the same thing."

The woman in the trench coat huffed. "I must admit, I had the same results with my crystals. But still…she's old."

Every muscle in Corey tensed. The bizarre discussion gave him the chills. It sounded as if this cabal was making plans…but for who?

When another figure came out of the woods, Corey got his answer.

Scott joined the group, and they actually applauded.

CHAPTER THIRTY-SIX

S cott felt like a movie star. Everyone wanted to shake his hand. Some of the women kissed his cheek like a grandmother would. Men hugged him, slapping his back with pride the way he hoped his parents would if they were alive today.

It surprised him a little to be so warmly welcomed. He'd thought he was doing a decent job but had kept second-guessing himself now that some things had not gone according to plan. But that was exactly the sort of thing Dad had taught him to expect. Improvisation was key because even the best-laid plans never played out perfectly. He may not have kept diligently on target, but it wasn't entirely his fault. The universe was full of randomness. Things were still mostly on track, and night was just now falling, the first few stars appearing beyond the rustling maples.

"Well, look at you," the little woman said. "Scott Dwyer, all grown up. Last time I saw you, you were just a little taller than me."

Scott hadn't always remembered what happened in the basement. It wasn't until his father told him everything that the buried memories slowly began to return. He'd suppressed them for so long. Digging them out of his subconscious had taken more than words. Fortunately, Dad had filmed it all back in 1988 and kept the tapes. Seeing was believing.

"You must be Reba," Scott said.

He held out his hand, and she slapped it away playfully, holding out her arms for a hug. He knelt down on one knee, and they embraced. Up close, he got a better look at the woman and saw what his father had told him about. Reba had condition known as hypohidrotic ectodermal dysplasia, which caused abnormal growth of the skin, hair, teeth, and nails. She'd been born hairless and without fingernails or toenails, and her teeth were pointy and undersized. Because of her skin problems, she'd always been wrinkled and splotchy, and so she looked relatively the same now as she had on the recording, despite it being over thirty years old.

"You've done a great job," Reba said. "Some of us had our doubts it would be possible for anyone to get all your old friends back to Redford. You're somethin' else, Scott."

"Thanks. It was nothing."

"Don't be so humble. You must've really laid on the charm to get them back here to begin with, but then to get them in the woods too? That's really impressive."

The tall man put his hand on Scott's shoulder as he stood up.

"What's the status on the old flame?" he asked.

Scott's heart sank a little further. It would take time to mourn her properly, just as it had taken time to mourn Katie after his wife's accident.

"It's done," Scott said. "Jenny's gone."

The tall man smiled, flashing immaculate dentures. "That's excellent news. I knew you had it in you, son. How'd you do her? Like your folks wanted?"

"Not exactly. It happened so suddenly. I felt like I needed to seize the moment, so…I stabbed her in the belly. I hope you that works for you… and for them."

"I'm sure it's fine. Don't worry about that right now. Be proud, Scott. If your mother were here to see this…boy, I tell you what. Lord, how she hated that little bitch."

"Can you blame her?" Reba asked. "Susie Dwyer just wanted what was right for her boy. That Jenny Parks girl got in the way. And that little shit Mark Goranson… Hell, I wish I'd killed him that night. I was so damn close, but I just wanted him to feel that fear a little longer, ya know? Make it all the more valuable to them. I just—"

"Now, Reba. There's no sense beating yourself up about it again. You've been doing that for decades now. We all made mistakes that night. But now, thanks to Scott's ingenuity and dedication to his parents' final wishes, we have the chance to redeem ourselves. Let's focus on the positive."

Reba grinned a yellow row of piranha teeth. "Yeah. Always look on the bright side. That's what your Mama always said, Scott. And she was right! Just look at you now."

Scott blushed, not used to praise. He'd lived a simple life, never even leaving his hometown. He'd traveled a little, of course, and had moved to the other side of Connecticut for a few years to attend college. Then he'd come right back to Redford, and after his parents passed on, he'd moved right back into the house he'd grown up in. His business was only moderately successful. He had enough to live on, provided he kept to a budget, but it was nothing to celebrate. If the house hadn't been paid for, he wouldn't have been able to afford the mortgage, and he was still struggling to put enough money aside to pay the property tax. He'd never done much to deserve praise. The only ones who really gave him any were his parents and Katie, but they were all gone now.

The woman in the coat turned to the tall man. "Fred, why don't you rally the others, okay? It's getting cold and I don't want to be out here any later than we have to."

"You got it, Julia."

Fred wandered off to gather the rest of The Congregation. Scott had only been dealing with Fred and Julia up until now, but looking at the crowd, he recognized some of the faces from his youth. The old black man was George Payton. He and Scott's father had been on the same bowling team. Once a month, Dad hosted a poker night at the house, and George was always there. Scott hadn't seen him in so many years, but he recognized him just the same. He even remembered his wife, Telma. She'd sometimes picked up Scott's mother for bingo when the ladies carpooled. Another woman he remembered as his junior high school librarian, and the one carrying the brass infuser was Mrs. Richardson, the elderly widow who still lived across the street. The final man was Dave Shrinner Jr., the county sheriff. Scott knew him from his re-election campaign signs, which were scattered all over town. His father had been sheriff too, and had only retired seven years previous, after nearly four decades of police service.

Like Julia, Shrinner Jr. was one of the few who weren't senior citizens. He was about Scott's age. Julia looked to be in her early thirties.

"I'm so glad you two have finally met," Reba said, looking at Scott and Julia. "You both were always such good kids." She smiled her possum's grin. "And who knows? Maybe you guys could, you know, *give it a shot*. If it doesn't work out with the other girl."

TRACI FELT as if someone had just walked over her grave. The sensation was constant and growing stronger. She cringed, biting the inside of her cheek as she followed Mark's lead, his hand in hers. It was full dark now and the moon draped the forest in a grim light the color of gunmetal. The trail was thinning, the thicket closing in on them.

"This can't be the right way," she said. "We would've been back to the house by now."

Mark stopped. "How long do you think we've been out here? I feel like time is, like, sliding or something."

Traci looked at her phone. "This says four o'clock."

"That can't be right. It's dark."

"I know."

Mark checked his and it read the same. "They're frozen. What is going on?"

"It's these woods…"

"But how?"

"Demons, Mark. Black magic."

"Why would they scramble our phones?"

"If we can't measure time, it just makes us all the more disoriented."

He sighed. "Well, should we keep on this trail or go back the way we came?"

"If we backtrack, we'll be in that awful deadening again. This trail may not lead to Scott's house, but at least it won't lead us to that clearing."

Mark looked grim. "Unless we've been going in a circle."

"Don't say that."

"Sorry. Just being practical."

"Or pessimistic."

"Sometimes that's the same thing."

They shared a small laugh then, if only to make each other feel better. When she looked into Mark's eyes, she felt a warm affection for him she wouldn't have expected as recently as this morning. She put her palm to his cheek. She almost wanted to kiss him. Not in some sort of romantic or sexual passion, but as a way to express the renewal of a connection long severed. They were in this together. They were here when they needed one another most, just as they'd been when they were young.

Both of them had unstable home lives back then, their parents being the sort of people who shouldn't have had kids in the first place. Without really knowing it, they'd taught each other they had worth, that they deserved someone who cared for them. Mark may have had many, great flaws, like being a rowdy malcontent who cared more about getting high than achieving any foreseeable goals, but he'd always been very protective of her. That was something other guys hadn't been—with the exception of Scott, of course. Mark was overprotective, actually, but she'd found that endearing, if a bit scary. Now, here they were again, after so much time, and he was protecting her to the best of his ability, same as he'd done back then. In at least this one way, it was a good thing he hadn't changed.

Traci didn't kiss him, though. She felt it would be too much. Worse than that, it would be distracting. They had to stay alert. So she hugged him—*really* hugged him, expressing it all physically since she knew words would fail her.

As Mark put his arms around her waist, there was a strange noise in the distance. They looked up at the woodland behind them. The sound was fluid, a murky resonance. It sounded like an electric guitar being strummed.

Traci tensed, recognizing the melody.

Mark held her tighter. "No…"

But there was no mistaking it.

"Don't Fear the Reaper" was coming for them.

THE TALL man they'd called Fred had a portable radio. It was little more than a loudspeaker attached to his hip, wirelessly connected to his phone. As the first notes of the song echoed through the dark, Corey put his hand over his mouth to keep from screaming. He took two steps back, catching himself just before he would have fallen into the brush.

"Nice throwback," one of the others said. "I'd forgotten about that. Wasn't it you who found the kid's boombox that night?"

Fred grinned. "And used it against them pretty well, if I do say so myself."

Corey held his head. His brain was as scrambled as an egg, too many thoughts going at once as he tried to understand all he'd seen.

Some kind of cult, he thought. *Some weird, satanic cult out to get us.*

And Scott was one of them—an important member at that. The others were acting like he was some sort of prince come to roost. And Jennifer…dear God…Scott said he'd *stabbed her to death*! It sounded like he'd planned to kill her all along.

Corey swallowed hard, his saliva sour. These people had wanted to kill them all that night. He felt certain they'd murdered Robin. Maybe they'd murdered lots of young people out here. Maybe *they* were the true demons, not monsters of supernatural force but monsters of the mortal variety. They were sadistic predators with some nefarious goal he didn't fully understand, and now they were going to try and kill him, Traci, and Mark.

Corey looked at the man who'd been his best friend growing up. Scott didn't look any different. He didn't seem malevolent or bloodthirsty. No darkness had fallen upon him, no red eyes or other signs of possession. He didn't come off as some kind of clone or robot version of himself. This was Scott Dwyer. He actually looked happy, even excited. He wore the farm boy grin that had always melted women's hearts as the song kicked in with vocals, the lyrics all too appropriate for what was happening all over again.

Fred pulled back the lapels of his army coat, revealing enormous hunting knives on both hips. The woman named Julia drew back her trench coat and took out a weapon with a curved blade. She passed it to Scott, and when he held it up, Corey realized it was a handheld scythe.

Don't fear the reaper, Corey thought with dread.

Smoke billowed from the infuser. Fred turned up the volume and the music filled the forest in a disturbing swansong. Julia reached into the crate that had been wheeled in on a pull-along wagon. She lifted a live chicken out by its feet and used a straight razor to slit it open from its wattles to its underbelly. It flapped and cawed as it was eviscerated, and as Julia's coat came all the way open, Corey saw she was nude from the waist up. She raised the chicken above her head, dousing herself in the steaming blood, coating her face, the drops rolling down her small breasts and belly.

George and Telma Payton cheered raucously. More blades appeared in the hands of the others, shimmering like stars when they caught the moonlight, clinking together in a grim, martial harmony.

Corey ran.

The hunt was on.

CHAPTER THIRTY-SEVEN

Mark felt like a child again. Such a feeling wasn't a good thing for everyone. When he felt like a little boy, it was as one cowering in a corner as his father screamed in his face. That was his boyhood—*fear*. His father's intimidation was a constant presence in his life until Mark finally ran away from home, just before his twentieth birthday, hopping in a van with friends and never coming back. The feelings of helplessness he'd had under his parents' roof, those feelings of always being in danger, had turned him into an angry young man.

All through his adult life, he continued to hear his dad's insults and degradations in his mind. Even though his father had died many years ago, he continued to hurt Mark through those painful memories, always telling him he wasn't good enough, that he would always fail, that he was a fuck-up, a moron, a total piece of shit beyond redemption. And it had become a self-fulfilling prophecy, hadn't it? Fear had ruined him, for it had poisoned him from the start.

Now the fear was back with the same intensity he'd felt when his dad pushed him into walls, the same terror he'd felt on that Halloween long ago. He thought of the crazed dwarf and the jack-o'-lantern that had sailed after him. He thought of Robin Reeves hanging from the sycamore. For years these same images had returned to him in nightmare after nightmare, keeping him awake until he'd learned to pass out drunk as often as possible. Most of all, he thought of his children: Dalton, who had essentially disowned him, and Jamie, who was not so far behind. It dawned on him that it might not make much difference to them if he wasn't around anymore. They might mourn him dying, but in the end, it wouldn't change their lives much. If anything, they might benefit from the lack of endless disappointments.

He wondered if neglect made him an abusive father too.

Running through a batch of dead branches, his depression slithered in, burrowing and coring, clinging to his soul like fishhooks. While all these thoughts about his life were valid, they'd been pounding at him with uncommon relentlessness since they'd returned to Suicide Woods.

The demons, he thought. *They're using our innermost heartaches against us. We're adults now. We've had years to acquire more failures, regrets, and insecurities. We have far more anxieties than the young, so much more to worry about, and far less time left. That's why people have a midlife crisis at my age.*

He knew he had every reason to be afraid, but he had to fight these crushing feelings of defeat. Otherwise, he would never succeed here. He knew that from experience. It would be the self-fulfilling prophecy of failure all over again. Mark couldn't afford to fail this time, for if he did, it would be the final failure. He couldn't let that happen to him and couldn't let it happen to Traci either. Letting people down again was not how he wanted to leave this world.

Sliding the knife from his pocket, he flicked the blade open and held it out in front of him as they journeyed deeper into the woods. They'd outrun their stalkers before. They could do it again. But if it came down to a confrontation, Mark Goranson was ready to strike first.

WITH THE slaughter done, Julia joined Scott, her butcher knife slick with chicken gore. She dragged her fingers across the flat of blade, dipping them in the blood, and brought them up to Scott's face.

But before she could decorate him, Telma snatched her wrist. "Easy now, child. Don't get carried away."

Julia lowered her hand. "I thought war paint was ritual. That's what I was taught."

"In most situations it would be, but right now we need him to look straight. If he runs into his friends tonight, we want them to believe he's still on their side."

"Right," Julia said, disappointed. "That makes sense. I'm sorry, I—"

"Don't worry it, girl," Telma's husband George said. "You've been doing great, especially this being your first time. You didn't hesitate with the animal sacrifice, so I think you're ready for the next step."

Telma agreed. "Oh, she's ready. And Scott's ready to, ain't you, child?"

He nodded. "Yes, ma'am."

"Such a good boy," she said, grinning motherly. "Your folks done raised you right. I wish Susie and Carter could be here tonight. They'd be so proud of you. This was their life's work, you know."

Scott nodded again. "Dad told me everything before he died. I want to finish this for them."

"Just know that even if you finish this, there will always be more to do. We must always work on the ingress. We must not falter."

From the same pull-along wagon, Julia handed Scott black fatigues to change into, to make him harder to spot. He thought this odd, seeing how Telma had said it was important for his friends not to suspect him of anything, but there were a lot of ritualistic elements to The Congregation's way he did not yet fully comprehend.

Fred joined them, brandishing a massive hunting knife with holes in the center, enabling blood to sluice through more efficiently, thereby draining a victim quicker. Reba followed behind him like a puppy. She had stripped naked—part of her personal ritual—and her unusual form made Scott avert his gaze.

"Reba says she senses one of 'em nearby," Fred said. "Let's get a move on."

Telma gave Scott a quick hug, bouncing with excitement.

"Go get 'em, boy," George said, pumping his fist in the air. "Us old folks will be right here, working the ritual."

Scott took a deep breath, and Julia took his hand. Hers was tacky with blood. Fred moved to the edge of the circle and entered the thicket, and Scott followed him with his scythe held at his side. His pulse raged, making the veins in his neck stand out. He wondered which of his old friends

Reba had picked up on. Would it be any easier to kill them than it was with Jennifer? Not physically, but emotionally? He'd stabbed Jennifer so suddenly she hadn't had time to react. She only gasped and whimpered, and then she went entirely rigid, her whole body flexing as a single muscle. He had hugged her into him, sending the knife deeper into her stomach, her throat making wet clicking sounds. Scott had shushed her then, running his free hand over the back of her head like he was petting an infant to sleep.

"It's okay," he'd said. "The hard part's over, Jenny. There's no more pain now."

She didn't combat him. She didn't even speak.

"Don't be afraid," he'd told her, kissing her forehead.

The words had come to him naturally, like some incantation that had been lying dormant in his subconscious, waiting for the right moment to be set free. And it was entirely appropriate. He hadn't wanted her to be scared.

It wasn't like her death was his idea. Jennifer would always have a special place in his heart. Mom knew that. That's why she'd let Jennifer Parks live. She couldn't bear to break her son's heart by taking the girl away, even though it would have made all the difference to the cause. Scott's love for his parents and determination to honor their dying wishes was the driving force that had enabled him to kill Jennifer. Without this motivation, he wouldn't have had the intestinal fortitude to stab her. Someone else would have had to commit the murder, and that wouldn't be nearly as potent an offering as having her killed by Scott. The offering would miniscule, not the powerful token it became under his direction. Killing the others was central to this night as well, but he felt Jennifer was the most vital of all their prey. Any member of the cabal could kill the others, but ideally it would be Scott who snatched their life force from them.

And already his reward was taking effect. The energy of the woods invigorated him.

"Spread out," Fred said.

The man was clearly an experienced hunter. Scott figured there would be much to learn from him. Even Julia, who was relatively new to The Congregation, just as Scott was, had an aura of wisdom and power. It thrilled him. Being part of such an exclusive event really got his fur up.

For the first time in his life, he was experiencing the benefits of nepotism. His lineage mattered here. Being a Dwyer really meant something. After a lifetime of mediocrity, he'd discovered he was more important than he would have ever imagined.

The sheriff appeared. Though he wore a pistol on his belt, he carried a machete held out before him like a Viking with a battle sword. It was best if the murders were intimate. Firearms made killing too impersonal. They had to get close to their prey and look into their eyes as the light went out of them. That was the way it had always been done. Tradition was crucial to the ceremony.

The past forges a path to the power. That's what his father had said.

And Scott's past had come full circle.

COREY WAS too winded to go on without a rest. He wasn't as young as he used to be and had never been athletic. His body didn't get along with running. Even the flight of steps up from his garage to the kitchen could wind him sometimes, so hauling ass through the forest was exhausting. He had to catch his breath.

He scanned the grove, moving through piles of leaves so thick they covered his ankles. When he stepped upon a large, fallen branch, he snatched it up, testing its sturdiness. It was solid.

The song had started over again. It was much louder now. Whoever was playing it, they were closing in on him. Taking his makeshift club, Corey went to the largest tree he could find—a hundred-foot sycamore with a split trunk, two thick shafts reaching for Heaven. He sat behind it and pulled mounds of leaves over him, covering his legs with their natural camouflage, and held the club to his chest.

The song grew louder, lyrics clearer. They said that all times had come and all that was would soon disappear. Corey thought about his life and wondered if he'd spent it wisely. If he were to lose it tonight, would he be leaving with regrets? Had he spent too much time in the escapism of fictional worlds, dedicating himself to comic books and sci-fi movies? Had he not pursued actual experiences as much as she should have by traveling more often and engaging in new adventures? Perhaps he'd been too much of a homebody. Perhaps his constant need for entertainment hadn't allowed him time for quiet introspection. Maybe his wife was right to resent him.

Somewhere in their marriage, he had disappointed her, and they'd never bounced back from it. She'd never adored him as much as he had adored her, but her apathy regarding their relationship had deteriorated into disinterest that bordered on distain. The marriage had rotted like a pumpkin on a porch, caving in on itself as it corroded. Again, he wondered if Gretchen had only stayed with him for the sake of their son. But now, for the first time, Corey had to ask himself why *he* had really stayed with *her*. He'd always told himself he was too old and strange to find someone new, but even if that were true, wouldn't being a solitary man be better than staying with a woman who hated the fact that you loved her? Maybe instead of waiting for her to hit him with divorce papers, he should have been the one to write them up.

The music was an audio ghost that drifted aimlessly. Corey wasn't sure if his predator was coming closer or getting farther away. Did it matter? His grip on the club began to loosen. He was so tired—tired of everything. Would putting an end to a life of exhaustion be such a bad thing? It would be the ultimate sleep. That's why it was called "laid to rest." Oh, to really rest. He wouldn't have to worry about sales at the store or clearing his margins enough to be profitable. He wouldn't have to sleep beside a woman comprised of concentrated disdain. He wouldn't have to watch Luke outdo him in every possible way until the sight of Corey made his son sick.

Maybe it was time to let it all go.

Don't fear the reaper, Corey.

He was tired of running. He'd been running all his life. Everything made sense to him now though. It had come to him in a sudden, golden epiphany as he sat there in the heart of Suicide Woods and—

Corey gripped the club. He straightened out of his slouch, his eyes wide once again. He gritted his teeth against the dark thoughts he'd been having.

This is why it's called Suicide Woods, he thought.

The woods did something to people. It got into your head and warped your perspective like a bipolar depression. Steven had been right—these woods were demonic. Tonight, Corey hadn't seen the three-legged monstrosity that had chased him that Halloween, but he did feel its evil presence. The demon had simply changed form. What frightened him as a teenager was not the same as what frightened him as an adult. The demon didn't always have to be a physical beast, like some scary movie special effects come to life. It had evolved to tailor his adult terrors, transforming into a psychic force aimed to torture his soul instead of his flesh. What did a demon need with violence if it could make its victim see self-violence as a better alternative to the horrors it wrought?

The music lost volume. The song wasn't fading away as it ended; it was being turned down manually. Someone couldn't see Corey, so they hoped to hear him. And Corey knew that while the demons were more of a force than a being, whoever had chased him here was of the mortal realm. He couldn't fight them just by blocking out negative thoughts. He had to fight physically. There had to be blood.

"Hey, kid," a man's raspy voice called out of the dark.

Corey held his breath. He gripped the club so tightly it shook.

"Welcome back," the man said, still out of sight. "I don't mean any disrespect calling you kid. It's just what we always called your little group—'the kids.' It's been a long time. Too long for me. I gotta admit, I gave up hope years ago. Never thought this day would come."

The man paused, no doubt listening for a whimper, a shuffle of feet. Corey had become inhumanly still. He suddenly pictured himself as a corpse with rigor mortis taking effect. Just a dead body lying out here in the woods to be ravaged by maggots, his eyes eaten out, the sockets doorways for field mice as they made a home of his skull. He was surprised by the serenity of this mental image, of returning to the earth from which all life had sprung. There was such poetry to it, such beauty. He saw snakes looping over and under his exposed ribs, his shirt and flesh torn free by vultures, his remaining guts gone black from days under the sun and his—

Stop! He bit his bottom lip so the pain would drive the morbid thoughts away. *Get out of my head!*

He focused on the physical discomfort and the footsteps crackling brittle leaves as the man inched closer to Corey's hiding spot.

"I'll make it fast," the man said. "You save us both the exertion of me chasing you, and I'll take you out quick and clean. I promise you that, and Fred Thomas is a man of his word. I've got a knife here with a blade as big as your forearm, and it's sharp enough to do surgery on a termite. I'll just sever your aorta and you'll bleed out quick and easy. Very little pain."

Moonlight revealed movement to Corey's left. He readied himself.

"Nobody wants you kids to suffer, least of all me," Fred said. "I have no beef with you. Look, I can understand why you don't want this, but you need to listen to what those voices in your head are trying to tell you. We're only trying to show you the way, son. We're only trying to show you there's nothing to fear."

The man paused. Corey predicted what he would say next.

"Don't be afraid," Fred told him, his voice low, sounding like a father sitting by his child's bedside on a stormy night. "Someone else told you that once, didn't they? Right here in these woods on a certain Halloween night?"

Robin Reeves' face flashed across Corey's mind. She was forever young there, pretty and innocent for as long as there were people left to remember her. He'd always done his best to block the memory of Robin hanging dead, but he did allow himself to remember her the way she'd been while alive. He even welcomed it. Remembering her paid her some sort of service. When she'd died, Corey had clipped her obituary and still had it in a photo album he'd never shared with anyone, not even his wife. In the newspaper clipping, there was a black and white photo of her sitting cross-legged on the floor with a small dog snoozing in her lap. Even though the picture was colorless, her hair and freckles were so bright, the girl's radiance impossible to mute.

"Little Robin was a clean vessel for those voices," Fred Thomas said. "Too young to resist them but too pure to be corrupted by them. Must've made her seem mighty strange to you that night, huh? I'm not sure what all she told you, but I can guess, and I promise you she spoke nothing but the truth."

The girl's final words remained vaulted in Corey's heart. They had forged a secret path for him. Yes, he'd wandered far off course, but however strongly he tried to reject it there always remained the memory, her words lingering eternal, echoing a riddle that had yet to find an answer.

Fred Thomas moved briskly, tromping through the leaves instead of tiptoeing. He was growing impatient. The noise he created was enough to cover the sound of Corey rising from the pile of leaves, his back staying pressed against the tree, club in both hands like a batter stepping up to the plate.

"C'mon out!" Fred demanded. "I know you're here. I'm too old for this cat and mouse crap. You've had twenty-five years more than you were supposed to. Consider that a bonus, son. Don't be greedy. You were a hell of a lot luckier than most of the other kids who came here back in those days. But your time is up. If we don't act soon, there's gonna be—"

Corey lunged, swinging the club. It snapped in half as it crashed across Fred Thomas' face. Dentures flew from his busted lips, blood gushing from a nose now pointing far to the right. The senior's eyes rolled white and he wobbled on his feet, those combat boots struggling to stay in one place. Corey swung what was left of the branch into Fred's gut, making him bend over, and then brought the end of it down on the back of his neck. When Fred fell forward, he dropped his knife so he could put out both palms to catch himself. Corey grabbed for it with speed and courage the likes of which he'd never known. His need to survive seemed to heighten every reflex.

The knife was so long it might as well have been a pirate's saber. There were strategic holes punctured through the blade and the edge formed alligator teeth. It was the kind of weapon he would have rolled his eyes at in a flea market, thinking it was just another totally unnecessary Rambo toy for rednecks, a flashy accessory for insecure males, same as an AR-15 or a pickup truck the size of a school bus. But looking at Fred Thomas, Corey doubted the knife was decoration. He had no doubts it had been used for more than whittling.

As Fred struggled to get up, Corey moved away. His first impulse was to run. The man was much older than him and he'd just been knocked senseless. This was an opportunity to escape. No matter what Fred and his weirdo friends wanted to do to him, Corey didn't want to hurt the man any further. He didn't even entertain the idea of killing him. It was too chilling on a karmic level. Corey just didn't have it in him. He loathed violence, and his moral principles set him against the very idea of murder, even in a case like this. He was no hippie, but he believed in peace. And though no theologian, he believed in the sanctity of life. So while he would fight to protect himself, he wouldn't stab an old man in the back while he was down. He had the hunter's weapon now, and that had rendered him mostly harmless. Time to haul ass again, before the other lunatics showed up.

As Corey turned to leave, a hand shot out and grabbed his ankle, pulling his foot out from under him. Pain exploded through his kneecap when it hit the cold, hard ground. He managed to roll over. Somehow Fred Thomas had the knife again, and—

No, wait. Corey realized he still held the knife. The man had another one that was identical.

This psychopath brought two! How many other weapons does he have?

Corey didn't want to find out. Pacifist or not, his life was on the line. He had to counterattack. There was no other choice.

Both men were on their knees. Fred swung his monster knife. He came too close for Corey to dodge the attack, so he raised his arm to protect his throat. The sleeve of his coat tore apart. Hot pain raced through him as his flesh opened and the wound dribbled blood.

Fred stumbled as he came at him again and Corey gripped his own knife upside down, raised his arms high, and stabbed the blade down where the man's shoulder met his neck. Fred's eyes bulged with shock, pale lips curling over exposed gums. A white tongue fluttered in his toothless mouth, and a red geyser exploded from his wound, dousing them both. Fred had threatened to cut one of Corey's arteries, but it seemed Corey had beaten him to it.

Fred dropped his knife and Corey pulled his out of the man's neck. Fred clutched his puncture, stacking his hands over it as if he might plug the oozing flesh. But it did not dribble like a leaky faucet. The hole in him was erupting blood. He let out a horrible, wheezing cry, a look of cosmic fright coming across his face. Corey realized, just as Fred did, that the man was bleeding to death.

And so Corey ran, his exhaustion forgotten. The woodland raced by in a black blur, his legs pumping furiously to get him as far from the dying man as possible.

The man you killed.

The realization kept returning to him as he tried to deny the terrible reality of all this night had wrought. The blood was still warm as it dripped down the knife and onto Corey's trembling hand. And he knew there would be more bloodshed tonight, much more. It was unavoidable. He could not hope for a non-violent conclusion. All he could hope was that the next blood spilt would not be his own.

Everything was different now. Everything.

He slowed down as he emerged from a cluster of shrubs. The dead branches had clawed at him, ripping his clothes and slicing into his hands and cheeks. But he hadn't noticed. He'd just kept on running.

When he entered a small clearing, he assessed his injures. The gash Fred had made in his arm was the only serious one, even though the prickers in the branches had made him bleed too. Corey used the knife to cut away the rest of his mangled sleeve and wrapped it tight around his stab wound, an improvised bandage and tourniquet in one.

He looked in all directions, hoping to find a trail. There had to be more of them. When he was a kid, there had been several different locations in the neighborhood where the trails led into Suicide Woods. All of them would offer a clean exit. These damn woods didn't go on forever. Even without a trail, he could make it out if he walked in one direction without straying. But without a compass, that wouldn't be easy. Some men seemed to think they had one built into their head, but Corey never succumbed to this fallacy, and therefore didn't get lost the way others did. But he was lost in here tonight. He hoped his Scout training would serve him well.

He looked at the knife and wondered if Fred Thomas had been a veteran, maybe an infantryman in Vietnam or something. At the very least, he had to be a buck hunter. Corey got nervous just playing paintball (once had been enough). If Fred hadn't been a senior citizen, Corey may not have gotten the upper hand. His head may have ended up on the man's wall, mounted on a plaque next to Bambi and Thumper.

Goose bumps scattered across his skin. There was a low growl coming from the briar in front of him. He could tell it was not an animal, but the snarl of a human being imitating one. His chest became weighted by a sluggish heartbeat. Corey gripped the knife with both shaking hands, ready to lunge with it like a bayonet and, by God, ready to kill again.

In the light of the moon, the face that emerged from the trees appeared purple. But Corey knew its true color was deep red. The skin had faded and cracked, as if bleached by time, but it bore the same warts and thorn-like horns. Elongated teeth rose from the pouting bottom lip like shark fins breaking the sea.

This was the visage of every bad dream. This was everything Corey feared boiled down to a purer, more concentrated evil. And it knew he was afraid, that he'd never stopped being so.

The demon's eyes flashed, blue as the waning moon.

Corey screamed.

CHAPTER THIRTY-EIGHT

Within the mask, his breaths created condensation. Scott had brought it along in his backpack, keeping it hidden from his old friends when they'd left the house. It was the exact same one Corey had worn when he'd emerged from the woods that Halloween, and that made it very special. He'd dropped it in Scott's yard, and Scott had picked it up and brought it into his room, intending to return it to Corey later. But everything had changed in the days and weeks that followed, and somehow the mask had never gotten back to its original owner.

Corey hadn't asked for it either. There were times Scott thought about just throwing the mask in the trash, but for whatever reason he had grown to think of it as some sort of evidence of what had happened, and so he'd decided to hide it in his room. He'd slid one of the mineral wood and fiberglass ceilings tiles out of place, having tossed the mask up there, and then he'd put the tile back. At times he'd thought of destroying it, but he'd never done it, though he wasn't sure why. And so there it had stayed, even when he'd moved out.

When his father first began telling him about The Congregation, he hadn't believed it. He'd thought Dad had gone mad. But the evidence revealed otherwise.

Mom and Dad had been in the woods that night too. Word had gotten back to his parents that Scott and his friends would be in Suicide Woods. Barbara Blankenship—Traci's mother—had overheard her daughter talking with her boyfriend about their Halloween plans and notified

Carter Dwyer. Because of this, the sect they belonged to had changed their course for the evening. This had been a golden opportunity for them to make great progress. Four children up for the slaughter.

But things hadn't gone exactly the way they'd hoped, and a large part of that was the fault of Scott's mother. Dad had told him this reluctantly, the embarrassment his wife brought him that night still lingering. He'd come to forgive her failings, even empathize with her over them. Once she was gone, Carter Dwyer had felt like he understood his wife better than he ever had while she'd been alive.

"It was your mom and I who found you and Jenny making out in that clearing," Dad had told him. "We wore ill-fitting clothes and ski masks. We figured, in the dark, you wouldn't recognize us. Besides, you'd never suspected us to begin with. I gave your mother the handheld scythe I'd bought just for this occasion. That was the kind of tool she'd asked for. She romanticized it for some reason, you see? I didn't mind. As long as she killed Jenny, it didn't make any difference what the murder weapon was.

"It's vital that the mother take the temptress away from the son. She is the first woman he loves, and therefore it becomes her duty to keep him from falling for the wrong girl. At first, we left your thing with Jenny alone, figuring it would run its course. But after a while, well...you know.

"The Congregation really put pressure on your mother to end it. And by God, I thought she was ready that night. I think she thought so too. The plan was I would hold you while she cut Jenny's throat. That's the way she liked to do it. She'd killed little Donnie Slater that way. Remember him? Nice kid. He played soccer with the twins. Think he was twelve or so when we...you know...*took* him.

"Anyway, when your mother saw you being...*tender* with Jenny, it just plucked her heartstrings. She saw how much you loved the girl, despite her not being the one, and your mother, well...she just couldn't stand to take her away from you. She backed out. So, I did the only thing I could. I tried to sneak up on you two myself, but you heard me and bolted like running backs outta there. Your mother held me back, but I was too old and fat to catch you anyway."

After his father told him this story, Scott had gone to the basement room and lifted the ceiling tile. The demon mask was still there. That was when it finally made sense to him why Corey had been wearing it. It had given Corey a false sense of security. And in truth, it hadn't hurt to try and confuse the demons. Hiding among them might have saved Corey's life.

It also finally made sense to Scott why he'd never gotten rid of the mask. He'd been saving it for this reunion long before he knew it would happen. The woods wanted it that way. He understood that now.

The sound of his breaths bouncing off the latex was like a saw whispering through bone. Enshrouded by the image of a demon, Scott began to feel he was becoming one in a way. As a child, he'd imagined himself as whatever he dressed up as on Halloween night, always more focused on the fantasy than gathering candy. The same feeling returned to him now. Was he reliving Halloweens past, or had the very forces he was trying to appease by killing Corey Pickett entered his soul? The thought made Scott quiver, and the scythe jangled at his side.

"Stay back," Corey said, brandishing the huge knife.

Scott recognized it as one of Fred's. That it was slick with blood concerned him. People were unpredictable in a crisis. Even Corey could surprise him.

Staring at his best friend from childhood, Scott realized he was going to have the same emotional difficulty killing him as he'd had with Jennifer. He loved her in a different way, but he loved Corey too. Even though he hadn't seen him in so many years, it had felt like no time had passed when Corey walked through his door last night. The bond had always been strong. Even when he'd outgrown Corey and started hanging out with cooler friends, Scott had never been able to push him away. Hell, he hadn't wanted to. It wasn't until the night Robin died that their friendship began to disintegrate. Suicide Woods had been enough to break them.

And this time it would break them for good.

"You stay the fuck away from me!"

Scott didn't reply. Corey would recognize his voice, and he didn't want him to know it was him behind the mask and black fatigues. Anonymity would make murdering him a lot easier. The look of betrayal and shock that had come across Jennifer's face would haunt Scott forever. He didn't need Corey's to haunt him, too. Scott's victims did not need to know who was taking their lives. They didn't need to know why either. Scott's identity was important to the woods alone. These sacrifices were a long time coming. That it was the firstborn son of the Dwyer family making these offerings was the only thing that could redeem the sect's past failures.

Destiny called him with a tongue thirsty for blood.

"Why're you people doing this?" Corey yelled. "What do you want?"

Scott inched closer. It's not that he wanted this; it just needed to happen. They'd dodged fate long enough. He wished he could explain it all to his friends, but there simply wasn't time. They wouldn't have believed it, anyway.

Corey flashed the knife, cutting the air between them. "Stay back, I said!"

Scott raised his scythe overhead and swung, just missing Corey as he jumped out of the way. There was an intensity behind his eyes that Scott had never seen before, the determination to survive giving him the strength and courage he'd always lacked. Scott was proud of him. At least Corey would die a noble death instead of cowering in the dark the way people would have expected.

When he spun back with the scythe, Scott caught the lapel of Corey's coat but didn't pierce flesh. The blade got caught in the fabric as he tried to retreat with it, and this gave Corey the opportunity to slash at his face. The teeth of the blade ripped open the mask and tore into his forehead and the bridge of his nose. Scott stumbled back, leaving the scythe hanging from Corey's jacket, and took the remains of the mask off.

Corey stared at him. "You son of a bitch."

Scott held his shredded head, pressurizing the wound. "I'm sorry, Corey."

"You're *sorry*?" Corey's eyebrows drew closer together. "Are you kidding me? You're trying to kill me, Scott! You killed Jenny! What the hell is wrong with you?"

He sighed. "This isn't about me. Or you or Jenny."

"Who are these people? What do they want?"

Scott's other hand inched toward the knife in his pocket, the same one he'd slain Jennifer with. Perhaps he'd have the same luck using it again.

"Look, Corey. This thing is bigger than any of us. The Congregation goes back hundreds of years. It serves a great purpose."

"They're a cult of murderers!"

"It's not a cult. You don't understand."

"It's *a cult*, Scott, and you're part of it. You...you killed Robin that night, didn't you?"

Scott was taken aback. "Of course not! I had nothing to do with that. I didn't learn the truth until recently. It was all kept from me, the same way it was from—"

"Get that hand out of your pocket!"

Scott froze. He gripped the knife but would still have to open it.

"Corey, please. Let's do this the easy way." Scott took a cautious step forward. "You can't win. Just give up. That way, you'll experience as little pain as possible. I promise."

He carefully took his hand from his pocket, trying to tuck the pocketknife so Corey would not see it. The shadows were a powerful ally. He eyed the scythe still hanging from Corey's coat and had a desire for it that bordered on obsession. It linked him to his mother, and it was important to honor her tonight.

"You come any closer," Corey said, "and I'll kill you. I mean it."

Scott stared him down. He took another step.

"Don't make me do this, Scott!"

In his palm, Scott slowly slid open the blade of the pocketknife. He tried to do it silently, but it clicked when it locked in place. From the look on his face, Corey recognized the sound. He swung, but Scott was faster.

Scott jabbed Corey in the ribs, but the blade bounced off the bone instead of going in. Corey retaliated, cutting Scott's bicep, and hacked cruelly at his neck, slicing the flesh open but failing to stick him. Their weapons gleamed red in the moonlight as they slashed and stabbed, puncturing holes and separating skin from sinew. They grunted as they battled for their lives, two men who'd been like brothers now exhibiting a most fatal rivalry.

Scott cut at Corey's face, opening one cheek like it was butter. Corey spat out a glob of blood and bits of skin. Scott kicked Corey's knee, making

291

him stumble. The scythe flew from his coat into the dirt. As Corey fell, Scott seized the moment and stabbed the knife down, going for the eyes. Corey brought up his hand to protect himself, and the blade went right through his palm and out the other side, the exit wound spattering blood across his screaming face.

But he didn't quit. As Scott withdrew the knife, Corey lunged upward with his own, punching a nasty hole in Scott's side that dropped him. Scott rolled as he hit the ground, the side of his abdomen weeping red upon the leaves, and Corey tucked his mangled hand into his coat, tears streaking his blood-soaked cheeks. He was torn and broken, but furiously alive. Standing above Scott now, he gritted his teeth, blood seeping through every gap. He stomped on Scott's wrist so he couldn't use his pocketknife and was just about to stab him when the first gunshot went off.

CHAPTER THIRTY-NINE

The sound reverberated like a thunderclap. It was an even more threatening noise than "Don't Fear the Reaper." Traci wanted to scream, but didn't dare. It would give away their position to anyone listening. She and Mark froze, crouching as if to dodge an attack.

"Someone's *shooting*?" she said.

Mark nodded. "They're after us."

"Who though? I mean, demons don't use guns, right? That wouldn't make sense."

"Nothing makes sense anymore. Nothing."

Mark bent over, hands on his knees.

"We've got to keep moving," Traci told him.

"I know. But I'm running out of steam here. I'm not in the best shape of my life, you know. I'm middle-aged and I've been smoking since I was eleven."

Traci enjoyed the occasional smoke, mostly in social situations, to relieve the anxiety they brought. But in spite of cigarettes and her more intense vices, she was obsessive about her appearance and went to the gym three times a week, doing yoga at home on the off days. She was also on her feet forty hours a week at the bar. She'd only been pacing herself tonight for Mark's sake, and it pained her to think she might have to leave him behind. She didn't want it to come to that.

"You've got to push yourself, Mark."

"I'm trying. Really." He stood up straight. "Traci...who on earth do you think is shooting that gun?"

She looked him in the eye, seeing her own sadness and fear reflected back at her.

"I don't know," she said, "but I'm pretty sure there's more to all this than we thought. I think we're facing more than one threat, that there are more than demons in these woods. I just have this feeling there are people out here too, and I don't think they're on our side."

Mark's mouth grew small and tight. She remembered that look. It was the one he always got when he was getting angry. He stared into the forest for their invisible enemies.

"What if these people and the demons are one in the same?" he said.

A gust of witch's wind made the trees rattle, sounding like falling rain. Traci felt incredibly cold then, in body and soul, and she found herself thinking of her small apartment and the basic comforts she took for granted. Her life wasn't what she wanted—not by a long shot. But it wasn't as horrible as she sometimes saw it. She'd adjusted to being on her own. She'd certainly had more than enough practice at it. This self-reliance had carried her through many tumultuous years. Would it be enough to see her through another night in Suicide Woods?

There was a second gunshot. Then a third.

"Come on," she said, snagging Mark's arm.

And just like that, she was the one leading the way.

THE MAN shouted at Corey to freeze, but only after the first shot. It had been so close to hitting him that he heard the air split before the blast of the pistol. The man had appeared out of nowhere just as Corey was about to drive his knife through Scott's chest. He hated the idea of doing it, but he was also cut to ribbons and didn't know how much longer he could take this. Pain burned throughout his body. His mind throbbed from the stress of horror. He'd actually been in a *knife fight*. This was insane. What kind of hellscape was he in here?

"Freeze! Police!"

He recognized the man as one of the cult members he'd seen earlier. He had the short buzz cut and moustache of a cop, and was in a shooting stance like one, but Corey didn't want to believe he was the law. That would add a whole other level of terror to this.

And so he ran.

As he bolted through the trees, the trunk of a maple burst, spraying bark as two bullets entered it. Corey ran harder than he ever had in his life, his swollen knee screaming, lungs aching until his entire left side went tight with pain. But still he ran. Fear was the most powerful fuel. The man gave chase, but he was overweight and obviously out of shape. Corey wasn't in good shape, but he was carrying around one hundred pounds less than his pursuer. He managed to gain ground. He went for a canopy of trees where the shadows were thickest, cloaking him so the shooter couldn't take aim. There were more shots, but they missed him by far. And he kept on running. Running, running, running until the act of escaping death threatened to kill him anyway.

Something twisted within him, and he clutched his chest. Worried he might have a heart attack, Corey hid inside a half circle of boulders, panting like a sunstroke dog as he tucked into the rocks. He was drenched in sweat and tacky with blood, some of which wasn't his own. He tilted his head back against the boulder and looked up at the branches through a veil of tears. The treetops spun as one giant wheel, his lack of breath dizzying him.

Corey looked at the hand he'd clutched into the bottom of his shirt. It throbbed in agony as he unclenched his fist. The center of his palm was like a coin slot of flesh. Turning his hand, he examined the smaller exit wound on the back. He'd never bled so much in his life. The hole was still dribbling. At least it was his left hand, the non-dominate one. He could still wield the hunting knife with the other. Cutting away his coat sleeve, Corey wrapped his hand the same way he had his opposite arm. There was nothing he could do for the rest of his wounds. The flesh would just have to seep until they crusted over. He spat out another red glob and tongued his torn cheek. Bright pain burst through the exposed nerves.

He wondered if Scott was dead. Had stabbing him in his side been enough to bleed him out? Corey had no way to know if the knife had punctured anything vital. Scott was trim, so the side of his belly didn't offer much protective fat. Had he perforated the intestines, poisoning Scott with his own bacteria? Corey wasn't an expert on human anatomy, but he doubted a torn length of guts wouldn't pose an immediate danger. It hurt him to wish this upon Scott, but he did. And not just because Scott dying would remove one of Corey's adversaries, making it easier for him to escape. He hated Scott now, hated him more than any man he had ever known. It astounded him that Scott could be so explicitly evil.

And what was all that talk about being sorry and wanting to kill Corey as painlessly as possible? What kind of sick nonsense was that? Had Scott always been a psychopath and just hidden it very well, or had he developed this dangerous mental illness later in life? The stuff he'd said didn't make sense.

This thing is bigger than any of us…it serves a great purpose.

What purpose could mass murder possibly serve?

The Congregation goes back hundreds of years.

Corey thought hard about this. Maybe Scott hadn't been behind Robin Reeves' death, but this cult had to be. He was sure of it. They'd been behind a great and secret slaughter of Redford's children, for whatever nefarious purpose. In the early '90s, they'd taken several lives, but for some reason they'd stopped after Robin's murder. At least, until now. The children who'd escaped them had returned home, and the killers aimed to finish what they'd started decades ago.

A rustle in the brush made him tense. The knife trembled in his one good hand as he peered around the boulder, vision distorted by tears. He hadn't even realized he'd been crying. There was another rustle. Someone was walking through leaves, getting closer. Corey gulped, swallowing blood. If it was the man with the gun, Corey would surely die. No amount of adrenaline could get him to run as fast as he'd been going again.

A shadowy figure appeared, followed by a larger one. They walked in silence. Initially, Corey thought Scott had joined the man, but as the figures passed by, he realized neither was fat enough to be the shooter. Corey wiped his tears away to get a better look, but it hardly helped.

Here there was only darkness.

THE TRAIL thinned until it disappeared entirely. Traci took them through a copse where they had to snap away a web of twiggy branches to pass through the trees. They'd only go in circles if they turned back. Mark didn't resist her lead. He had no idea where he was, no idea where to go next. He was just an idiot, practically useless to her. Maybe if they kept walking, the trail would appear again. Perhaps it had only grown over in parts. As they moved out of the tangled shrubs, they passed by an arrangement of rock that formed a half circle. Traci hushed and gripped his hand tighter. It seemed she'd felt the presence too. They weren't alone here.

Just keep walking, he thought, hoping to somehow pass this message to Traci with his mind. *Keep walking and keep your eyes peeled.*

He clutched the knife in his other hand. A lot of good that would do against a gun.

Rock, paper, scissors. Bullet beats blade, Mark-o. You lose.

Exertion was bullying him. His nerves were shot, and he needed a cigarette, but didn't want the glow of the cherry to give them away. Pain pulsed in his knees. His feet were throbbing. Mark Goranson felt every bit his forty-three years.

And the woods continued to trouble his mind, filling him with doubt and self-disgust. He almost wanted to just sit down in the dirt and wait for death to come. Mainly, it was wanting Traci to be safe that kept him pressing on. In the back of his mind, he understood that he should want to stay alive, but more and more, the suicidal thoughts were flooding his head with darkness, and that made him even more afraid.

They passed through the grove, leaving the rock arrangement behind them as they marched through the underbrush and into the basin. The feeling of another person's presence faded, but it did little to diminish Mark's trepidation. Death was creeping through every corner of the forest. Its bony fingers clicked upon every branch, its cold breath breezing through the trees, whispering its promise.

"I'LL CALL in a medic," Sheriff Shrinner said, putting pressure on Scott's wound. "You just rest here."

Scott struggled to sit up. "I'm fine. I have to go after them."

"You've been stabbed, buddy. And you're all cut up—you should see your face. Let the others get 'em. You keep your strength for the ceremony. That's what's important."

Scott stood up anyway. "That's not the only thing that's important. I need to see this through. It means everything to me."

"I get that, but—"

"No, you don't get it, Sheriff. I promised my father on his death bed I would sacrifice my old friends."

The sheriff stood up straight, hands at his hips. "You've already killed—"

"That's not enough. There are more remaining, and I can't rest until I see them die."

He found the scythe resting in a patch of dirt and picked it up. Blinking blood from his eyes, Scott touched the wound in his side and winced. It was trickling blood down his leg, but at least it was starting to go numb. He might not be able to run, but he wouldn't be limping much either.

"Well," Sheriff Shrinner said, "if it means that much to you, I won't stand in your way. A man's gotta do what a man's gotta do, and I respect that. But watch yourself, okay? And get 'em fast. I tried to chase that one who stabbed you, but he got away. And he was heading east. He keeps going and he'll reach the neighborhood before we know it."

Scott furrowed his brow. "You sure?"

"Sure, I'm sure. I've been out here more times than you can imagine. My father was dedicated to The Congregation and taught me everything there was to know about this place. I know it like I know my own dick."

Scott remembered Dave Shrinner Sr. He'd headed all the investigations involving Suicide Woods in the '90s. He'd grilled Steven about Robin's death. It had shocked Scott to realize the lawman had known the truth all along. And now the torch had been passed to his offspring, just as Scott's dad had passed it on to his son.

The sheriff reached out with his pistol, handle toward Scott. "Sure you don't want this?"

Scott shook his head. "No. You know the tradition."

"Don't have to kill with it. You could just use it to slow 'em down."

"Thanks. But that's too risky." He clutched the scythe to his chest. "I have to take them out in a more...personal way."

The sheriff smirked. "You really go for the poetry of all this, don't ya? Well, that's all fine and good, long as you remember the importance of the ceremony. *That* is the priority, not some grand poetic gesture. Don't let those pricks get away just 'cause you can't kill 'em in your ideal manner."

"I know, and I won't."

"Good. Then go on, time's a-wasting."

"And what about you?"

The sheriff smirked again. "I've done all the running I can tonight. Any more and I'll have an infarction. I'm gonna circle back and call for extra help."

"Extra help? What do you mean?"

"Just what I said." He pointed in the direction Corey had fled. "Wayland Street is that way. It's rural, but it's a neighborhood."

"I know the area."

Shrinner nodded. "Oh yeah, that's right. Well, if he breaks outta the woods, we'll need our people to be there, waiting for him."

CHAPTER FORTY

The trees above seemed to spin in a swallowing vortex, like a giant dust devil forming leaves into a cyclone. The sound of the stream teased her, and she smacked her gummy lips. Clutching her stomach with one hand, she put out the other to crawl in short, hopping movements toward the water, then planted her knees in the sandbar and cupped water in her hand to drink. The act of swallowing made her wound pulse hot. Hopefully she could keep the water down. The crisp flavor reminded her she was alive.

Jennifer pulled her hand back from the hole in her stomach and it poured blood like a spout. Her lower body was soused in red. When she tried to stand, her stomach contracted, the pain so brutal it reminded her of going into labor. It rose up her gullet and shot down through her thighs, seizing her entire body. Had something been ruptured? Had the contents of an organ flushed her abdominal cavity? She held the wound again and the blood sluiced through her fingers, warm and thick. She wondered how much of her bleeding was internal.

Lying down beside the stream, Jennifer looked at the branches above again. They were making a tornado of the stars, and she realized it wasn't her lightheadedness that made them swirl.

The woods really were twisting on their own, branches writhing like angry snakes against the night sky, and the moan of the wind was not wind at all but the ghost howl of a hungry demon of the earth that had broken the bounds of Hell. It hovered all about her in a gathering shroud, a monster of pure shadow, and when its belly rumbled, it was the sound of thunder echoing off mountains.

Jennifer closed her eyes in fright, but the sounds it made were worse when she could not place them. Her eyes snapped open again, crazed and bloodshot, and what she saw made her scream. But the pain in her stomach muted it to nothing.

She was surrounded.

They were humanoid figures comprised of tree roots that ran up from the ground like cornstalks. The roots lapped over themselves again and again, contorting knots into knees and elbows, scattering twigs into ribcages and making features from crumpled, dead leaves. When the demons moved, their wood creaked like an old ship in a storm, and the crackling sound of their curling fingers made Jennifer's flesh crawl.

They're real, she realized. *The demons of the woods are real.*

As twigs and leaves formed their faces, Jennifer's eyes went even wider. She recognized these creatures. There was the white birch face of Susie Dwyer, Scott's mom, staring down at her with acorn eyes, baring her splinter teeth in a horrible rictus. Beside her lumbered Mr. Dwyer, all knobbed sycamore and yellow foliage, moss serving as body hair. His eyes were tiny, blue rose buds, the kind you would put on a memorial wreath. Still rising from the dirt was the upper torso of Traci's mother, Barbara Blankenship, her hair a stream of russet pine needles, her breasts two warped knots of tree bark.

Jennifer inched away, crawling on her back. The faces of the demons contorted, transforming into the faces of Scott and Traci and Corey. They were manipulating her, playing with her in an effort to mangle her emotions. And it was working. When the largest woodland demon transformed into a puppet of her husband Roger, she shrieked and scurried away, spitting up blood.

Jennifer tried to get up, pushing through the white-hot pain, and the wooden demons took on the appearances of her own children, Devin clawing at her legs and Alex growing impossibly tall, hovering over her like a gnarled streetlamp. They clawed at her legs, splitting the jeans and the flesh beneath.

You've failed them, Jennifer thought. *You're a terrible mother and you deserve this. You asked for it. You've been asking for it your whole life.*

THAT NIGHT IN THE WOODS

The thoughts rattled her. She'd never thought like this before. Negativity seemed to possess her until death seemed like the only solution. Again, she tried to scream but could not make a sound as the deepest despair made a fist around her heart.

Alex drove her branch finger into Jennifer's knife wound, twisting deep and filling the puncture with splinters and dirt. Roots broke from the ground and slithered around Jennifer's wrists and ankles in rickety tentacles. She had just enough strength left to release a true scream before she was taken. Then Jennifer was gone, lost in the woods forever, like so many who'd come before her.

CHAPTER FORTY-ONE

S omething lurked within.

Traci froze and Mark stopped behind her, looking over her shoulder at the pale thing in the brush ahead. It was small and meaty, half hidden in the darkness, making it difficult to identify. His heart rose in his throat when he saw tiny feet caked in filth. They were human but had no toenails.

When the creature stepped toward them, he saw it was female, the crotch hairless, the chest flat, nipples sagging. Its plump hands were at its side, also without fingernails. As her face emerged, Mark moaned in fear.

This was the nightmare woman, the troll who had stalked him through the woods twenty-five years ago.

No, he thought. *It's not possible!*

But there she was, slinking upon them, her warped forehead like a fleshy peanut, the caveman brow sunk low across beady eyes. Her jaw hung open, showing off yellowed dog teeth. She wiggled her sausage fingers in a wave.

"Hi, Mark."

Her voice was like an axe running along a stone. The sky rumbled as if in agreement, shaking the trees and the ground. Mark and Traci fell speechless. Horror made his throat close up.

"I always knew this night would come," the little woman said in a seductive manner, rubbing her hands along her body's rolls of errant flesh. "I knew you'd return to me."

Mark felt bile rising in his esophagus. As she took another step, he moved in front of Traci, brandishing the pocketknife. His chivalry surprised him, a morsel of courage in the face of a horror that had haunted him for most of his life. Looking at the little woman, he realized there was much about her he'd forgotten, details like her lack of nails and her pronounced brow. Time and trauma had smoothed the roughest edges. Sometimes the mind forgets because it must do so to stay sane.

"Don't be afraid," the little woman said.

But he was afraid. He'd never stopped being afraid.

A terrible moan came from the branches above them, the sounds of sex and death merging into one, like an orgasm in a hospice bed, a kiss before dying. Traci whispered in his ear. "The shadows…they're *alive!*"

Even the little woman glanced skyward. The woods had become a spiraling mass of darkness, the tree branches forming skeletal hands of rotted wood. They swayed like drowning men in a current. The earth rolled beneath their feet.

Mark glanced back at the little woman. Her mouth hung open in shock, her eyes wide with realization. She turned milky white.

"Nothing…" she muttered. "It's just…*nothing.*"

And Mark understood what she meant. The dark force was more felt than seen, a sort of static electricity of pure blackness that altered reality, spinning it like water going down a drain. Thoughts of self-harm riddled him. The groan in the dark returned. It tore the night apart, growing louder, until it was the roar of a mountain lion. But it came from the trees. Their knots and knobs had morphed into fierce mouths—*hungry* mouths.

The little woman's eyes brimmed with tears.

"Wait," she said, turning her head side to side, addressing the woods itself. "Wait…there's still time. Please, we still have time!"

She looked to Mark as the shrubs and earth trembled and popped. The look on her face made Mark gasp, and he knew instantly she would attack, so when she raised her hands and came at him, he was ready with the knife. Even though she appeared to have no weapons, she came at him anyway, snarling like a wolf, still telling him not to be afraid. She was a madwoman, he realized. Not a goblin or demon, but a person who'd had some sort of psychotic break. But this realization didn't stop him from stabbing. When she seethed at him, the blade sank into her left eye, splitting in down the center. The socket filled with blood, and he planted his palm on the end of the knife and pushed it in deeper. The little woman shrieked.

An ill wind blew, smelling of decay. Mark could swear he could actually feel the earth spinning on its axis. He struggled to stay standing as the little woman backed off. She put both hands on the knife in her skull and pulled hard, expunging it in a splatter of blood and ocular fluid. She foamed with rage as she came back at him, the bloody knife darting and slashing. As he backed up, Mark saw Traci was no longer behind him.

Had she run away?

He put up his fists in a boxing stance, but when a wave of depression hit him like a tsunami, he dropped them. Maybe it was just his time. Maybe he had it coming. A single, deadbeat dad had little use in this world, and even less to live for. His death might be the best thing he'd ever done for the people dumb enough to care about him, if there were even any left.

Traci reappeared, snapping him out of his inner darkness. She held a rock in her hands the size of a football. As their attacker returned and lunged, Traci swung at her blind side and cracked the rock against her skull. The little woman fell into the leaves, twitching. The wind picked up. Something howled like a whale song, and the wind gushed like a hurricane, lifting the little woman into the air as Traci and Mark grabbed onto a pine tree. The little woman's one good eye went wide with terror as the hands of the tree branches passed her higher and higher into nebulous blackness, and she yelled to whatever waited in that merciless dark, begging for more time.

But hers had run out.

COREY WAS almost positive he recognized this area. There was a distinct assortment of pignut hickory trees here that he remembered for their rich tangerine color every fall, and how they seemed to line up in a purposeful row. There wasn't a trail here, but he recalled using it as one as a child, a hallway of trees pointing an arrow into a nearby neighborhood they'd once called the boonies.

"Pleeezz," he muttered, his mouth a mangled hole. It continued to fill with blood, making him hack and spit.

He didn't want to give in to hope. It would just make it all the more crushing to find out he was wrong about where he was. Until he saw the roofs of houses, he would consider this a mere illusion, either created by evil forces or just his tired, traumatized mind. But as he kept moving forward, he grew more confident. The land dipped and then rose up higher, just as he recalled from days gone by when he, Scott, and Ryan played *Masters of the Universe* here.

Whenever Ryan hadn't been around, Corey even got to be main hero, He-Man, because Scott always preferred to be villains. He'd loved being Skeletor, Cobra Commander, Dr. Doom, and Boba Fett. Corey figured they were precursors to his love of horror icons such as Leatherface and Pinhead. Had these leanings led him to this real-life villainy? It seemed preposterous to blame pop culture for criminal acts. Corey knew plenty of non-violent people who loved those characters too, including himself. Blaming scary movies, heavy metal, video games, and gangster rap was just a pathetic effort to explain and understand human atrocity. If someone had murder in them, their influences were irrelevant. They would have gone on to kill no matter what. Lust, greed, and politics were the true instigators.

And so was religion.

This cult of maniacs was certainly ritualistic. They performed animal sacrifice with chickens (and who knew what else). Was human sacrifice also on their list of commandments? Scott had referred to them as a congregation, a group assembled for religious worship. What horrible lord were they in service to? What archaic faith would call for the spilling of blood? This was the twenty-first century, not the age of Vikings or the Inquisition.

Limping along, Corey began to cramp. His wounds throbbed, burrowing an ache into his entire body. Still he pressed on, ignoring his physical desire to quit. He wouldn't give up, despite the whispers of suicide that occasionally snuck into his consciousness. He wouldn't give Scott the satisfaction.

As children, Scott always seemed to win whatever games they played outdoors. Corey could whip his butt in *Battleship* and *Monopoly*, but Scott had always been the manhunt champion, besting Corey at hide-and-seek missions and outwrestling him when their showdowns commenced. He was perpetually the more powerful soldier.

Well, not this time, Corey thought. *How's that wound in your side treating you, old friend?*

The other cult members would still be after him, but Corey was confident Scott was down, at least for tonight. He couldn't imagine someone continuing their hunt with that serious of an injury. They'd have to be...

Insane, he thought. And suddenly he wasn't as confident anymore.

A witch's wind wailed, throwing walls of leaves against his back. When he looked up, he saw the cosmos were still undulating. He was beginning to wonder if it was only lightheadedness causing the effect. The trees creaked in the wind like rusty hinges on a cemetery gate, and there was a dull moaning sound that hollowed Corey's chest. He heard a scream in a familiar voice.

Traci?

He scurried toward the sound, his heart pumping. He was shaking uncontrollably, and he thought again of that twister in Tennessee, of his new bride crunched into a motel bathtub with him. The image changed. She was wearing a smock with her legs parted, their baby boy's head crowning out of her. Despite everything she'd done to him (and worse yet, hadn't done), Corey still loved Gretchen. He dreaded the idea of never seeing her again. But much more than that, he dreaded never seeing his son again, never attending his graduation or wedding or the births of his own children, never seeing him achieve all the success Corey knew would come to him. It didn't matter if Luke outdid him in manliness or any other facet of life. Corey *wanted* his boy to better than his father. He wished him a greater life than Corey ever had, which was not such a bad one when he really looked at it.

Now Corey knew he was almost out of the forest. His dark thoughts were fading, the depression easing off as the vicious influence of Suicide Woods began to dissipate. He heard Traci scream again and was not only motivated to save his own life but driven by the need to rescue her too. He just hoped he had enough fight left in him.

Corey clenched the hunting knife.

There was movement ahead. The two shadows he saw looked to be the same ones that had passed by him when he was crouched behind the wall of rocks. They were the same size and shape, and as he drew closer, he could make them out more distinctly—a woman and a man. But there was another presence here, something bigger, blacker. Something cruel. He could feel it hovering all about him, a suffocating veil of menace.

It's the woods, he realized. *It's one single great demon.*

Everything spiraled. Branches clawed the air. The leaves sung of death and hatred. A pale-blue flicker appeared in the firmament, the moonlight ripping through the eye of the darkest hurricane, and there were Traci and Mark, crouched beside a pine tree. Mark's pocketknife was wet with blood. Corey slinked back into the shadows.

Could they be in on this too?

He hadn't seen Traci and Mark amongst the cult, but that didn't mean they weren't a part of it. It didn't add up, though. Scott had been the one with all the secrets and lies. He'd drawn them all back to Redford on false pretenses and had rather incredibly lured them into the woods. Mark had no reason to have faked such apprehension. And if Traci's tears had been forced, then she'd missed her true calling as an actress. Even now, the look of absolute horror on their faces was so raw and primal it chilled Corey's marrow. He had seen a hell of a lot of movies, but no one on screen had ever captured this look as convincingly. His old friends were wrought with fear.

He tried to call out to them, but his mouth was a mush of torn meat and his lungs were raw. So he shuffled along, waving from the shadows, but they did not see him.

But Corey saw something.

He froze again and swallowed hard, tasting blood and uncontrollable drool. Every hair on his body stood, for he recognized the man coming out of the forest, approaching Mark and Traci.

CHAPTER FORTY-TWO

Traci gasped at the sight of him. "Scott?"

He was slick with blood, his face split down his forehead and nose, making him look like a change purse of red flesh. He was pushing one hand to his side in a failed effort to hold back the bleeding. For some reason, he was wearing torn black fatigues. This confused her, but the intensity of his injuries was her main concern. It was as if he'd just staggered out of a brutal car accident.

"Traci!" Scott said. "Mark! Thank God I found you guys."

"What happened to you?" She had the urge to run to him, to take him in her arms, but she worried she'd only hurt him further. "What happened? Where's Jenny and Corey?"

"I don't know. We were attacked and had to split up."

He staggered closer, and now she did step toward him. The desire to take his pain away flooded her like divine, white light. All the questions could wait until later. Right now, her precious Scott needed her, and that was all that mattered. Her love for him bloomed within her breast, warm and bright and beautiful, and the creepy aura she'd felt about him earlier was instantaneously vaporized. How could she have ever expected him of anything other than goodness? From the look of him, he obviously had fought to save Jennifer and Corey's lives, risking his own in the process. Truly an incredible man. Her heart swelled until it felt like it would burst.

Mark snagged her wrist. "Traci…wait."

He pulled her back toward him, back toward reality.

The sudden spell evaporated. Traci shuddered. The intensity of that brisk love had been overwhelming, and the further she got from Scott, the more curious she became.

"Why are you in those clothes?" she asked.

"Please...you have to help me." His face contorted in pain. Blood dribbled over his eyebrows and dotted around his nostrils. "I'll explain everything. Just help me first."

Mark came beside Traci. The knife was still in his hand, but he held it loose and low at his side. It seemed he too was confused—maybe even suspicious—but their friend was severely wounded and needed assistance.

Scott had been acting weird tonight, but he hadn't done anything wrong that they knew of. Traci told herself not to be silly. Dread had made her irrational. Scott was no threat to them. He had brought them here with the best of intentions and someone had really made him pay for it. They had to help him. They had to get out of these woods alive. All of them.

"Jesus, man," Mark said, approaching Scott. "Who did this to you?"

A groan rose from the surrounding thicket, turning everyone's heads. It wasn't the beastly howl the forest had made while sucking the little woman into oblivion. This was the cry of a man in fright. He sounded frantic. He sounded familiar.

"Traayyy-seee! Maaahhhk!"

Mark turned toward the shadowy figure. "Corey? Corey!"

"Maahk! Ruuhh....ruh..."

"He's in trouble!" Mark said to Traci. "C'mon, we gotta help him!"

He made a quick dash toward the thicket, urging the others on.

"Ruuuuhhhnnn!" Corey cried from the dark.

There was a blue flash as a moonbeam reflected off the blade Scott had drawn from behind him. It swung overhead, a weapon like a crescent moon descending upon Mark. He spun back to face Scott, but then only stared at him, his eyes wet and lost. He looked so defeated, so willing to surrender.

Traci gasped when he dropped the knife. Mark shrugged.

"Then kill me," he whispered.

The scythe tore his chest and into his belly, his shirt fluttering open as his torso burst with blood, his innards spilling as the blade carved down and out, filleting him alive. Steam emanated from the fresh concavity.

Traci threw her hands to either side of her face, screaming. The urge to vomit came and she gagged, running backward, unable to take her eyes off the grisly scene. It couldn't be real. It just couldn't. It was not only grotesque, but also incomprehensible. Scott's actions were entirely motiveless. The level of brutality was beyond anything she would have thought him capable of. Mere moments ago, she had been flushed by affection for the man she'd once dated, the first boy she'd ever kissed with actual passion. She'd been enamored by his kind demeanor in adulthood, even if she had grown somewhat suspicious. He was just as gentlemanly as ever. Now, she realized she didn't really know him at all. Perhaps she never had.

Corey yelled to her again. "Ruuuunnn!"

Her feet pounded the earth with everything she had. There was a sick, squishy thud behind her. Mark's body must have hit the dirt. She heard Scott pursuing, but he was wounded and slow, his footsteps fading. Traci leapt over fallen logs and scrambled up an incline of rock, all those hours in the gym paying off.

What is happening? She kept asking herself. But she had no answer. This night was utter insanity, and it was still unfurling in all its godless horror. She cried as she ran, thinking of Mark and how he simply had given up. It seemed the dark thoughts had finally convinced him to give in to the call of death. They came and went in sudden flashes, the intensity rushing and ebbing like a tide.

How long had they all been out here? It felt like an eternity.

A disturbing thought hit her: had the past twenty-five years of her life been a mere illusion? Had they never gotten out of the woods that Halloween? Were they trapped in a loop without end, some cosmic figure-eight track that hurled them through this alternate dimension of pure horror? It seemed entirely possible. If Scott Dwyer could be a ruthless killer, then anything was possible. That's what frightened her more than anything else—the uncertainty and solipsism. The world she lived in could no longer be trusted or even known. In these woods...there was only madness.

COREY WATCHED Traci hurtle by until she was nothing but a blonde spec in a sea of shadow. He was glad she'd run for safety instead of trying to find him. Though he wanted to be with her, he wanted her to get away even more, and taking the time to look for him would have ruined her chances at escape. And if they were to band together, he would only slow her down. Scott was too damned close for that luxury—too close and too frenzied.

Seeing Mark disemboweled had caused Corey to bend over and wretch, the vomit rushing through the wound in his mouth, his stomach acid stinging the open cuts. He'd shut his eyes tight and flinched at the sound of Mark's body collapsing. There was such a dreadful and crushing finality to it. Mark would never have another laugh, never chug another beer or eat a good meal or rock out to Judas Priest. He'd never see his children, never reconcile with a lost love or find a whole new one. Everything he amounted to was extinguished in less than a minute. The sheer profundity of it took Corey's breath away.

And he was trying to save you, he thought.

Mark Goranson's last act was an effort to rescue Corey Pickett. It boggled the mind. It surprised him, but perhaps he shouldn't have been so surprised. Mark was far from perfect, but he wasn't all bad either, especially now that he'd matured. It was Mark's lack of fight that upset Corey most. He'd given up and accepted his fate. Well, Corey wasn't going to let his death be in vain. He would get through this. He would save Traci. And Scott was going to pay.

He wobbled through the brush, queasy and in pain. The hunting knife seemed to weigh a hundred pounds now.

Scott had slowed to a stop, unable to keep up with his fleeing prey. There was no sign of Traci now. She'd vanished into the woods like a gazelle. Corey had never seen anyone run so fast, but he'd also never seen someone with such a strong motivation to do so.

As Corey reached the other end of this leafy cluster, Scott surprised him by walking to the array of bushes on the other side. He wasn't chasing Traci and wasn't looking for Corey either. He lumbered into the wilderness as if he were looking for a place to hibernate. But still there burned a malevolent determination behind his eyes, and his blood-slicked face spoke of more violence to come.

The mask of the red death, Corey thought.

As soon as Scott was gone, he started toward the last spot he'd seen Traci.

YOU JUST left him there.

The guilt smacked Traci hard. She'd known Corey was nearby, and Mark had been right—he did sound like he was in trouble. He sounded hurt, like he could barely talk. What if he was even worse off than Scott? What if Scott had done something to him? What if he was stuck in a bear trap or...*hanging from a tree.*

Her chest ached. Her entire soul did.

Atop a small hill, she boosted herself upon a tree trunk and scanned her surroundings. She listened for any sounds of a pursuer, of Scott's labored breath or that Blue Oyster Cult song that had become a horrible funeral dirge, as threatening as a shotgun loading its chamber.

The woods were silent. She turned in every direction for a panoramic view. Her heart sank. She was lost in the labyrinth of a primeval forest. This wasteland was a phantasmagorical quagmire seemingly without end, and the maze's Minotaur was still snorting fire, trampling anything that got between them. After seeing what Scott had done to Mark, she had no doubts what he had in store for her. Scott was hunting them down for slaughter. That part was clear. But for what batshit crazy reason, she did not know.

Surely this wasn't part of Steven's last request, was it? Had Steven even left any last requests at all, or was it all just a figment of Scott's demented mind? Was Steven Winters really even dead? There'd been no evidence other than Scott's word. All he had was Steven's weird journals written from the perspective of the suicide victims, who she now wholeheartedly believed hadn't been suicides at all.

She tried to come up with any kind of logical explanation for Scott killing Mark. Had he planned to do it all along or had it been a spontaneous eruption of violence? Had the evil presence of the woods infected him somehow? Was he possessed? Or did he believe Mark was out to get him for some reason, or maybe even all of them? Even if Scott felt killing Mark was necessary, that didn't justify the gruesome way he'd executed it. He'd gutted him like a deer, as if he were planning to...*eat him.* Her stomach gurgled, but she managed to keep it down.

Suddenly she remembered the flask in her pocket. She grabbed for it with both hands, unscrewed the top, and drank with vigor, washing away the bile in her throat and sending instant relief through her jangled nerves. She realized she'd been experiencing mild withdrawals and again wondered just how long she'd really been out here.

As the vodka entered her blood, Traci steadied herself and stared down the slope in the direction she'd just came. Scott was down there somewhere, but so was Corey. She looked for something she could use as a weapon and settled on a thick fallen branch, which she snapped over her knee so one end would be jagged.

This is crazy.

But she had to do it.

She trotted back downhill, holding the branch out like a spear. Scott was bigger than she was and had a better weapon, but he was badly hurt and wasn't nearly as athletic as she was. She would be faster and more dexterous. And though he would normally be stronger than her—and was still strong enough to eviscerate Mark—he wouldn't be at his full strength with all that bodily harm .

Traci believed she could take him. She had to believe it.

CHAPTER FORTY-THREE

Scott was thunderstruck.

If what he'd done to Mark wasn't an adequate sacrifice, nothing would be. He'd done to his old friend what Julia had done to the chicken, splitting him vertically and expunging his insides. His own capacity for violence stunned him. Although he'd killed before, he'd never committed murder with such brutality. After the knife fight with Corey, he just didn't want to take any chances, and so he'd struck hard, going for the kill immediately. He'd felt electric as he'd done it, like a force of nature reminding humankind they were just helpless dust specks in an indifferent universe. He was a vital cog now in the transition of darkness into light, the impetus for a great exchange of power. And though he felt lethal, he also felt divine.

Let Traci run. He knew what lay ahead. She would find it, and he would find her. So fine, let her run, and let Corey bleed to death in the woods. Though he would prefer to kill Corey himself, Scott had to prioritize here, just as Sheriff Shrinner told him. If Corey didn't die from his injuries, the others could terminate him.

What mattered now was Traci, only Traci.

SHE DUCKED down when she saw movement. The figure shuffled along, every move grueling. Traci exhaled when she ascertained the man was too short to be Scott. Rising again, she came forward gingerly, keeping the spear in both hands just in case she'd been mistaken or the demons had more tricks in their cauldron.

"Trayyy-see?" the shadow called.

The voice was distorted, but definitely Corey's. She moved faster. When she got close, she saw why he was talking funny. His mouth was in tatters. His lip was split, and one side of his face had been sliced open. Even in the dark, she could see the whites of his teeth through his cheek.

"Oh my god…" she said.

She lowered her weapon, and he fell into her, sobbing. When she put an arm around him, she felt the stickiness of blood gone cold. Cuts and gashes peppered his body, his one hand wrapped in a soaked jacket sleeve and the other limply holding an enormous knife. Still apprehensive, she reached for it slowly. Corey let her take it, making her trust him all the more.

"Corey, what in the hell's happened to you?"

He spat to better speak. "Scott. He's…he's out to kill us. All of us. He's parta dis crazy cult. They're murderers."

Her mind seized around the new information. She needed another drink for this, but it would have to wait.

"A cult?" she said. "That's insane. What do you mean by 'a cult,' Corey?"

"Theezz people. They're behind all of it. And they're out here…with Scott."

"How many?"

"I dunno. Maybe sevun or eight. But I killed one. I had to. He wuz gonna kill me."

She looked him over. "Where are you most hurt?"

"Everywhere…"

"I have alcohol. We can sterilize the—"

He shook his head. "We have to move! Before they kin catch up ta us."

"Where is Scott?"

"Don't know. Walked off." He pointed into the distance. "He gave up runnin' after ya. But he won't stop comin'. I'm sure of it. Ya gotta believe me."

"Don't worry, I do. There was a woman who attacked us. She was small, disfigured… I don't know. But the trees just, like…just *swallowed her up.*"

She directed him toward the slope she'd come down from, worried if he could make it up the hill or not. Traci could help him, but not carry him. Gently, she put his arm over her shoulder to ease him along.

"Where's Jennifer?" she asked.

Corey went rigid and, at first, he didn't answer. "She's…"

"Maybe we can find her too."

He sniffled. "Scott said…he murdered her."

Now it was Traci who went rigid. Shock detonated through her. She flashed upon Jennifer Parks' kind face and warm demeanor, which no one would be lucky enough to enjoy again. The poor woman had *two children* who would never see their mother again. And while Traci had never been interested in being a mother herself, she felt a coring grief thinking of teenagers losing a parent.

They trenched on, struggling but steady, and when they reached the crest of the hill, Corey had to catch his breath. Fearing he'd mysteriously disappear, Traci kept her hands on him, brushing his matted hair and stroking his back in a soothing manner. This sort of tenderness had been foreign to her for so long. She didn't even show this kind of affection to her boyfriend, and Kordell was equally unromantic. Danger bonded people together. It was sad how it took such extremities to bring out the compassion in some people.

"Come on," she said. "We really have to keep mov—"

A soft whisper cut her off. Its voice was female. Corey must have heard it too, for his head turned in the same direction.

"This way," the voice said.

But they saw nothing. Not a shadow lurking or a face appearing. Traci held the knife out in front of her with both hands, her arms flexed. "Who is that?"

The voice called them forward again, and then there was another whispering voice, then another and another, each coming from the dip in the land ahead, urging Traci and Corey to come to them.

"Is it the cult?" she asked Corey.

"I don't think so," he said. "They all sound so…"

"Young," she said, finishing for him. "They all sound like teens, don't they?"

He nodded, his face wan and bloody. As the voices continued calling, the first voice grew loudest, drowning out the others' mantra.

"Don't be afraid," it said.

"WHO ARE you?" Corey demanded.

He could no longer take the insanity. His physical wounds were excruciating, but it was the strangeness of all he'd witnessed that finally threatened to break him. Feeling as if he might fall down weeping, he gritted his teeth against sadness and frustration, honing them into a sharp rage. It might be the only thing that would keep him alive.

Now the voice was a whisper directly in his ear, and though there was no one there he felt the breath on his ear, soft and sweet like a lover's. His body locked up, hairs rising at his neck.

"We dress up like monsters to trick the real monsters," the girl's voice said.

Bizarre phosphorescence swayed beside him, side to side like a pendulum. Traci clenched him tighter. The celestial image swung back and forth, recreating the last time he'd seen Robin Reeves. Corey felt it more than saw it, visualizing the scene like a forced dream.

"Don't be afraid," Robin's voice said as she hung. "Just don't...be...afraid."

And the strangest part was that he wasn't.

The voices of Suicide Wood's lost souls rose in a murmuring chorus. The forest stretched and popped, roots crawling along like giant earthworms, dragging the sycamores and lining them in formation like the ones that had always led him out of the woods.

"It's a path," he told Traci.

Surprise seemed to have hushed her.

Robin's voice returned, her words labored. "The truth...here is the *truth*."

The opening widened, blowing leaves away to reveal a freshly carved trail. Corey took Traci's hand and moved forward, but she held him back.

"What if it's a trick?" she said. "The demons."

"I don't think so."

"But what if you're wrong? What if—"

Once again, she was silenced, this time by a low snarl rising from the hillside behind them. They looked back, and there was the crimson demon, the same one he remembered; or perhaps there were many who looked this way. The thing's three legs were clawing up the slope as it snorted and drooled over extending fangs. Its horrid face was no mask. This was the true monstrosity.

"They hear us…" Robin told them. "Go…*now*."

The demon turned his head up at them. When it opened its eyes, they filled with blood. Traci shrieked as the creature's eyeballs pushed out of its head like babies being born, a gush of optical afterbirth following as they fell from his skull. The sockets sprouted tiny teeth, turning into crying baby mouths.

Traci rushed Corey along, taking him into the trail for there was nowhere else left to run. As they fled, the trees behind them twisted and contracted, creating a complex briar wall to shield them from the rear. Robin whispered for them not to be scared, instructing them more forcefully. Something about the way she said it comforted Corey in a way the words never had before. When coming from demons, the words had a different meaning. They wanted him not to be afraid of dying, whereas Robin didn't want him to be afraid because it would weaken his resolve. He hoped Traci received this same message, for it was one he could not explain. There was no clear logic or evidence. It was a mere vibe, one that calmed his pulse and cleared his head.

The trail came to an end, and Corey gazed up at their salvation.

"DO YOU see what I see?" Traci's heart pounded at the sight of it.

"Is that…a *house*?" Corey asked.

A deck on stilts hung above a rocky bluff, overlooking where they stood. Squinting in the dark, Traci could just make out the back of a house, the moonlight gleaming off the windowpanes.

"Oh my god!" she said, nearly squealing.

They moved quickly, even Corey finding his second wind now that they were this close to rescue. The building loomed like a utopian vision.

Traci kept telling herself it wasn't a mirage. What they saw was a solid reality, as true to life as they were. They were at the end of this hell night. They were saved.

"Help!" she yelled toward the house. "We need help!"

They tromped up the slope, shouting to whoever might be inside. She picked up a handful of pebbles and started tossing them at the windows. She turned back, making sure the horned ghoul wasn't on their tail, but the woods had closed like a castle gate. The only sound was Corey calling to the owner of the house. When they didn't get an immediate answer, they scrambled up the crag and onto the deck.

Just being on the deck was a relief in itself. It was a symbol of civilization, an affront to the labyrinth of Suicide Woods. This was her world, not the world of woodland creatures and satanic cults. Reality had come back.

There was a sliding glass door at the rear of the house. She and Corey banged on it and looked though the small section not covered by vertical blinds. Traci cupped her hands to her head and pressed into the glass. A living room in darkness—a sofa and coffee table, some framed photos over a fireplace. There were no lights on, not even one above an oven many people left on at night. There was no faint glow of a clock or the illuminated red dot of a TV's *on* button. It was as if the house had lost power.

A porch light was suspended over the deck. It was dark too. Maybe the owner was out of town. But wouldn't they have left some lights on if that were the case, to make it look like they were home? Wouldn't they have at least kept the outside lights on? Maybe the bulbs had burnt out. There were too many possibilities. None of them mattered to her now. They'd found a house and they were going in, invited or not.

She tugged at the door handle. Locked.

"We can't just break in," Corey said.

"What else are we gonna do? Maybe they have a phone that actually works and we can call the cops."

"Or maybe they're home and *they'll* call the cops on *us*."

"Good! I'd rather be in jail than dead. Besides, we can explain what's happened. We'll be protected. Safe."

He winced when he opened his mouth, but he was speaking more clearly now. It seemed the numbness was doing him a favor. "What if they have a rifle and shoot us?"

She grabbed him by his ravaged coat. "After everything we've seen tonight, I'll take that gamble. Mark was *fucking gutted*, Corey. There are dwarves and demons and God knows what else after us. It's a miracle we got out alive. I think the voices were guiding us here, don't you?"

He shrugged. "Yeah, I think so, but I dunno. If you hadn't heard them too, I'd have thought I was hallucinating."

They looked all around them, gazing into the woods and sky, holding hands. They called for Robin, but she didn't answer. The ghost voices were gone. She thought about what Robin had said about the demons hearing them. Was that why they'd been silent until that moment, to thwart the malevolent beings? Or did they have to use their ability to communicate sparingly?

She put the hunting knife into the jam where the door met the frame. She forced it up and down, trying to tumble the lock, the paneling warping as she nicked and tore it. But the damn thing wouldn't budge.

Traci scowled. "Screw it."

She turned the knife around so the handle faced the door and pounded the glass until a bullet hole-like splintering appeared. Then she darted the tip of the blade into the center of the rupture and drove the knife in. The glass broke into chunks that shattered when they fell upon the hard wood floor.

Traci reached through the hole she'd made, unlocked the door, and slid it open, more glass flurrying. Drawing her phone from her pocket, she turned the flashlight on. She found a light switch on the wall, but it offered nothing when she flipped it.

"Shit. No power."

"There still might be a *working* phone somewhere."

Her eyes went wide. "Or maybe even car keys."

They trotted to the front window and peered outside. The driveway was empty, and the neighborhood was deserted, no other houses in sight, only a street riddled with potholes running through more horrible, vacant woods.

"The garage," Corey said.

They shot through the kitchen, ignoring a rotten smell, and Traci rushed through the door. In the garage was a green Jeep Cherokee, an older, boxier model. Traci flung open the driver's side door.

No keys in the ignition. She searched the glove box, drink holder, armrest, visor, and under the mat. No goddamned keys.

"They must be in the house," she said.

They went back inside, and that's when Traci first heard the buzzing. It was low at first, but as they moved through the kitchen, it intensified, several drone noises zipping past. She held up her phone and the light revealed an orgy of flies whisking around the trash bin. This was where the stink had come from. She pointed the beam into the bin and her stomach soured. There was grayed ground meat in the trash that writhed with maggots, and an army of parental flies harvesting moldy cheese and black banana peels.

Corey recoiled and they moved out of the kitchen. "Place must've been empty a while."

"C'mon. Maybe we can find those keys. Even if the owner has them, there is probably a spare around."

They checked for a hook or bowl at the front door. Nothing. So they searched through the downstairs rooms, choosing to stick together rather than split up. Even if they were out of the woods, she didn't want to lose sight of him. They returned to the living room, Corey opening the drawers of end tables while she went to the mantel above the fireplace.

When the flashlight fell upon the framed photos, Traci gasped at who smiled back at her.

CHAPTER FORTY-FOUR

"Corey...Corey, come look at this."

He came beside her, and she aimed her light upon the row of framed photos on the mantel. Corey's heart rose into his gullet.

"It's him, isn't it?" Traci asked. "Tell me that's not him."

He was older, but there was no mistaking Steven Winters. His arched eyebrows and perfect jaw line were dead giveaways. In every picture, there was a much younger girl with him. Sometimes she was a teenager, other times just a toddler. And she had those same arched eyebrows and wavy hair.

A daughter.

Corey took one picture in his good hand. "Jesus. This is Steven's house."

Traci's eyes misted. "What is going on?"

"The truth."

"What?"

"When Robin led us here, that's what she'd said; that we would find *the truth.*" He put the frame back. "Scott's been lying to us this whole time, hasn't he?"

But it was more of a statement than a question. Traci tugged him back from the mantel. "Let's keep looking. I'd rather have car keys than answers."

He followed her around the sofa. "That girl. She must've been his kid. She looked so much like him. I didn't see any pictures of a mother though."

"Keys, Corey. Keys."

THEY FOUND nothing on the bottom floor. They headed upstairs. In the stairwell, Traci reflected upon the one in the Dwyer house that led to Scott's basement room. It made her shiver. A fraction of her nightmare returned to her then, a vision of an orange-tinted underworld where naked bodies hovered over her as a young boy was…

The dream segment vanished, dismissed by a terrible odor far fouler than that of the neglected kitchen trash. She put her hand over her nose and mouth.

"Oh, God. What is that?"

Behind her, Corey coughed the stench away. The cough was wet.

We should go to the bathroom, she thought, *find him some hydrogen peroxide and bandages*. Maybe they could plug their nostrils with wadded toilet paper too.

"I don't like this, Traci. That stench…it's a bad sign."

"We have to check. If we can't get a car or a phone to call 911, it'll be like we haven't gotten out of the woods at all."

On the upper landing, a door was open to a small bedroom. The walls were plastered with posters of movies and pop stars. There were also many charcoal drawings—faces, birds, bowls of fruit and other still life. There was a short desk with several stacked books and an open laptop covered in stickers, two video game controllers next to it. A blouse and skirt were draped over the back of the chair. The bed was unmade.

"This is a teenage girl's room," Traci said. "No doubt about it."

"So he did have a daughter."

Corey tried the laptop to see if they could contact the police with it, but like everything else in the house, it was stone dead. They returned to the hall, peeked in at a bathroom and closet, and then came upon another bedroom, which had been turned into an office. There was a large L-shaped desk with a computer on one end and an old-fashioned typewriter on the other. Bookcases hid the walls, jammed full of hardbacks and paperbacks and chapbooks and magazines. She noticed many of the books were multiple duplicates, fifteen or twenty copies of just one title.

"These must be the books he wrote under pen names," she said.

There were books on New England history and local legends, a few movie novelizations, and some co-written and ghostwritten biographies. But the one that really drew her eye was called *Modern Studies in Demonology: A Guide to the Underworld and its Spirits*. When they came inside, they spotted a table that had been hidden behind the door. It was stacked with black, bound journals identical to the ones Scott had read from the night before. She opened the cover to one, seeing the pages were blank, awaiting Steven's scribbled handwriting. There were also piles of loose papers—letters, faxes, photocopies of articles, and yellowed newspaper clippings. All were related to the suicides in the woods.

"He never let it go," she said. "It haunted him his whole life."

"Too many questions left unanswered." Corey fingered the journals. "I don't think he was imagining these entries. I think the same voices we heard tonight were actually communicating with him, trying to tell him something. Maybe that's why he bought this house in the boonies, so he could be close to them. So there'd be little interference."

Traci said a silent prayer. Supernatural involvement was no longer a possibility to her; it was a certainty. She longed to dig deeper into these revelations, but time was wasting, so she led Corey out of the room and journeyed on to the door at the end of the hall.

The master bedroom.

Here the putrid reek was thickest. It wafted from the crack in the doorway where a sliver of moonlight glowed an ethereal blue. She put the collar of her sweater over her nose and aimed the phone's flashlight forward. With Corey right behind her, she nudged the door open with her foot.

They groaned in unison.

Splayed out upon the bed was the body of Steven Winters. A ring of flies danced upon his head in a sickening halo. Others climbed the walls. The corpse was lying on its back, dressed in a t-shirt and lounge pants, its arms and feet gone ashen from rigor mortis. The mattress was covered in dried blood. When Traci shined the light closer, she saw the concavity of Steven's chest where something had crushed and opened it. Insects had made their home in the gaping wound, and a pool of maggots writhed in the deepest caves of the purpled flesh.

"No…" Corey muttered.

She turned the light away, and the beam was reflected at them from the nightstand. She focused the light again, seeing a ring of keys laid atop a wallet. The remains of a crushed cell phone were beside them. Corey saw it too. His eyes went wide, his face slack.

She gripped his hand tighter. "C'mon."

Traci swallowed hard and squinted against the flies that buzzed about the room in an electric choir. Bile swam in the back of her throat, but she tried to stay focused on the keys, keeping her eyes off the decaying corpse just inches away. Tears rose from fright and grief and the overpowering vapors of rot.

The nightstand was specked with blood, and a small chunk of bodily meat was crusted to the wallet. Globules of gore were caked onto the bed-side lamp. Traci held her breath. She snatched the blood-flecked keys and turned around quickly, eager to leave the room, leave the house in the woods, and leave the hellish world of Redford forever.

She and Corey screamed.

Scott Dwyer stood in the doorway. "I'm sorry it has to be like this."

There was no menace in his tone. His expression was remorseful, eyebrows drawn close, a frown dimpling his chin. He was holding the blood-encrusted scythe to one side. Traci dropped her phone so she could grip the hunting knife with both hands. The phone fell to the floor face-up, the light creating a harsh glow that illuminated their faces from beneath like a pale white campfire. She tried to speak but could only whimper.

Scott exhaled. "I didn't want you to have to see this, Traci."

"Please…don't…"

"It pained me to take part in Steven's death a few nights ago. I wasn't the one to swing the axe, but I was here. I really wanted all of us old friends for the reunion. But he'd gotten too close."

Corey held up his fists. "You sick bastard. You murderer!"

"Look, I wanted all of us to have the chance to be with Steven at least one more time before he died, but The Congregation felt we had no choice but to end him sooner. He'd spent his life researching the deaths in the woods. He was always trying to understand why Robin did what she did. And when his daughter was taken, well—"

"Taken?" Traci asked.

"Look…the voices were speaking to Steven—all the voices of the dead. I think they figured he would be the best one to tell their story, him being a writer. All of this brought him too close to finding out the truth."

"The truth about your demented cult?" Corey asked.

"No. The truth about what had to be done."

"What truth?"

"I guess I do owe you guys an explanation." Scott released a long sigh. "The deaths in Suicide Woods weren't suicides, at least not for the most part. Sure, there were one or two depressed kids who wanted to jump on the bandwagon when they took their own lives, so they went out there to die. But for the most part, the suicides were actually sacrifices."

"Human sacrifices."

"That's right. A necessary evil. We—"

Traci snapped. "Who the hell are you people? What do you want?"

"It's not what we *want*. It's what has to be done." He shrugged. "It's been done for centuries. Maybe even longer. Take the Aztecs, for example, or the ancient Egyptians. They sacrificed to their gods. But it was the druids who discovered who we really must make offerings too. They knew the harvest season was when the land of the living was closest to the border of the land of the dead. The portal opens in the latter half of October. The demons of Suicide Woods are real. If they're not appeased, we—"

"You worship Satan…"

He moved closer. "No, we don't. It's—"

She slashed the air between them, and he stepped back. "Don't come any closer! Please, Scott…please…"

He shook his head. "Traci…you don't think I'd hurt *you*, do you?"

She blinked away a tear. "What?"

"Traci…oh, honey, you've got it all wrong. I'm not going to sacrifice *you*! Listen to me. My father explained it all to me before he died. That night in the woods when we were teens…they found out we were going. I wasn't part of The Congregation yet and didn't know anything about it, but my parents were members. So were a lot of people we all knew—teachers and neighbors, a dentist and a librarian, and others. In fact, even your mother was a member of The Congregation."

"No!" she said, tears falling. "You're lying."

"She was a well-respected priestess. Her promiscuity served a purpose, Traci. She was—"

Corey seethed. "Shut your damn mouth! Stop saying these horrible things! You're crazy, Scott. You need help! Give us the scythe. We can all go to the police. There's still time for you to do what's right. You can't just kill us."

"Damn it, I told you—I'm not going to hurt Traci. I wouldn't dream of it." Scott smiled his warm, charming smile at her, the one that had always melted her. In this context it was morbid, grotesque. "She's vital to The Congregation. Our parents knew it even back then. That's why they hated Jenny, you see? She got between Traci and I, who were destined to be together. Jenny was the one who was supposed to be sacrificed that night, but my mother couldn't bear to hurt me by doing that. So the demons came. They used their power to confuse and misdirect us, to separate us from each other. The Congregation was only able to appease them by taking Robin. They coaxed her along perfectly. We always thought Steven sacrificed so much for us that night by saying he was out there alone. But it was Robin who made the true sacrifice. Who knows how many souls were spared by hers being taken? She was a perfect sacrifice—a *virgin*. Without her as an offering, we never would have gotten out of Suicide Woods alive. The demons would have slaughtered us all."

Traci choked back a sob. She wanted to run, but Scott blocked the only exit, unless she was going to jump through the two-story window. She'd been so confident she could take Scott down, but now that she was facing him, she had doubts she could stab another human being, and the aura of criminal madness emanating from him made her tremble. The man had the advantage of insanity.

"Because of me," Scott said, "my mother failed. So, in a way, I failed, even if I didn't know it. I'm part of The Congregation now, and an important part. I had to make things right. That's why I brought you all back here, to make an offering like no other. I'm giving back the souls the world beyond never got to claim."

"You're out of your mind," Corey said.

"After all you've seen and heard and *felt*, can you really doubt these things?"

"I believe in the demons," Corey said. "And I believe in spirits. We've all experienced them, it's true. But that doesn't mean you have to serve them. You turned on all of us, man. All your friends. We grew up together for God's sake. You were like a brother to me, Scott."

Traci was surprised to see Scott tear up. She knew then that his remorse wasn't faked. However crazy or confused, Scott was also hurting inside. Perhaps she could use that to her advantage.

"I'm sorry, Corey," he said. "You'll always be a brother to me. But unfortunately, that's exactly why they want you. It makes my offerings all the more valuable if they're someone I care about."

"Is that why you killed Steven and his daughter?"

Scott's eyes fell. "That's not what happened. The Congregation influenced Stephanie to take her own life. A new youth was needed and she was highly suggestible after her mother died suddenly of pancreatic cancer. Stephanie was deeply depressed. She knew her own death was coming and wrote it all out exactly the way it happened before it happened." He pointed to his temple. "She was *touched*…just like Robin Reeves.

"Steven was getting too close, so his daughter went first. She was a warning. But her suicide only made him all the more pursuant. So he was killed too, and not too kindly." He clutched the scythe to his chest. "Please, Corey. I ask you again. Let me make this quick and easy. It's for your own good. It's for the good of *the world*. Don't you see that? Let my sacrifice be yours as well—the greatest sacrifice of a true suicide. That's why, whenever we can, The Congregation tries to trick the evil ones into thinking the murders were suicides with hangings and slit wrists. But if you really offer yourself for the slaughter, Corey, you'll be keeping the demons at bay. That will prevent the portal from opening this harvest season. I can't begin to tell you how important that is. For over twenty years, other congregations have handled the demons in all parts of the world. But now the ancient evil has returned to Redford. We must rise again."

Corey stood speechless. He seemed so tired and defeated. Traci hoped he wasn't succumbing to blood loss or, worse yet, succumbing to Scott.

Scott continued to plead. "I tried to make you all understand the truth by reading Robin's journal. I told you as much as I could without chasing you away."

He reached out to Traci with his free hand, as if asking her to dance. She raised the blade higher, ready to strike at his first move.

"Come with me, Traci," he said, his soft eyes begging. "Let's begin our new life together—the life we were always *supposed to have*."

"No…"

"The Congregation chose us for greatness long ago. That's why they put us together as lovers at such a young age. It's time we fulfill our destiny. Let's make our parents proud."

Her chest went hard and breathless. Every muscle in her body tightened as memories she'd suppressed into oblivion emerged from the ether of her mind. For so long she'd been unable to remember when exactly she and Scott had first gotten together. It seemed he'd always been in her life somehow. She credited this to the passing of time erasing old memories to make room for new ones. But the horrors of coming home and Scott's chilling words had resurfaced the trauma, her bad dreams unmasking themselves as actual memories of being coaxed into a partnership with Scott Dwyer, who was equally controlled by their parents and other members of the community. They'd pushed the children into ritualistic mating, and now Traci realized it had all been some sort of forced consummation of a marriage made only in the eyes of The Congregation.

But as the children grew older, the cult had been unable to reinforce this union. Doing so would have been too risky. As teenagers, Traci and Scott's minds were almost fully formed. They'd be more capable of resisting and understanding the cult's intentions. They could go to one of their teachers or to the police. So the cult had to influence them in other ways, but Scott's mother had deviated from the plan, and that had changed everything.

Traci's hands sweat around the handle of the knife. She wasn't an abused little girl anymore, and she wasn't a damaged teen either. She was a woman. The fact that she was functioning at all after everything life had thrown at her just showed how strong she was. Despite all the horror and pain she'd been forced to endure, she'd survived and, better than that, she'd escaped. Running away from Redford was one hell of a victory for a young woman with no prospects. And still she'd managed to make it on her own. Okay, so maybe she didn't have it all together. Maybe she drank too much and too frequently hopped from job to job. Maybe she suffered from deep emotional scars that inevitably ruined all her relationships. But she wasn't anyone's victim anymore, and she damn sure wasn't going to be one again. She'd sooner die than have her humanity stripped away.

Slowly, Traci lowered the knife, but only just enough. Scott took another cautious step, his fractured face illuminated by the phone's light. His lips parted in a small smile, eyes filled with somber hope. As his outstretched hand came within reach, Traci slashed at it, the blade lacerating his palm.

He winced and stumbled back. She lunged at him, shoving the weapon in an effort to spear him. If she could just hurt him enough to send him to the floor, she and Corey could get to the jeep and drive as far the hell away from these woods as possible.

Scott raised the scythe, but only in an effort to block her attack. He did not swing it at her or rush her. Instead, he backed into the dresser, stumbling again, and Corey grabbed the amber lamp from the nightstand, pulling the plug from the wall, and swung it from its cord like a shot put. The lamp just missed Scott's face and the porcelain burst against the dresser, spraying him with shards so he closed his eyes.

Traci seized the opportunity.

The knife entered Scott's ribs. He didn't scream, but he gasped so deeply his face flushed, veins standing out on his neck. Having done such a horrible thing, Traci cried out, even though she'd had no other choice than to assault him. She wasn't proud to momentarily hope she'd punctured Scott's lung. Despite everything, she didn't want him to die. She told herself it was because of a deep-seated belief in the sanctity of life, but it was more than that. It was a feeling so ingrained it caused her physical pain to deny it.

She still cared about Scott.

She knew she shouldn't, but she did. It was ironed into her very soul, impossible to erase. His hold on her was staggering. It's how he'd lured her back to Redford, gotten her into his basement despite her hesitation, and brought her back into Suicide Woods. She thought of what he'd said about their parents putting them together as lovers, and then came the mental image of naked adults hovering over them while they...

She tried to withdraw the knife but Scott grabbed the handle, holding the blade still in his chest while he struggled to remain standing. Darting for the door, Corey ushered her out first, a chivalrous act that would cost him dearly.

COREY GASPED for air as a stinging sensation pierced his neck. His chest went warm and wet. Blood was funneling out of him, a slit across his throat opening like a second mouth.

Scott's swing of the scythe had ripped in front of Corey when he was just a foot away from the door jam. Even being stabbed in the chest had yet to stop this psycho. He was just that determined to see his blood-dream fulfilled. And so he'd cut Corey's throat.

Falling back, Corey put both hands to his neck, ignoring the pain in his punctured palm in an effort to stop the bleeding, telling himself it wasn't pointless, that he could stay alive if he just remained calm. But as he hit the wall behind him and slid to the floor, he felt the slick heat of blood pouring all the way down into his lap. When he breathed, he coughed a red mist. Trying not to panic, he reached for the sheets on the bed beside him. They were covered in Steven's dried blood and swarming with flies, but Corey pulled them to his throat regardless, trying to bandage the gushing wound.

In the hallway, Traci was staring at him with tears running down her cheeks. He tried to tell her to run but could hardly hear himself. His words were a whisper, not unlike the voices of the dead. *Soon I may be one of them*, he thought. He tried to shake the notion from his mind, but it persisted, a relentless promise that he would see the reaper at last.

Don't fear the reaper...

Scott lumbered forward. He stared down at Corey with those blue eyes of his in one last, silent apology. And then the scythe came down, falling and rising and falling, slinging ropes of flesh into the air. Bits of his own body splattered across Corey's face, and yet he felt no pain. His pain was over. Now there was only the crippling dread of approaching the ultimate end.

Corey thought of the words that had haunted him since that Halloween so long ago. He'd never been able to tell anyone what Robin Reeves had said that night. Instead, he'd kept it locked inside his heart where it could creep and fester, poisoning him from within. He'd long told himself they were just the ramblings of an intoxicated girl with serious emotional problems, especially considering they'd found her hanging a few hours later. But deep down he'd always known she'd spoken the truth, and that's why the words had stayed with him, and stayed secret.

"We're both going to die in these woods," she'd told him.

Corey's head fell to one side, facing the window, and as Scott finally lay off his attack, Corey gazed out at the moonlit sycamore swaying in the October breeze. The woods were waving him in. They were there for him, had always been there for him, ready to welcome him back forever.

CHAPTER FORTY-FIVE

Traci nearly collapsed as she raced down the stairs. Her hand slid down the banister, streaking it with Scott's blood. She leapt down the last four steps and ran through the living room, the keys clutched in her fist and poking through her fingers, a makeshift weapon she'd learned about in a women's self-defense class.

As she passed through the kitchen, she heard Scott thundering down the staircase. He called her name as if he were her husband just coming home from work. She darted into the garage and gently closed the door behind her, hoping he wouldn't know where to look for her.

There was no key fob, so she had to open the door of the jeep manually. Having left her phone behind, she now had no flashlight, and she struggled in the dark to make out which keys belonged to the Cherokee. She tried one and failed. Switching to another, she heard Scott knocking into things in the kitchen. She pictured him staggering as a punctured lung was flooded by blood. Was it possible she'd hurt him that badly? The next key failed. She whimpered through clenched teeth and pushed in another. It turned in the keyhole, and the lock popped up behind the window. She could almost kiss it.

The door to the jeep flung open just as the kitchen door to the garage did.

SCOTT CAME through, smearing the door with blood. He'd pulled the knife out of his chest before coming down, but it may have been a mistake to do so. He was bleeding profusely. At least he was breathing okay. Traci had stuck him good, but it seemed he'd been lucky enough not to have anything vital rupture, but he was mutilated and exhausted. Every inch of him was raw with pain. He was growing lightheaded, and the world seemed to swirl around him like a bad acid trip. But he could still see Traci climbing into the jeep.

Scott lunged just as she slammed the door shut. Grabbing the handle, he tried to pull it open, but she grabbed the door with both hands and slammed it shut again, surprising him with her strength. He slipped and fell hard onto his tailbone, giving birth to a whole new agony that shot up through his colon and into his lower back.

As the jeep started, he swung at the driver's side window with the scythe in a last-ditch effort. The glass shattered, little shards spraying Traci. She was searching through the interior. The rolling garage door was still closed. In her hurry, she'd forgotten to open it, and now she was scrambling to find a remote inside the Cherokee. This would buy him some time.

Using the scythe for leverage, he hooked it onto the windowsill and pulled himself up. "Traci…. Traci, stop."

But she only groaned, tears leaping from her eyes as she pawed through the glove box, throwing out the registration and old maps.

Scott reached for her, trying to calm her down, but when his hand landed on her shoulder, she turned and sank her teeth into his fingers. He pulled back, but she clenched harder, shaking her head back and forth like a birddog with a fresh duck. Even as his blood filled her mouth, she refused to let go, so he had to rip his hand free, her teeth peeling his fingers like carrots.

"Traci, please! *I love you!*"

But his bride only snarled. "Get the fuck away from me!"

Scott grimaced. He couldn't be gentle about this anymore. The others had warned him Traci might not go quietly. Despite the indoctrination she'd received in her youth and all the programming her mother had done, she'd been gone so many years and was bound to have reservations, doubts, suspicions. Of course, seeing him kill the others would lead her to believe he had the same plans for her, no matter how much he tried to explain he would never hurt her. It annoyed him that she was making a liar out of him now, but he had no choice but to take her by force.

He grabbed her by the hair, twisting those beautiful blonde locks in his skinned fingers. She didn't try to bite him again. She didn't punch at him or even scream. She flinched at the tugging, but that was all, and for a moment Scott thought she just might be coming around, that she'd realized at last that he was doing all of this for them. But this sweet delusion didn't last long.

The tires spun as the jeep went into reverse, even though the garage door was still closed, and suddenly Scott was being dragged across concrete.

THE GARAGE door collapsed on top of the jeep in a blanket of twisted metal. Traci slammed down the gas pedal, and the Cherokee roared down the driveway, flinging off the garage door and other debris. But Scott's grip on her hair did not loosen. He held it in one hand and the scythe in the other, still hooked onto the windowsill. His lower body was being pulled down the driveway, his legs flopping as he was chaffed by road-rash.

Traci's neck arched in his direction as he pulled harder on her, trying to climb through the window. Some of her hair began to free itself from her scalp. She could feel drops of blood seep through.

The driveway was in disrepair, and when she hit a broken section, the jeep bounced and she flinched and spun the wheel, screaming as blood dribbled down her forehead, her head feeling as if it might snap off at the neck. The rear of the jeep swung wide and the front driver's side tire bounced over something, as if she'd hit a raccoon.

Scott cried out and lost his grip completely, his leg crushed under the wheel.

Traci's scream turned into a manic, high-pitched laughter when she saw him lying in the driveway all gnarled and smashed. It was the laughter of a cracked mind, and she knew it, so it quickly turned into crying as she switched gear into drive and gunned it, the roar of the engine like a cougar's , so loud and freeing she could not help but smile behind the tears.

339

The first light of day was breaking on the skyline, a gray fall morning greeting her like a kind, familiar face. She raced toward it, swerving around the street's potholes and cracks where grass had grown through the gravel. She was relieved to be driving a jeep that could handle a shitty road while going at such a high speed. It vibrated beneath her, shuddering her very core, and she laughed and cried and screamed and pounded the steering wheel and spat pieces of Scott's flesh that had caught between her teeth as she drove on, so out of her mind she didn't notice the police car until it was right on top of her.

THE LIGHTS swirled and the headlights flashed. At first, Traci went rigid—a reflex—but then a waft of joy burst through her.

She was saved. By the grace of God, she was saved. She pulled over, so happy she could almost squeal. It took all she had not to just jump out of the jeep and run to the officer with open arms, a sudden move that could get her tased or even shot. But she didn't have to wait long anyway. Not one but two officers came out of the police cruiser. They had their guns drawn and were standing behind their car's open doors.

Traci's relief faded.

One officer yelled out. "Let me see your hands!"

Traci put them up.

"Come out, nice and slow!"

This couldn't be happening. She'd escaped a vicious killer! She was the victim here. Had they seen the hit and run? She had to explain it all—*fast*.

Opening the door, she did as she was told, and the officers closed in on her, keeping her at gunpoint as cuffs were snapped around her wrists.

"Officers, please. You have to listen to me!"

"Just calm down, miss."

"There's been multiple murders! I just barely escaped with my life. These people…and a man named Scott Dwyer…that house back there…"

When she looked back there was another police vehicle at the foot of Steven's driveway. An officer knelt beside Scott, holding a flashlight over him.

Oh, God, Traci thought. *He's dead. He's dead and they're going to think I just killed him, that I killed them all.* She glanced at her blood-spattered clothes. Drops had streaked her face. She could still taste the salt of gore on her tongue, the stench of copper in her nostrils.

"There's a cult!" she said in a panic. "They killed everyone. They've been doing it for years. Remember the history of Suicide Woods? Human sacrifice for demons! You've gotta believe me, please, I—"

"Just calm down, miss. We're gonna take you back to the station."

"Am I...Am I under arrest?"

"Just come along and we'll straighten this whole mess out."

He guided her toward the police cruiser, still cuffed. The other officer had holstered his pistol.

"Please," she said. "You have to arrest that man back there! He's a killer, I'm telling you. He has this hook weapon thing. He killed my friends Corey and Jenny and Mar—"

"Okay, okay. Take it easy." They came upon the back of the police car, and the officer held the top of her head as he tucked her inside. "Just calm yourself. Everything's okay now."

She felt some small relief, but it vanished with what he said next.

"Don't be afraid."

CHAPTER FORTY-SIX

Medics were tending to Scott as the cruiser drove past Steven's house, but there was no ambulance, only a high-topped, unmarked station wagon, like a hearse with a gurney in back instead of a coffin. Traci stared out the window of the police car, trying to get a better look, but she couldn't tell if Scott was alive or not. He wasn't moving, but the medics were still working on him, seemingly trying to save his life after all the cuts and stabs and bone crushes. Traci wished she could walk over there to both raise a toast with her flask and spit in his face. She'd gladly visit his grave to do so if only he wouldn't be buried in Redford, a town she vowed to never return to.

Hopefully, she'd have the chance to leave it once and for all. She had an uneasy feeling, being locked in the back of this cop car with her hands cuffed behind her back and her knees pressed against a slanted wall so she could not kick. The officers' behavior was alarming, particularly the one's choice of words. *Don't be afraid.* She rambled on, telling them everything that had happened, urging them to search for Jennifer Parks in case she was still alive. The driver just continued to tell her to calm down. The other didn't speak at all. They didn't turn their heads to look at her or even glance at her in the rearview mirror. Worse still, they didn't ask any follow up questions when she told them of carnage and death and a cult of demon worshipers that had been murdering children for decades.

They think you're crazy, she thought. *Or they already know what's happened and won't tell you.*

Maybe they know far more than you do.

Traci didn't give up. She went on and on, telling them about the past as well as the present. They continued through the neighborhoods, and soon she recognized the streets. Turning onto Union Drive, she saw the old Goranson place—Mark's house when they were teens—and a pang of grief went through her. Instead of allowing the image of him being disemboweled to return to her, she thought of him young and wild, of his farm boy grin and shaggy hair, of the way he'd let her wear his jean jacket with all the metal band patches on it, and how he'd always found ways to make her laugh even in those bleak high school days.

They rounded Crestline Avenue, the street she'd grown up on. She'd learned to ride a bike on this street, and had even broken her ankle doing it. She'd made out with Joel Carlson in that treehouse right over there. On those porches, she'd smashed pumpkins on Halloween and watched jealously as other kids' fathers hung Christmas lights while her house never even got a Christmas tree. When the cruiser passed by the house she'd once lived in, Traci bit her bottom lip. She'd avoided this street while she'd driven to Scott's, not wanting to remember. Now that the house was right there in front of her, she was raked with conflicting feelings.

In contrast to all the good memories of the street, the house seemed to pulse with filth and shame. She remembered the sounds of strange men having orgasms in the next room, the noise of her mother having sex with another stranger while Traci was trying to sleep. She flashed back to the thick, hairy man who'd crept into her bedroom one night when her mom had passed out drunk. He'd put his finger in Traci's mouth, and she'd screamed. The man went running out of her room and then out of the house. Her mother had never mentioned it. Traci remembered always sneaking into the bathroom to cut herself with a penknife because psychical pain took away the emotional pain.

This house was not haunted, but it was a house that haunted her. She watched it roll by and vanish into the long shadows of dawn. The sky was dull and gray now, and the pale morning light revealed ghosts made of sheets hanging from rain gutters and faux graveyards with foam tombstones. Rubber zombie heads poked out of the dirt. Jack-o'-lanterns were showing the first leprous sores of rot, and an oak tree was draped in toilet paper.

God, I hate Halloween. If she never saw another it would be too soon.

She regretted the thought almost immediately. Not seeing another Halloween sounded too much like *not living to see* one. Just because she'd escaped from the woods did not mean she was out of the woods yet.

As a troubled teen, she'd been arrested a few times. Once was for spray-painting a bridge, another time for possession of a dime bag, and another for shoplifting clothes at Kmart by putting them on and just walking out, a tactic that had worked for her countless times before. So she knew where the police station was. If that's where she was really being taken, they weren't going in the right direction.

When they turned down Belmont Street, it became clear where they were really headed. Her stomach soured, and she had to bite her tongue so not to scream.

Just ahead, the sun was rising over Scott Dwyer's house.

STILL GROGGY, Traci stirred. When she opened her eyes, there was an older black woman hovering over her. She wore glasses and had short-cropped hair tied up in barrettes. The woman was somehow familiar, but she could not place her.

Traci realized she was lying in bed, dressed down in just her t-shirt and panties. She tried to sit up.

The old woman put a hand over Traci's chest and guided her back down. "Easy now, child."

Traci didn't ask where she was. She didn't have to.

"You got a little beat up last night," the old woman said. "Not as bad as poor Scott, but you still sprained your neck and got cut up. Seeing what happened to everybody else, I'd say you had God on your side."

Traci blinked. "God?"

The woman's eyes were kind, her smile warm as melted butter. "Jesus looks out for us always."

"You…you believe in Jesus?"

"Of course, I do." The woman looked surprised. "Boy, they must've doped you up good."

Traci gulped. Her mouth had a minty taste, but she didn't remember having brushed her teeth. She tried to remember if someone had brushed them for her. She'd certainly been cleaned up, but she couldn't recall much after being taken into the house.

When she'd stepped out of the police cruiser, one of the officers had kept her close and pushed the butt of his pistol into her side. "You scream or try to run and I'll blow a hole clean through you. Just stay calm and get in the house."

She'd thought of her women's self-defense class then. The instructor had told the students that no matter what a man threatened you with, you should never, *ever* get in the car with him. Once you were in his possession, you were likely to never get away from him without being raped, assaulted, or killed. It was always better to scream and draw attention to the situation as much as you could, rather than comply by going with him. The same rule applied to houses.

So she'd screamed for help. It was a nice neighborhood. Even though there had been no activity in the streets, someone had to be awake, starting on coffee and breakfast. She had screamed as loud as she could, her lungs aching, voice cracking.

And she hadn't been shot for it. That meant they wanted her alive. But a vicious jolt had gone through her, making her muscles constrict. Hot pain had exploded through her body as she was tased and she collapsed into the officers. They had held her up and dragged her into the house. It had never occurred to her then that, even if someone had heard her screams and looked out their window, they would only see a woman resisting two police officers. Whom would they call if they saw a need to call anyone at all?

"Dope me?" she asked the old woman now. "Who doped me?"

She heard dripping, and the woman came up with a bowl and produced a warm, wet rag. She placed it over Traci's forehead like a nursing grandmother. "Now, now. It was for your own good, child."

"I'm not a child."

"Sorry. Force of habit. You're right. I'll call you Traci."

"How do you know my name?"

"My stars, we've known you since the day you was born. Don't you 'member me?"

Traci looked from side to side. There were a lot of things she didn't remember clearly, especially about her childhood. "You do look familiar."

The old woman patted her hand. "Oh, that's okay. It's been a lotta years. Last time I saw you, you was knee-high to a grasshopper. I'm Telma Payton. I was a friend of your mother's."

Traci wanted to believe she'd been rescued, that everything was going to be all right. But she was lying upon the bed in Scott's basement room, and Telma had said she'd been drugged for her own good. Nothing about this felt safe.

"Why am I here?" she asked.

"Don't fret over that just now. You need more rest."

Traci got up on her elbows despite the woman's suggestions. "I want to leave. Now."

"That isn't the right thing to do at this time, but soon, you—"

Traci swung her legs over the bed. When the old woman touched her, Traci shook her off. "If you don't let me go, it's kidnapping." She knew how empty the threat sounded, given all the heinous crimes committed in the past twenty-four hours. "You can't hold me against my will."

Telma stood. "Traci, listen to me, please. The worst is over. I know you've been through a lot. Believe it or not, I know what you're going through."

"You can't possibly understand what—"

"Don't tell me what I know and don't know! Now, I am trying to help you. Can't you see that? If you'll just sit back down and listen to me…"

Traci crossed her arms. The old woman had been tending to her, and they were alone in the room. She suspected the woman was part of this group all right, but perhaps she'd gone rogue and was trying to give her a way out. Traci figured if she tried to run, those crooked cops would stop her again, and maybe give her another taste of that taser. Perhaps if she heard the woman out, she'd learn there was a better approach.

"All right," she said. "I'll listen, but I'm standing."

"Fine by me, long as you're listening." Telma sat back in her chair. "Now, like I was saying, I know you've been through a lot. Not just tonight, either. But the worst of it is over. I'm sorry your friends are dead, but the demons are appeased. They won't come for you now." She took a deep breath and stared into space, into a world she'd once known but was forever gone. "I've lived in Redford all my life. And all my life, I've been what you'd call *gifted*. When I was a little girl, my parents were fine, upstanding, dedicated members of The Congregation. My grandparents were leading elders of the northeast sector of these United States. The Congregation has always been very liberal-minded, you see? Even when water fountains were segregated based on a person's race, The Congregation never discriminated. My grandfather became the first colored leader of a region, as they called it then, all the way back in 1922. And The Congregation has always embraced female leadership, too. It's always women who read the talismans and charms. It's they who foretell the coming of all things. My mother was a such a priestess, and by the time my father was in his mid-forties, he'd become one of the head noble executors in Connecticut."

Traci held her arms tighter across her. "Executors?"

"I know how that must sound, but allow me to explain." She straightened up. "I was very proud of my family, and very proud of my lineage. So I was willing to make sacrifices of my own."

"So you're an executor too then?"

Telma's eyes went wide and she touched her chest. "Heaven's no! Good grief, I could never do anything like that. I just don't have it in me to be violent. When I say I made sacrifices, I mean I gave up certain things, for the greater good. Things like my friends, or choosing my own gentleman callers, just for example." She sighed. "I know what it's like to be in your shoes, Traci, 'cause I walked in them long before you. Many people have. I had my first ceremony when I was just eleven years old. My George was already sixteen by that time. I was lucky in that he knew what he was doing. And he was gentle with me. Still is. And from what I remember about Scott, he was gentle with you too, even though he was a virgin like you, both of you being so young."

Traci's mouth went dry. She wanted to say something, but all words escaped her.

"And I also know what it's like to see your friends die," Telma told her. "To see them killed by your elders and have their souls taken to the world beyond the world by creatures you could never have imagined. I survived my own night in the woods, back in 1969—the summer of love." She raised her eyebrows. "Boy, the woods were much larger in them days. Now there's a highway and a whole mess of shopping malls where the portal was back in my day. But you still won't ever catch me there. I take all sorts of back roads just to avoid that part of the highway. Even though I know the portal has moved, it's still too upsetting to go back to the place where it all happened." She paused and had a little laugh. "Oh, how I ramble on, though. What I was trying to say is, you aren't the first pretty, young thing to be chosen."

Traci grimaced. "Chosen for what?"

The older woman's eyes lit with surprise. "You mean to tell me you don't know?"

Traci shook her head.

"Sweet mercy, I thought you would have sensed it or that Scott would've told you by now."

"Is he alive?"

"God willing."

"Thought you people worshipped the Devil."

Telma furrowed her brow. She seemed to go gray. "Don't ever say things like that again. Do I look like a Satanist to you? I have always been a devout Christian. I love the Lord, for he is an awesome and caring God. If The Congregation worshipped demons, why would we try to keep them at bay?" She returned to her previous subject. "You've been chosen for *greatness*, child. Why, that's what the ceremony is all about. It's what bonds you to Scott forever. And the two of you were always meant for The Birthing."

A chill snaked up Traci's vertebra. "What is..." But unfortunately, she felt she already knew. "What in the hell is The Birthing?"

Telma stood again. She placed her hands over Traci's. "You and Scott are like me and my George. You come from a long line of faithful members of The Congregation. Decades of devotion to the cause. The blood in your veins is purified by your lineage. You're meant for each other. All our sector's priestesses foresaw it. As soon as your mother said you were ready, you and Scott were put through your first ceremony. We were—"

Traci backed away from her. "You were trying to force me to…to have a baby?"

"No, no," Telma said. "Not exactly. The ceremonies begin as soon as one of the lovers is ready. You and Scott were the same age, but he started having….well, I always want to be a lady, but we're both adults…. he started having *erections* when he turned eleven. You didn't reach your menarche until a year and a half after the ceremonies began. You couldn't have gotten pregnant yet."

Traci felt dizzy as the ceremony returned to her in all its visceral intensity. Scott on top of her, thrusting, and the feeling of being kicked in her most private area. The adults surrounding them, nude and staring, and in the throng, there was her mother and Scott's parents, and a black couple standing beside them, Telma looking young and radiant.

"Why then?" Traci asked. "If you didn't want a baby, then why?"

"The ceremony is key, my dear. Even if your union doesn't create a child, it does create an energy, the combined force of two young lovers from two noble bloodlines, generations of devotion coming down to one beautiful act of love. That power keeps the demons back. It's like a shield that not only protects you but everyone around you. Villages across the world have been saved by the ceremony."

"And what about The Birthing?"

Telma gave her the motherly smile again, eyes twinkling. "That's the most beautiful sacrifice of all, to have a child to offer up."

Traci's heart dropped into her stomach. "No…you don't mean…you can't—"

"The Birthing has been ritual for centuries. Some say even millenniums. The firstborn child of the chosen lovers is always offered up to the demons. The more innocent the sacrificial lamb, the more powerful the gesture. Such an offering keeps the demons satisfied for years, and the portal stays closed."

"Oh, dear God," Traci fought the urge to be sick. "You kill *babies*!"

Telma put up her hands—calm, passive. "One life to save thousands. And you've owed this for a long time. Scott told us you never had children. Said you seemed proud of it. All these years, you didn't know it, but you were saving your eggs for Scott. For that is your destiny."

There was the rumble of someone coming down the stairs. Traci stepped back into the wall, clutching both hands beneath her chin. She wanted to shrink into herself until she didn't exist. She wanted to turn back time and never reply to Scott's message, to continue to be haunted by the mystery of that night rather than know the awful truth. The basement seemed to close around her like a tomb, and when Robin Reeves appeared in the stairwell, Traci opened her mouth to scream but could only whisper.

"Robin?"

As the woman came into the room, Traci realized it wasn't Robin at all. Her eyes had played tricks on her because of the woman's red hair and freckles. The ginger turned to Telma, her eyes cutting.

"What's she doing out of bed?"

Telma gave a small smile. "We were just talking. Seems no one told her what she'd been chosen for."

The woman returned her attention to Traci. When she stepped closer, Traci clenched her fists at her sides.

"You think I'm Robin?" the redhead asked, smirking. "Robin Reeves? Guess I should take that as a compliment. They say the Reeves girl was special—that she could perceive things about the woods even our priestesses couldn't. Made her an even better sacrifice, right, Telma?" She didn't wait for the old woman to answer. She squinted at Traci. "If only she'd known about The Congregation before they dragged her up that tree. She might've been a chosen one and they would've given up on you. But Robin's gone, princess. Has been for a long time. And if I had it my way, you would be too."

Telma's tone grew stern. "Julia, you back off now, child."

"It's not fair, Telma. All these years I've worked so hard, waiting to be chosen, only to be runner up now, an understudy to this whore."

"I said back off." Telma glowered. "Traci became a chosen one decades ago. You know this."

"She's a deserter. A defector."

"She didn't know what she was doing when she left."

Traci's jaw clenched. "I knew exactly what I was doing. Leaving here was the best thing I've ever done. Fuck Redford and fuck your little cult."

Julia's eyes grew even sharper, and Telma grabbed her arm to prevent her from lunging.

"You see this?" Julia said to the old woman. "She'll never respect what we do. Her mind is too weak to comprehend. She thinks we're evil. Hell, she doesn't understand what real evil is."

Traci sneered. "Well, I know what crazy looks like."

Julia put her hands on her hips. "You're the one who's crazy, princess. Here you have an opportunity most of our women can only dream of, and what do you do? You nearly killed Scott."

"Only nearly?"

Julia flashed a sadistic grin, reveling in her nemesis's failure.

"Things have been touch and go with Scott," Telma said. "But we remain hopeful. We're praying for his speedy recovery."

Julia went to the liquor cabinet, retrieved a square glass bottle with a silver bulb on top, and poured a full tumbler. The booze was clear as crystal, making Traci's mouth water.

Julia smirked. "This is Kilian Vodka. Runs for hundreds of dollars. It's the kind of booze you find at Saks Fifth Avenue." Julia took a drink and swished, really rubbing it in. "Bet you'd like some of this right now, huh?"

Traci's coat was nowhere in sight. Her flask was still in the pocket.

Julia teased her with another sip. "This bitch's body is no good, Telma. The way she guzzles vodka, her eggs are probably pickled. And besides, she's old."

"We know she's fertile."

"Maybe the talismans are wrong."

"They're never wrong."

"Okay," Julia huffed. "So maybe she can still have a kid, but what if it takes a long time for her to get knocked up? She's over forty. There might be complications. She might need all sorts of treatments. She might have miscarriages."

Traci bared her teeth. "Fuck you."

"That's what Scott should be doing. I'm thirteen years younger than you. I'll bet I could have six or seven successful Birthings. You'd be lucky to pump out even one little bastard."

Telma got between them. "Julia, that is *enough!*"

Julia's face flushed, and for a moment Traci thought she was going to turn her aggressions on Telma. But the kind expression the old woman had shown Traci had darkened now, turning her granite-hard, and Julia stepped down. She looked like a schoolgirl caught smoking in the bathroom. There had been insubordination here, and Julia had been called out on it.

"I'm sorry," she told Telma. "It's just that I—"

"We'll discuss this later. There are more important things to tend to. Fred and Reba are gone, and we all need to pick up the slack. Now get back upstairs and make yourself useful."

"Wait. Sheriff Shrinner actually sent me down here to get you."

"Oh?" Telma looked at her expectantly. "What is it?"

Julia gave Traci the side-eye, then whispered in Telma's ear. Traci couldn't make it out. She watched the old woman's face for a reaction, but she was unreadable. When Julia was through, they both looked at her. Telma's smile was friendly, Julia's wicked.

Telma started upstairs.

Julia put her drink on the counter and pointed at it with her thumb. "Help yourself, princess. You're gonna need it."

She followed behind Telma.

Traci came forward, but by the time she reached the door, they had locked it behind them. The basement room had always locked from the inside, not the outside. Someone had adjusted it.

They planned to keep her.

CHAPTER FORTY-SEVEN

Traci stared at the bottle.

She'd already drunk half of it. Her nerves demanded booze. She wanted to stay sharp, but without the alcohol, she would go into withdrawals. Besides, she told herself, it would take a whole lot to get her drunk, her tolerance being so high. So she poured another. The Kilian was quite good, but flavor was of little concern to her. She'd drink rubbing alcohol right now if it were all that was available.

How long had it been since Telma and Julia left? It couldn't have been more than an hour, could it? The windowless basement played with her. How long had she been down here? Having been drugged to sleep, it was impossible to know. Reality itself had become difficult to discern, a malleable figment that refused to solidify. Time and reality—little more than concepts, both vague and fleeting.

Finishing her drink, Traci poured another.

Help yourself, princess. You're gonna need it.

Looking around the room, she again tried to choose something to use as a weapon, even though she knew it would be futile to fight. She was so tired and weak from the drugs and overall exhaustion, and so crippled by grief and fear she could barely think straight. She supposed she could break one of the liquor bottles for a weapon. But even if she managed to kill one of these freaks, she still had little chance of escaping. She was outnumbered and outgunned. Resisting this cult would more likely result in punishment than victory.

But she couldn't just give up, could she? Hadn't she had enough losses in her life? She was tired of letting intimidation drive her down, whether it was someone else threatening her or if she were merely threatening herself, always ready to assure herself she would fail at whatever she tried. Self-doubt was so corrosive. It caused the very failures it predicted, making itself stronger in the process.

Traci stared into her drink. It's calming effect was fading now, giving way to the end result of all depressants. Despair arose from deep within her. Finishing the drink, she stood to fetch another and the room spun. She was on the threshold of drunk now. Once again, she'd failed. She let the glass fall to the floor and it rolled instead of shattering. Sitting back down, she pulled the blanket over her bare legs, hoping it was Telma who had undressed her. She hated to think of one of the policemen stripping her down to her t-shirt and panties. Even the thought of that bitch Julia putting her hands on her made Traci's skin crawl.

If this cult got their way, there'd be more than just hands on her. She would be forced into sex, raped until she was swollen with child, and made to carry the baby to term, only to have it massacred. For the first time in her life, she wished she'd reached menopause. Maybe then they'd let her go.

Or maybe they'd just sacrifice you.

As soon as the thought came to her, she knew it was true. If she weren't fertile, she'd serve no other purpose. They wouldn't trust her to keep her mouth shut. Nor should they. Maybe some of the cops in Redford were in on this, but there was bound to be law enforcement agencies elsewhere who'd have a problem with multiple, ritualistic murders. She could contact the state police or even the FBI. She'd take this all the way to Washington if need be. This Congregation, as they called it, had good reason not to let her go, no matter if she could deliver a baby or not. She had to ask herself what was worse—being forced to give life or forced to have her own taken away. It would be an easy decision if they just wanted a child instead of a human sacrifice. Rather than die, she would give them a baby, if they intended to raise and nurture it. The only option they had given her was to have her newborn child killed or be killed herself. Would it be better to live with something this terrible or not live at all?

And what if she couldn't deliver one? How long would they wait for a positive pregnancy test result before they cut their losses, and then her throat? And what would become of her if she did have a baby? Would she be expected to get pregnant again and do the whole thing over again? Or would they see her as having served her purpose and throw her corpse to the demons? What was the lesser of these evils?

Traci wanted to cry but couldn't. She'd run out of tears after a night of unprecedented sobbing. She needed to concentrate. A strange thought had hit her. There could be some way out of this nightmare, even if there wasn't a way out of this basement.

The stairway rumbled again. Footfalls. Lots of them.

Traci sat upright upon the mattress, pulling the blanket up to her chin, a little girl hiding from the boogeyman. A sense of finality enveloped her, telling her there would be no more options, no more resisting. She swallowed back the lump in her throat as the lock turned in the door, sounding as loud as a bullwhip to her, and as The Congregation filled the basement room the horrid déjà vu returned.

They were all naked and carrying candles—Telma, Julia, the two officers, as well as a man Traci guessed to be Telma's husband, George, and a big, fat man with a buzz cut. And there were others too, including Mrs. Richardson, a neighbor she remembered from childhood. The old woman smiled and said hello, but Traci only stared at her with vacant eyes. Mrs. Richardson wasn't the only one smiling—they all were. Their faces were warm and inviting, the faces of a family reunion all gathered around a Christmas tree. Even Julia wore a welcoming expression, likely having been given a tongue-lashing for her crude behavior.

They didn't say anything, because they didn't have to.

George flicked off the lights, and the basement fell in shadow, lit like the inside of a great jack-o'-lantern by the orange glow of handheld candelabras, a sinister vigil. And though she understood the horror of it all, Traci did not tremble. Like crying, she was all trembled out. The fear and the sadness were there, but prevailing over them came a numbing sensation of acceptance. She felt like a patient in hospice. This was her cancer. She could die right away or buy some time with treatments that caused other problems.

The Congregation gathered around her. Traci let the blanket fall to the floor. She pulled off her t-shirt, scooted out of her panties, and waited.

357

Telma took her clothes for her, the old woman smiling from ear to ear as she kissed Traci on the cheek.

"Don't be afraid."

And now when they said it, Traci didn't mind so much. Sitting there nude, she was a child again. Only this time the feelings of shame and violation were flooded by a newfound certainty of her fate. Her life had been planned out since childhood—perhaps since birth. Everything between her first ceremony and the one about to happen was merely an intermission, empty and directionless. This wasn't what she wanted, but nothing had ever been, whether her mother controlled her life or Traci controlled it herself. She'd been fighting against fate all her life, and she was tired. She'd been asked to return here, and she had come. But had there ever been a choice?

What if there was no free will? What if this was all part of God's divine plan? She knew now that the demons were real. That they had to be satiated was not much of a stretch. In fact, the more she thought about it, the more it made sense—terrible but perfect sense.

It was time to let self-doubt go. There was no point in losing forever.

The sound of footfalls filled the stairwell again. A shadow lumbered down the staircase and Traci watched as fate stepped through the doorway. It was too familiar to deny any longer.

Scott was naked but for his bandages. His torso was covered in cuts that were scabbing over, his side wrapped with gauze. His left leg had been removed at the knee, replaced by an artificial, metallic one. A line of thick stitches ran from the top of his head down to his chin, his once handsome face now split in half forever.

But still he smiled at her, and told her the same words that had endeared her to him for so long. They seemed more appropriate now than ever before.

"You don't have to do anything you don't want to," he told her. "Never."

Looking up at him, she realized with crushing certainty that he was the only boy she had ever truly loved. Maybe The Congregation had drilled that love into her brainwashed mind long ago, but if so, the feeling was the truest lie she'd ever felt. And now he would be the only man she would ever love. There was no choice. She gazed upon her destiny, falling into the blue oceans of his eyes, hoping she could float freely there, that she could get lost in what he had once been instead of the monster he had become. Maybe she could bring that sweet boy back. Maybe he was here already.

She looked into his eyes. "I'm not afraid."

SCOTT CLIMBED on top of his new bride.

There was no need for an expensive wedding and honeymoon like he'd had with Katie. What he and Traci shared wasn't as superficial as that. That sort of ceremony was virtually meaningless. One only needed to look at divorce rates to see how empty vows really were. Not like this ceremony. This was the true expression of being joined forever. There was no bond like the bond of sacrifice.

Katie had thought she'd understood that. She'd waited until she was eight and a half months pregnant before driving off a bridge to drown herself and their unborn daughter in the Housatonic River. He'd not known The Congregation had influenced her. She didn't mention it in her suicide note. It was only once he'd become a member that he learned what had really happened, that The Congregation needed both the sacrifice of an innocent baby and the elimination of Scott's wife if they were ever going to move forward. The demons had to be appeased, and Scott had to be open to new love, and that couldn't happen until his wife was dead and buried.

As it turned out, this new love was his first love, and the purest of all. At one time, he'd thought Jennifer Parks had been his first love. Later, he'd thought Katie was his soul mate. But with Traci Rillo below him now, he realized she was both. The other women had been nothing more than distractions and obstacles. There was only one true bride who could hold his heart, the one who had been there from the very beginning. Together, they would seal the world against all that was evil, their union the very pinnacle of The Birthing, and when their beautiful baby left its sweet mother's womb, Scott would be there with his own mother's scythe, ready to continue the legacy, ready to embrace the white light of destiny.

When he kissed Traci, she kissed him back and put her arms around his neck, for there were no more reasons to let go.

Scott smiled. "Welcome home, Traci."

ACKNOWLEDGEMENTS

THANKS TO all my fans and readers, especially those who take the time to write reviews and spread the word about my work. Thanks to everyone who contributed to my fundraiser for the chemo for my dog Bear. Thanks to all the other kids who grew up on the wrong side of the tracks with me. Thanks to all my writer, publisher, producer, and editor pals I've made in the horror industry. Thanks to my few close friends who keep me sane, or at least as sane as someone like me can get.

Big appreciations to Kevin Lucia and the team at Cemetery Dance for giving this book a proper home and making it shine.

Special thanks to Sadie Hartman and Brian Keene.

And big thanks to Tom Mumme—always.

KRISTOPHER TRIANA is the Splatterpunk Award-winning author of *Gone to See the River Man, Full Brutal, The Thirteenth Koyote, They All Died Screaming,* and many other terrifying books. His work has been published in multiple languages and has appeared in many anthologies and magazines, drawing praise from Rue Morgue Magazine, Cemetery Dance, Scream Magazine, and many more.

He lives in New England.

Kristophertriana.com
Twitter: Koyotekris
Facebook and TikTok: Kristopher Triana
Instagram: Kristopher_Triana

Visit TRIANAHORROR.COM

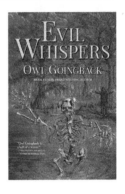

Printed in the USA
CPSIA information can be obtained
at www.ICGtesting.com
LVHW071110160923
758334LV00007B/80